DATE DUE

THE PATHS OF THE AIR

THE PATHS
OF THE AIR

Alys Clare

severn
House

This first world edition published 2008
in Great Britain and the USA by
SEVERN HOUSE PUBLISHERS LTD of
9–15 High Street, Sutton, Surrey SM1 1DF.

British Library Cataloguing in Publication Data

Clare, Alys
  The paths of the air
  1. D'Acquin, Josse (Fictitious character) - Fiction
  2. Helewise, Abbess (Fictitious character) - Fiction
  3. England - Social life and customs - 1066-1485 - Fiction
  4. Detective and mystery stories
  I. Title
  823.9'14 [F]

ISBN-13: 978-0-7278-6636-3   (cased)
ISBN-13: 978-1-84751-090-7   (trade paper)

*This book is dedicated to all the loyal readers who have
stayed with Josse and Helewise all the way.*

Feror ego veluti	I am borne along
sine nauta navis,	like a pilotless vessel,
ut per vias aeris	like a soaring bird
vaga fertur avis	on the paths of the air
Carmina Burana;	
cantiones profanae	(Author's translation)

All Severn House titles are printed on acid-free paper.

Typeset by Palimpsest Book Production Ltd.,
Grangemouth, Stirlingshire, Scotland.
Printed and bound in Great Britain by
MPG Books Ltd., Bodmin, Cornwall.

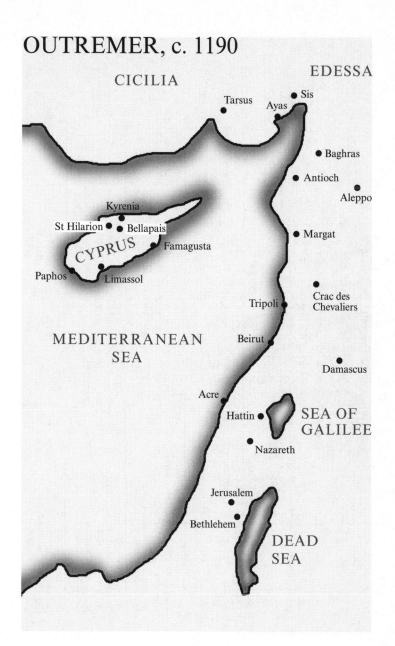

OUTREMER, c. 1190

CICILIA

EDESSA

Tarsus

Sis

Ayas

Baghras

Antioch

Aleppo

Kyrenia

St Hilarion · Bellapais

CYPRUS

Famagusta

Margat

Paphos

Limassol

MEDITERRANEAN
SEA

Tripoli

Crac des
Chevaliers

Beirut

Damascus

Acre

Hattin

SEA OF
GALILEE

Nazareth

Jerusalem

Bethlehem

DEAD
SEA

The Family Tree of Gerome de Villières
showing the Antioch and Sussex branches

Robert de Villières = Mathilde de St Denys
1088–1137   1089–1169

m. 1103

went on the First Crusade (1096–1102) and won lands in Antioch;   daughter of a wealthy family of champagne merchants turned noblemen;
married a wealthy heiress,   made her home in Antioch and died there aged eighty after a visit to the
settled and raised his family in Outremer.   newly refurbished Church of the Nativity in Bethlehem.

Antioch

Sussex

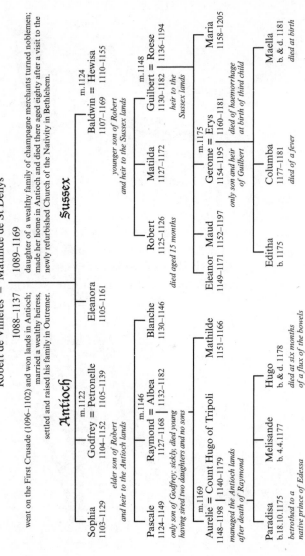

Sophia
1103–1129
*elder son of Robert
and heir to the Antioch lands*

Godfrey = Petronelle
1104–1152   1105–1139
m.1122

Eleanora
1105–1161

Baldwin = Hewisa
1107–1169   1110–1155
m.1124
*younger son of Robert
and heir to the Sussex lands*

Pascale
1124–1149

Raymond = Albea
1127–1168   1132–1182
m.1146
*only son of Godfrey; died young
having sired two daughters and no sons*

Blanche
1130–1146

Robert
1125–1126
died aged 15 months

Matilda
1127–1172

Guilbert = Roese
1130–1182   1136–1194
m.1148
*heir to the
Sussex lands*

Aurelie = Count Hugo of Tripoli
1148–1198   1140–1179
*managed the Antioch lands
after death of Raymond*
m.1169

Mathilde
1151–1166

Eleanor
1149–1171

Maud
1152–1197

Gerome = Erys
1154–1195   1160–1181
m.1175
*only son and heir
of Guilbert*
*died of haemorrhage
at birth of third child*

Maria
1158–1205

Paradisa
b.18.10.1175
*betrothed to a
native prince of Edessa*

Melisande
b. 4.4.1177

Hugo
b. & d. 1178
*died at six months
of a flux of the bowels*

Editha
b. 1175

Columba
1177–1181
died of a fever

Maella
b. & d. 1181
died at birth

Prologue
November 1196

The night had been still and cold. The approaching dawn had brought a rise in temperature and now, as the first faint silvery light appeared in the eastern skies, mist rose in spiralling wisps and curling folds from the lake in its shallow valley.

The track around the lake was clear of vegetation but only a few paces back the undergrowth began, dense and dotted with stands of birch and alder. The leaves had fallen but the thickly growing bracken still provided rust-red cover. Boar made their heads-down, single-minded, trotting progress through the under-growth; roe deer stood, heads raised and checking for threat, before resuming their browsing.

It was not only animals who were making use of the Vale's cover.

Suddenly, silently, a tall figure appeared. One moment there was nothing; the next it was there, standing quite still in thigh-high bracken, its outline shimmering in the mist like some phantom of the woods. Very slowly it turned its head, as if making sure no human eyes observed its movements. Then, apparently satisfied, it stepped fluidly through the bracken and emerged onto the path.

The mist swirled around its feet and legs, obscuring them so that an observer would have thought the figure floated, or perhaps flew. Its progress was swift; in a matter of moments it had reached the huddle of simple buildings at the end of the Vale. It gave this human habitation a wide berth, although this was scarcely necessary because most of the inhabitants were still asleep, and it made no more sound than an adder sliding through the grass.

It reached the path that led up the rise and swiftly climbed up to the walled settlement on the brow of the hill. Without hesitation it turned left and, following the line of the stonework, reached the place where the wall turned a corner. Here there were apple trees within the walls and, on the outside, its branches reaching towards the apple trees as if they were yearning arms, an ancient yew.

The figure reached up and caught hold of a thick branch about a tall man's height above the ground. With a movement that suggested great strength, it swung off the ground and climbed up into the yew, coming to rest astride a high branch. It settled itself as comfortably as such a perch allowed – which was scarcely comfortable at all – and then it froze.

It had sat there in that watchful pose all the previous day and the one before that. It had an urgent purpose and it did not allow bodily discomfort to impinge on its concentrated attention. Pushing back the dark headdress, it gazed down into the enclosed settlement that spread out on the other side of the wall.

Towards the end of the day the man in the tree – it *was* a man and he was fully human even if he moved and acted like a lost spirit – had seen enough. He began the long and painful process of restoring feeling to his numb limbs, for the descent was potentially fatal and he could not risk an accident. Too much depended on him, and besides – for the first time there was expression in the gaunt face as a wry smile faintly touched the mouth – why risk taking his own life when so many others were lining up willing, eager and very well equipped to do it for him?

He gritted his teeth through the agony of returning sensation in his feet, legs and hands. Then, very carefully, he climbed down the tree. He had to stand leaning against the trunk for some time before the shaking stopped and while he did so he ran his hands over himself, checking on his clothing. The ground-length dark brown woollen tunic was dusty and travel-stained, but that was all to the good as the dirt concealed its quality. Beneath it he wore garments which for very good reasons he chose to keep covered; he felt to make sure that the brown over-tunic had not become caught up and that the neck fitted snug to his throat. Then he smoothed the generous folds of his dark headdress, pulling it down low over his brow and up over his nose so that only his eyes, watchful in the deeply tanned face, were visible.

When he was fully satisfied that he looked exactly as he wanted to look, he stepped out from beneath the yew tree and, following the path, walked light-footed around the walls until he came to the gate. Then, slipping into line behind perhaps a dozen others, slowly and steadily he shuffled forward until his turn came.

The big woman in the voluminous white apron was tired. She had been on her feet since early morning and hadn't had a moment to call her own. It was a busy time, as it always was when the first hard days of late autumn bit and people began falling foul of the miasmas that lurked and jumped out as soon as hunger and cold revealed underlying weakness.

Quickly she dealt with the first of the sick and the needy, dishing out to the trio at the head of the queue a vermifuge, cough syrup and her patent earache cure. Then came a heavily pregnant woman, a man with bellyache, a boy with a wheeze, a baby with a bad case of cradle cap, a woman with a huge red sty. And, last in the line, a tall, broad-shouldered man in a long, dusty tunic, his head swathed in a concealing headdress. What she could see of his face suggested he was dark-skinned. In the failing light his eyes might have been any colour.

He stood before her and, putting one hand to his heart, gave her a courteous bow.

She waited but he did not speak. 'What ails you?' she prompted.

Very slowly, as if his vocal cords were stiff from disuse, he said, 'My . . . chin.'

'Your *chin*? What's the matter with it?'

'Pain. Much pain.'

'Let me see.'

He glanced around as if to make sure nobody was watching – the other patients had gone and he and the large woman stood apart – then very carefully he reached up and lowered the cloth that covered the right side of his face. She went to help but, with a gentle but very firm hand, he pushed her fingers away. Holding the headdress so that most of his face was still hidden, he turned his head and she saw his chin.

The skin under his jaw was red raw, swollen tightly, weeping and blistering. The dreadful wound must have been agonizing. She said very softly, 'You poor soul.'

He made a sound in his throat; it might have been in response to her sympathy.

She led the way to a small table where she had laid out freshly boiled water, lavender oil, ointment and pieces of clean white linen. She made up a strong solution of the oil in water and then, with the tenderest of touches, began to bathe away the dead skin and pus. He winced – she was hardly surprised – but made not a sound. The shadowed eyes, she noticed, were focused on some object in the middle distance. A fighting man, she thought, trained to take pain in his stride by detaching from it. She changed the foul and bloody water and began again, and this time the man took her ministrations without a flicker.

When at last she had finished, she gave a nod of satisfaction and turned away to dispose of the soiled cloth. She heard a tiny sound and, spinning round, saw that the pain had overcome him at last; he had slumped against the wall.

She hurried to crouch down beside him. 'I will find you a bed for the night,' she said, 'for you are faint, weak with suffering.' He also looked as if a square meal and a decent night's sleep wouldn't be unwelcome. 'Come, let me—'

But he was struggling to his feet, backing away from her hands that wanted to help. Repeating his hand-to-the-heart gesture, he murmured, 'No, lady. No.'

'Oh, but why won't you let us care for you?' She too was whispering, as if she had caught his fierce desire not to be seen or overheard.

He shook his head. 'You have cared for me already.' Then, his speech broken and hesitant once more: 'Pain is less. I thank lady.'

He bowed again, deeply this time, and then before she could stop him he spun round and hurried away.

The relief was exquisite. The pain was still considerable but the woman's lavender oil and ointment – witch hazel and St John's wort, he thought, with a few precious drops of poppy – had greatly reduced it. He had known that the wound was infected; now, thanks to her, it would mend. He would have a scar but scars did not matter and anyway he already had plenty.

He walked quickly, for he had a long way to go. His business with the foundation on the top of the hill was done. Not only had he watched for long enough to work out which people were influential and important, who did what and how the place operated; in addition, he had spoken to some of the visitors and listened carefully to the gossip of the inhabitants, which had probably told him more than everything else put together.

Yes. He had found out what he needed to know. But he had been there for three days and it was very dangerous to stay in one place. Death stalked him; it might be a quick execution, or a long drawn-out agony while they tried to get him to tell him what they knew he had stored away in his head, or it could be a bloody mess of severed flesh designed for maximum effect. It all depended who found him first.

Night fell. Soon Hawkenlye Abbey was left far behind.

Part One
The Quarry

One

Josse was bored. The November day was cold but bright and there were a dozen reasons to get up from his chair and out into the fresh air. A man more involved in his acres – a farmer or a conscientious landlord – would have been out at dawn on his daily inspection to make sure that everyone was working hard and everything was running smoothly. Josse, whose estate of New Winnowlands ran as smoothly as any thanks to his man Will, knew full well that any inspection tour *he* made would be seen for what it was: a complete waste of his and everyone else's time.

Josse knew next to nothing about agriculture. He was a soldier; a King's man. With King Richard engaged in keeping Philip of France out of Normandy and with no threat of war looming, Josse had little purpose in life.

He scowled. Perhaps *none at all* would be nearer the mark.

He knew he should pray daily in gratitude for the steadfast Will, who, over the years that they had been together, had grown into a thoroughly dependable, capable and authoritative figure, whom the many people who worked Josse's land obeyed almost as readily as they would Josse himself. Other than having to weigh in occasionally in some small matter that was beyond Will's diplomacy and skill to solve, Josse knew that he did not need to be at New Winnowlands at all.

He was very tempted to pack his gear, saddle his horse and set off for France. King Richard would pretend to know who he was and put him to work on some task aimed at furthering the Plantagenet cause. The King, they said, was building a wonderful new castle called Château Gaillard, situated on a bend of the Seine to the north of Paris and designed to pen Philip into the Île de France. Philip, naturally, took exception to this and had been provoked into renewing hostilities with all the energy and force he could muster.

The trouble was that Josse had absolutely no enthusiasm any more for fighting King Richard's battles. He told himself that this was a perfectly understandable reaction, King Richard having proved to be a man more concerned with winning glory than with the well-being of his people. And just look at that business of his capture, Josse thought, and the enormous ransom we had to stump up!

But this was only one of the complex set of reasons why Josse did not want to re-enter his monarch's service in Normandy. The main cause of both his peevish discontent and his lack of enthusiasm for a foreign venture was that he wanted very much to be in two other places and he was not sure of his welcome in either.

He wanted to be with Joanna and Meggie. Joanna had kept her word and usually she would be there in her little hut in the forest when Josse went to visit her after each of the eight annual festivals that her people celebrated. She had been there at Yule and he had even been allowed to join in one of the lesser feasts; something he was quite sure he had enjoyed although he couldn't really remember. Those forest people certainly knew how to brew up a good mug of mead. He had not seen her at Imbolc; he had been summoned to Hawkenlye Abbey to help in a minor crisis and there hadn't been time. Then when he'd gone into the forest at the spring equinox she hadn't been there; it was only with great difficulty that he'd even been able to locate her hut, as she seemed to have become very skilful at casting some sort of hiding or camouflaging spell over the place when she wasn't at home. At Beltane he had been allowed to take Meggie away with him for a couple of days. Joanna had given some vague explanation about having been summoned for an important role in some ritual that was too powerful for a small child of three years to attend.

Josse enjoyed being alone with his daughter even more than being with her when her mother was there too. There was something very *awesome* about Joanna these days; he could tell that she shielded her power when she was with him but sometimes she didn't do it very successfully and quite often he felt quite . . . Quite what? he wondered.

Quite afraid, was the honest answer.

He did not want to think about that.

Meggie had power, too. They had explained to him about

her ancestry on her mother's side (on her father's too, they said, although he didn't want to think about that either) and he knew from personal experience that what they said was true. But when she was alone with him she was just a bright and pretty little girl with a wonderful sense of fun, an infectious giggle and a way of twining her arms around his neck in a loving hug that just about made him melt. During the two days they had spent in each other's company – he'd taken her to the Abbey overnight, where they knew about her and asked no awkward questions – they had ridden together, walked in the woods and fields tracking small animals and birds, waded into streams and climbed trees. They had talked non-stop. Returning her to her mother and riding away had all but broken his heart.

There had been no sign of either of them when he went visiting in midsummer and at Lammas they had had half a day and one night together before Joanna announced she had to go off somewhere. He and Joanna had made love that night; she had been as ardent, as loving as ever, although he sensed some sort of reserve, as if she wanted to give more than she felt she could. Or should . . .

He had been invited to attend the daytime celebration at the autumn equinox and he had had a great time. Joanna's people seemed to accept him for who and what he was and nobody ever made him feel like an outsider; well, not intentionally. Then when Joanna had gone off to do whatever it was she did, he had taken Meggie home to the hut, where he fed her, bathed her, cuddled her, told her five stories and then put her to bed.

He had not even looked for them at Samhain; Joanna had told him not to bother as they wouldn't be there. He didn't know where they had gone. He didn't know where they were now and he didn't know when he was going to see them again.

It made him angry.

Some time later he resumed his seat by the hearth, a mug of ale in his hand. He had tried to divert himself by going out into the courtyard and checking that Will had dealt with the dead leaves blocking the gulley – of course he had – and by pretending an interest in Will's woman Ella's preserve-making.

The other place he wanted to be was Hawkenlye Abbey.

But he had been there only a couple of weeks back on the flimsy excuse that perhaps they'd like help in raking up the leaves.

They had accepted his offer with gracious kindness and given him a besom and a rake, and for four or five happy days he had worked alongside the lay brothers in cheerful companionship.

Abbess Helewise must have realized that it was Samhain and that he visited Joanna and Meggie around the time of the festivals. She had been too tactful to mention it.

He did not want to risk going back to the Abbey so soon. If he kept turning up there like a puppy wanting attention they would see the underlying neediness. He really didn't want them – oh, all right, he didn't want *her* – feeling sorry for him.

He took a long pull at his ale. I'm no use to anyone, he thought mournfully, I'm idle, I'm miserable, I'm full of self-pity and I'm—

His ruthless catechism of faults might well have run on for some time, but Will tapped at the door and announced that there was a stranger at the gate and would Sir Josse come out to see if it was all right to let him in?

It did not take Josse long to leap out of his chair, put his mug discreetly out of sight, brush down his tunic and wipe a hand across his beery lips. He hurried out through the door and down the steps. Beside him Will muttered, 'There he is, sir. Wasn't sure I liked the look of him.'

'I see,' Josse murmured.

'Fellow looks as if he could do with some Christian charity, though,' Will observed piously. 'Never seen a man so weary and still on his feet.'

Josse had to agree. The stranger was tall, wide in the shoulder and ought to have had the confident stance of one well able to take care of himself. Instead he was trembling with exhaustion. He wore a travel-stained brown tunic that reached almost to the ground, held in at the waist with a leather belt. His satchel of soft leather must have cost a pretty penny but was scratched and battered. The skirts of the brown tunic were generous; if the man were carrying a sword, it was concealed and, Josse thought grimly, it would take him a moment or two to extract it.

Josse had a long knife in a sheath on his belt. He did not expect to use it but it was reassuring to know it was there.

What could be seen of the stranger's skin, between the hem of the headdress low over his eyes and the fold that covered his mouth and nose, was a sort of brownish-olive shade. Might he be from Outremer? Former crusaders often returned accompanied by servants they had picked up and it was all too common for these poor souls to be cast off once their masters were safely home. As Josse gave the stranger a tentative smile, the man put his right hand over his heart and bowed. The gesture was so alien, so unlike anything a native Briton would offer, that Josse decided his guess was right.

'I am Josse d'Acquin and you have arrived at my estate of New Winnowlands,' he announced, speaking loudly and clearly. Keeping his tone friendly, he added, 'What do you want of me?'

The man lowered his eyelids and dropped his chin. 'I seek shelter, master,' he said huskily.

'I see.' Josse was playing for time.

'I work,' the stranger said eagerly, risking a brief bashful upward glance. 'I chop wood, I sweep floors.'

He looked as if he could hardly even hold an axe or a broom, never mind wield them. 'I have all the men and women I need for such tasks,' Josse said.

The stranger seemed to sink into himself. 'Very well, master,' he muttered. 'Thank you for your time.'

He turned to go.

'Wait!' Josse called. 'Come back. You may sleep in an outhouse and we will feed you.' Beside him he sensed Will stiffen. He plunged on regardless. 'Rest here with us,' he urged, 'build up some strength and, when you are restored, go on your way.'

The man spun round to face Josse once more, already sunk low in a bow. 'May God bless you,' he said in a hoarse whisper. God, Josse noted, not Allah; perhaps the man had adopted the faith of the master who had brought him so far from his homeland? 'May he rain down gifts on you, on your sons and on the sons of your sons,' the stranger was adding, 'even until the tenth generation.'

'Aye, well, I don't know about all that,' Josse said, embarrassed. 'Come in, and Will here shall see about feeding you.' Will sucked air through his teeth, a sound so eloquent of disapproval that Josse sighed in exasperation. 'Won't you, Will?' he added pointedly.

'Aye, sir.' Will looked the stranger up and down. 'You'd better follow me,' he said grudgingly.

Josse watched the two of them walk away. Will was heading for one of the outbuildings that were used to store surplus produce in the late summer. It was now empty and it smelt pleasantly of apples. It had a rudimentary hearth so the stranger would be able to have a small fire. He could—

Something occurred to Josse; something he should have thought of earlier. Running to catch up with Will and the stranger, he called out, 'You'd better tell me your name.'

The man stopped, turned and, looking Josse coolly in the eye, said, 'I am John Damianos.'

The presence of a strange foreigner sleeping in his outbuilding disturbed Josse far more than he had anticipated. As much as he had thought about it – which was not very much at all – he would have said that he'd probably have forgotten all about the man after a couple of days, leaving Will and Ella to see to the stranger's well-being.

But it did not happen like that at all.

Will and Ella certainly looked after him well enough. Despite his initial misgivings, Will seemed to want the foreigner to regain his health and strength as quickly as possible. This might have been with the aim of seeing the back of the fellow but Josse thought not. He concluded that Will was concerned with the reputation of New Winnowlands and, indeed, of Josse himself. It was as if it was up to Josse's household to respond to the man's faith in them and do their utmost to provide that which he had humbly come seeking.

Ella, who normally did no more than silently obey whatever orders were issued to her, also seemed affected by this generosity of spirit. Josse noticed the sudden variety in the dishes that were brought to his table; they all seemed to have the most delicious and mouth-watering smells. Josse checked with Will, who confirmed that the same dishes were being sent to the outbuilding. 'Hope it's all right with you, sir, only you did say as to feed him up.'

'Aye, Will, of course it's all right,' Josse assured him. 'I had—' I had never imagined Ella to be such an imaginative cook, was what he nearly said. But since it was hardly kind or flattering to the mild and chronically unselfconfident Ella, he held back.

But Will seemed to understand. 'Makes a change from pie, sir,' he observed in an undertone.

'Nothing wrong with Ella's pies,' Josse said stoutly. Then, grinning, 'But aye, it does.'

Will's contribution to the stranger's comfort was to furnish the outbuilding. He had knocked together a crude bed frame from old hurdles and stout pieces of wood and stuffed some sacks with straw for a mattress. He – or perhaps Ella – had provided woollen blankets. To help keep the night chill at bay, he had repaired the hearth, adding more stones to its circle, and he kept the stranger well supplied with firewood.

With regular and nourishing meals and a warm place in which to sleep, the stranger ought to have recovered some strength. Which made it all the more peculiar that instead of rising in the morning with the rest of the household and offering to help with the chores – even a relatively weak convalescent could have done *something* – John Damianos continued to sleep through the short November days as if all the food and rest had no effect at all.

Far from being able to ignore the presence of a stranger in their midst, then, Josse – and, he was quite sure, Ella and Will and everyone else at New Winnowlands – found that John Damianos was perpetually on his mind.

It was *odd*.

Days passed. Soon the stranger had been at New Winnowlands for a week, then ten days. Ella continued to provide him with large amounts of food and drink. Will had approached Josse bashfully one morning and asked if it would be all right to broach the new barrel of small beer, only the previous one had gone down so fast, what with one thing and another. Josse had noticed that the amount he had to fork out for flour had gone up considerably; Ella seemed to be constantly baking . . .

It was time to go and see for himself.

Early the next morning he went to the outbuilding. He tapped on the door – it was closed and latched – but there was no answer from within. Josse was about to tiptoe away but then a flash of anger got the better of him. Rapping smartly on the wooden door panel, he said loudly, 'Are you awake in there?'

There was a snort, as if someone were being roused from deep sleep, then sounds of rustling straw. 'A moment,' said a sleep-dazed voice.

After quite a long time the door opened and John Damianos

stood in the doorway. He was fully dressed in his tunic and the concealing headdress. Behind him, the straw mattress had been shaken up and the blankets neatly folded on top of it.

The stranger made his hand-to-heart bow, bending low so that Josse could not look into his face. 'Master,' he murmured. 'You wish to speak?'

'Er – aye, I do,' Josse replied. 'I wanted to ask you – to see if you—' His momentary anger had vanished and now, put in the position of a host who had revealed all too clearly that he wished his visitor to depart, he felt nothing but embarrassment. 'How is your health?' he rapped out, his tone made brusque by his unease. 'Are you feeling stronger?'

The man bowed again, but not before Josse had glimpsed the brief, sudden smile that creased up his eyes. 'Master, I offer honour and respect to your esteemed household, for I, a stranger, have been treated like a prince.'

Josse waited, not speaking, and the man straightened up and for an instant met his eyes.

John Damianos looked exhausted.

Fear slid down Josse's back. Dear God, the man's sick of some dread disease, he thought wildly, and I've let him into my household so that I and all my people are endangered! But then common sense returned: sick men did not eat like healthy horses.

Dumbly he stared into the stranger's eyes. His puzzlement must have been easy to read; after a moment, John Damianos said, 'I am stronger than before, master, but still I need to rest. If I may beg your indulgence a little longer . . .' He left the sentence unfinished.

Josse waved a hand. 'Of course!' he heard himself saying. 'Stay as long as you like! I am sorry to have disturbed you.'

Then, cross with himself for his cowardice and for lacking the good sense to have seized the chance to ask a few questions – as well he might have done, given all that he and his people were doing for the stranger – he backed away, turned round and hurried back to the house.

Josse was not to know but others burned with curiosity about the foreigner in their midst even more than he did. Ella in particular, cooking for him, spent rather more time than was good for her in dreaming about him. She did not tell Will, but in the privacy of her own thoughts she made up a long, romantic and highly unlikely story. Fed by the tales and legends told to her when she was a child, her account of how the stranger had ended up begging at the gates of New Winnowlands involved frost giants, flying horses and a bridge the colours of the rainbow. Her fascination had an edge of fear for, as Will had remarked, it 'ain't natural for a flesh-and-blood man to eat like what he does and sleep both the night and the day away like a new-born babe'.

Ella thought that John Damianos might be under an enchantment. According to Will, the foreigner kept the door fast shut and it could not be opened from the outside. It surely followed – or at least it did according to Ella's fairly limited powers of logic – that the stranger locked himself inside the outbuilding because he had *something terrible to hide*.

What could it be?

Ella took to pondering this fascinating question as she peeled vegetables and drew the guts out of chickens. Was the stranger really a man or was he an animal spirit who took on a different form in the night hours and went out hunting as an owl, or a wolf? Was this why he had to sleep through the day, out of sheer exhaustion? Was he cursed because he had done something very, very wrong, something that had aroused the fury of some dark spirit of the deep forest? Was he under a spell that meant he ate and ate and still did not grow strong?

Shivering with delicious fear, Ella let her mind run free.

And presently just *thinking* was not enough.

She waited for a clear sky and a generous moon. She lay beside Will until he was asleep, then she got out of bed, wrapped her cloak around her, picked up her wooden shoes and silently let herself out of the warm little room off the kitchen where she and Will slept.

She crept across the stone floor, lit only by the remnants of the fire in the hearth, and opened the door. Putting on her shoes, she scurried across the courtyard towards the outbuildings, her heart beating fast. She was amazed at her own courage. What was she doing out there, all by herself in the still, cold night? For a moment fear gripped her and stopped her in her tracks. She ought to go straight back to her cosy bed and forget all about this mission . . .

Slowly she walked on.

As she approached the outbuilding, it seemed that the door was not as tightly fastened as usual. Was there a tiny gap between door and lintel? Or was it just her imagination?

She had to look; she *had* to.

She crept nearer.

The door was closed but it was not fastened from the inside. Instead, a loop of twine held it shut. She untied the twine and opened the door.

The fire had been banked down but it gave enough light for her to see by. The straw mattress was puffed up and the blankets lay draped across the foot of the bed.

Of John Damianos there was no sign.

Fear raced through Ella like fire through a bunch of dry kindling. The atavistic, unspoken, unacknowledged terror of the weird and the unknown that lay deep in her countrywoman's soul took her over completely and her simple mind translated an empty bed into a savage and bloody tale of shape-shifting werewolves, malevolent spirits, cruel creatures of the night that soared up into the black starry sky to descend on their helpless prey to tear out their throats and suck their blood.

He's not here, she kept thinking, over and over again. *He's not here.*

Hand to her mouth to suppress her scream of horror, Ella backed out of the outbuilding. Terror made her clumsy; she tripped and fell. As she hastened to stand up again, a sob broke out of her. Then, with a wail, she flew back across the yard and in through the kitchen door, recovering sufficient presence of mind to stop her noise as she entered the house and to make sure she closed and fastened the door without a sound. Then, trembling violently and longing only for the blessed safety of her bed and Will's snoring presence beside her, she took off her shoes and her cloak and crept into the little room off the kitchen.

She would have tried to bar the door, only Will would have noticed in the morning and been suspicious.

She scolded herself. She had been unbelievably foolish and look where it had got her. Why, the foreigner was as much of a mystery as ever!

But at least – and in the silent darkness it seemed quite a lot – at least nobody knew what she had done.

*   *   *

Ella was wrong. Someone did know, for he had both heard and seen her.

He had been setting off on his regular night-time mission, carrying the usual burden. Ella had guessed more accurately than she knew, for the reason that he slept the day away was indeed because he was out all night.

Tonight he had done as he always did and waited until well after the household had gone to sleep. That time always seemed to him unbearably long but he knew this was an illusion, brought about by his desperate need to be on his way. To ease the agony of having to wait, he would sit quite still on his straw mattress and make body and mind relax until he could walk in the quiet inner pathways in the way they had taught him in that mysterious land so far away. Sometimes it worked; sometimes it did not.

Finally he got to his feet, shouldered his satchel and the pack and let himself out, fastening the door so that it would look closed to a casual glance. He crossed the courtyard to the place in the wall where it was possible to climb over and was actually sitting astride, about to drop down onto the frosty grass on the other side, when he spotted her.

The only reason he saw her was because of a slight change in the light. Perhaps she had cast a momentary moon shadow; perhaps he had caught a fleeting movement out of the corner of his eye. Up on the wall he froze.

She had not seen him; she was intent on the outbuilding. He watched as she unfastened the twine, eased the door open and looked inside. He heard her suppressed sob and for a moment he felt her terror, as if the emotion was so powerful that it blasted out of her and assaulted everything and everyone around. He was sorry for her then; sorry for her suffering and her extreme fear.

She stumbled off, back the way she had come. He sat quite still on the wall, and when he was satisfied that she had really gone inside, slipped down on the far side and hurried away, breaking into an easy, loping run that covered the ground with surprising speed.

When he was some distance away he stopped and turned around, looking back the way he had come. He sent a silent thank you to the generous, unquestioning souls who lived in that place where he had been taken in.

Then he slung his satchel over his shoulder and hitched the pack higher on his back. His sword was in its scabbard beneath his tunic, his long dagger in its sheath at his waist. Everything he possessed in the world was either on his person or in his satchel. Not for the first time, he was thankful that he always took everything with him when he went out at night. This time this deeply ingrained habit would serve him well.

Two

They could not comfort Ella. When they discovered the stranger had gone, at first she kept her silence. But it was clear something was gravely wrong, for she bit her lips and frowned, muttering to herself under her breath, and she jumped at the slightest noise. Eventually she burst into tears, threw herself into the meagre comfort of Will's scrawny arms and confessed what she had done.

Will decided to put the matter before his master.

'Ella reckons she knows summat about the foreign fellow's disappearance,' he said to Josse, apprehending him on his way to the stables and firmly clasping Ella's hand in case she decided to cut and run. 'She says he'd gone from the outbuilding last night and his bed hadn't been slept in.' He turned to Ella. 'That's right, isn't it?' He gave her a shake, not ungentle. 'Go on,' he added in exasperation as her face crumpled, 'Master won't bite!'

'Ella?' Josse said, surprised. 'Is this true?' What on earth had she been doing out there in the darkness?

Ella raised her eyes to meet Josse's. She nodded. Then, encouraged by his smile, she burst out, 'I reckoned he were a spirit of the night, see. One of those shades that sleeps all day because they're out a-haunting through the hours of darkness, and I just wanted to find out if what I feared was true because if so then we – then we—' But, overcome, she pulled up her apron and buried her face in it, shoulders heaving.

Will, after a moment of staring at her in mystified incomprehension, put his arms round her thin body. 'Come on, old girl,' Josse heard him mutter.

But Ella seemed incapable of further explanation. With a shrug and a lift of the eyebrows in Josse's direction, Will led her away.

He left Josse frowning and puzzling over the strange ways of women, in particular those such as Ella in whom the deep and unshakable superstition of the peasant was so strong. One of those creatures who haunted through the night and lay up all day? Well, that would explain John Damianos's habit of sleeping the daylight hours away. And Josse realized there *had* been something slightly unearthly about the man . . . those unfathomable eyes, shadowed by the headdress so that it was impossible to determine colour or expression. His speech, sometimes just the few hesitant words of a man speaking an alien tongue and sometimes – very occasionally – fluent and grammatically accurate. And where had he come from? Josse had not gone beyond his initial assumption, that John Damianos was a native of Outremer brought to England by a returning crusader.

Why did I not ask him while I had the chance? Josse thought. Had I known his history, I could now be comforting Ella and telling her not to let her imagination run away with her, because our mysterious stranger was no more than a body servant from Acre brought home by Sir Somebody of Somewhere and released from his master's service to find his own way home.

He wondered briefly whether to tell her this anyway; it would be a kind lie if it succeeded in removing her terrified anxiety. But he knew he was a poor liar, and if his brief explanation brought forth a torrent of questions he would soon be floundering.

No. Best to let Will take care of his woman. She'd soon forget all about John Damianos.

But she didn't. Three days later, she was still afraid of her own shadow and she refused to go anywhere near the outbuilding. Since she had to pass it to get to the hen house, the root-vegetable store, the little shelter where Will stacked bundles of kindling and the earth privy, this meant life was becoming quite trying for everybody, especially Ella herself.

Summoning Will after overhearing yet another outburst of hysterical weeping, Josse asked wearily if there was any chance of Ella seeing sense.

'None at all, sir,' Will said bluntly. 'Me, I've kept hoping the fellow would come back, then I'd have pinched him, punched him or snagged him with my knife to show her he was no spirit but felt pain and bled just like any other man.' There was considerable vehemence in Will's tone and Josse sympathized; it must be hell having to live cheek by jowl with a woman in Ella's current mood, not to mention having to empty a daily bucket for her while she was incapable of using the yard privy. 'But he's gone,' Will concluded. 'Gone without a kiss my arse – er, gone without a word of thanks. We shan't see him back here, sir, that's my opinion.'

Josse had a suspicion that Will was right. He also suspected he knew just why John Damianos had vanished into the night: because he had seen Ella and knew his nocturnal habits were no longer a secret. If, that was, he had regularly gone out at night and the one occasion when Ella had gone looking had not been the exception.

'I wonder,' Josse said musingly.

Will voiced his indignation. 'It's not right, after we cared for him, just to vanish into the night. Is it, sir?'

'No, Will.' The odd thing was, Josse thought, that John Damianos had appeared better than to accept kindness and care without expressing his gratitude. The more he thought about it, the more it seemed likely that the stranger had intended to come back; that he would have returned before morning – just as in all probability he had regularly done – had it not been for Ella. With a flash of understanding, Josse realized that Ella must have worked this out too. A man had come to them for help and they had fed him, given him shelter and helped him recover his strength. The healing process was well under way but then through her own irrepressible curiosity, Ella had frightened him away.

What she was suffering from was not only superstitious terror but also a very human sense of guilt.

Poor Ella.

Josse waited another day and night, during which he prayed fervently that either John Damianos would return or Ella would come to her senses. Neither happened.

In the morning he went to the kitchen, stopped Ella's weeping with an imperiously raised hand and announced, 'Ella, you can't go on like this.' And nor can the rest of us, he might have added. 'If there is nothing we can do to help you, we must take you to others who are skilled in such matters.' Turning to Will, standing open-mouthed with the heel of an ageing loaf of bread in one hand and his knife in the other, Josse said, 'Will, saddle Horace and prepare the mule and the smallest of the working horses. You and I are going to take Ella to Hawkenlye Abbey.'

The very act of riding out on the old mule in the clear morning air did a lot to restore Ella's spirits. Twisting round to look at her, Josse observed that she was staring around with interested eyes as they rode along the track he knew so well. He realized that this was probably the furthest she had been in the years since she had come to the manor, and that must be . . . He did not know, for Will had been there in the days of the previous tenant and, for all Josse knew, so had she.

What a narrow world she inhabited.

They reached Hawkenlye Abbey in the early afternoon. Josse instructed Will to take the horses and the mule to Sister Martha in the stables. Taking Ella's arm and giving her what he hoped was a reassuring smile, he led her across the wide courtyard.

He was very aware of her fear. As he opened the door and ushered her inside the infirmary, he tried to observe it with eyes that had never seen it before.

He saw a long room with windows set high in the walls. On either side were low beds, many of them occupied, and at each end were curtained-off recesses where treatments were carried out and where patients could be isolated. There were several nuns: all wore black habits, with white wimples that covered neck and throat and were drawn up around the face and across the brow. Some wore white veils and some black. Each wore a simple wooden cross around her neck. There must have been perhaps thirty-five or forty people yet the impression was of serenity. The nuns walked soft-footed, their pace unhurried so that they seemed to glide over the scrubbed flagstones. The patients – comforted, cared for, loved, perhaps – did not moan, cry out or complain, but instead lay passive and quiet, apparently well aware that the nuns were doing their best for them.

It was, thought Josse, a haven.

Beside him he sensed Ella relax. Then a big nun in a black veil, a crisp white apron tied over her habit, came towards him, a smile on her face and her arms open in welcome.

'Sir Josse, how good to see you again so soon!' she said, embracing him. 'I am sure we can find some more leaves for you to sweep up!'

He returned her smile. 'And right willingly I'll do it,' he said. 'But I have come on a different mission. Sister Euphemia, this is Ella, who is in charge of my kitchen at New Winnowlands.' Ella was staring up at the infirmarer, awestruck, and now she gave a bob curtsey. 'Ella, Sister Euphemia here and her nursing nuns will be able to help you.'

'What ails you, Ella?' Sister Euphemia asked gently; she must, Josse noted, have picked up Ella's fear and chronic shyness and she had turned from a large, confident and some-times overbearing woman into a soft-spoken soul whose only wish was to soothe and to comfort.

To be able to change one's very essence so swiftly and seam-lessly was, he reflected, quite a talent.

'Ella has—' he began.

But with a smile Sister Euphemia shook her head. 'Thank you, Sir Josse, but I would prefer it if she told me herself,' she said.

Then, without a backward glance from either of them, the infirmarer and her shy companion walked away to one of the curtained recesses and disappeared from sight. Josse stared after them and wondered just what to do next.

He found Will waiting for him outside the infirmary.

'Ella's being cared for,' Josse said. 'By the infirmarer herself, who is very good at reassuring those who are disturbed. Don't worry, Will, we'll soon have our Ella back again and restored to her usual self.' Will muttered something under his breath. 'Go and get yourself something to eat,' Josse ordered. 'Over there – ' he pointed – 'you'll find the refectory, and they serve food to those who ask. Tell them you're with me,' he added, unable to prevent the instant of pride.

Will suppressed a grin. 'Right you are, sir,' he said. Then, turning to go: 'You'll be off to see the lady Abbess, no doubt.'

'I—' But the protest never came. It was exactly where Josse was going.

Will's smile was wider now. 'See you later, sir.' With what might well have been a wink, he turned and was gone.

Slowly Josse walked across the open space to the cloister, at the end of which Abbess Helewise had her little room. Tapping on the door, he heard her low 'Come in' and opened the door.

She looked as delighted to see him as she always did.

'Sir Josse,' she exclaimed, getting up and striding around her wide oak table, 'you have come back! What can we do for you?'

'It's not me, it's my servant Ella,' he said hastily. 'She's given herself a bad fright and we just can't get her out of her terror.'

'How dreadful for her! What on earth happened?'

'We had a stranger staying with us at New Winnowlands. He came to us asking for work, although he looked so sickly and weak that I didn't reckon there was much he could have done. Anyway, we offered him an outbuilding to sleep in and we fed him up a bit.' He was aware of her nod of approval and it warmed him. 'It was odd, because for all he ate everything put before him, still he did not seem to grow any stronger. Instead of getting up in the mornings, he kept to his bed and slept for most of each day.'

'What was the matter with him?' asked the Abbess. 'Oh, Sir Josse, it wasn't some frightful sickness . . . ?'

'No, my lady, I am sure, for no sick man ever ate like our stranger.'

'Go on,' she commanded. 'What happened to scare Ella so badly?'

'She was intrigued as to *why* he slept all day,' Josse explained, 'and I guess she imagined he might be up to some secret nocturnal task. Anyway, she got up one night and went to see for herself and she discovered he wasn't there.'

'Did that not serve only to confirm her suspicions?'

'So you'd have thought,' Josse agreed ruefully, 'but unfortunately she made up her mind that our stranger was some sort of malevolent spirit who hid from the light and emerged by night to do whatever such entities do.'

'Had she any reason to believe the man was malevolent?' asked the Abbess.

Josse shrugged. 'If so, she has not revealed it.'

The Abbess was studying him closely. 'Have *you*?'

Josse considered the question. 'I don't know,' he said slowly. 'He's a mystery, that's for sure – I'm pretty certain he's been brought back from Outremer and abandoned, for he looks, acts and for the most part speaks like a foreigner. That's really what prompted me to take him in, my lady – too many returning crusaders use a man they've engaged out East for as long as it pleases them, only to kick him out once they're home with their own servants again.'

'I see,' she said. Then: 'And this strange guest of yours has definitely gone?'

'Aye. Vanished into the night, taking everything he owns with him.'

'If it is indeed true that he is engaged upon some clandestine mission,' she said thoughtfully, 'then could it be that Ella's sudden interest caused him to flee?'

'Just what I thought,' Josse agreed. 'I visualized him on the point of setting out, then spotting Ella tiptoeing across the yard to spy on him. Fearful that she'd report back to me, he ran.'

'Yet you say he took all his belongings with him,' she pointed out. 'Does that not suggest to you that he was planning to leave anyway, even before he saw Ella going out to check up on him?'

He rubbed a hand across his jaw. 'Aye,' he acknowledged gruffly. 'Aye, it does.'

She smiled suddenly. 'Sir Josse, does it matter? You did what you could for him, and it appears you helped him recover his strength. The important thing now is to make Ella see that her fears were unfounded; that this mystery man was no more than a stranger whom you took in and saw on his way. If we here at Hawkenlye can achieve that, we can call the matter closed.' He did not answer. 'Yes?'

He looked up and met her eyes. There was, he detected, the beginnings of amusement in her expression. 'Suppose so,' he muttered.

'Excellent!' she cried. 'Now, you have had a long ride in the cold – let me order some refreshments.'

Ella remained closeted with the infirmarer for most of the afternoon and by the time she emerged – smiling shyly up at Will, who was waiting for her – it was too late to set out for New Winnowlands. Josse and Will were offered accommodation with the monks down in the Vale and one of the nursing nuns said she would prepare a shakedown bed for Ella in the infirmary.

In the morning Will was up early to ready the mounts. Josse, who had been enjoying a chat with Brother Augustus while he finished his breakfast, followed him a little later up to the Abbey to seek out Ella, who was making herself useful in the infirmary by helping Sister Caliste take food and drinks to the bed-bound patients.

Will brought out the horses and Josse went to say farewell to the Abbess. He, Will and Ella had already mounted up and were setting out through the gates when Josse heard the sound of hurrying hooves. He drew rein, waiting.

A horse and rider came into sight from the direction of the forest. The horse was pushed to its limits and, despite the chill morning air, sweating. The rider was white in the face and looked shocked and sick.

Josse slid off Horace's back, handing the reins to Will. Stepping forward, he went to meet the rider as he pulled his horse to a skidding halt at the gates.

'Is this Hawkenlye Abbey?' the man shouted. He was young – little more than a boy – and the poor quality of his garments compared with the splendour of his horse suggested that the animal was not his usual mount.

Laying aside the instant suspicion that this lad might be a horse thief, Josse put a hand on the horse's bridle and said, 'Aye, this is Hawkenlye.'

'Oh, thank God!' The lad all but fell from the saddle, stumbled and would have collapsed but for Josse's supporting arm. 'It's terrible! I've never seen anything so ghastly in all my born days, and that's a fact!' His eyes were wide with horror and Josse smelt vomit on his breath. 'It fair turned my stomach and I don't normally quake at the sight of blood.' His pallor increased and Josse stepped back just in time as the lad threw up on the frosty grass.

A small crowd had gathered. Sister Martha, frowning and with her pitchfork in her hand, stood beside Ella, who was mounted on the mule; Brother Saul and Brother Augustus, who had come to see Josse's party on their way, stepped forward. In the background the Abbess was walking slowly towards the source of the commotion, eyebrows raised.

Josse nodded at Augustus who, understanding, took charge

of the lad's horse. Then Josse put an arm around the shaking boy and said, 'Let's have it, then. You've seen something bad and you've come here for help?'

'Yes. *Yes,*' the lad stammered. 'Me and the master, we're riding along the track that skirts the forest on our way down to Tonbridge – Master, he's a merchant and he had some goods he were taking to sell – and all of a sudden his horse starts and almost throws him. We could smell it ourselves then, both of us – the stench was like a butcher's block, I'm telling you.' He shuddered. 'Anyway – ' he rallied – 'Master dismounts, goes to have a look and I follows. It – he – is lying there under the trees and there's blood and spilled guts and he's—'

But trying to describe the horror was beyond him. Dumbly shaking his head, the lad began to weep.

'Your master told you to mount his horse and come on here for help?' Josse suggested. 'Is that what happened?'

'Yes, sir, it were just like that,' the boy said, turning pathetically grateful eyes on Josse. 'Me, I ride a mule but he's a lazy old bugger – sorry – and it takes all my strength to get him moving, let alone hurrying, so Master says to ride his horse.' The lad glanced up at the horse, now being soothed by Brother Augustus. 'He's all in a sweat,' the lad said. 'Master'll be cross.' His face crumpled anew.

'I'll see to the horse,' Augustus said kindly. He glanced at Josse, who nodded again, and then he led the horse away to Sister Martha's stables.

The Abbess had now joined the group. 'I don't think this poor boy is capable of telling you any more,' she murmured in Josse's ear. 'Would it perhaps be wise to get him to take you to where this accident occurred? Perhaps if you were to take Brother Saul and Brother Augustus, they could carry a hurdle on which to bring the unfortunate victim here to us?'

He turned to her. 'Aye, my lady,' he said quietly, 'that was exactly what I had in mind.'

Sister Martha volunteered to take over the big sweating horse. Will took charge of Horace and his own and Ella's mounts, following Sister Martha to the stables with Ella clutching on to his arm. Very soon Josse and the two lay brothers were ready to leave. The lad still seemed overawed by Josse and so Brother Augustus – much closer in size and age – quietly fell into step beside the boy. Josse and Brother Saul, walking behind, heard him say cheerfully, 'They're good people at the Abbey and you did well coming to us for help. I'm called Brother Augustus but my friends usually call me Gussie. What's your name?'

The boy looked up with the very beginnings of a smile and said something – it sounded like 'It's Dickon' – in reply. Then Gussie, exhibiting an unexpected gift for small talk, began to chatter about the weather, the quality of the food at the Abbey and just what a lay brother's daily round consisted of and quite soon the lad was joining in and even giving the occasional chuckle.

Josse observed it all. He was grateful to Augustus for making the boy relax – people in shock weren't much use for anything – but nevertheless he felt deeply disturbed.

He was lying there under the trees.

So much blood and spilled guts.

Glancing down at the hazel hurdle that the silent Brother Saul carried under one arm, he wondered if it would be a living man or a corpse that they bore back to the Abbey.

He thought more likely the latter.

Three

The body had been savaged.

It was naked and the wounds were clear to see. There was a large lump on the forehead, and bruising and a couple of grazes on the jaw. There was a series of deep cuts across the chest and the right arm had been all but severed just above the wrist. It was as if the dead man had defended himself – with sword, with knife? – and his attacker, or more likely attackers, had gone for the right arm to prevent the defensive blade thrust.

The belly had been sliced open, allowing the purplish-white folds of the guts to push out. This would have undoubtedly killed him but his murderers had been merciful. They had slit his throat.

Not just slit it; they had carved out a wide slice from jaw to larynx, leaving a terrible gash in the shape of the young moon.

Dear God, Josse thought.

In front of him Dickon and Brother Augustus had stopped. Josse and Brother Saul drew level and all four stood staring. Josse glanced at Dickon, pale as new snow beside him. 'Go and stand on the track down there where it curves round to the right,' he ordered. 'Stop anyone coming along the path.'

Dickon's look of gratitude was eloquent reward. Not only was he excused from going any nearer to that terrible thing under the trees but in addition Josse had saved his pride by giving him a job to do.

Leaving the lay brothers on the path, Josse approached the bloody body. There was a cloaked figure standing some distance beyond it, next to two mules tethered to a tree. The man hurried forward.

'You are from Hawkenlye Abbey?' he called.

'Aye,' Josse said. 'I am Josse d'Acquin. The brethren with the hurdle are Brothers Saul and Augustus.'

The man nodded. 'I am Guiot of Robertsbridge, on my way to Tonbridge with nutmegs and cloves for the market. That's my lad Dickon. He's a tad lacking in the wits but he's willing and he has a way with a heavily laden mule that I've rarely seen bettered.' Having thus identified himself – a wise notion, Josse reflected, when standing over a mutilated corpse – Guiot of Robertsbridge dropped his voice and muttered, 'Someone had it in for this poor fellow.'

Josse had crouched down over the body. 'Aye.'

'I've been wondering if—' began Guiot. But, evidently sensing that Josse would prefer silence, abruptly he shut his mouth and stepped back a pace.

Slowly and steadily Josse took in the details of the dead man, from the top of his head to his pale, bare feet. His shoulder-length hair was so dark that it looked black, lying slick and smooth on his skull. His eyes, partly open, were also dark; having noted this detail, Josse gently lowered the lids. The man's nose was sharp and the cheekbones were set high, giving a hawkish look to the face. The skin was olive in tone. His chest was well muscled and he was broad-shouldered, with a toned belly and long legs with sturdy thighs. The penis, flaccid below the smooth black body hair, had been circumcised.

Josse looked up at Guiot. 'Any sign of his clothing?'

'No. This is exactly how he was when the lad and I stumbled across him: mother-naked, unarmed and no pack, purse or wallet.' Unable to curb his curiosity, he added, 'Robbery, do you think? Some wretch jumping out on a man travelling alone in the early hours of the morning?'

Intrigued, Josse said, 'How do you know he was attacked in the early hours?'

Guiot looked smug. 'Because Dickon and I left home around dawn and Dickon had been up some time before that getting the mule packed. He pointed out that it was a good thing we didn't set out earlier because we'd have been caught in the downpour we'd just had.' The smile spreading, Guiot went on, 'The body's wet, so it was lying here when the rain fell, but the ground under the body is dry, so he must have fallen just *before* the rain shower.'

Josse was impressed. But he could see a slight flaw in the argument: 'Could there not have been another shower earlier in the night?'

'No,' Guiot said firmly. 'I'm a light sleeper and I'd have heard rain on the roof. D'you reckon it *was* a robber killed him?' he persisted. 'Seems likely, since whoever did for him took his belongings and every stitch of clothing.'

'Aye,' Josse agreed. He was not really listening; he was trying to make up his mind about something.

It was difficult to say with certainty, for with the clothing and the satchel missing there was nothing to go by. The face was exposed, that was true, but then Josse had nothing with which to make a comparison. Still, the height and the general build were right, as was the swarthy skin tone.

And the man he was thinking of was, after all, missing . . .

Making up his mind, Josse stood up. He looked at Guiot and said, 'We must take him to the Abbey and prepare his body for burial.'

He turned and beckoned to the two lay brothers who, with no display of emotion save that their touch on the dead man's body was noticeably gentle and respectful, loaded him onto the hurdle.

'We can't carry him into the Abbey like that,' Josse said, gazing down at the corpse. He unfastened his cloak and was about to cover the body with it when Guiot said, 'Wait.' Then, looking slightly ashamed: 'Pity to spoil a good cloak. Let me fetch a bit of sacking to absorb the blood, then your cloak can go on top of that.'

It made sense. Josse gave a curt nod, and the dead man, decently covered, was borne away to Hawkenlye Abbey.

'I think,' Josse said to Abbess Helewise, 'that the victim may be John Damianos.'

'I see,' the Abbess said slowly. 'You are not sure?'

'I cannot be, my lady, for John Damianos wore a headdress that kept his brow, nose and mouth concealed and his eyes in shade. Our dead man was naked when he was found and his garments are missing.'

'On what grounds, then, do you believe him to be this John Damianos?'

'Right build, right height, same olive skin tone, and John Damianos is missing. Also the dead man was circumcised, which suggests he was possibly Muslim, and, as I told you, I believe the man who took refuge in my outbuilding was a servant brought home from Outremer.'

'Yes, yes, so you did,' she murmured. Then, frowning, 'But is such scant information sufficient for us to bury him as John Damianos?'

Josse shrugged. 'I do not know, my lady.'

Abruptly she stood up and, walking around her table, said, 'Come, Sir Josse. Let us go and join Sister Euphemia.'

The corpse had been taken to the infirmary and Sister Caliste had washed it. Now, as the Abbess parted the curtains and led the way into the recess, both Sister Caliste and the infirmarer were bending over the dead man.

Sister Euphemia glanced up as they stepped inside and let the curtain fall behind them. She gave the Abbess a bow and said quietly, 'I've tidied him up. I hope that was all right, Sir Josse, only . . .' Her lips tightened.

Josse looked at the long, strong body lying on the cot. The guts had been pushed back into the abdomen, the flesh held together with a neat row of large stitches. A roll of linen had been placed beneath the head, so that the chin was tucked down against the upper chest, partly closing the awful wound in the throat. Meeting Sister Euphemia's eyes, he nodded. 'Aye. It was quite all right, Sister. I saw him by the road and I know what was done to him.'

The Abbess's face was white. He could hear her soft mutter as she prayed for the dead man's soul. When she had finished, she turned to Josse and said, in what he thought was an admirably controlled tone, 'What can have prompted such savagery, Sir Josse? This man must have suffered agony.'

He hesitated, not because he had no answer but because that answer added more horror. But she was waiting. 'My lady, to torture a man before killing him is usually done to extract something that it is believed he knows, or to inflict maximum punishment before the death blow.'

She nodded. Putting out a hand, she let her fingertips rest on the dead man's shoulder in the lightest of touches. 'Did he bear an awesome secret?' she said softly. 'Or had he done a wicked deed?'

Not sure whether the question was rhetorical – he would have had no answer even if it were not – Josse held his silence. After a moment, the Abbess said, 'If indeed this man is your John Damianos, then we know he was going out secretly by night. He fled once his nocturnal habits were known. Were those not, Sir Josse, the actions of a fugitive with something to hide?'

'Aye, my lady.'

'Then we must assume that those who sought him have found him.' She sighed. 'Is there any more to be gained from further study of the body?'

Josse met the infirmarer's eyes. 'Sister Euphemia? Have you completed your inspection?'

'I have,' she confirmed. 'He was a man in his late twenties or early thirties, tall and broad and very well-muscled. I would say that he was a fighting man.'

'Aye,' Josse agreed.

'His feet and legs in particular are powerful,' the infirmarer continued, 'suggesting that he did a great deal of walking. His skin is darker in tone than is common among us, indicating that he comes from a foreign land. His eyes are dark brown and his hair black. He suffered multiple wounds before his throat was cut.' She looked quickly at the Abbess, then her eyes returned to Josse. 'It wasn't an easy death or a quick one.'

'Thank you, Sister,' the Abbess murmured. 'Sir Josse? Have you anything to add?'

Mentally Josse ran through the many wounds on the body. The horror of the man's death prevented him thinking about anything else, but he knew he must force his brain to work. 'I am trying to recall anything I observed of my visitor that might help us to determine whether or not this is his body,' he said. 'But I have not come up with anything. John Damianos was most scrupulous in keeping his head and face covered and I just don't know . . . '

There was a short silence. Then the Abbess said, 'Will further contemplation of this poor, ruined man help you?'

He realized belatedly what she was asking him. 'No,' he said firmly. 'I am attempting the impossible, for I am trying to compare something I can see with something that was carefully kept from my eyes. The sooner we put this man in his grave' – and out of our sight, he might have added – 'the better.'

She nodded. 'Very well. Sister Euphemia, if you will prepare the corpse, it shall be taken to the crypt to await burial.' She was still staring down at the dead man, her eyes wide and dazed, and Josse could see that it was with some effort that finally she tore her gaze away.

She turned and strode out of the recess. Josse, with a quick smile to Sister Euphemia and Sister Caliste, hurried after her.

Helewise wanted more than anything to escape to her private room, close the door and bring herself under control. The dead body had disturbed her far more than she had let on and as she walked swiftly across the frost-hard ground, after-images of horror floated in front of her eyes. As she reached the cloister she was aware of someone hurrying after her – Josse, for sure – and, biting down her impatience, she turned.

It was not Josse; he was standing in the arched doorway to the infirmary, staring after her with a faint frown on his face. It was old Brother Firmin.

She forced a smile. 'Brother Firmin, good day.'

'I am sorry to detain you when I know you must yearn for a moment to yourself,' he began – oh, dear Lord, she thought, how fast news travels in this community! – 'but I fear I must tell you. It's not only the other brethren and me – Sister Ursel and Sister Martha were asked too, and so were two of the refectory nuns, and I am told they were also seen outside the infirmary so they must have pursued their enquiries with the nursing sisters, and I – that is, we – just thought you ought to *know*, my lady.'

His honest eyes in the deeply creased old face were looking up at her anxiously and her irritation vanished as swiftly as it had come. 'Of course, Brother Firmin,' she said kindly. Taking his hand and tucking it under her arm, she added, 'Come along to my room, where we shall be out of the draught, and you shall tell me what it is that troubles you.'

'But—'

They had reached her door and she opened it and ushered the old monk inside. She seated herself in her chair. 'Now, Brother.' She folded her hands inside the opposite sleeves of her habit and gave him what she hoped was an encouraging smile. He seemed to shrink in alarm so she relaxed her fierce expression a little. 'What is the matter?'

Eyeing her nervously, he hesitated and then said in a rush, 'Three men have been here asking questions. They are brethren of the Order of Knights Hospitaller and wear the white cross upon breast or sleeve.'

Her mind had leapt ahead as soon as Brother Firmin spoke his second sentence. Knights Hospitaller. Outremer. Returning knights and abandoned servants. Dead man with a secret. John Damianos.

Brother Firmin was looking at her warily.

'Go on!' she snapped. Then, instantly penitent, 'I am sorry, Brother Firmin. Please excuse my impatience. These men were asking questions, you said?'

'Yes, my lady. They spoke to the monks and pilgrims down in the Vale, then like I say they came up here and spoke to the sisters in the refectory and the—'

'Yes, quite,' she interrupted. 'What did they want to know?'

Brother Firmin's eyes widened like a storyteller approaching the most dramatic point of his tale. 'They're after a runaway!' he breathed.

'Really?' She felt her own excitement rising. 'From where and what has this man fled?'

'I cannot say, my lady,' the old monk admitted, 'save that the knights implied their chase had been most arduous and lengthy.'

Had they trailed their quarry all the way from Outremer? she wondered. Was it likely that three warrior monks would follow a runaway all that distance? Was it even possible to dog a man's footsteps for all those hundreds and hundreds of miles over both land and sea . . . ?

'They did say,' Brother Firmin added darkly, 'that the runaway was an English monk.'

'Did they?' She was not sure why she was surprised. Wouldn't it be the obvious thing, for an English fugitive to run for home? But then she realized that her surprise was because she was still obsessed with the body of the dark stranger: he, clearly, was no Englishman, and consequently she was now faced with the fact that her instant conclusion – that the runaway Knight Hospitaller was the man in her infirmary – could not be the right one. 'I see,' she finished lamely.

Brother Firmin waited to see if she was going to speak again and when she did not, he ventured tentatively, 'We all thought it was very strange, my lady.'

'What was?'

'That these men should creep about asking questions of just about everybody except for the person they ought to have approached.' His frown expressed his disapproval. 'They are vowed monks and they ought to know how such things are done.'

'You mean they should have asked me first?'

'Indeed they should, my lady! Why, we all assumed they had your permission to interview us! Had we known that this was not the case, we should have refused!' His very body language spoke of his indignation. 'I do hope that no harm has been done?'

'No, Brother; none at all.' She got to her feet. 'Do you know where they are now? Because I think it is about time that I too heard what they have to say.'

The three Hospitallers, she discovered as she crossed the cloister with Brother Firmin panting along by her side, had found Josse. Or perhaps, she thought with a smile, Josse had found them. Either way, they were all standing in the lee of the long infirmary building and Josse appeared to be giving the oldest of the trio a considerable piece of his mind.

'. . . not the way things are done here, however you might

carry on in Outremer. Here it is considered good manners to speak to the Abbess first, and only proceed when and if she says you can!'

He and Brother Firmin must have been taught the same rules. Suppressing her smile, she glided up to the group and said, 'I am Abbess Helewise. May I help?'

Two of the three knights had the grace to look abashed. The third – a lean, pale man whose extreme thinness gave an illusory impression of height – stared straight at her with hazel eyes that did not look down as he gave a perfunctory bow. 'I am Thibault of Margat, of the Order of the Knights of the Hospital of St John of Jerusalem,' he intoned. 'These – ' he indicated the other two with a wave of his hand that was almost insulting in its indifference – 'are Brother Otto and, er . . .' he paused, frowning, 'Brother Jeremiah.'

Helewise wondered which was which, for their superior did not deign to enlighten her. All three were dressed in dark robes that were dusty, mud-spattered and very well worn. She waited for Thibault to continue.

'We are hunting for a runaway monk,' he said in a curiously expressionless tone. 'He is an Englishman.'

'An English Hospitaller,' she said. 'And what does this man look like?'

'He will be dressed as we are,' Thibault said, 'in a dark robe and black cloak – ' he held out a fold of his own cloak – 'or scapular – ' he pointed to one of the brothers – 'marked with the distinctive white cross of our Order.'

Slowly she shook her head. 'I have seen no such man,' she said. Then, for Thibault's look of disdain was profoundly irritating, she added, 'I will ask my nuns and monks if they have noticed a man dressed as you describe. Unless, that is, you have already done so?' She fixed Thibault with a hard stare.

His lips tightened. 'We have asked both in the settlement down by the lake and here in the Abbey,' he acknowledged.

'And have any of my community or its visitors been able to help you?'

'No.' The single word was curt.

Although she knew it was unworthy, she was enjoying his discomfiture. 'To describe a man simply by the garb he wears is not of much value,' she said, forcing a helpful expression, 'since it is the easiest thing to remove one garment and put on another.'

'I had thought of that, my lady.' Thibault sounded as if he was speaking through clenched teeth.

'Can you not tell us more?' she prompted. 'What age is this runaway? What is his name? And what does he look like – is he fair or dark? Tall, short, fat, thin?'

Thibault raised his chin and squared his shoulders. 'I do not know,' he said.

For an instant Helewise was blessed with additional perception and she knew without doubt that this was a lie. Then the moment passed.

She glanced at Josse, watching the exchange with close attention, and drew him towards her. 'This is Sir Josse d'Acquin,' she said, 'a King's man and a loyal friend to Hawkenlye Abbey. Have you asked your question of him?'

Thibault looked at Josse, who stared levelly back. 'I have. Like you and your people, he says he knows nothing of a robed Hospitaller.'

There was a very faint emphasis on *says*. Helewise felt her anger boil up. She waited until she had herself under control and then said quietly, 'If that is what Sir Josse says, then, Thibault of Margat, it is the truth. If there is nothing else you want of me or my community, then allow me to wish you God's speed.'

She watched the protest rise and fall again in Thibault's face. He is torn, she thought grimly. There is more – probably very much more – that he could tell us that would help us to identify this runaway monk, should he ever come this way. Yet this information is sensitive, for Thibault cannot bring himself to divulge it . . .

As she waited for the Hospitaller to make up his mind she was struck forcibly with the thought that whatever the fugitive monk might or might not have done, she was on his side. But that was not a thought that a nun – an abbess, indeed – should entertain.

Thibault must have been working out his parting remark. Now, sweeping his black cloak around him, he jerked his head at his two silent companions and they walked off towards the gates. Thibault, turning to look at first Helewise and then Josse, said, 'We make now for Tonbridge, whence we shall set out for our Order's English headquarters at the priory of St John in Clerkenwell.' Then, in a voice of soft intensity, he added,

'You will send word to me if the English monk comes here. We will not be hard to find for we make no secret of our comings and goings.'

And that also is a lie, Helewise thought coolly.

Thibault, after the briefest of reverences, strode away after the two brothers.

She felt Josse stir beside her. 'Not so much as a farewell,' he muttered.

Without thinking, she said, 'He'll be back.'

Josse's expression suggested that he was almost as surprised as she was by the remark. 'My lady?'

'Oh – er, I just meant that here at Hawkenlye we have the biggest concentration of people for miles, so Brother Thibault is hardly likely to be satisfied with a few brief questions.' It sounded unsatisfactory even to her ears.

Josse went on staring at her and now he was looking decidedly suspicious. She gave him a smile – she could not have explained how she knew, even had she wanted to – and after a moment he muttered, 'Have it your own way.'

Her need for solitude had grown out of all proportion; a great deal had happened this morning and she urgently needed to think. Leaning close to Josse, she said softly, 'I must send for Father Gilbert to arrange for the burial. I had thought that perhaps the man those Hospitallers are seeking might be our dead man, for I believe that the brethren do recruit soldiers from the native population in Outremer.'

'Indeed, my lady,' Josse relied. 'They are known as turcopoles, and the military orders put them on a horse, give them a bow and, after scant training, fling them into battle.'

She hid a smile; evidently Josse did not approve of such practices. 'But then they said the runaway is an Englishman,' she said with a sigh, 'so that was the end of that bright idea.'

He was frowning, clearly thinking.

'Sir Josse?' she prompted.

'Oh – I was thinking of John Damianos. If what I suspect is right and the dead man *is* him, then perhaps he accompanied the missing Hospitaller? He – John Damianos – might have been the monk's body servant, brought to England and abandoned.'

She considered the idea. Then, with an impatient shake of her head: 'It's all too vague, Sir Josse! Nothing but ifs and maybes.'

He looked quite hurt. 'I'm sorry, my lady, but it's the best I can do.'

She smiled. 'No, Sir Josse; *I* am sorry, for my bad mood. There is much that I need to think about. I do not mean to be mysterious and I will try to explain later, but for now I really do need to be alone.'

He studied her, his head on one side. After a moment – and she had the clear impression he knew exactly how she felt – he said, 'Off you go, then, my lady. I'm going to return with Will and Ella to New Winnowlands. Send for me when you feel like some company.'

His low and respectful bow put Thibault's to shame. Then he gave her a cheerful grin and strolled away.

Outremer, September 1194

He did not know at first why they had selected him for the mission. Initially he felt nothing but pride that he, not even among the fully professed, had been singled out for such an honour. It was only afterwards that he realized why: for two qualities that of all the company only he possessed . . .

The mission was a hostage exchange. Such things occurred quite frequently and often the brethren acted as escorts. As avowed men of God they were honest and impartial, and their presence ensured fair play by both sides. Moreover, sometimes the prisoner had been wounded in battle, in which case the brother who had cared for him would be in the escort. Saracen prisoners were exchanged both for Frankish knights and for gold.

This time it was going to be different.

It was rumoured that the order had come from the Grand Master himself but the young man was used to the way gossip flared within the community and he wasn't sure he believed it. As far as he was concerned, it was his superior who gave the instructions, and Thibault was a tight-lipped man who never wasted a word.

They sent for him in the night.

He fell into step behind five other Hospitallers, the senior monk leading the way. Despite the heat of the late summer night, all six were swathed in black surcoats, hoods drawn up over their heads and hiding their faces. Beneath the surcoats each man carried a sword and a knife.

They reached the stables, where the sergeants had prepared their mounts. The bridles were bound with twine to prevent noise; the smallest sound of jingling metal carried a long way in the still desert. Then the sergeant unbolted the door and they set off down the long covered passage to the outside world.

It was a fine night and the stars were dazzling in the black sky. The air retained much of the daytime heat although he – who had been in Outremer for nine long years – knew how quickly the temperature could plummet in the hours before dawn.

They had picked up the prisoner as they emerged from the vast gates. He was broad-shouldered for a Saracen, hooded and dressed in pale robes. He sat on a beautiful Arab gelding. His manacled wrists were attached by a short chain to the pommel of his saddle and two longer chains linked him to armed guards riding either side. Otherwise the man was treated with respect.

They rode for perhaps an hour. The land was so different by night – it smelt different, the sounds were not those of the day, and night vision had a way of playing tricks so that distant things seemed suddenly near and something apparently a stone's throw away proved to be on the far horizon. Or perhaps, the young man thought with a shiver, there was magic in the air. In this distant land full of strange ways and secrets, that would hardly surprise him . . .

The first sign of their destination was the faint glimmer of a fire in the vast desert in front of him. He narrowed his eyes to see how far away it was, but with no other point of reference it was impossible to tell. They rode on and soon he began to make out shapes. A simple tent had been put up, and beside the fire there was a picket line to which ten horses had been tethered. As the party approached the campsite, two Saracens emerged from the tent and, with courteous bows, invited the monks and their charge to dismount and enter.

He was the last to go inside and what he saw took his breath away. The desert sand had been covered with rugs and carpets in delicate geometric patterns of purple, red and gold, and low divans, covered with gold and purple silk throws, had been set around the curving fabric walls. Light came from a series of iron lanterns from which candle flames shone through jewel-coloured panes of glass: amethyst, garnet, ruby and sapphire. A copper pot was bubbling on a small brazier, emitting a strong aroma of orange and cinnamon.

For the young Hospitaller standing awestruck by such opulence, this was the sole jarring note. As a child he had once gorged himself on marigold, saffron and cinnamon cakes and been violently sick. Ever since he had been unable to stomach the taste of cinnamon.

A very large man lay on one of the divans and as the prisoner was led into the tent his face lit up in a smile of welcome. The prisoner raised his manacled wrists and threw back his hood and the young monk saw a beautiful youth, tall, lithe and strong. The olive skin of his cheeks and jaw looked too smooth to require a razor, yet there seemed to be a sharpness to the bones of the face. With a couple of years' more maturity, this man would look very different. The near-black eyes, set slightly on a slant, stared out from beneath a thick sweep of lashes and fine, gracefully curved eyebrows.

The fat man, staring intently at the prisoner, said how happy he was to be reunited with his beloved little brother. The Hospitaller, positioned as he was behind the prisoner and to his left, was in exactly the right place to see the long look that the fat man bestowed on him. And the young knight experienced one of those sudden flashes of sure but unlooked-for knowledge which, here in Outremer, occurred quite frequently. He knew that the beautiful youth was not the fat man's brother but his catamite.

The fat man indicated that the Hospitallers and the prisoner should sit on the remaining divans. Then they were offered glass cups of the drink that had been simmering on the fire. The young monk accepted his with a polite bow. While everyone else drank to a satisfying outcome for the night's business, he held his breath so as not to inhale the scent of cinnamon and only pretended to sip. Then he put his glass down out of sight beside his feet.

Swiftly the fat man on the divan put the courtesies aside. His expression suddenly serious, he began to speak, so rapidly that the young Hospitaller had to use all his wits to keep up. When he had finished the senior monk replied, speaking the same tongue but in a more controlled manner. There was a further exchange of terms and then, both parties apparently satisfied, a toast to seal the agreement.

Then to the young knight's amazement his superior turned to him and gave him a curt order.

It was only then that he realized that this was no ordinary hostage exchange.

As he prepared to do as he had been commanded, his eyes ran around the Saracens in the tent. There were four servants. Including the fat man, that made five.

Why, then, were there ten horses tethered outside?

The first chill finger of fear slid up his spine.

Four

In the course of the ride back to New Winnowlands, Josse was very relieved to find that Ella appeared to be herself again. Not that it was easy to tell, for she was a diffident woman. But Will, Josse thought, seemed far more relaxed and happy than he had done for days. The Hawkenlye magic had worked, then. Maybe he would suggest that she cook him a particularly toothsome dinner today to celebrate her recovery.

Presently his thoughts snapped guiltily away from gravy-rich, steaming pies and back to the worrying subject of the mutilated corpse. The Abbess had been deeply disturbed, even though she had striven not to show it. But then we were all disturbed, he thought. No decent human being could fail to react to such savagery. It was no wonder she had been so eager to seek out a little solitude. There was no need for me to have taken offence, Josse told himself firmly; none whatsoever. No matter how distressed she might be, she was constricted both by her position and her own proud and self-reliant nature and she was not a woman who habitually took comfort in the arms of a dear old friend.

More's the pity, he thought morosely.

She had been angry with him because he could not be more

definite as to the identity of the dead man and he understood
well enough why that was: she disliked sending an unnamed,
unknown man to meet his maker. But there was nothing I could
do! Josse cried silently. For the life of me, I just *don't know* if
the dead man was the man who lived for almost a fortnight in
my outbuilding!

Now he too was feeling angry. Dear Lord, he thought, but
she can be an unreasonable woman!

They were nearing New Winnowlands now and he heard the
rare sound of Ella laughing. Well, the mission had achieved its
purpose and that was something to be glad about.

He rode into the courtyard and slipped down off Horace's
back. In the hall a fire was blazing; he went across to the hearth
and held out his hands to its warmth. She'll send for me if she
needs me, he thought. If those Knights Hospitaller return and
start giving her trouble, she knows she can call on me. I'll be
here, eager and waiting and more than ready to go to her aid.

And that, he reflected as he sank down into his big carved
chair, was the trouble.

The next day Josse experienced a strange sense of events
repeating themselves. In the late morning Will announced there
was someone wishing to speak to him. Josse leapt up, quite
convinced that the visitor must be John Damianos; that he had
come to apologize for running off in the night, to offer belated
thanks and to explain himself. Which would all be splendid
because then Josse could gallop over to Hawkenlye and tell the
Abbess that the dead man certainly was not John Damianos.

These thoughts ran through Josse's head in the time it took
him to hurry out of the hall and down the steps into the yard.

Where it instantly became clear that he was wrong.

He had not one visitor but two. Both were Saracens and wore
headdresses of elaborately wound cloth, immaculately white,
folds of which passed beneath their chins and around their
necks. They were clad in warm travelling cloaks over well-
worn but fine-quality tunics whose fabric must once have been
dazzlingly bright, and their scuffed boots were of expensive
leather. They were mounted on small but beautiful Arab horses
and attached to the saddle of each was a round shield. Both
men bore a short, curved sword.

Josse approached them. 'You wish to speak to me?'

The elder of the pair responded. His dark eyes, deep-set under strong brows, were intent on Josse and he said in accented French, 'You are Sir Josse d'Acquin?' Josse nodded. 'Then yes, we do.'

Josse felt wary. Instead of immediately issuing the expected invitation to dismount and come inside, he said, 'Who are you and what is your business here?'

The two men exchanged a glance. Then the elder said, 'I am Kathnir and my companion is Akhbir.' Both men touched their fingers to their lips, their brows and their hearts, bowing their heads as they did so. 'We seek a man. We ask whether you have seen or heard of him. We have followed our quarry for many hundreds of miles and now – ' the man gave a wry smile – 'he will be as dusty and as travel-worn as we are. He wears a long brown robe and an enveloping headdress that conceals most of his face and overshadows his eyes and he carries a leather satchel that he is always most careful never to let out of his sight.'

The description perfectly fitted John Damianos.

Josse took his time in replying. 'This man is a Saracen like yourselves?'

Kathnir hesitated. Then: 'Yes.'

Josse watched the pair steadily. With another smile, Kathnir said, 'May we dismount?'

Josse nodded. Kathnir slipped down from his horse and Akhbir did the same. They bowed again, this time more deeply, and as they straightened up Josse noted absently that they were both short men. Short but wiry and strongly muscled.

Fighting men.

He made up his mind. 'Come into my hall,' he said, 'and, if you will, accept refreshments. My kitchen woman makes a tasty drink that warms the heart after a ride in the cold.'

'We drink no intoxicating liquor,' Akhbir said reprovingly.

Josse looked at him. 'I was not offering you any,' he replied coolly.

He nodded to Will, who took the reins of the two horses, then led the way up the steps and into the hall. He called to Ella and asked her to prepare a jug of her special ginger infusion. Then, turning to the two Saracens, he indicated that they should sit down on the bench opposite his chair. 'Why do you seek this man?' he demanded.

Again, the swift exchange of glances. Then Kathnir said, 'He has a – treasure that does not belong to him. We are commanded to find him, take back that which he stole and return it to our master.'

'I see.' It was an empty comment, for Josse did not see at all. 'You have come a long way, you said?'

'We come from Outremer,' Kathnir said softly.

'Then what was stolen from your master must be priceless indeed,' Josse observed.

Neither man took up the clear invitation to elaborate. Neither, in fact, spoke at all.

Josse was thinking hard. If the dead body at Hawkenlye was that of John Damianos and he *was* the man who had stolen the treasure, whatever it was, then Josse could dispatch these two tough and ruthless warriors in his direction with a clear conscience. Nobody could hurt him any more.

'What is the name of the man you seek?' he asked.

Kathnir eyed him, his face expressionless. 'We do not know his name,' he said. 'We describe him by his appearance. After all' – his smile seemed warmer now but Josse would have put a bag of gold on it being nothing more than a skilful act – 'a man may change his name more easily than his raiment.'

The Abbess, Josse reflected, had made a similar remark . . . A runaway Hospitaller and a thief. Both had fled to England from Outremer. Both were being pursued by men who were as relentless as hounds on a fresh scent. And surely it was too much of a coincidence to suggest that the monk and the Saracen thief were not connected?

Ella appeared with a jug emitting clouds of fragrant steam and three earthenware mugs and, at a nod from Josse, she poured her ginger concoction. He was grateful for her arrival; it had given him some much-needed thinking time.

When she had disappeared back down the passage, he raised his mug to the two Saracens and all three drank. With a small part of his attention he responded to their polite appreciation. The rest of his mind was working on what he was going to tell them.

I *liked* John Damianos, he thought, perhaps only now appreciating the fact. He was evasive, mysterious, he told me nothing concerning himself or his business and he disappeared without a thank you, but there was something about him to which I

warmed. If he is *not* the man who lies dead at Hawkenlye –
and some irrational instinct told Josse that this was so – then
I will not throw him to the dogs until I know a great deal more.
Even then, I might choose to save him.

He was in no doubt that the two men sitting calmly in his
hall would not hesitate to kill the man who had stolen their
master's treasure if it proved necessary; perhaps even if it *wasn't*
necessary . . .

He made up his mind.

'I do know of a man who answers the description of your
thief,' he said.

Two pairs of very dark eyes shot to meet his own. It was,
he thought, a little like facing a quartet of sword points. 'You
do?' breathed Kathnir.

'Aye. But I warn you, the man I speak of was found stripped
of garments and of possessions and it is only from the tone of
his skin and the near black colour of his eyes that I deduce
him to have been a Saracen.'

'Was found?' Kathnir echoed quietly.

'Aye. He is dead: murdered close by Hawkenlye Abbey, half
a day's ride from here. You know of it?'

'We have heard tell,' Kathnir said. He leaned towards Akhbir
and the two men muttered in what Josse assumed was their
own tongue. Then Kathnir said, 'We do not believe this dead
man to be our quarry.'

'You *what*?' Josse was astounded; he had been so sure that
at last he was to have some answers to his many questions.
'How can you be so sure? There aren't many stray Saracens
wandering through the countryside, I can tell you! Should you
not at least go to Hawkenlye and ask to see the dead man before
he is put in the ground?'

But instead of a reasoned response, Kathnir exclaimed, 'You
do not understand the gravity of the crime that this man
committed! If you did, then you would help us!'

'It makes no difference what I understand,' Josse began, 'for
I—' For I cannot tell you what I do not know, he was about
to say.

He stopped himself. There was something he *did* know but
that he had chosen not to tell the Saracens, but he had decided
not to mention his former guest to this sinister and threatening
pair.

Kathnir was still watching him intently and Josse had the uneasy feeling that the Saracen saw straight through the subterfuge. Forcing a grin and a shrug, he said, 'You say I do not understand the gravity of what this man has done. Won't you tell me?'

There was a long pause during which the two Saracens muttered to each other, their impatience and their frustration clearly evident even though Josse did not understand a word. Then Kathnir turned back to Josse and said, 'My master's younger brother was taken prisoner. He had been wounded in the fighting and he was taken to Margat.' His mouth twisted into its wry smile. 'Margat,' he added, 'is a fortress held by the Knights Hospitaller and even after the disarray that followed Hattin, the great Saladin did not succeed in taking it.'

'I know,' Josse said softly, 'about Margat.'

And, he could have added, I heard the name only this morning. That was something he was going to have to think about very carefully.

But not now.

Kathnir was speaking and Josse made himself listen.

'My master loves his little brother dearly,' the Saracen said, 'and it was against his wishes that Fadil – that is the brother's name – went off to fight, for my master judged that he was too inexperienced.'

'Where did the young man fight?' Josse's soldier's soul was intrigued by this talk of war.

'In Antioch and Tripoli, on the eastern borders of those territories,' Kathnir said. 'When Saladin signed the Peace of Ramla with the Frankish kings, we sent an arrow high in the sky to show our enemy that they need not fear the flying arrow.' His lean face creased in an ironic smile. 'But a treaty signed in Jaffa has little effect upon a war of attrition being waged two hundred miles to the north, and many of my master's kinsmen joined those who fought to push the Franks back towards the coast.'

'Aye, that I can understand,' Josse murmured. He had heard tell of such skirmishes where, under the general aegis of fighting off the Christians, Muslim landowners took the opportunity to add to their territories.

'My master prayed for Fadil's safety every day of his absence,' Kathnir continued. 'His grief when he learned that Fadil had fallen in battle was limitless, as was his joy at being told that he was not dead but merely injured. He had been unhorsed by a lance thrust and a Frankish sword bit deep into his shoulder. He was taken prisoner but, because of the severity of his wound, he was given into the care of the Knights Hospitaller, first at Crac des Chevaliers and then in their fortress of Margat.'

'And the Hospitallers nursed him back to health?'

'They did.' Kathnir's acknowledgement was grudging, as if it pained him to praise the enemy for their skill. 'But then during the monks' time in Outremer they have learned much of medicine from Arab doctors.'

'Aye, true,' Josse agreed. Kathnir shot him a glance, surprise in his eyes. 'Credit where credit is due,' Josse murmured softly.

Kathnir continued to stare at him for a moment. Then, resuming his narrative, he said, 'For many long months there was no news of Fadil but then my master was notified that his little brother had been proposed for a hostage exchange.' Suddenly his black eyes lit up with fire and with fury in his voice he cried, 'But from the outset it was—'

Akhbir dug him very hard in the ribs and abruptly he swallowed the words he had been about to say.

Josse bit back a curse. After a moment he said, 'But from the outset, you were saying?'

'There was a – a complication,' Kathnir said neutrally; he seemed to have regained control. 'My master's brother disappeared and was almost certainly killed and my master barely escaped with his life.'

'And it was during this complication that the Saracen whom you are seeking stole the treasure from your master?'

But Kathnir was not to be drawn. His dark eyes steady on Josse's, he said, 'I do not know.'

Oh but you do, Josse thought. There is much more that you could tell me of this hostage exchange that went so disastrously wrong. Of Knights Hospitaller and Saracens involved in some *complication* that took a man's life and robbed another of a treasure so precious that he sent two tough and resourceful warriors thousands of miles to get it back.

He studied first Kathnir and then Akhbir. Their dark eyes in the bland, impassive faces stared right back and he knew they were not going to say another word until and unless they decided it was appropriate.

And hell will probably freeze over, Josse reflected, before *that* happens.

He needed to think. He wanted to race back to Hawkenlye and have another look at the dead man before they put him in the ground. He wanted to go all around the spot where the body had been found, on his hands and knees if necessary, to see if he could find something – some small, overlooked thing – that might help him start to unravel this mystery.

He wanted to talk it all through with the Abbess.

He stood up and immediately the two Saracens did the same. 'I cannot be of further assistance to you,' he said flatly. 'I have told you of the dead man found near Hawkenlye and I can only suggest that you go there. It is not too late to look at him before he is buried.'

'But—' Akhbir began.

It was Kathnir's turn to stick an elbow into his companion's side. Smiling even as the abruptly silenced Akhbir winced, Kathnir said, 'We are grateful for your help and for the most excellent ginger drink. Now we will be on our way.' He bowed.

Josse saw his visitors out into the courtyard and watched from the steps as the two men mounted, gave him a final valediction and rode out through the gates and onto the track.

Thoughtfully Josse went back to his chair. He was going to return to Hawkenlye as soon as he could, and he would have yelled for Horace there and then except that he did not want to ride out alongside the two Saracens. He would give them some time to get away, then he would be on his way.

There was no danger that he would catch up with them on the road to Hawkenlye, even if he could have urged old Horace to the sort of speed necessary to overtake a couple of light, swift Arab geldings; quite a big *if*, he thought with a grin.

Because the Saracens weren't going to Hawkenlye.

He had realized something as he stood watching them ride away; something that he ought to have worked out sooner. Those two men were first-rate trackers. They had followed their man all the way from Outremer and somehow they were aware that the corpse at Hawkenlye was not that of the man they hunted. *We do not believe this dead man to be our quarry.* There was no need for them to view it.

They might not know where their man was now but they

knew perfectly well where he had been: they had tracked him to the exact spot where he had only recently been hiding.

New Winnowlands.

No, Josse thought, they won't be going to Hawkenlye. They'll be staying right here and as soon as they get the chance they'll be creeping through my outbuildings like rats after corn searching for any sign my late guest might have left behind. His grin widened. And they won't find a thing, because I've already looked.

He sat by the fire a while longer.

Then he sought out Will, informed him he was going back to Hawkenlye and, as soon as Horace was ready, hastened on his way.

Outremer, September 1194

He could feel the sweat of extreme anxiety running down his back and leaking from his armpits. When he drew breath he could smell himself.

His superior had given him a totally unexpected order. As the urgently muttered words had sunk in, a detached part of his mind had thought: yes, I understand now why I was chosen for this mission. Although accurate, his understanding was, however, only part of the story.

The fat man on the divan began to speak. The young monk strove to do his appointed task. In the flickering light of the coloured lanterns it was hard to see clearly and the effort added to the tension building up in his neck and shoulders. Soon his head was pounding like a battle drum. Eventually the fat man was done. With a wave of his hand, set with rings in which the huge stones twinkled in the lantern light, he commanded his servants to fill up the visitors' glasses with the cinnamon-flavoured drink. The young monk hastily reached for his own glass and, pushing aside the edge of the rug, poured the contents into the sand, holding up the empty vessel with what he hoped was a winning and innocent smile. The glass was filled by a supercilious servant and, after another pretend sip, the young monk hid it out of sight. He was nauseated by the drink. Even the smell all but turned his stomach and, given the tension and the vivid sense of danger that thrummed and hummed in the air, this was no time to be crouched over, vomiting in the sand.

The Hospitallers and the fat man were raising their glasses to each other's health. The prisoner's manacles were removed and the fat man, beaming, opened his arms in welcome. One of the guards leaned close and muttered something in the prisoner's ear. The prisoner nodded.

The young monk was watching him. He does not want to go, he realized suddenly. This night's business is not his choice, for his time as a prisoner has removed him from the fat man's spell. To return to his former state will be moving from one captivity to another, infinitely worse. It was as if the prisoner picked up the young monk's flash of understanding. Slowly he turned his head on its long, graceful neck and his eyes stared straight into those of the young Hospitaller.

The dark eyes held such a depth of anguish that the monk felt himself shrink away. As if the prisoner was making quite sure that the monk knew what he was going to have to endure, pictures began to form in the monk's mind; alien pictures that he knew without a doubt had been put there by the prisoner, for the things they showed were not actions that he had ever envisaged. He saw the fat man, sweating, grunting, eyes closed as he approached the moment of ecstasy, the loose flesh of his swelling belly slap, slap, slapping against the beautiful youth's lower back and round, firm buttocks. He saw the youth's face, a rictus of horror and disgust. He felt the youth's pain.

The youth's eyes slipped down to where the monk's short but deadly sword lay beneath his habit, pushed awkwardly behind him as he sat on the low divan. It was as if the youth could see straight through the black cloth. And suddenly his voice spoke inside the monk's head: Help me.

How can I? the monk responded in silent anguish.

Now the mental pictures were worse. The fat man was kissing and caressing the bare buttocks but then in a flash his mood changed and, with an expression of naked sexual desire and brutal savagery, viciously he brought a short, whippy cane down onto the olive-toned flesh. Once. Twice, three, four, five times, each stroke leaving a deep red welt that oozed blood.

Then the prisoner lowered his head and turned away and the horrific images faded.

The young monk tried to shake off the echoes of the prisoner's despair. There is nothing I can do, he told himself. Nothing. He forced himself back to the present; soon we shall be finished here, he thought, and we'll be outside in the night and riding off in the darkness. Then, as soon as we are safe within our own fortress, they will send for me.

Will I be ready? Will I be able to justify their faith in me and give them what they want?

He hoped he had achieved what had been asked of him, but it seemed wise to think over what he had just done. There was a great deal of excited chatter going on around him – the fat man was arranging an entertainment, it seemed – and while everyone else was preoccupied, the young monk took a few moments of quiet reflection.

And then the sounds around him grew distant and faint as, for the first time, he thought he understood what this meeting in the tent was truly about. Could he be right? No – oh, no; surely he had made a mistake? They could not even consider something so terrible, so barbarous!

Could they?

Perhaps they could . . .

The feverish heat died out of him and his sweat cooled on his skin.

He sat in the gaudy, glittering luxury of the tent, eyes wide in horror, and his blood turned to ice in his veins.

Five

Josse reached Hawkenlye, with some relief, just before the early November darkness descended. It wasn't that he was afraid; not exactly. But images of the mutilated body kept coming unbidden into his mind and that brutal slaying had, after all, occurred not far from the track on which he now rode.

He handed Horace into Sister Martha's care and made straight for the Abbess's room. After the courtesies, he said – and it sounded rather too demanding – 'I need to know if you've put him in the ground yet.'

She stared back at him, her face expressionless. Then he caught the smallest twitch of a smile at the corner of her mouth. 'No, Sir Josse. Father Gilbert is coming tomorrow.'

'Thank God,' he said.

She raised an eyebrow. 'Do you think to extract some more information from the poor man's body?'

'Aye, my lady. I should have explained, only I was overcome with my need to know whether it was too late. I apologize.'

'No need for apologies. What do you hope to find?'

He told her about the two Saracens. 'Somehow I have the feeling,' he said, rubbing his jaw, 'that we are not going to get anywhere until we know if the man who was brought to the infirmary is John Damianos.'

'But why is that so vital?' she asked.

He shrugged. 'I don't know,' he admitted. Then, with a rueful grin, he added, 'Perhaps the reason won't become clear until we've got the answer.'

She got to her feet. 'Your instincts, Sir Josse, have served both of us very well in the past and I for one am happy to indulge you. Come along.'

She swept out of her little room and he followed in her wake.

The infirmary was busy, the nursing nuns and some of the refectory nuns dishing out supper and warm drinks. Sister Euphemia gave the Abbess a deep bow of reverence and said, 'My lady? You wished to see me? Good evening, Sir Josse.'

'Good evening, Sister.'

'We have come to view the dead man once more,' the Abbess said in a low voice. 'Is he still here?'

'He's over in the crypt,' the infirmarer replied quietly. 'Let me fetch a light and I'll show you. You didn't say, my lady, but I thought it best under the circumstances to lock the door down to the crypt.'

'That was wise, Sister,' the Abbess said gravely.

'I can't explain it,' the infirmarer muttered as she held the door of the infirmary for the Abbess and Josse and then fell into step beside them, 'and I know it's silly, but I keep thinking someone's watching us and I'll bet we've not seen the end of all this yet.'

'I'm afraid you may be right, Sister,' Josse agreed. He too

had the repeated feeling that watchful eyes were constantly on him. The funny thing was, however, that he was not at all sure they were hostile, which really made no sense at all.

The infirmarer led the way into the church and unlocked a small door to the left of the altar. Inside, she took a torch from a bracket on the wall and, lighting it from the candle in her lantern, handed it to Josse. One by one they made their careful way down the narrow spiral steps, the infirmarer and Josse holding up their lights.

Stepping out into the crypt, Josse saw that the body on its bier had not been abandoned to the darkness. Surrounding it was a semicircle of tallow lamps. He felt uneasy. The crypt was bone-achingly cold and smelt of death.

He sensed the Abbess shiver. 'I will make haste to do what I came to do, my lady,' he said.

She nodded but did not speak. Sister Euphemia stood close beside her, as if drawing comfort from her presence, and the swift smile which Josse saw the Abbess bestow on the infirmarer as she tucked Sister Euphemia's arm under her own suggested the comforting might go both ways. He advanced to the bier and, folding back the linen covering the face, stood looking down at the dead man. Who are you? he asked silently. Are you the man who sought refuge at New Winnowlands? Are you the man whom those two Saracen warriors sought? Are the two identities one and the same?

Of all of us here, he thought, only I have seen both men. He had an idea. The sheet draped over the body was generously sized and, careful not to disturb the body any more than he had to, he arranged it in an approximation of the headdress that John Damianos had worn. He worked away silently for a few moments and then stepped back to look.

It was hard to tell; John Damianos's face had been animated with the movement and the vitality of the living. Josse stared at the deep eye sockets. I really don't know, he thought. I don't think this is the same man, but I just cannot be certain.

Sister Euphemia cleared her throat nervously and said, 'Sir Josse, what are you doing? Can I help you?'

He spun round. He had almost forgotten the two nuns. 'Sister, I should have explained,' he said. 'A stranger was lodging with me at New Winnowlands shortly before this poor soul was found dead on the track. There are similarities between this man and my lodger and I am trying to decide whether they are one and the same.'

'You know the name of your former guest?'

'Aye.'

'And if this were him,' the infirmarer said eagerly, 'then we should have a name by which to bury him.'

'Indeed. But I don't *know*—' He broke off to glance down at the corpse. 'The man who came to New Winnowlands was clothed in garments that enveloped him closely from throat to feet and he wore a dark headdress that covered all but his eyes, and they were ever in deep shadow.'

Sister Euphemia had gone very still. 'When did this man arrive on your doorstep, Sir Josse?'

'Oh – it must be more than a fortnight ago.' He felt a twitch of excited apprehension. 'Why do you ask?'

She did not answer immediately. He guessed she realized the import of what she was about to say. Then: 'Such a man came here about two weeks back. He was clad just as you describe and he was most reluctant to remove even sufficient folds of his clothing for me to treat him. He carried a leather satchel and he kept the strap slung across him even while he was in the safety of my treatment room.'

Josse let out his breath. 'It sounds exactly like John Damianos,' he said. 'He could have been treated here, gone on his way and later, when he could go no further, sought out the first house that he came to asking for lodgings.' He remembered something. 'He was exhausted,' he murmured. 'I do not think that he could have gone any further; he was on the verge of collapse.'

Sister Euphemia was nodding vigorously. 'Yes, yes, as was my patient!' she exclaimed. 'I could see how weak he was and I offered him a bed for the night. He needed rest and sustenance, for I could tell that both had been in short supply for him of late.' She sighed. 'But try as I might, I could not persuade him and he left that same evening.'

'And then he happened to pass by New Winnowlands,' Josse said, 'where he—'

But the Abbess interrupted. 'I am not sure that he *happened* to do any such thing, Sir Josse,' she said. Her face broke into an affectionate smile. 'Is it not more likely that he sought you out deliberately?'

'Why in the Lord's name should he do that?' Josse

demanded. 'He did not know who I was any more than I knew who *he* was!'

The Abbess turned to the infirmarer. 'Sister Euphemia, how did you come to treat this man?'

'He presented himself with the sick and the ailing late one afternoon,' she said. 'He was at the end of the queue and, if my memory serves me right, he was the last patient to be treated.'

'Last in the queue,' the Abbess said. 'Which would have given him ample time to listen to the chatter around him, both among the nursing nuns and also among those seeking their help.'

'What are you suggesting?' Josse asked.

The Abbess looked at him. 'That among the names bandied about, yours probably featured quite prominently,' she said. 'You had recently been with us and, dear Sir Josse, you make an impression on people. They remember you and they talk about you.'

He felt himself blushing. 'Do they?'

'Yes.' Her smile widened. 'In the most favourable of terms, I might add. Do you not agree, Sister?'

'I do,' Sister Euphemia said stoutly. 'A good friend to us you are, Sir Josse, and I for one do not hesitate to say so.'

'Oh,' he responded lamely. The awkward sensation of being the subject of the two nuns' approval was interrupted – much to his relief – by a sudden exclamation from Sister Euphemia.

With a swift 'May I?' directed at the Abbess, who, frowning in puzzlement, nodded, the infirmarer stepped up to the bier and gently removed the makeshift linen headdress from the dead man's face and throat. She stood looking down at him for some time, compassion in her face. Then, turning back to Josse and the Abbess, she said, 'This is not the man whom I treated.'

'How can you be sure?' the Abbess demanded.

'Because the man I saw had a frightful wound on the under-side of his jaw, extending down his neck,' the infirmarer answered firmly. She laid a tender hand on the dead man's shoulder. 'Although this poor soul's throat has been savagely carved out, I can see from the flesh on either side of the gash that there is no sign of the wound I treated for our mysterious stranger. *That* wound was extensive and suppurating. I bathed it with lavender oil and then put some of my special ointment on it and I hurt the poor man so much that, for all he never made a sound, he all but fainted when I was done.'

'What had caused such an injury?' Josse asked.

'It looked like a burn. A bad burn, going right down deep into his flesh, as if someone had lit a pitch-soaked brand and held it flaming under his chin.'

'He was a Saracen,' Josse said slowly, 'or, at least, that is what I surmised from his dress, his speech and his mannerisms.' He met the eyes of the Abbess. 'I am thinking of how they burn heretics in Europe. Could the man have been a member of a fanatical sect whose preaching antagonized some over-zealous French bishop?'

The Abbess shook her head. 'It is a large conclusion to draw from slight evidence, Sir Josse. And, besides, those who are condemned to the stake do not habitually escape it.'

'No, I suppose not.' He sighed deeply.

'He'd had the burn for some time,' Sister Euphemia volunteered. 'Month or more, I'd say. The flesh was quite putrid around the margins of the wound and the pus—'

'Thank you, Sister,' the Abbess said softly.

'Sorry, my lady. Just trying to be helpful.'

Josse watched as the Abbess gave her infirmarer one of those generous, loving smiles that endeared her to her nuns and said, 'You have, dear Euphemia; oh, you have.' Turning back to Josse, eyes bright in the soft light, she added, 'We have achieved our purpose, have we not? We might not know who this poor man is, but we do at least know who he is not.'

'Aye,' Josse agreed. And he thought: my instinct was right, then. John Damianos is still alive. Hard on the heels of that thought came another: where is he, then?

Helewise was so glad to have Josse's solid presence back at Hawkenlye that she insisted on seeing him as far as the track down to the Vale; he was going to seek out his usual overnight spot with the lay brothers. The visit down into the crypt had brought back all the horror she was trying to forget.

Her common sense told her that there was no danger to anyone at Hawkenlye, for this was surely not a random killing. You did not torture a man if he was a stranger. If the motive was robbery – the likely cause of most random killings – then you would hit your victim over the head and make off with his purse or his horse, or both, without even going to the bother of stopping to see if he was still alive.

No. Whoever had attacked the man on the forest track had known him and had wanted something from him.

It was, in a way, a reassuring thought. But all the same, whether or not there was a direct threat to the Hawkenlye community, it felt good to have Josse with them. He was standing with his hand on the gate, looking at her with a faint frown. She knew him well enough to know that, far from suggesting he was frowning at *her*, this probably just meant he was deep in thought.

'And so, Sir Josse, what next?' she asked.

'Hm?' He came out of his reverie and she hid a smile. 'Sorry, my lady, I was thinking.'

'Yes, Josse,' she murmured.

But she didn't think he heard. 'Tomorrow,' he said, 'I'm going back to where the dead man was found. It's unlikely I'll find anything, because both that merchant fellow and the lay brothers had a good look round. Then,' he added more decisively, 'with your permission, my lady, I shall send for Gervase de Gifford and see what he makes of this.'

'I have already done that,' she said. 'Brother Saul rode down to Tonbridge first thing today to tell him about the brutalized body and ask him to come up to the Abbey. Sabin told Saul that her husband was away from home and expected back late this evening, and she undertook to ask him to ride up here in the morning.'

Josse was watching her, slowly shaking his head. 'I should have realized,' he said. 'A foul murder so close to the Abbey? Of course you would inform the sheriff. I'm glad, my lady, for it means we shall have the benefit of Gervase's wisdom all the sooner.'

He had gone through the gate now and was closing it behind him. 'Make sure you bolt it,' he warned.

'I am doing so.' She shot the two heavy bolts home.

'Until tomorrow,' came his voice from the far side.

'Sleep well.'

She heard the jingle of his spurs as he hastened away down into the Vale. Then she turned and walked quickly back to her room.

*　　*　　*

Josse watched Gervase de Gifford ride through the Abbey gates early the next morning.

Gervase had married Sabin de Retz in the spring and Josse had danced at the wedding. It had been a joyful day, for Sabin and Gervase were deeply in love and, having taken the decision to stay in Tonbridge rather than return to her native Brittany, Sabin appeared to have every intention of throwing herself wholeheartedly into her new life. Her old grandfather had come to England with her. Like Sabin, he was an apothecary and he was going to continue to teach her as she set about practising her skill in Tonbridge.

Josse had heard that Sabin was pregnant. He would have liked to congratulate the prospective father but now was hardly the time. It seemed wrong to celebrate the conception of a new life when one had just been so savagely brought to an end.

He stepped forward to greet Gervase as he dismounted. The two men embraced and Josse muttered, 'It is good to see you, Gervase. A dreadful thing has happened and—'

'Josse, I am sorry but I bring more bad tidings. Shall we find the Abbess?' He glanced at Sister Ursel, hovering close by, and at Sister Martha, holding out her hand for the reins.

Understanding, Josse led the way to the Abbess's private room. She was seated at her big table and she got up to greet the sheriff. 'Gervase, thank you for coming. We—'

'Something else has happened, my lady,' Josse said. He glanced at Gervase, whose handsome face wore a sombre expression. 'Gervase?'

'In the early hours of this morning there was a fire in the new guest quarters of the priory at Tonbridge,' he said baldly. 'They are still busy with building work and it is suggested that the fire may have started in a brazier left smouldering when the workmen left the site last night.'

Josse thought that it sounded unlikely, since for one thing, braziers did a good job of containing fires, even fierce ones, and for another, workmen were fully aware of the risk of fire to timber-framed buildings and were extremely careful with it. He heard the Abbess ask the question which he too should have thought of first: she said, 'Was anyone hurt?'

'One man killed, my lady. Two injured, one very badly. There were but the three of them in the guest accommodation last night.'

'Are the wounded men well enough to be brought here? My infirmarer has great skill and undoubtedly she could help them, unless transporting them is impossible?'

'I was hoping that perhaps Sister Euphemia might come down to Tonbridge,' Gervase replied. 'My initial thought was indeed that the survivors would be best off here at Hawkenlye, but I would prefer to have a healer look at them before they are moved.'

'Sister Euphemia is skilled in the use of analgesics,' the Abbess said. 'It would be best to dull their pain before attempting to move them.'

The ghost of a tender smile crossed Gervase's face. 'Sabin has already administered one of her concoctions,' he said. 'Both men are now sleeping.'

'Thank God for your Sabin,' the Abbess exclaimed warmly.

'Amen,' murmured Gervase.

'I will ask Sister Euphemia to accompany you back to Tonbridge,' the Abbess announced, walking towards the door. 'Do you need me to send some lay brothers to help bring the men back here?'

'No, my lady, thank you. One of my men is already organizing a cart.' Gervase opened the door and then turned to Josse, standing silent by his side. 'Will you come with me, Josse? I am disturbed by this fire, which so neatly destroyed only the guest accommodation.'

'You don't suspect it was started deliberately?'

'It is a convenient way of killing someone,' Gervase answered. 'And we both know of another fire, in another land, where the motive was murder, although that time the murderer did not succeed.'

'Aye,' Josse said. He knew that Gervase referred to an episode in Sabin's past. 'It is a grave accusation.'

Gervase shrugged. 'I will say no more now. Come and see for yourself, Josse.'

They turned to hurry away but the Abbess called them back. 'I do not wish to detain you, Gervase,' she said, 'but is the identity of these three men known?'

'Yes, my lady. Neither survivor is in a condition to speak, but I asked the canon in charge of the guest quarters. He told me they are Knights Hospitaller and their leader's name is Thibault of Margat.'

'Then they are the trio who came here!' she cried. 'They arrived a couple of days ago and were going on to Tonbridge and then to their Order's headquarters at Clerkenwell. Why did they not ask to stay here with us? We have excellent facilities in our guest quarters or, if they preferred something simpler, they could have put up with the brethren down in the Vale. Either way, we would have made them welcome! Oh, if they had done so, this tragedy would have been avoided!'

Josse pitied her anguish. He knew why the Hospitallers had elected to stay with the canons at Tonbridge rather than the Hawkenlye community: because at the priory there were no women. Thibault of Margat, Josse had observed, was a misogynist whose revulsion for the female sex appeared to extend to nuns.

But he wasn't going to say so.

Gervase's brow had creased in a frown. 'I do not know, my lady. Apparently the trio were trying to find a runaway monk and they had based themselves there in the priory while they pursued their search. The canon who told me this added something odd: he said, "They were like hounds after the quarry, but it seems their quarry has turned round and bitten the hounds." '

'Then this canon too suspects that the fire was started deliberately?' Josse asked.

And Gervase said simply, 'Yes.'

Part Two
The Warrior Monks

Six

The fire had been very particular in what it had consumed. The priory's guest wing had been completely destroyed, leaving no more than one or two charred uprights and a strong smell of burning. The remaining buildings of the new foundation, for all that they were but a short distance away, had scarcely been singed; the wattle-and-daub walls and the reed thatching were intact.

As Josse and Gervase approached the smouldering ruin, Sister Euphemia and Sister Caliste riding behind them, Josse reflected that for once the priory's proximity to the river had worked in its favour. When work had commenced on the foundation, locals had remarked pessimistically that it was nothing but folly to build on low-lying ground so close to the water, where the heavy clay was soggy for most of the year and where the yellowish mists brought a man nothing but colds, catarrh, coughs and consumption. When the rumours had spread that the canons had trouble singing the daily round of offices because at any time at least half of them were suffering from sore throats, the locals had nodded wisely and said, told you so.

Well, Josse thought, that might be the case. But before dawn this morning, the river that made the canons' existence a permanently damp and rheumy one saved not only most of their new foundation but also their lives. If, that was, the fire had been an accident and not intended to burn down no more than the guest wing . . .

A short, stocky man dressed in a hooded black cloak over a white surplice was striding to meet them. Raising a hand to Gervase, he addressed Josse. 'I am Canon Mark,' he said. 'Are you Sir Josse d'Acquin?' Josse nodded. 'Then glad I am to see you, for your reputation has gone ahead of you.'

'Oh – er, thank you,' Josse said.

'And you have brought the nursing sisters!' Canon Mark exclaimed, beaming up at the nuns.

'Two of Hawkenlye's finest,' Josse confirmed. 'This is Sister Euphemia, the infirmarer, and this is Sister Caliste.'

'Ladies, gentlemen, please dismount and I will call someone to see to your horses.' Mark looked around, spotted a brother apparently doing nothing but staring at the new arrivals and called him over. As the young canon led the horses away, Mark said, 'Now, first let me take the two nuns to see their patients. Mistress Gifford is tending them with great skill but they are a sorry sight and I am sure she would welcome some support.' Turning on his heel, he led the way to a low building only a few paces from the burned-out guest quarters. 'We've put them in here because it was closest,' he said over his shoulder. Then, ushering his visitors through the open door: 'There they are.'

Josse saw a body lying on the ground, covered from head to toe with a muddy length of darned linen. Two other men lay on low cots. They were filthy, the remnants of their garments charred and sticking to their skin. Their faces were badly burned, swollen and unrecognizable. Both were asleep or unconscious.

Between them stood Sabin de Gifford.

Her eyes flew first to Josse and she murmured, 'Josse, I am glad to see you.' Then she moved to greet the two nuns, and Josse saw that Sister Euphemia put a concerned arm around the young woman's waist as she muttered some urgent question. 'I am quite all right,' he heard Sabin reply. 'Thank you for your concern, but I am neither overtaxed nor overtired.'

Word of her condition must have spread, Josse thought. With a surreptitious glance, he observed that any bump she might be showing would not be visible beneath her cloak and her voluminous white apron.

'We hope to take the wounded men up to Hawkenlye,' Josse said. 'Are they fit to make the journey?'

He might have directed the question at Sabin but it was the infirmarer, bending down and studying the two men in turn, who answered. 'Sabin has done a fine job,' she announced. 'What did you give them?' she asked, and Sabin replied with a string of ingredients out of which Josse understood only poppy and monkshood. Lord, I thought monkshood was a deadly poison, he thought in alarm. But the infirmarer was nodding her approval; presumably Sabin knew what she was doing and whatever she had given the two Hospitallers had succeeded in sending them into a deep and hopefully pain-free sleep.

'I think,' Sister Euphemia was saying, 'we may safely take them up to the infirmary and I suggest we make haste about it before the drugs wear off and they begin to feel their hurts once more.'

Canon Mark needed no further instruction. Already he was hurrying out and Josse heard him shouting to his brethren, issuing orders for the sheriff's man and his cart to be brought up and for straw palliasses, pillows and blankets to be loaded onto it. Very shortly afterwards, the two unconscious men were tenderly carried out to the cart. The nuns volunteered to accompany them and a sister sat beside each of the patients to watch closely over them during the slow journey up to the Abbey. The man driving the horses was given final instructions to go as gently as road conditions allowed, and then they set off.

Gervase went to see Sabin home and Josse watched as he gave his wife a kiss and took her leather bag from her. Josse was about to go over to where the horses were tethered and organize leading reins for the two sisters' mounts when Canon Mark caught his sleeve.

'A word, Sir Josse, if I may,' he said. 'I wanted to speak to de Gifford as well, but he has gone . . . '

'He is escorting his wife home,' Josse said.

'Ah, yes, of course.'

'I will pass on to him anything that you tell me.'

Josse guessed that the canon was going to voice his suspicions about the fire and he was correct. 'I am worried about how this blaze was started,' he said quietly, lowering his voice and leaning close to Josse. 'There is a suggestion being bandied about that it was caused by carelessness with a brazier, but this simply cannot be so because I take it upon myself to check that all the workmen's braziers are dead at the end of each day.' No wonder the poor man is so agitated, Josse thought; he senses that his own reputation is at stake. 'I know the dangers of fire,' the canon added, 'as do we all, and as soon as the alarm went up, the fire drill that I myself devised was set in motion. All of us were ready with our buckets, forming a chain from the river bank. Canon John and I soaked our garments, covered our noses and mouths with wet cloths and dashed into the guest wing, where we were able to grab the two Hospitallers nearest to the door and drag them outside. But, Sir Josse – and this is what both puzzles and disturbs me – the fire showed no inclination to spread to neighbouring buildings! There we all stood, water at the ready, yet once it was done with the guest wing, the fire went out!'

'*Went out?*' Josse could not believe it. 'Was it not rather that you and your men had already soaked the walls and roofs of the neighbouring buildings so that the fire could not take hold?'

'No, no, *no*, there was no time for that!' Mark insisted, agitated. 'I was at the head of the chain and I *swear* to you that only I and perhaps a dozen others had thrown the contents of our pails before the flames died. What do you make of that, Sir Josse?'

'I am not yet prepared to say,' Josse replied cautiously.

Mark tutted impatiently. 'Then come and look at this,' he said, grabbing Josse's arm and dragging him back to the small room where the patients had been put. Striding across the floor, he drew back the linen that covered the dead man. 'This one was Brother Jeremiah. God rest his soul,' Mark said, and so great was his urgency that Josse decided the last four words were an afterthought. 'Look, Sir Josse.' Mark was turning the dead head on the muddy ground. 'What do you say to this?'

Josse crouched beside him, staring down at the left side of the dead monk's head where Mark was pointing.

'I see nothing,' he began, 'and I—'

Mark tutted again. 'Don't look, *feel*.' Grabbing Josse's hand, he pushed the fingers down into the smooth, dark blond hair. 'There!'

Under Josse's fingers he felt a huge swelling.

Something – or someone – had struck Brother Jeremiah very hard behind his left ear. And that was not all: as Josse continued to probe, he felt a deep depression right in the middle of the back of the skull. Sickeningly, he detected sharp splinters of bone.

'It could have happened as he tried to escape the flames,' he said. 'It was dark; he had been wakened from profound sleep. He probably panicked, tripped and fell.'

'Think again, Sir Josse,' Mark said darkly. 'I was first into the guest room once it was possible to enter. Brother Jeremiah had not even sat up, never mind tried to get out. He lay dead in his bed and his poor smashed skull rested on nothing harder than his straw mattress.' His eyes, round with horrified astonishment, met Josse's. Just in case Josse had missed the point, Mark breathed solemnly, 'He was dead before the fire began. Somebody murdered him and then started the fire in an attempt to hide what he had done.'

As Josse and Gervase rode briskly back up the road to Hawkenlye, Josse related to his companion everything that Canon Mark had told and shown him.

'You agree that this dead Hospitaller was murdered?' Gervase asked curtly.

'Aye,' Josse said. There was no other explanation for Brother Jeremiah's staved-in skull.

'And you do not think Canon Mark is inventing this tale in order to cover up his own negligence in allowing a fire to start in his guest wing?'

'No,' Josse said firmly. 'I cannot vouch for Canon Mark's honesty, having only just met him, although I must say that I gained the impression of a conscientious man who insists on things being done according to his own careful rules. If he says he always makes sure no fires are left smouldering at the end of the day, then I believe him. Also' – and this, he thought, was what clinched it – 'how else did Brother Jeremiah get those fatal wounds to his head unless by another's hand? He cannot possibly have fallen, for he was found in his bed.'

'We only have Canon Mark's word for that.'

Josse's irritation spilled over. 'Well, go back and ask the others! I did not think to do it, Gervase, but Canon Mark didn't fight that fire all by himself and I'm sure his companions will vouch for the truth of what he told me.'

Gervase grinned. 'Sorry, Josse. Yes, you're right; I'm just thinking around the problem.' His expression becoming rueful, he added gloomily, 'As if one violent murder wasn't enough, now it seems we have another.'

Gervase and Josse had decided to speak to the surviving Hospitallers in the hope that they might have seen or heard something suspicious before the fire broke out. It seemed quite possible for, as Josse pointed out, the murderer must have hoped that his fire would kill all three of them – it was only thanks to the quick-thinking and courageous Canon Mark and his fire drill that two had been saved – and therefore there was a good chance that the killer had not bothered too much about keeping out of sight.

On reaching the Abbey in the early afternoon, Josse had asked Sister Ursel to send word to the Abbess that they were back and then they had gone straight to the infirmary, where Sister Euphemia had put the Hospitallers on adjacent cots in the curtained recess at the far end of the long ward. The patches of cloth had been sponged off their flesh and now both appeared to be naked, covered as far as the waist with clean white sheets. Their burns were red and shiny.

'This man – ' Sister Euphemia indicated the monk on the left, who Josse identified as Brother Otto – 'is the more badly wounded and he breathes only with great difficulty. His burns are extensive and he would now be in agony were he conscious. I thank the merciful God for Sabin de Gifford's skill.'

'Amen,' Josse muttered. Gervase, he noticed, gave a faint smile at this praise of his wife.

'The other one – ' the infirmarer turned to look at Thibault of Margat – 'suffered less damage and I guess this is because he was pulled out first. His burns are not so deep, and although he has been coughing and wheezing, his condition is not as severe as his companion's.'

'How soon before he is able to talk?' Gervase asked.

'He is very sick. Although I said his condition is less severe, that is relative, for he too will be in a great deal of pain when he recovers consciousness and I shall do my best to keep him asleep for as long as I think fit.'

'Sister, the monk who died did not perish in the fire,' Gervase said in an urgent whisper. 'He was murdered, and I must set about trying to find the man who killed him. These two lucky survivors – ' he must have noticed her instinctive protest, for he held up his hand to silence her – 'yes, I know full well they will suffer agonies before they are healed but at least they are alive! These two may have seen or heard something of the attacker who killed their brother, and the sooner I can speak to them, the sooner I can get on his trail!'

The infirmarer nodded. 'I understand,' she said quietly. 'All I can promise is that I will monitor my patients' condition when they wake up.' She stared down sadly at Brother Otto. 'I fear it is *if* he wakes up, in this poor soul's case,' she added. Then, her eyes returning to Gervase's: 'If I deem it suitable for you to speak to either of them before I sedate them again, be sure that I shall send for you.'

'But—' Gervase began.

The infirmarer put both her hands on his chest and pushed him out of the recess, Josse following. Once she had ensured that the curtains had fallen closed behind her, she looked at Gervase and said, her voice exasperated, 'That's the best I can offer you. Go and ask that pretty wife of yours about the treatment of badly burned patients and I'm sure she'll tell you I'm doing the right thing. It's the shock, you see – burns hurt so much that the pain alone can kill you even if whoever is caring for you manages to keep you clean so that you don't suppurate to death.'

'Oh,' said Gervase. Josse felt quite sorry for him; he looked like a scolded child.

Sister Euphemia must have thought so too. She smiled and put a motherly arm around Gervase's waist. 'Just be patient,' she said kindly. 'The older monk is lean, wiry and tough as an oak tree. I'm not making any promises but I reckon it'll take more than a few burns and some lungfuls of smoke to kill him off. We'll see how he is in the morning. A good night's sleep can do wonders, and we'll all be praying for them both, so we'll have the good Lord on our side.' She nodded encouragingly, her face full of such trust that Josse was moved.

'Come, Gervase,' he said gently. 'There's nothing more we can do here. Everything the Hospitallers had with them, including the shifts they slept in, undoubtedly went up in flames, so we can't even go through their belongings in the hope of finding some clue as to who wanted them dead. Let's leave the nursing nuns to their task.'

Gervase let out his breath in a long sigh. 'Very well.' Then, belatedly remembering his manners, he turned to the infirmarer. 'I am sorry if I appeared heartless, Sister, and I did not mean to bully you.'

'I know,' she replied serenely.

'You will let us know the instant we can speak to one or both of the monks?'

'I will.'

He stared down at her for a moment or two. Then, with a

curt nod, he turned and strode down the long ward and out of the infirmary.

Outside in the crisp air, Josse recalled something he had intended to do today. Now seemed as good a time as any, and having a purpose might help Gervase's all too evident frustration.

'I was going to suggest we went to report to the Abbess,' he said, 'but before we do that, there's something I've been meaning to check.'

Gervase looked at him. 'What?' he said eagerly.

'I'd like to go over the ground where the first victim was found,' Josse replied. 'I'd like to do so with you, my friend, for a fresh pair of eyes may pick up something that others missed. After all,' he added, 'in mitigation, we who brought the dead man here to the Abbey were greatly disturbed by what had been done to him and it is quite possible we did not search around as thoroughly as we might have done.'

'Indeed it is, Josse!' Gervase cried. 'Show me the way and let's go!'

Josse went first along the track that ran beneath the forest fringes. He did not speak; he was reliving the moment two days ago when he had first seen the dead body. He reached the place and stopped, Gervase beside him.

'He was lying just there,' Josse pointed, 'on the edge of the track. No attempt had been made to hide the body. He was naked and anything he might have been carrying on him was gone.'

'And you do not think that the merchant who reported the body stole anything? It's possible, Josse – I'm told that the fellow sent his lad to the Abbey for help, so could he not have stolen the dead man's pack and hidden it away before you all came along?'

'It's possible, aye,' Josse admitted. 'The merchant – he gave his name as Guiot of Robertsbridge and he was going to Tonbridge market with nutmegs and cloves – was insistent that they found the corpse robbed of every garment and possession, and I had no reason not to believe him. I—' He frowned, trying to put into words his conviction that the merchant had spoken the truth. 'It was just so awful, Gervase, that somehow I don't think any of us who saw that body lying there would have wanted to take anything, even something valuable. It would have been like picking up a piece of the victim's horrible death.'

Gervase was looking at him interestedly. 'I never thought you were superstitious, Josse.'

'It has nothing to do with superstition. You weren't there, Gervase. You didn't see or smell that terrible death scene.'

'You are probably right about the merchant,' Gervase said after a moment. 'The fact that he volunteered his name and his business so readily suggests he was honest. I suppose I could send one of my men to speak to him . . . '

'I don't think you'd learn any more from him than you will from me,' Josse said bluntly. 'But it's your decision and your man's time you'll be wasting.'

'Very well,' Gervase said meekly. Then: 'I'm sorry you have to come back here. Clearly it's upsetting you.'

Josse shrugged but did not speak. Then both men quietly crouched down and, eyes fixed to the hard ground, began to search along the track and through the fringing undergrowth.

The cramp in Josse's damp knees suggested they had been at their task for long enough. Josse had not found a thing; from Gervase's continuing silence, he guessed the sheriff had had no more success. Slowly Josse made his way back to the spot where the body had lain and, staring at the short, frosty grass at the edge of the track, he made out the large area where it had been flattened, first by the corpse and then by the booted feet of those who had come to bear it down to the Abbey. There were still a few smears of blood.

Smears of blood . . .

Josse straightened up. 'Gervase, he wasn't killed here!'

Gervase hurried over. 'There's not enough blood,' Josse said. 'With those wounds – and assuming he was still alive when they cut his throat – he would have bled copiously. So where is it? Where's the blood?'

Gervase was now staring down as intently as Josse had done. 'There's some there.' He pointed. 'And there.'

'Aye, but those patches are nothing but seepage from the dead body,' Josse said. 'When you cut into a man's wrist – and the dead man's hand was all but severed – the blood spurts out like a fountain.'

Gervase was looking at him respectfully. 'There, Josse, I must bow before your greater experience, for I have never seen a man's hand cut off. Nor a throat being slit,' he added, 'and I pray I never shall.' Then, as if deliberately steering his thoughts away from such horrors, he said, 'So, if he wasn't killed here, where? Is it worth our while looking around?'

Josse was thinking. 'If you are going to torture a man, you want to do so in an out-of-the-way spot.'

'In the forest?' Gervase suggested.

'Aye, perhaps, although—' Although the forest would not like it and would soon rid itself of your presence, he was going to say. Deciding it would sound impossibly whimsical to someone like Gervase, who had had very little experience of the Great Forest and all that went on within it, he said instead, 'Although if the slaying was done deep within the trees, why did they not leave him there? No – I think they probably jumped him on the track, took him a short distance into the under-growth and afterwards dragged his body back to this spot.'

'Why would they do that?' Gervase persisted. 'If he was hidden in the bracken, why not leave him there?'

It was a good question. Josse was considering it when, as if out of nowhere, the answer was in his head: *We did not want the residue of such brutality within the forest. It was we who brought him out to the track.*

And then he knew.

Would he be able to make Gervase believe him?

He could but try.

'The forest people put him here,' he said simply. 'They knew he would be found sooner or later, for the track is quite well used. They also knew he would end up at Hawkenlye Abbey.'

Gervase was looking at him wonderingly. 'You know that?' Josse shrugged. Gervase took it as an affirmation. 'Because of Joanna?'

But Josse did not want to talk about Joanna. He shrugged again and then said, 'I suggest we go along the track for a mile or so in each direction, looking for any spot where flattened grass or disturbed undergrowth points to a body having been dragged out of the forest. You go back towards the Abbey; I'll go on that way.'

Gervase, Josse noticed, had the puzzled frown of a man who wants to ask further questions but does not want to risk offence. With a private smile, he set off along the track and presently heard the sound of Gervase's footfalls as he strode off the other way.

It was Josse who found the place. Had he not been actively searching for it, he would probably have missed it, for the signs were faint: a heel print on the edge of a muddy puddle right off to the side of the track; a slim hazel branch that had been partially broken; and, when he hastened off the track and in under the trees, the shadow of a line through the dying bracken that might have been made by a boar or a deer but that, under the circumstances, Josse was absolutely sure was the work of human beings.

He had gone perhaps a hundred paces. Hoping Gervase was still in earshot, he loped back to the track and yelled, 'Gervase! *Gervase!* Here, to me!'

Presently he saw the sheriff coming running towards him. When he drew level, Josse said, 'In there,' and led the way back along the path through the bracken.

They came to a patch of open ground where short turf grew in a space between birch and hazel. There were the ashes of a small fire on which some lengths of rope had been burned; their charred ends were still visible at the edges of the burned circle. Stuck in the ground beside the fire was a bow made of layers of horn and sinew. It was strangely shaped and instead of taking the form of a single shallow arc, it curved back on itself.

It was broken.

The ground in front of the fire was drenched in blood. It had congealed and in places had dried to a crust. This was the place of torment and death they had been searching for.

Gervase had paled and Josse felt sure his own face must be just as white. He stared down at the blood. Had the ropes been used to tether the man? It seemed likely. Had whoever killed him tried to burn them to destroy the evidence of their brutality? But why do that, when the dead body spoke so eloquently?

There was something about the clearing. Something to do with the fire, and that broken bow stuck in the earth . . .

Gervase had stepped back from the blood and was standing beside the bow, staring hard at it as if trying to distract his mind from the horror behind him. 'Josse, what is this?' he asked, his voice a hoarse whisper. 'I don't know—'

The first arrow flew so close to Josse's cheek that he felt

the breeze. With a heavy clunk it struck an ash tree behind him, burying its head in the trunk; he reached up and wrested it free and quickly looked at it. The second arrow was for Gervase, who gave a cry of fear as it brushed his sleeve and flew on to lose itself in the underbrush. There came the faint creak of a large bow being drawn as the unseen archer prepared for another shot.

'*Come on!*' Josse grabbed Gervase's arm and raced back through the bracken to the track, so conscious of the presence of that unseen archer that instinctively he weaved to and fro as he ran, pulling Gervase with him. For some terrible moments it seemed that, as hard as they were running, the track came no nearer, but then the spell broke and they burst out from beneath the trees. Without even a pause, Josse turned to the right and pelted on down the path towards Hawkenlye. Only when the Abbey buildings were in sight did he slacken the pace and, eventually, draw to a standstill.

His lungs were burning, his chest heaving with exertion and the aftermath of danger. Gervase, bending over with his hands on his knees, was gasping for breath. When he could speak, he raised his scarlet, sweating face and said, 'He tried to *kill* us! Why, Josse? Why?'

Josse felt his racing heartbeat gradually returning to its normal rhythm. 'I'm not sure,' he said. 'Possibly we were about to stumble upon something that would have given away the killer's identity. Perhaps he watches over that place purely for that reason: to scare off anyone who gets too close. Or . . .' His voice trailed off.

Perhaps he watches over that place.

He saw again the fire with the partially burned ropes. The broken bow, sticking up out of the earth like a marker.

He turned calmly to Gervase, for now he knew. 'It's a shrine,' he said. 'The dead man's body may have been removed to a place out of the reach of his companions, but they have honoured him as best they can. They purified the tools of his torture – the ropes – by burning them, then they put his broken weapon in the earth as a memorial to his courage.'

'*They*, Josse?' Gervase looked doubtful. 'You refer to *them*, but how can you sound so certain? How can you know he had more than one companion? How do you know he had a companion at all?'

'Because the arrows came from different directions.'

'They almost killed us!' Gervase's face was suffused with anger. 'That arrow came so close that I—'

'No, Gervase. If they had wanted to kill us we would now be lying in that bloodstained clearing, as dead as the corpse at Hawkenlye. No – they merely wanted us to go away, for we were contaminating the sacred spot where they lost their companion.'

'But—'

'It is what fighting men do, Gervase,' Josse said patiently. 'In an earlier age, a man's broken weapon would have been buried with him as a mark of respect. These men are skilled fighters and, although I cannot speak for the others, the dead man at least was a Turk; one of the elite troops who use the recurved bow to such devastating effect.'

'That thing stuck in the earth of the clearing?'

'Aye. To use it well takes long training and the development of specific muscles. It's a cavalry weapon and both its penetration and range exceed the longbow.'

'You mean they fire these things from horseback?'

'Aye.'

'Then they are skilled fighters indeed,' Gervase whispered. Meeting Josse's eyes, he said, 'I would not be in the boots of whoever killed that Turk. If his companions ever find him, his fate does not bear thinking about.'

Josse straightened up. 'Then, my friend, we had better make sure we find him before they do.'

Seven

Helewise was awake early the next morning. Very quietly she dressed and left her bed in the long dormitory, treading softly so as not to disturb her sleeping sisters. In the silent church she knelt before the altar and prayed for help in unravelling the many strands of the trouble that had fallen into the community's lap.

A man tortured and killed; a fire started deliberately in an attempt to disguise the murder of a Knight Hospitaller. Josse and Gervase had stayed in her room for a long time the previous evening and she was aghast to learn of the manner of Brother Jeremiah's death. When they told her about their discovery in the forest and of the warning shots that had sent them running for safety, she was horrified at the peril in which they had placed themselves.

The three of them talked for hours but they came nowhere near any sort of conclusion. The dead Turk had known something, or perhaps possessed something, that his killers had tried to extract from him. A man named John Damianos was on the run and had taken shelter with Josse. Three Knights Hospitaller had come all the way from Outremer after a runaway English monk. One of the trio was now dead and the others badly hurt; I *knew* that Thibault of Margat would return here to Hawkenlye, she thought now, but I did not anticipate the dreadful circumstances under which it would happen. Two Saracen warriors, searching for a man who answered the description of John Damianos, had followed him all the way to New Winnowlands; they had known without having seen the body that the dead man at Hawkenlye was not the one they sought. Their quarry had been involved in some fatal incident in Outremer. Josse proposed that the runaway monk and the Saracen sought by the warriors Kathnir and Akhbir – whether or not this man was John Damianos, although they all felt it most likely that he was – must surely be connected. Perhaps they had travelled together on the long road from Outremer? Perhaps they had in some way both been involved in that mysterious incident?

Helewise frowned in concentration, all but oblivious to the ache in her knees on the cold, hard stone. If Josse is right, then perhaps one or other of the surviving Hospitallers – Thibault probably, for he is the senior – will know something of whatever it was that happened. Oh, but I do hope that Thibault—

She arrested the thought. She had been about to pray for Thibault of Margat not for the poor man's own sake but because of her own desperate need to find answers. Humbly she bowed her head over her clasped hands and asked to be forgiven. Only then did she compose the suitable words that prayed for Thibault and Brother Otto's swift recovery and release from their pain.

*   *   *

She made herself wait until after tierce before going to the infirmary. She knew that Sister Euphemia would have sent for her had either of the Hospitallers been ready to speak, but nevertheless she burned with impatience to go and see for herself. She offered up the suppression of her intense desire as penance for her earlier fault.

The morning sun was shining on the frosty ground as she walked to the infirmary. Sister Euphemia came to greet her. 'The older monk is stirring,' she said. 'He has slept well and his colour is a little better. I am going to try to get him to drink, perhaps even to accept a mouthful of broth if his throat can take it. Then I think that if he is agreeable you may speak to him. Should I, my lady, send word down to the Vale to summon Sir Josse and the sheriff?'

'Yes, Sister,' Helewise said. 'They should be here if poor Thibault can manage a few words.'

Sister Euphemia nodded and, catching the eye of one of her young nursing novices, whispered to the girl and sent her off. Then the infirmarer disappeared inside the recess where the two monks lay, Sister Caliste following her and bearing a laden tray.

Helewise stood quite still and waited.

A few moments after Josse and Gervase had arrived in the infirmary, Sister Caliste put her head around the curtain and beckoned all three of them over.

'Can they talk?' Josse hissed urgently.

'One can,' Sister Caliste replied. 'The senior monk has been asking repeatedly to speak to *you*. Sister Euphemia is occupied with her duties and she has left the care of both monks in my charge. My lady, Sir Josse, my lord sheriff, please come in.' Bowing, she held the curtain back.

Helewise stared at the two monks. The younger one still lay motionless beneath the crisp sheet, its slow and steady rise and fall the only sign that he was still alive. Thibault, however, was propped up on pillows and his eyes glittered with pain and anxiety in his burned face.

It was Josse who spoke first. 'We are here to help,' he said. 'Abbess Helewise, Gervase de Gifford and I will do whatever we can.'

Helewise, watching closely, saw the monk's eyes go first to

Josse, then to Gervase and finally to her. The antipathy – even the disapproval – that she had sensed at their earlier meeting seemed to have vanished. Now he looked like a man who was suffering deeply and who despaired because he could not continue his appointed task.

To her faint surprise, he first addressed her. 'My lady, you see me here punished for my arrogance in my treatment of you and your community,' he said. 'I thought to hunt for that which I seek within the walls of this Abbey; yet I skulked like a thief instead of coming openly to you and asking for your help. Well, I have been set low for my sins, and I beg you to forgive me and to listen to what I must tell you.'

'Of course I forgive you,' she said, 'although I do not fully understand what there is to forgive.' Nor, she thought, how anything could be so bad that the loving God I worship would punish a man so dreadfully. Thibault might have been under the influence of one of Sister Euphemia's analgesic concoctions but it was plain to see that even so he was in severe pain. With burns like those, Helewise thought, her eyes moving involuntarily over the extensive red and blistered patches on the monk's face, chest and upper arms, how could he not be?

'You are charitable, my lady, and I am unworthy,' murmured Thibault. 'I must ask your indulgence, for still I am not able to – well, never mind.' He frowned, as if he were having difficulty arranging his thoughts.

'Tell us about the fire,' Gervase said gently. 'Can you remember anything?'

Thibault turned his pain-darkened eyes to the sheriff. 'Oh, yes,' he whispered.

There was a pause. Sister Caliste helped the monk to take a few sips from a cup she held to his lips. He thanked her and after a few moments the taut lines in his face relaxed a little.

Then he began to speak.

'My tale does not start with the fire,' he said. 'It begins a long time before that and in another land.' He coughed and Sister Caliste gave him another sip of the drink. 'Originally I was based at our Order's great fortress of Crac des Chevaliers, in Syria. I had served there for many years, a member of the garrison which held out against the great advance of the enemy following the defeat of the Frankish armies at the Battle of Hattin, in the summer of '86.' His eyes met Josse's. 'Hattin broke the spirit of many who had seen themselves as invincible,' he went on. 'Groups of knights and their attendants who had come out to Outremer with such confidence and high hopes watched their dreams trickle away into the sand with the blood of the dead and the wounded. The Western forces gravely underestimated Saladin. It became evident very quickly that we just did not have sufficient manpower.' He sighed. 'After the defeat, most men with interests in Outremer scurried away to protect their own borders, and I suppose one cannot blame them. But the result was that our side was pushed back to the coast. Even northern states such as Antioch and Tripoli, which were well away from Saladin's main thrust, lost lands on their eastern borders.'

'Saladin took the Holy City,' Josse said glumly. 'And that led to the launch of King Richard's crusade to recover it.'

Thibault grimaced, an expression which, Helewise thought, stemmed more from remembering that disastrous episode than from any sudden stab of pain. 'Indeed it did,' he agreed. 'For those of us still battling with the Saracens, it was a grim time. Although help came from an unexpected source.'

'Which was?' Gervase prompted.

Thibault turned his eyes to the sheriff. 'I said just now that most of the nobles fled to defend their own estates. However, many of those who fought under them felt a more pressing obligation to the greater cause. Having no property or possessions of their own out in Outremer meant, I suppose, that they did not have to judge between the conflicting needs of God and their own interests.' There was, Helewise thought, a very faint suggestion of condemnation in the words. 'Anyway, be that as it may, after Hattin both we and the Knights Templar found that many young knights and soldiers came to us wanting to continue the fight. Some were freshly arrived out in the Holy Land and eager to make a name for themselves. I cannot speak for the Templars but, as for us, we were delighted to receive them.'

'You mean they joined your Order?' Josse asked.

'No, not permanently, although they lived and fought alongside us and were subject to the same routine and regulations.' He gave a small smile. 'Even the Saracens respect the warrior monks, for the majority of our soldiers are not only vastly experienced and knowledgeable in how to pursue the fight against the enemy but also, because we are avowed monks and must obey, we are considerably better disciplined than most of the crusading troops.' He lowered his eyes. 'I am sorry; I am proud and boastful and that is not seemly.'

'Perhaps not,' Josse said, 'but a little pride is deserved, Thibault, for your Order's reputation is a fine one.'

'Thank you.'

'So, you were based at Crac des Chevaliers and your numbers were swelled by more soldiers after the defeat at Hattin,' Gervase said. Helewise detected impatience in his tone.

'Yes,' Thibault agreed. 'Then two years on our King Richard and Philip of France arrived and they regained Acre and consolidated the other possessions held by the Franks along the coast. It was success, I suppose, of a sort; although the great prize remained in Muslim hands. Both we and the Knights Templar counselled against an attack upon the Holy City, but kings are kings and they do not necessarily welcome good advice. Eventually King Richard and Saladin agreed to a truce and for the most part the fighting came to an end.'

'Except for the persistent border skirmishes,' Josse said softly.

Thibault turned to look at him. 'You are well versed in the history of the Holy Land, Sir Josse. The term *border skirmishes* describes exactly what they were, for the Peace of Ramla did not stop the Saracens from pursuing the enemy who were trying to settle on what they perceived as their land.

'In the course of such fighting – in which my Order was sometimes called upon to take part – prisoners were taken by both sides. In the case of wealthy and influential knights and warriors, men whose families would do almost anything to have them back, there was always the possibility of an exchange. Usually the practice was for one or other party to come to us and express their interest in such an arrangement, offering in exchange either a prisoner of their own or a cash payment.'

Rather, Helewise thought ironically, in the manner in which our own king was captured and then purchased back by his own poor, suffering people.

'Such things are common in the aftermath of battle,' Josse observed. 'Go on, Thibault.'

He shifted on his cot and the sheet covering him from the chest down slipped a little. Helewise saw that the burns extended over his ribs and stomach. Dear God, she thought, is any of him *not* affected? Sister Caliste squeezed out a clean piece of linen in a bowl of water – it must, Helewise realized, include lavender oil, for the clean, sharp smell pervaded the recess – and, with a hand as gentle as an angel's, laid it on Thibault's scarlet flesh. He gave her a smile of gratitude.

She returned it. Then, turning to the Abbess, she said, 'My lady, he should not go on much longer.' She shot a concerned glance at her patient. 'He needs to rest.'

'I know, Sister,' Helewise said gently. 'Thibault? Would you like to finish later?'

But Thibault seemed agitated at the suggestion. 'No, my lady, I must tell you what I saw while it is fresh in my mind.'

'Can you not move straight on to the events of yesterday?' Gervase asked. 'Surely that is what we need to hear about, and—'

The Hospitaller shook his head. 'I will tell my tale in my own way,' he said firmly. 'It is not from the pleasure of hearing my own voice that I am giving you this information.'

It sounded like an admonition, Helewise thought, and for a moment she saw past the gravely wounded man to the author- itative warrior monk that stood beyond. He must, she reflected, have been an awesome man . . .

'After the Peace of Ramla I was commanded to go to Margat, where I was to take up a senior position, and I began my new duties,' Thibault said. His voice sounded stronger, as if, with the end of his tale at last in sight, he was drawing on his reserve strength. 'In September two years ago I was summoned to my superior's quarters and commanded to arrange a prisoner exchange. The man in question was a young Saracen who had taken a deep sword cut in an incident to the east of Crac des Chevaliers. Because his wound was infected he was given into the care of the Hospitallers and, after spending some months at Crac des Chevaliers, he was moved to Margat and he thus became my responsibility.'

'I do not understand,' Gervase burst out, 'how one moment you can be fighting a man and presumably trying desperately to kill him, then the next be doing your best to keep him alive!' Helewise saw Josse give a quick grin, as if the plain logic of the remark amused him. She waited to see what Thibault would say in reply.

The Hospitaller had turned offended eyes towards the sheriff. 'You are not,' he said, 'a fighting man.'

'I have taken part in no battle, I admit it.'

Thibault nodded. 'Then you cannot possibly understand. You, by contrast – ' he turned to Josse – 'know full well how it is, do you not?'

Josse, after an embarrassed glance at Gervase, said, briefly, 'Aye.'

It appeared that Thibault was not even going to attempt an explanation. 'We used our skill to nurse our young patient and, in time, he began to recover,' he went on. 'It was not a quick healing and Brother Michael, who nursed the young man, felt almost that the patient did not want to get better. We have observed,' he added, 'that a man who desperately wants to resume his life will recover much more speedily than, say, a man who knows that some feared event awaits him. But, be that as it may, eventually the young man was well enough to leave us and almost immediately the question of exchanging him occurred.'

'He was to be swapped for some Frankish knight?' Gervase asked.

'No. It was not as simple as that. The young man, it appeared, came from a very rich and powerful Saracen clan, a close and loving family who, because of their profound regard for him, badly wanted him home again. It was the young man's elder brother who made the approach. He sent his representatives to my superior and negotiations were opened. I was commanded to select six of my brethren to act as escorts, and the prisoner would be closely watched by two of our guards.' He paused, eyes unfocused. 'The prisoner was manacled and chained and the party set out into the desert by night, heading for the place where the exchange was to be made. Then—' Again, he stopped. 'I was not there,' he said, 'and I cannot tell you exactly what happened. All I know is that something happened – there was perhaps treachery on behalf of the prisoner's family and their men; possibly they tried to take both the prisoner *and* whatever they were offering in payment for him. I do not know and that is my best guess. A fight broke out, in the course of which the monks of the escort group and the two guards were attacked and cut down.'

He looked round at his audience, briefly studying each face. 'All but one of them perished out there in the desert. We sent out a search party at first light, when they had not returned, and I was ordered to lead it. We reached the place where our brethren were to have met the prisoner's party and we found carnage. We guessed that many of the enemy had perished – our monks do not go down without a fight – but there must have remained sufficient of their number to bear the dead and the wounded away. They had left our brethren where they lay in their own blood. I who was first off my horse to kneel beside my brothers saw straight away that there was no hope. Six were already dead; one was dying. I crouched beside him – it was dear Brother James; such a devout, caring monk and no mean fighter – and he tried to tell me what had happened. He was choking on his own blood and I could hardly make out the words, but he managed to say that Brother—' Abruptly he stopped, a shocked expression on his face as if horrified that he had nearly said something he shouldn't. 'He told me that one of the brothers had run away.' His voice was hushed. 'I could not understand, for it sounded as if Brother James was commending the brother's cowardly, shameful act! We do not *run away* whatever the danger, whatever the threat to our own lives. We stay and fight beside our brothers, and if they succumb, we battle on to our last breath at their side.'

'And so you set out to follow the runaway?' Helewise asked softly.

Thibault turned to her, looking slightly surprised, as if he had forgotten she was there. 'I returned to Margat first, my lady, and made my report,' he replied. 'Then, when we had tried to patch together a likely sequence of events, we realized that the monk who ran from the scene might by his desertion be responsible for the deaths of his brethren. My master declared that he must be apprehended and brought back to give an account of himself and face whatever punishment was deemed appropriate. I volunteered to lead the pursuit; Brother Otto and Brother Philip were selected to go with me.' He gave the ghost of a smile. 'We did not anticipate, when we set out all that time ago, just how long and how far the pursuit of our missing brother was going to take us.'

'Brother Philip?' Josse asked, frowning. 'I thought the third monk's name was Jeremiah?'

Thibault's eyes were unfocused again. He was clearly tiring rapidly now and he appeared to be staring back into the past. 'Brother Philip died,' he muttered. 'He took sick of a fever

soon after we left Constantinople and Otto and I were unable
to save him.'

'Then – was Brother Jeremiah not originally of your
company?'

Thibault's eyelids were drooping. 'We met Brother Jeremiah
on the road up from the coast.'

'The coast? Which coast?' Gervase rapped out.

The shadow of a smile played on Thibault's lips. 'Yours,' he
replied. 'Brother Otto and I recognized by his habit that he was
a brother Hospitaller and Otto asked where he was bound.
Jeremiah said he was heading for Clerkenwell, and that being
our eventual destination too, we decided to join up and travel
together. It's safer – ' he gave a huge yawn – 'to travel in
company.' Slowly his eyes closed.

'Then—' Gervase began.

But Sister Caliste stood up. Considering how slight she was,
Helewise thought, watching the young nun, there was a considerable presence about her. She knew very well what Sister Caliste
was going to say and, with a secret smile, she watched to see
how she would set about it.

'My lord,' she began quietly, 'enough. My patient is very
tired and he must sleep.'

'Sister Caliste, I am investigating not only the death of the
man found on the forest track but also that of his own
companion, this Brother Jeremiah!' Gervase protested in an
angry hiss. 'I must hear what he has to say of the fire in the
priory.'

Sister Caliste stood her ground. 'I understand that, my lord,'
she said. 'Nevertheless, you cannot hear it now.' She lowered
her voice. 'We have not yet told him of Brother Jeremiah's
death, although of course he may already know, and it would
be better if you wait until he is stronger before you discuss
such a tragic matter with him.' She added, with quiet dignity,
'I have been put in charge of this man – ' she looked down
and bestowed upon her patient a kind and loving glance – 'and
I will not allow you to endanger his recovery by keeping him
awake when his body is pressing him to sleep.'

'You—' Gervase looked furious.

Sister Caliste stepped forward towards him and, well-
mannered man that he was, even when angry, he moved back.
Sister Caliste pressed on and Gervase was soon outside the

recess. Helewise slipped out beside him and Josse did the same. Sister Caliste drew the curtains closed and held them together behind her back. Smiling sweetly up at Gervase, she said, 'I will watch over him as he sleeps. If he says anything, I will tell you. When he is awake and can speak to you, I will send word.'

With that she gave a low reverence to Helewise, slightly more perfunctory bows to Josse and the sheriff, and vanished back inside the recess.

The Abbess led the way back to her little room. Once the three of them were inside and the door closed, Josse burst out, 'It is the same event that the two Saracen warriors described!'

'Saracen warriors?' Gervase queried.

Josse turned to him. 'Aye. I had a visit from them – ' he paused, calculating when it had been; so much had happened that it came as quite a surprise to realize that it had only been two days ago – 'the day before yesterday. They gave their names as Kathnir and Akhbir and they said they were hunting for one of their own.'

'Another Saracen? Then surely the man they seek must be the dead man who was brought here!'

Josse sighed. 'No, Gervase. He isn't. That was what I suggested and they were sure he was not their man.' He looked across at the Abbess. 'I am sorry, my lady, to repeat what you already know but it is important to explain matters fully to Gervase.'

'Hmm?' She seemed to be deep in thought and it seemed to Josse that she had barely heard him. 'Yes, of course,' she said vaguely.

Swiftly Josse related to Gervase the tale that the two Saracens had told him. 'And during this exchange out in the desert,' he concluded, 'something happened and their master's young brother – who must be the Hospitallers' prisoner – disappeared and was probably killed. Their master managed to escape, but the man they're hunting stole some precious treasure from him.'

'Did they not say what this treasure was?' demanded Gervase.

'No,' Josse replied shortly. 'There was rather a lot that they did not say. Clearly they knew far more than they were admitting.'

'Could they have been at the meeting in the desert?' Gervase asked. 'Their master trusts them enough to send them after the thief and the stolen treasure; might this not mean that they form part of his personal bodyguard?'

'I don't know,' Josse said. He gave a wry smile. 'If so, then they are definitely holding back, for they would have witnessed the whole thing.'

'What could the thief have taken? Something portable, for it appears that the two men who hunt him expect to recover it. Gold? Precious stones?'

'Either is possible,' Josse agreed. 'My understanding of these hostage exchanges is that, if it's not a simple swapping of one prisoner for another, then usually the payment is in coin.'

Suddenly the Abbess spoke. 'How did they know it wasn't him?'

Josse and Gervase exchanged a glance. 'My lady?' Josse said.

'Your Saracens, Sir Josse. I've been puzzling over how they knew that our dead man here was not the man they sought. Was there anything in your description that would have enabled them to be so certain?'

Josse thought back. 'I told them I thought the dead man to be a Saracen, but that was solely on account of his colouring, since his clothes and possessions were missing.'

'You did not give away some detail such as that the dead man had long black hair?' she persisted.

Josse concentrated very hard. Then: 'I do not believe, my lady, that I mentioned any such detail.'

Her eyes lit up. 'Then they must have seen the dead man for themselves,' she said simply, 'for how else could they have been so certain?'

'They might have caught sight of their quarry *after* the dead man was killed,' Gervase pointed out.

'Yes, that is so,' the Abbess admitted.

She did not, Josse thought, look very convinced. 'My lady?' he said. 'Won't you share your thoughts with us?'

She looked slightly alarmed. 'Oh – no, I do not think I should, for what I am thinking amounts to a terrible accusation, and if I'm wrong I would be blackening two men's names for no reason.'

'There are only the two of us to hear,' Josse said softly. 'We won't repeat anything you say.'

She was frowning. Then her face cleared and she said, 'Very well. But bear in mind that I am probably right off the scent.'

'We will,' Josse and Gervase said in unison.

She took a deep breath. 'Well, when the two Saracens told you, Sir Josse, that they were hunting for a man like themselves, you instantly thought of the dead man, because he too was a Saracen and there are not many of them in these parts. I'm just wondering if they made the same swift judgement.'

Josse waited to see if she would go on but she did not; she sat in her imposing chair watching the two of them eagerly, as if waiting for them to agree. 'I'm sorry, my lady,' Gervase said, 'but I do not understand.'

She clicked her tongue in irritation but it was at herself and not them. 'I am sorry; I did not explain. What I am suggesting is that Sir Josse's Saracens caught sight of someone whose manner of dress and general appearance were that of the man they had hunted for so long. They assumed he was their quarry and without pausing to check they—'

'They jumped on him!' Josse finished for her. 'They believed he was the thief! They stripped him and searched through his pack and when they found nothing they tortured him to make him say where he had hidden it! When he did not tell them – he couldn't, of course, because, not being the thief, he didn't *know* – they killed him.' After a moment's reflection, he said, 'It is indeed a grave accusation, my lady.'

She looked anxious. 'I realize that, and—'

'Grave it may be,' Gervase said, 'but I think it is an accurate one.'

Josse looked at him. 'You do?'

Slowly Gervase nodded. 'As you said, my lady – ' he smiled at the Abbess – 'there just aren't that many Saracens around here. It seems only logical that Josse's pair thought the dead man was their thief.'

'If they did,' the Abbess said thoughtfully, 'then we are wrong about their having been present that night in the desert. If they had been, they would know what the thief looked like.'

'True,' Josse agreed. 'Unless either then or subsequently he adopted a disguise.'

Gervase gave a short bark of laughter, but there was little mirth in it. 'Oh, Josse,' he said, 'you turn a puzzle inside out and double its complexity!'

Josse grinned. 'Aye, I know.' Then, after a moment, 'I am trying to picture that night. Thibault's party of eight Hospitallers escorting the prisoner; his name was Fadil. The wealthy man, waiting with his bodyguard and clutching some valuable possession with which to buy back his beloved younger brother. Then something goes wrong. A fight breaks out, the prisoner is killed, the elder brother barely escapes with his life and all the Hospitallers die save the one who ran away.'

'Do you think that one side or the other might have tried to win both prisoner and ransom?' suggested Gervase.

'I would not think the Knights Hospitaller capable of such treachery,' Josse answered. 'Thibault implied that it is quite common for monks of the Order to act as brokers in such exchanges and that is, I imagine, because both parties trust them to ensure fair play.'

'I do not speak of the Order as a whole,' Gervase said. 'It would only take one man to instigate treachery.'

'He would have had to persuade seven other Hospitallers to go along with it,' Josse observed.

'Six,' Gervase said. 'One ran away.'

'Perhaps he was the traitor,' the Abbess remarked. 'He could have killed his brethren and fled the scene.'

'Perhaps the runaway monk stole the treasure!' Gervase exclaimed. He punched his fist into the palm of his other hand in frustration. 'Dear God, but we fumble around like blind men!'

The Abbess stood up and both men turned to her. 'We have made progress with our fumbling,' she said with a smile, 'and tomorrow Thibault will, I hope, be able to speak to us again. Let us think what we will ask him, for if we are allowed limited time, we do not want to waste it.'

It was, Josse thought a sensible suggestion. As the Abbess found a scrap of vellum and dipped her quill in the inkhorn, he and Gervase went to stand either side of her.

It was marginally better than doing nothing.

Outremer, September 1194

He sat slumped on the sand. Reality had slipped quietly away and he was in the middle of a nightmare.

He could not absorb what he had just seen. Its power was

sheer evil and a superstitious man would have said it came
straight from the devil himself.

But that was not the worst of it.

The worst had begun so slowly, so insidiously that at first
he had barely noticed.

Brother James had yawned.

It was quite funny to start with. So much excitement – the
incredible sight of what they had just witnessed; the tense situ-
ation out there in the black night beneath the stars; the bright
silken tent, the lanterns, the fat man's luxurious garments; the
sights, the smells – and there was dear old Brother James
looking as if he could barely keep his eyes open! How he would
be teased!

But then one of the guards standing beside the prisoner
suddenly slumped to the ground. He tried to stand up again
but his legs seemed to have turned to jelly.

Then right beside the young monk Brother Thomas gave
a sort of groan; turning, he stared right into Thomas's eyes
and saw in the flickering lantern light that the pupils were
widely dilated, so that blue-eyed Thomas looked dark-eyed
as a Saracen . . .

It was horrible.

But the horror was only just beginning.

Eight

In the afternoon, Gervase returned to Tonbridge. He said
testily that he could not kick his heels at Hawkenlye waiting
for Thibault to wake up. 'In the meantime,' he added, 'the
entire criminal population of the Medway valley may be
thieving, raping, pillaging and looting, and nobody there to
restrain them.'

Josse, understanding Gervase's frustration, walked over to
the stable block with him. 'Give my love to Sabin,' he said,
'and I'll send word as soon as there's anything to tell you.'

'Very well,' Gervase said. Then, with a grin, 'I'm sorry, Josse. It's just that—' He broke off, apparently unable to put his thought into words.

'I understand,' Josse said feelingly. 'All that we so badly want to know is beyond our reach behind the mist.'

Gervase's smile spread. 'I would not have put it so poetic-ally but yes, that's it. Farewell, Josse – I hope to be back soon.'

Josse watched him ride away. Then, for want of anything better to do, he strolled down to the Vale to pass the time of day with Brother Saul.

Late in the evening, Sister Caliste came to inform him that Thibault was awake, his pain was less intense and he had drunk a bowl of broth. 'Abbess Helewise is on her way to him,' she added, 'and asks that you join her.'

Josse saw the improvement instantly. And Brother Otto was stirring, although the nursing nuns were keeping him sedated. Thibault watched with intent eyes as the Abbess and Josse went to stand on either side of his cot. Then he said, 'You wish to hear about the fire. Since I awoke I have been thinking of nothing else. I have put my thoughts in order and I am ready to tell you.'

Josse said, 'We are ready to listen.'

'It was the second night that we were lodging at the priory,' Thibault began. 'We went to bed very tired, for we had searched all that day for the runaway monk, asking questions in Tonbridge and the neighbouring hamlets. My two brethren fell asleep quickly and I soon followed. Then something disturbed me; I cannot say what. I lay quite still, but it was dark and I could see nothing. Then as my eyes adjusted I made out the small square of the window; a lighter patch in the blackness. I listened to see if whatever had awoken me would recur and, after a while, it did.' He looked from one to the other of his listeners, making sure he had their full attention. 'It was the latch being lifted very gently from its hook. I could not see, but I could hear, and I remembered that the door was a little stiff, so that even with the latch free, one still has to push the door quite hard to open it. The timber is new,' he added, 'and has prob-ably swollen a little, so that it is tight in the door frame.'

'Someone was trying to get in?' Josse prompted.

'Yes. I sensed the door opening and then I saw the outline of a figure pass in front of the little window. I felt a waft of air as he swiftly moved further into the room. Brother Jeremiah was sleeping closest to the door and thus he was the first of us that the intruder came to.' His face fell and briefly his lips moved in a muttered prayer. 'Then I heard a sort of rustling sound, as of a man stirring in his bed, and a sort of muffled cry, presumably from poor Brother Jeremiah. There was the swishing, whistling noise of something heavy moving rapidly through the air and then those two hideous thumps.' He raised a bandaged hand and covered his eyes.

'You are quite sure that what you heard was the assailant attacking Brother Jeremiah?' Josse asked gently.

Thibault lowered his hand and stared straight into Josse's eyes. 'Oh, yes,' he said. 'Whoever came into our room murdered poor Jeremiah. That I will swear before God and before any court in the land.'

'But you did not actually *see* the deed,' the Abbess said. 'Could the sounds have had another source?'

Thibault looked at her. 'No, my lady. I could make out more by then. Either my eyes were becoming accustomed to the darkness or the dawn was lightening the sky; I cannot say. But I saw the outline of that raised arm and I knew without doubt the target of those dreadful blows.'

'And then the fire started?' Josse asked. It was clearly causing Thibault great distress to speak of his brother monk's murder and it seemed charitable to move on. He was also aware of time passing; Sister Caliste would soon step forward and say in that soft but imperious voice, 'Enough.'

'The fire; yes, the fire,' Thibault breathed. 'The two things seemed to happen simultaneously, although I do not see how a man can commit murder and set a blaze at the same time.' Josse could see one very obvious answer but, not wanting to interrupt, he kept his peace. 'I smelt the smoke,' Thibault was saying, 'and I heard the sound of kindling crackling. Then there was a whoosh and a great sheet of flame leapt up just outside the door.'

'Where was the murderer?' the Abbess asked. 'Could you see him in the light of the fire?'

'I saw a cloaked shape, black against the light,' Thibault replied. 'His hood was over his head and face and I caught no more than an impression as he whipped round and shot out through the open door.'

Knowing that the fire was about to start, Josse thought, the man had probably wetted his cloak and wrapped a soaked cloth around his nose and mouth. Thus prepared, he would have been able to dash through a sheet of flame with reasonable safety.

'I got out of bed and threw on my robe,' Thibault said. 'Brother Otto was on his feet and yelling at the top of his voice; well, until he breathed in the smoke and began to choke. He sings bass baritone, you know, and I think that may have saved us, for he has a good loud voice. We gathered up poor Brother Jeremiah and began to drag him towards the door, but already two of the walls and the roof were ablaze and burning reed straw was falling all around us. We put up our hoods but very soon our garments were singeing and beginning to burn. The canons had evidently heard Brother Otto's cries for help for they came running, and Canon Mark burst into the room through the fire and helped us pull Brother Jeremiah outside, where we laid him on the ground. The rest of the canons had formed a chain with buckets of water but before many had been thrown the fire went out.'

'That's exactly what Canon Mark told me!' Josse exclaimed. He still found it barely credible. 'You just said, Thibault, that the fire had taken hold of the walls and the roof. How, if there was still combustible material to be consumed, can it possibly have gone out?'

'There was in fact little left of the guest wing to burn, but the fire did not spread to neighbouring buildings,' Thibault corrected. 'Why, I do not know.' He spoke somewhat stiffly. 'All I can tell you is what happened.'

'I am sorry,' Josse said instantly. 'I do not doubt your word but I've never known a fire behave like that.'

'Neither have I,' Thibault agreed. He appeared mollified by Josse's apology. Then, thoughtfully, he added, 'Have you ever seen a fire-eater at the fair? That's what it was like, as if someone had lit their outward breath and, as soon as it had all been consumed, the fire went out.'

'Then it was some sort of a trick?' Josse asked.

Thibault shrugged. 'I do not know.' He sighed deeply. 'It took the life of one of my brethren, whatever it was.'

Josse met the Abbess's eyes. He was torn between the need to ask further vital questions and the desire to give Thibault a few moments to mourn the dead monk. Presently the Abbess gave a very small nod; taking this as encouragement, Josse said, 'Thibault, you say that Brother Jeremiah was not of your original company but that you encountered him on your way up from the coast?'

'That is correct,' Thibault said wearily. 'It was just after Robertsbridge. Brother Jeremiah was, as I said, bound for Clerkenwell and fell into step with Brother Otto and me. He had never left his native land – he was only a young man – and he was eager to hear our tales of Outremer and our long journey over land and sea. The good Lord filled his heart with zeal and after only a day or so he had made up his mind to ask permission to go on crusade himself.' He sighed again. 'That will not now come to pass,' he said sadly.

Josse knew what he must ask next. 'Thibault,' he began, 'you said that since Brother Jeremiah was sleeping in the bed closest to the door, it was he whom the murderer came to first. Do you think that is the only reason why he attacked Brother Jeremiah? Or do you think he deliberately targeted the poor young man?'

Slowly Thibault shook his head. 'I have asked myself that same question over and over again,' he muttered. 'If the assailant wished to kill Jeremiah – and I cannot for the life of me see why – then it would not have been difficult to discover which bed he slept in. As I told you, we had already spent one night at the priory and anyone could have looked in and seen which bed each of us occupied. We go early to our rest and we sleep deeply. Not one of us would have been aware of someone spying.'

Josse nodded. 'Thank you, Thibault. So, Brother Jeremiah could very easily have been the intended victim and, as Canon Mark suggested, the fire was started in an attempt to hide the fact that he had already been murdered. But *why* should anyone want to kill him?'

'He was eager, friendly, devout and, I believe, hard-working,' Thibault affirmed. 'I cannot imagine that in his young life he had done any harm to anyone.' His face crumpled. 'I grieve for him,' he whispered. 'God rest his soul.'

'Amen,' said the Abbess.

Josse was looking down at the sleeping Brother Otto. He could hear the wheeze and rattle of air in the monk's throat and chest. *He sings bass baritone*, Thibault had said. Would he ever sing again?

'He won't be ready to speak to you yet awhile,' Thibault said, mistaking the reason for Josse's interest. 'And he won't be able to tell you any more. He did not wake up until the flames started to roar.'

Josse put a hand on Thibault's shoulder; one of his few undamaged areas of flesh. 'I am sorry,' he said sincerely. 'It must have been unspeakable.'

Thibault nodded. 'It was.'

The Abbess was moving towards the gap in the curtains. 'We have disturbed you for long enough,' she said. 'Thank you, Thibault, for going through your terrible experience again. It cannot have been easy.'

'No, my lady, but it is done now.' Thibault's expression seemed to lighten and for a moment he was almost smiling. 'It's strange, but I feel better.'

'I will make sure that Gervase de Gifford hears your story,' Josse said. 'We will do whatever we can to catch Brother Jeremiah's killer; that I promise you.'

Thibault eyed him. 'It won't bring him back,' he said quietly.

There was really no answer to that. With a brief bow, Josse left the recess and the Abbess followed him.

He walked beside her to her room. She seemed deep in thought and it was with reluctance that he broke into her reverie.

'My lady,' he said tentatively, 'Thibault said he did not see how the assailant could have slain Brother Jeremiah *inside* the guest room and set the fire *outside* at the same time, but—'

'There must have been two of them,' she interrupted calmly.

'Aye, that was what I was about to say. Who were they? Why did they want poor Jeremiah to die?'

'It has been occupying me since we knew the poor young man had been so cruelly killed,' she said. 'He seems to have lived a short and fairly limited life. What can he possibly have done to earn such retribution?'

'We'll have to find out more about him,' Josse said glumly; he did not relish the prospect. 'No doubt Thibault will be able to tell us where he was based and, perhaps, what business was taking him to Clerkenwell. We shall have to notify his brethren of his death.'

'We shall,' she repeated dully.

He suddenly realized how tired he was. 'I am going to bed,' he announced. 'My head is full of shadows and vague shapes that I feel I ought to recognize yet cannot. I will see more clearly after a good night's sleep.'

She turned to him and he saw that she looked as weary as he felt. 'Sleep well, Sir Josse,' she said. 'I shall try to do likewise.'

Josse slept deeply for many hours. But then he fell into a vivid and alarming dream in which he and Abbess Helewise rode on a huge white horse along a narrow dusty track, following two shadowy figures. One of them was dressed in the black habit of a Knight Hospitaller; the other wore a flowing brown robe and carried a leather satchel. There was a great sense of urgency, for the figures kept disappearing in mist and sometimes when he caught sight of them there was only one of them. The Abbess was urging him on, and he dug in his heels so that the horse leapt forward with such a violent lurch that he was all but unseated and had to fling his arms around her waist. She felt slim as a reed in his arms and then she was no longer the Abbess but Joanna, naked, twisting round with a smile on her face as she pressed her flesh against his and he began kissing her, caressing her, until—

Beside him in the lay brothers' sleeping quarters somebody began to snore.

And Josse, flinging himself over onto his back, clutched the covers around him against the cold of the night and wondered how long it was until morning.

He must have dozed and when he woke again, Brother Augustus was stirring a pot of porridge over the hearth and whistling happily. Josse too felt happy; not as cheerful as Augustus perhaps, but with the quiet satisfaction of knowing his next step. Hurriedly he went to wash as much of himself as the cold morning and the even colder water allowed – which amounted to his hands, face and neck – and he joined Gussie, Brother Saul and old Brother Firmin for breakfast. Then he took his leave of them and hurried to suggest to the Abbess that they ask Thibault about the runaway monk whom they had come so far to find.

The improvement in Thibault's condition appeared to be continuing. Helewise thought, as she and Josse entered the recess, that his face had lost its deathly pallor and his eyes were brighter.

'Thibault,' she began, 'when you came here before you said you were searching for a runaway monk from your Order; an Englishman. When I asked you to describe him or to tell us his name, you said you did not know these things. I realize,' she added softly, 'that you must have had very good reasons for your reticence, but I must confess I did not believe you; for how would it be possible for you to hunt for someone if you didn't know what he looked like? And surely you must know his name as well as you know your own, for he was of your Order and, I presume, served with you in Outremer.' She paused, watching Thibault's face, from which he had carefully removed all expression. 'I appreciate that those of us in holy orders must obey our superiors,' she went on, 'and I do not expect you to reveal information that you have been commanded to keep secret. However, the situation has changed now. A monk has been murdered and you and Brother Otto were badly burned. Will you not share your burden with us, Thibault? Can we not help you carry it for a while?'

Thibault did not answer for some time but stared silently into her eyes. She read yearning in his, as if he longed to confide but knew that he could not. Eventually he said, 'I appreciate the offer. There is little that I may tell you of *why* we hunt our runaway. However . . .' He paused, as if testing his decision. 'However, I feel that I may at least tell you something of the man's life in Outremer.'

She shot a glance at Josse, to discover that he was unsuccessfully suppressing the same excitement that she felt rise up in herself. She said calmly, 'Very well, Thibault; if you are prepared to do so, then Sir Josse and I are listening.'

Thibault glanced at Brother Otto in the next bed. Otto had his eyes open but Helewise did not think he was aware of them. He looked vacant and she suspected that he was still being dosed with the infirmarer's sedative and analgesic mixture.

Then Thibault began to speak. 'The English monk was not a Hospitaller when he arrived in Acre. He came out to Outremer in a company of twenty-five knights and their attendants, all in the service of an English lord who was going to the support of his kinsman in Antioch. The kinsman was a wealthy landowner but his wife had given him only daughters and, hard pressed, he had sent home to England for help in defending his lands. The Englishman fought for his lord at the Battle of Hattin, and in the aftermath of the defeat his master retreated to his kinsman's home in Antioch to lick his small wounds and recover his strength. According to the Englishman, his master had not enjoyed his experience of fighting and was not keen to repeat it. He had the excuse that his kinsman needed his and his knights' help in defending his property, which was after all why the lord had come out to Outremer in the first place. Our Englishman, however, felt differently. He made his way from Antioch to Crac des Chevaliers where, in the early autumn of 1187, he was admitted to the Order of the Knights of the Hospital. He was strong and blessed with a fit and healthy body, and worked hard, training his less experienced brethren in the arts of war.'

'I thought you said he was young?' Josse asked. 'How was he able to teach such skills?'

Thibault smiled. 'Young he might have been – he was eighteen or nineteen when first I met him – but in the year he had spent in Outremer he saw a great deal of action. Moreover, he had received the training that prepares a man for the life of a knight. There was much he had to teach and I observed that once the monks had overcome their disinclination to be drilled by a younger man, they learned to appreciate him. He was modest and he did not permit the role to inflate his sense of self-regard.' For a moment Thibault stared into the distance. 'Then,' he resumed, 'King Richard arrived and we began the next major onslaught against the enemy.'

'You were in the fighting?' Helewise asked.

'Yes, my lady. I was in the army that took back the great fortress and port of Acre from the infidel and the English monk was of my company. We rode together on the march from Acre to Jaffa and we fought at the Battle of Arsuf, where the Hospitallers formed the rear guard; we and the Templars took it in turns to be the advance guard and that day it was their turn. Despite this, it was our Grand Master himself who led the charge.' His face glowing, he added quietly, 'The English monk and I rode side by side.'

Helewise, glancing at Josse, noticed that his face too was alight with excitement. Men, she thought.

'As we routed the last attacking Saracens, the English monk encountered an old friend. It was his former lord and he had been stricken with dysentery. He was so unwell that he could not sit his horse and the Englishman was ordered to take him back through the lines to where he could be treated. But the lord showed no sign of a speedy recovery and it was decided that he should go back to Acre and thence to his kinsman's estate in Antioch. Our army was indebted to him; he had supplied a strong force of knights and men-at-arms, most of whom remained to fight with us, and in recognition of this the Hospitallers were ordered to provide an escort to see him safely home. The English monk was selected to care for his lord, and although the task was not to his taste and he would have preferred to remain with the army, he had to do as he was told.'

'Was that the last time that you saw him?' Helewise asked.

'No, my lady. When the fighting was over and King Richard set sail from Acre after the Peace of Ramla, we returned to Crac des Chevaliers and quite soon after that I was posted to Margat. The English monk turned up there one day late in 1192. He had, apparently, been there on and off for the past year, alternating his duties with nursing his lord back to health in Antioch. By December his lord was well enough to go home to England and our monk, not wanting to go with him, came back to us.' Thibault frowned. 'He was different,' he said. 'Something deep within him had changed. He was still dutiful and conscientious; he took on any duty that was laid upon him, however arduous, without complaint and he would carry out the task to the best of his ability. But it seemed to me that his heart was no longer in it.'

'And it was at this time that he was selected for the mission in the desert?' Josse asked. 'The prisoner exchange that went so wrong?'

'Yes,' Thibault replied. 'I selected him to be part of the escort because I thought that the experience would be something out of the ordinary. Something with a dash of excitement, which might help him draw the sundered parts of himself back together again.' He looked at Helewise. 'My intention was good,' he said quietly. 'But it ended, as you know, in disaster.'

There was a short silence, as if all three were honouring the memory of those who died. Then Josse said, 'Thibault, it seems that you liked this English monk?'

Thibault closed his eyes, his expression grief-stricken. 'I did. He was a good man and I both liked and respected him.' He opened his eyes again and glared at Josse. 'I find it all but impossible to believe that he can have acted in such a cowardly way!' he burst out. 'He was the last man I would have expected to run away and leave his dead and dying brethren to their fate!'

Helewise had remembered something. 'Did you not tell us that there was something odd about the dying brother's last words?' she asked. 'Brother James, wasn't it?'

'Yes, Brother James. And you are right, my lady. I had the impression that James was trying to say that Brother – that the English monk had done well to run off as he did.' He shook his head. 'I have thought about it so much – if only poor Brother James could have explained more thoroughly! – and I cannot envisage a situation where running away was the right thing.'

'Perhaps—' Helewise began. But then, aware of the two fighting men beside her, both of whom knew so very much more about these matters than she did, she stopped.

Josse said, 'Go on, my lady. What is your thought?'

'Oh – I am sure it is nothing.'

'Tell us, anyway,' Thibault invited. 'It cannot be more far-fetched than some of *my* ideas.'

She returned his smile. 'I wonder whether something even worse would have happened if this English monk had stayed with his brothers. If they had each received a fatal blow and he had escaped injury, he would have been the only Hospitaller left to carry out the mission.'

'The prisoner exchange, you mean?' Josse asked.

'Yes. You said, Thibault, that the knights and men of your Order are renowned for their obedience?'

'Yes, indeed.'

'Then as the sole survivor, would not this Englishman have taken upon himself the task of fulfilling the mission?'

'Ye-es,' Thibault said slowly.

'The knights and the enemy had both suffered many casualties,' she said, excited. 'You said, Thibault, that the surviving enemy removed their dead and injured?'

'That is correct,' Thibault confirmed.

'It must have been a terrible fight,' she said. 'In the midst of it, the Englishman could have seen that although it was too late to help his brethren, he might still get the prisoner away to be exchanged at a later date. Wasn't that the purpose of the night's excursion?'

Thibault was thinking. 'I suppose it could have happened like that,' he murmured. 'It *is* possible that the English monk regarded the order to guard the prisoner as more important than attending to his brethren.' His eyes lit up. 'He might even have been *ordered* to take the prisoner away – perhaps that was what Brother James was trying to tell me!' He turned to Helewise. 'Thank you, my lady. You have given me something to think about while I lie here.' He added something else; she was not sure she caught the words but it was enough to make her feel a sudden heat in her face. She turned away and suggested to Josse that they leave Thibault to rest.

She thought he said, 'I was wrong about you. You are a woman to reckon with.'

She would have to confess and do penance for the sudden rush of pride the remark had brought in its wake . . .

Outremer, September 1194

He had to get away.

Those few who were left alive of the enemy had removed their dead and wounded and gone. He had heard their wails as they had ridden away. The servant with the deep cut to his cheek had stemmed the blood and managed to get the fat man to his feet and outside to the horses. The fat man, groaning and wheezing, had been clutching his right arm, into which Brother Andreas's sword had bitten deeply as the fat man drew his vicious, curved knife and sliced into Brother Theobald's throat. The fat man would live; Theobald would not.

Brother James was still alive – just – although the poor man could not have very long. The young man knelt beside him, his face close to James's mouth, for he could see that James was trying to talk.

'You must – go,' he whispered.

'No! I will look after you until help comes!'

'NO. That is an order and you will obey me. Take the prisoner and go.'

'But—'

Brother James steeled himself for a last effort. 'If you stay here, others will come and they may arrive before our brethren come looking for us. Then you too will die, the prisoner will be lost and, most important, that which you now carry will not reach its destination.'

'I can't leave you!' he whispered.

'You must,' Brother James said. 'God bless you, my brother, and keep you safe.' Then, with one last direct look into the young monk's eyes, his lids fluttered down and he turned his face away.

It was an order, the young monk thought in anguish. I have been given a direct order by a senior monk. I must obey.

They had to get away . . .

He looked across to the prisoner, huddled on the sand with his thin arms clutched around his raised knees and moaning softly. He strode over and took him not ungently by the arm.

'Are you hurt?' he asked in Arabic. The boy shook his head. 'Then we must leave.'

The boy stood up and trotted along at his side. Outside, all the horses had gone – the wounded servant must have cut them loose after he had grabbed mounts for himself and the fat man – but the young monk stood quite still and presently he heard the sound of a tentative neigh. He called out softly the words he had heard the native grooms use and out of the darkness a group of ten or twelve horses slowly appeared. Some of them were the Hospitallers' mounts but he passed them over, instead selecting two of the smaller, lighter horses of the enemy which travelled so swiftly in desert conditions.

He told the youth to mount up. He put his hand on his leather pouch to make sure the contents were secure, then he patted the horse he had selected for himself, put his foot in the stirrup and mounted. He paused to lengthen the stirrup leathers – he was considerably longer in the leg than the animal's former owner – and then, with one last look at the silken tent, kicked his heels into his horse's sides and, with the youth at his side, galloped off into the night.

Part Three
The Saracens

Nine

Josse was with the Abbess in the refectory finishing the noon meal. They were seated apart from the rest of the community, discussing Thibault's story.

'I keep returning to the conclusion that this runaway English Hospitaller and the Saracen whom Kathnir and Akhbir are hunting just have to be together,' Josse said. 'And I feel sure that the man calling himself John Damianos is Fadil.'

'Fadil?'

'The prisoner who was to be exchanged.' He frowned. 'Although I thought Fadil was a younger man.'

'The meeting in the desert was two years ago,' the Abbess pointed out. 'Fear, privation and a hard road can greatly age a man in two years. And you never saw John Damianos's face.'

'That's right.'

'Well, then. For the time being, let us work on the principle that the runaway monk and his charge – Fadil, going under the name of John Damianos – have travelled all the way from the desert outside Margat to the south-east corner of England.'

'Where are they going?' Josse demanded. 'Why would the Hospitaller bring the prisoner so far? The obvious thing to do was go straight back to Margat, return the prisoner and make a full report.'

She thought about this. Eventually she said, 'Thibault suggested that the prisoner's family might have tried to cheat the Hospitallers so that they went home with both Fadil and whatever they were offering in exchange for him. Is it not possible' – she had softened her voice to a whisper – 'that the Knights Hospitaller did the same?'

'Gervase suggested something similar,' he whispered back. 'When I protested that the Hospitallers were renowned for their honesty and dependability, he replied that it only takes one man to instigate treachery.'

'I agree,' she said. 'If the English monk knew that the tragedy in the desert had been caused because a senior Hospitaller had decided to cheat both his brethren and the prisoner's family, then returning meekly to Margat and the monk who had sent his brethren into danger would have been the last thing he would do.'

'It's possible,' Josse said reluctantly, 'although I still find it hard to believe the great Order of the Knights Hospitaller would behave so shabbily.'

'*One* of them might,' she persisted. 'Keep an open mind, Sir Josse. As to why the English monk made for England, why, I can think of two reasons. One: he is, as we keep saying, English – he went out to Outremer in a party of knights with an English lord who has kin in Antioch – so he could merely be coming home. Two: we have heard mention of the Order's headquarters at Clerkenwell, so might our man be heading there? It is a very long way from Margat and he might think it is therefore a safe place to deliver his charge.'

'Either is possible,' Josse said. 'But we cannot confirm anything until we see more clearly.'

'Sir Josse?' she said after a moment.

He turned to look at her. 'You sound as if something has just occurred to you. Let's hear it.'

'It has,' she said eagerly. 'Why don't we ask Thibault if he knows the name or the dwelling place of the English monk's former lord? If he could provide either, then we can perhaps discover where the English monk came from.'

'How would that help?'

She sighed. 'Because he would very likely be making for the place,' she said. 'We could look for him there.'

'Aye, so we could,' he said slowly. Then: 'John Damianos – Fadil – came to New Winnowlands. If his monk companion is also hiding out in the area, that suggests he might have come from around here.'

Her eyes widened. 'Of course!' she said. 'Do you know of any families in the area with kin in Outremer?'

He grinned. 'Not offhand, my lady, although I dare say I could find out.' He wiped his platter with a crust of bread. 'I'll ride over to see Brice of Rotherbridge; he knows most of the big households of this corner of England, by reputation if not personally.'

He had just put the bread in his mouth when Sister Martha came to tell him that Will was looking for him. Hastily standing up, he chewed and swallowed his mouthful and said to the Abbess, 'Excuse me, my lady.'

'Of course, Sir Josse,' she replied. 'Hurry – he would not have come to find you unless it was important.'

Josse ran to the gates where Will, dismounted and holding on to his horse's rein, was waiting for him.

'Will, what has happened?'

Will touched his shapeless bag of a hat and gave him a sketchy bow. 'Those two foreigners have come back. One's got an arrow sticking in his chest.'

He said two, Josse thought swiftly, so he must mean Kathnir and Akhbir. 'The men who came before?'

'Aye. It's the one who did all the talking that's been wounded. The other one is afeard for him – rightly, I'd say – and he brought him to New Winnowlands because it was the only place he knew. Reckon they must have been nearby,' he added. 'Stands to reason.'

'Aye,' Josse agreed. 'Has anything been done for the wounded man?'

'Not much,' Will admitted. 'Couple of the lads helped me and Ella get him into the hall and Ella's keeping the fire fed. But none of us knows anything about arrows and we thought we'd do more harm than good.'

'I'll come back with you straight away,' Josse said. 'I'll ask the Abbess if she'll send a nursing nun with us. Go across to Sister Martha and get Horace ready for me, Will. We'll leave as soon as we can.'

They reached New Winnowlands in good time. Sister Euphemia had ordered Sister Caliste to go and tend to the wounded man and, with a small leather pouch of medical equipment at her waist and mounted on the golden mare that had been left in the care of the Abbey, she rode as swiftly as Josse. They had soon left Will behind. The stable lad came out to meet them, staring at Sister Caliste as if he had never seen a nun before. He took the two horses and led them away to the stables.

Josse escorted Sister Caliste inside the house. Kathnir lay on a straw mattress by the fire. Akhbir was kneeling beside him as still as a statue, his eyes closed and his lips moving silently. Josse walked up to him and touched his shoulder. The man's dark eyes flew open and he stared up at Josse. Then, still without speaking, he inclined his head in the direction of his fallen comrade.

Kathnir was on his back, breathing shallowly, the shaft of the arrow and its feathered end sticking up out of his chest about a hand and a half's span from his shoulder. The arrow must have missed his heart but it was a good shot all the same. His garments were soaked with blood and his skin felt cool and clammy.

Sister Caliste was standing right beside Josse. 'What should we do, Sir Josse?' she asked in a calm voice. 'I have never extracted an arrow before, although I did once deal with a spear wound.'

'The problem is in getting the arrowhead out,' he replied. 'Too often men wrest at the shaft in panic and it breaks away. Then you have to probe around to make a path through the swollen tissue until you get to the arrowhead.'

He knelt down and heard the swish of Sister Caliste's wide skirts as she did the same. He put a careful hand on to the arrow and Kathnir moved slightly. His face was ashen, his eyes closed. 'He is far down in unconsciousness,' Josse whispered. 'Awake, even that small touch on the arrow would have hurt like fury.'

She was leaning forward, a small knife in her hand. 'We should cut away his garments,' she said. 'It may be that the arrow has not penetrated deeply.' She did so, and then laid back the cloth to expose the embedded arrow. They both looked. 'Oh,' she said.

It was no minor wound that they were dealing with. Josse said, 'Sister, have you any tool with which to hold the sides of the wound apart?'

She opened her pouch and looked. 'Yes,' she replied, holding up an instrument like a pair of tongs, about the length of her hand and formed of a U-shaped band of metal whose two blades had narrow, slightly flattened ends. 'If I hold the two blades tightly against each side of the arrow shaft and push them inside the wound, I can lever them apart when I reach the arrowhead so that perhaps we shall be able to see how it is lying. If I then open the pincers along the wide side of the arrowhead, you will have an unimpeded channel through which to pull it out.'

It sounded appalling. But he could think of no better idea

and she, after all, was the healer. 'Very well,' he said. He swallowed nervously.

She leaned down over the exposed shoulder and chest and very carefully inserted the ends of the pincers into the wound. Concentrating hard, she applied pressure and kept the two blades firmly placed against the shaft. Slowly they followed the arrow inside Kathnir's flesh. Still he made neither sound nor movement; I am afraid, Josse thought, we are wasting our time. He watched to see if Kathnir was still breathing; the rise and fall of his chest was all but imperceptible.

He's dying, Josse thought.

Sister Caliste gave a soft exclamation: 'I can feel the arrowhead,' she said. Very carefully she opened the blades of the pincers and began to move them around the arrow shaft. She frowned, then her face cleared. 'Yes! I've got the shoulders.' She changed her grip and pulled the pincers apart. There was a squelching sound and a great deal of blood flowed out.

Josse stared into the wound. He could see all the arrow and its head. The pincers were holding the wound open where the arrowhead flared out, giving it a clear and unimpeded route out of Kathnir's flesh. Clutching the shaft as close to the arrowhead as he could, he tensed his arms and shoulders and tugged. The arrow resisted at first but then suddenly yielded and he fell over backwards with it in his hand.

He stared at it. He had seen one just like it not very long ago . . .

'*Sir Josse!*'

He crouched beside her. The blood was flowing out of Kathnir like a flood, pulsing lazily with each beat of his heart.

Sister Caliste had grabbed a wad of linen from her pouch and was pressing it hard to the wound. It seemed she was stopping the flow for, after quickly soaking the cloth, it appeared to slow down. She removed the cloth.

The blood had stopped.

She put her fingers to Kathnir's throat, just below his ear. Then she crouched down, her cheek to his slightly open mouth. She stayed like that for some time.

Then she straightened up and said, 'He's dead. I'm sorry.' Respectfully and as if this were still a living, sentient man, she removed her pincers, wiped them on the cloth and put them back in her pouch.

Akhbir had maintained his stone-still, silent pose. Now, starting slowly and quickly escalating, a moan rose up out of him. He threw himself down beside Kathnir's body, his arms around the shoulders and his face against the deathly pale cheek.

Josse caught Sister Caliste by the hand. Squeezing it gently, he whispered, 'Best leave him be, Sister. We'll step away and presently he'll come and find us.'

She wiped her eyes, nodded and allowed Josse to lead her outside into the chilly sunshine.

Akhbir came out to them quite a long time later. They had left the courtyard and were seated by the fire in the kitchen. Ella, shy with strangers, had made herself scarce and she and Will could be heard from their own little room off the kitchen exchanging the occasional remark in low, awed voices.

Akhbir bowed very formally to them both in turn and said, 'You try. I thank you. I am grateful.'

'I am sorry we could not save him,' Josse said.

The ghost of a smile crossed Akhbir's thin face. 'He say no use. When arrow go in he say he feel something very bad, very deep. He say leave me, bury me here but I put him on horse and come here.' His face crumpled. 'I do my best. But no good.'

There was so much that Josse wanted to ask. So much that, he was sure, Akhbir could tell him. But the man was grieving and in shock; he needed food, drink and rest. Josse stepped towards him and put an arm across his narrow shoulders. Akhbir flinched, then relaxed.

'We will look after you,' Josse said. 'Tell us what you want to do with the body and we will carry out your wishes. Then we will give you food and drink and a place to sleep.'

Akhbir was crying now. Covering his face with his hands, he said, 'You are good people. I stay for now.'

Sister Caliste went to stand on his other side and together she and Josse escorted him slowly back along the passage and into the hall.

They buried Kathnir in a corner of the orchard at New Winnowlands that caught the westering sun; before the last of the light fell below the horizon, he was in his grave. Josse, Will and a couple of labourers who had helped Akhbir dig the grave and bear out the body stayed with bowed heads for a little while and then they crept away and left Akhbir to his grief.

Josse insisted that Sister Caliste accept his bed and he had Ella make it up with fresh linen. He set out shakedown beds for himself and Akhbir in the hall. A long time after he had settled down for the night, he heard Akhbir come in. He had neither eaten nor drunk, although food and drink had been offered. He had stayed out there alone in the cold night beside his companion's grave.

As he lay down, Josse could hear him sobbing.

Josse and Sister Caliste returned to Hawkenlye the next morning and Akhbir borrowed Will's horse and rode with them. He was silent, deathly pale and the flesh around his dark eyes looked bruised. Sister Caliste, watching him anxiously, asked Josse in a whisper if he had accepted anything to eat. Josse shook his head.

As they covered the miles to the Abbey, he wondered what on earth they were going to do with the poor man.

On arrival, his half-hearted suggestion that he take Akhbir to the Abbess so that she and Josse could ask him a few questions was met with a shake of the head from Sister Caliste. 'I am sorry to contradict you, Sir Josse,' she said, 'but Akhbir is not fit to answer questions, no matter how gently put. I fear he is very near collapse.'

'Is he ill?' Josse asked. He was quite relieved that Sister Caliste was being so decisive; asking delicate questions of a man so obviously in shock was not a prospect he relished.

'I do not think so,' Sister Caliste answered. 'He has neither eaten nor drunk, you tell me, and he has suffered the terrible strain of seeing his companion wounded and trying, unsuccessfully, to save his life. He needs to rest in a quiet and safe place. Once he is himself again, then you may speak to him.'

'May I make a suggestion, Sister?'

She was already blushing; he guessed, at having given what amounted to an order to someone who greatly outranked her. She lowered her eyes. 'Of course, Sir Josse.'

'It is possible that Akhbir and his late companion may have some involvement in the death of the man out on the forest track. There is also the matter of the fire at the priory, which it seems was deliberately set. Two of the victims of that act lie in the infirmary; their brother monk died in the fire. I suggest that—'

'That we do not house Akhbir anywhere near the two Hospitallers,' she finished for him. 'I will ensure that he is kept well away.' She looked across to the infirmary and then her gaze went on past it. 'He does not need any treatment, other than someone making sure he drinks and eats,' she mused. 'Should we ask the lay brethren in the Vale to look after him?'

'Aye, Sister,' Josse agreed. The suggestion suited him very well. Since his own accommodation was down in the Vale, he could make sure that, with Akhbir being housed there too, he was the first to know when the man was ready to talk. He could also put the word around that Akhbir was to be subtly watched; Gervase de Gifford would undoubtedly wish to interview him as soon as he was up to it. It was probably just as well for Akhbir, Josse reflected, that the sheriff was not there with them now because he would not be as considerate as Sister Caliste and Josse with a man suspected of being involved in two murders. 'I will come with you to install him in the lay brothers' quarters,' he added.

'Should we not first ask the Abbess?'

'I will report back to her as soon as Akhbir is comfortable,' he assured her. 'You have my word.'

His word was, apparently, good enough; Sister Caliste gave a relieved smile and, with Josse trying to form the words of a simple explanation to inform the stunned and silent Akhbir what was happening, they set off for the Vale.

'The arrow that killed Kathnir was of the same manufacture as the one I pulled out of the tree,' Josse said to the Abbess a short time later. 'Whoever killed him was one of the pair who aimed the warning shots at Gervase and me to drive us away from where their Turkoman companion died.'

'You are certain?'

'Aye, my lady.'

She raised her hands in a gesture of frustration. 'What are we to make of it all, Sir Josse? We now have two bands of murderers in the area.'

'It appears that they are busy killing off each other,' he said grimly. 'First one of the group of archers is tortured and killed, and his companions value him enough to return to the spot and make a simple sort of shrine. Then one of their arrows kills Kathnir, whom we already suspect of knowing about the death of the Turk and who might well have killed him. I think we can now be sure of that. Kathnir – the leader out of him and Akhbir – mistook the Turk for his real quarry, whom we believe to be Fadil, going under the name of John Damianos. Kathnir and Akhbir capture the Turk and try to extract from him the whereabouts of whatever it was that the runaway monk stole.'

'They are surely aware that the English monk and Fadil are in league,' the Abbess said. 'They must be, since they assumed that Fadil knew where the treasure is hidden.'

'Aye. So, Kathnir fails to extract the information he seeks – because the victim isn't Fadil – and he murders him. The Turk's companions find his body and they know who killed him. They bide their time and when the moment presents itself, one of them fires an arrow which finds its mark and kills Kathnir. Vengeance is done.'

'Vengeance is mine; I will repay, saith the Lord,' the Abbess quoted softly.

'I do not think, my lady, that the Lord comes into this very much.'

There was a short silence. The Abbess broke it. 'What of the man Akhbir?'

Josse shrugged. 'He is broken, a soul in despair. Whatever he has done, he is suffering grievously. Sister Caliste said quite rightly that we should not attempt to question him yet.'

'Sister Caliste is charitable,' the Abbess said neutrally. 'But Akhbir was present at a brutal scene of mutilation and death.'

'Aye, my lady. I know.' He paused. 'I have the advantage over you in that I have met and spoken to Akhbir,' he said diplomatically. 'Had you too had that experience, I am sure you would agree that he is not a ruthless, vicious killer and that it is best to accord him time to absorb his grief and begin to recover himself.'

He watched her nervously and soon a slow smile spread over her face. 'How tactful you are, Sir Josse,' she murmured. 'Very well.'

'I will not hesitate to inform you when that time comes,' Josse said, relieved. 'My lady, we must send someone down to Tonbridge in the morning to tell Gervase what has happened.

He will want to come straight here to speak to Akhbir, but we will instruct our messenger to explain that the man is unwell and that it would be better to wait for a day or so.' Something occurred to him: there was another mission he had been going to pursue when Will brought news of the wounded Kathnir and drove everything else out of his mind . . . Ah yes! 'I will go to see Brice of Rotherbridge and ask about local interests in Outremer. Unless, that is, you have anything from Thibault concerning the English monk's lord?'

'No,' she answered. 'I did ask him but he says he does not know.'

There was something in her tone that made him pause. 'But?'

She smiled again. 'But,' she echoed. 'Yes, Sir Josse; there is indeed a *but.*' She drummed her fingers on her table and he could sense her impatience and tension. 'I asked Thibault a very simple question: did he know the name and domicile of the English lord in whose company the runaway monk had gone out to Outremer?' Her eyes met Josse's. 'I expected an equally simple answer: yes or no. It was not what I got.'

'What did he say?'

'He made a great show of appearing to think, but I am sure it was only to give himself the time to make up a credible lie. Then he said he hadn't known the English monk that well and when they were together it was usually in the press of battle and they had never got round to talking of the past. It was,' she added dismissively, 'a shower of words that said precisely nothing. He knows the identity of this English lord perfectly well, Sir Josse; but for some reason he doesn't want to tell us.'

Ten

Josse took a guilty pleasure in his ride over to Rotherbridge the following morning. There had been a hard frost overnight and now the sky was a clear, brilliant blue and the early sunshine was making diamond sparkles of the melting drops of water

on tree and grass. It was a relief to leave the complex problems at the Abbey for a few hours. There was, he told himself,
nothing that he could do for the time being, anyway. Akhbir
was still refusing food and water and he lay curled up on his
side, his face to the wall. Sometimes his voice could be heard
keening in a peculiar high-pitched, animal-like wail. It was
unnerving, to say the least.

Brother Augustus had volunteered to ride down to inform
Gervase de Gifford of Akhbir's presence at Hawkenlye. When
Josse had asked if he could manage to deter the sheriff for a
day at least, Augustus had replied glumly, 'I'll tell him about
that inhuman howling that kept us all awake and chilled our
blood. That ought to do the trick.'

Josse smiled at the memory. Gussie was a solid and dependable young man and, in his own modest way, as much of a
force to be reckoned with as the sheriff himself.

He clucked to Horace and encouraged him to a reasonably
sprightly canter. Rotherbridge was still an hour's ride away and
the morning was advancing.

He was shown into Brice's hall by a young maidservant with
a shy smile and a dimple. Brice's wife Isabella sat on a settle
before the hearth, a girl of about two and a half sitting beside
her and a baby of perhaps a year clutching on to its mother's
skirts as it tried to stand up. At Josse's approach, the smaller
child, a little boy, turned and gave him a wide and endearing
smile that displayed four top teeth and five bottom ones.

'Josse,' said Isabella, 'how lovely to see you! Tilda, bring
some mulled ale and some of those little cakes, for Sir Josse
will be hungry and thirsty after his ride and it is a chilly
morning.'

The maid gave a bob curtsey and hurried away. At Isabella's
invitation, Josse sat down beside her. The little girl immediately scrambled over her mother's lap and held out a rag doll.
'E'nor,' she said. Then, peremptorily: 'Kiss!'

'E'nor?' Josse repeated, lifting up the doll and placing a light
kiss on the cloth face.

'Eleanor,' Isabella said. 'Fritha has grandiose plans for her
doll.'

Fritha had now elbowed her way onto Josse's lap. She leaned
her head against him and, after a slight hesitation, he put his

arm round her. To have a little girl treat him with such affection was a poignant reminder of his own daughter and for a moment he did not feel able to speak. Fortunately he didn't have to. Not only was Fritha keeping up a long monologue about her doll's likes and dislikes – of which there seemed to be an unreasonable number – but in addition Isabella was chatting away about her little boy's progress.

'And just yesterday he clambered up onto the end of the settle and jiggled around pretending it was a horse, so you can imagine how delighted Brice was about that since he just can't wait to have another man in the family to go hunting with!'

Josse smiled. 'How old is Olivar now?'

'He'll be a year old next month,' she said. She held out her arms to the child and he threw himself at her. She sat him on her lap and he put a thumb in his mouth, regarding Josse with wide dark brown eyes.

'You named him for Brice's brother,' Josse said.

'Yes. I never met him, although you did, Josse?'

'Aye.' It was an old tragedy but Josse still remembered the tormented young man. 'I hope his little nephew here will tread an easier path through life.'

'Amen,' Isabella whispered. Then, her smile breaking through, she said, 'The omens are good, Josse. I know he is mine and therefore I am probably prejudiced, but I have never encountered a child with a sunnier nature.'

The maid brought in a tray containing mugs of warm, spiced ale and a platter of small cakes. 'The cakes are Tilda's speciality and quite delicious,' Isabella said, dismissing the maid with a smile of thanks. 'The main ingredient is dried marigold petals.'

Both children were eyeing the cakes and Josse decided he had better help himself quickly before they disappeared. He ate one, then another, then one more; they were indeed delicious. Then he brushed the crumbs from his tunic and said, 'Where's Brice?'

'He has taken Roger and Marthe out for a ride,' she replied, referring to her children by her previous marriage. 'They'll be back soon, for they set out early and have been gone some time. You wish to speak to him?'

'Aye. I've a question for him but – ' he grinned at her – 'there's no reason why I shouldn't ask you.'

She returned his smile. 'Ask away.'

'There's an unpleasant business at the Abbey. Some people are hunting for a couple of men who have returned to England from Outremer. One probably went out to the East with a lord from this area, and I wondered if Brice – or you – knew of anyone locally whose family have interests in Outremer?'

Isabella considered. 'I can think of families who sent a son or a husband off to the crusades,' she said after a while, 'but in each case save one the man has returned, and the one who did not died at Acre.'

'Oh.' It was disappointing.

'Unless,' Isabella added, 'you mean the de Villières clan?'

'The de Villières?'

She laughed. 'Oh, Josse, I thought everyone knew about them! They're famous and people have been known to commit murder for an invitation to one of their grand gatherings. I'm joking,' she added.

He grinned. 'Sorry, Isabella. I'm not much of a one for socializing.'

'Oh really, Josse?' The irony was unmistakable. Then she took his hand and squeezed it affectionately. 'Don't worry,' she murmured, 'as long as you don't stop coming to see us, I shan't complain.'

He returned the squeeze. 'Thank you.' Then: 'Who are they, then, and what can you tell me about them?'

She settled Olivar more comfortably on her lap and said, 'They hold estates to the west of Robertsbridge. They manage their land efficiently and carefully and their wealth has grown accordingly ever since Robert de Villières was awarded it back in the middle of the last century.' This Robert, Josse thought, must have been one of the Conqueror's Normans. 'He went off to fight in the First Crusade,' Isabella was saying, 'and he won lands in Antioch. He married the daughter of a wealthy family of Champagne merchants who, like so many others, turned themselves into noblemen out in Outremer, and she and Robert settled down in Antioch and raised their family.' She turned to look at Josse. 'They say that Mathilde de St Denys was a woman in the mould of our own Queen Eleanor,' she added, 'a matriarch who lived to the ripe old age of eighty and died in Antioch after fulfilling her ambition of visiting the newly refurbished Church of the Nativity in Bethlehem.'

'Quite a pilgrimage for a woman of eighty,' Josse remarked.

'Indeed it was, but apparently nothing deterred Mathilde once she had made up her mind. What was I saying? Ah, yes. Their elder son inherited the Antioch lands. The second son, whose name was Baldwin, was sent home to Sussex. He married the daughter of another noble family and they had several children, although the eldest son died young, I believe. Their son Guilbert inherited the Sussex lands and he was the father of Gerome de Villières, the present lord.'

'And Gerome went to Outremer?'

But Isabella was going to tell her story in her own way. 'Meanwhile,' she said, ignoring Josse's interruption with a smile, 'in Antioch, Robert and Mathilde's elder son had inherited the title and it passed down through his son to his grandson. He, however, was a sickly man who did not cope well with the climate of Outremer. His wife gave him two daughters, one of whom, Aurelie, was a redoubtable woman and the true descendant of her great-grandmother. She married the Count of Tripoli and produced two daughters and a son, but sadly the son died young. *So*' – she had obviously picked up Josse's impatience, for her eyes were twinkling with mischief – 'when the redoubtable Aurelie and her count began to feel hard-pressed after Saladin's victories, they sent home to Sussex to ask Gerome to come out with a company of men to help defend the family lands.'

'So this Gerome had sons?' Josse asked.

'No.' All levity had left Isabella's face. 'He and his wife – she was called Erys – had two girls, Editha and Columba. Columba died when she was a little child and Erys produced another baby girl late that same year. But Erys fell sick of a fever soon after the birth and both she and the baby died.'

'Yet still he left his surviving child on her own and went off to Outremer!' Josse cried. Such things happened, he knew full well, but still it seemed heartless.

'Josse, all this happened fifteen years ago,' Isabella said gently. 'Editha – Gerome's daughter – is a woman in her twenties now and she manages her father's household with effortless efficiency, so they say. And what a household it is – Gerome may not have sons of his own but he maintains a company of well-trained knights and a number of foot soldiers drilled to perfection.'

'And it was this company that Gerome de Villières took out to Outremer?'

'Yes. Gerome led his knights into the fighting at Acre and

then on the march south to Jaffa, although he fell ill and was taken to his kinsman's home in Antioch to recuperate before taking ship home to Sussex.'

Dear Lord, Josse thought, but this is the very man! He heard Thibault's voice in his head: *The English monk encountered his former lord and he had been stricken with dysentery. It was decided that he should make his way back to Acre and thence to his kinsman's estate in Antioch. The English monk was selected to care for him.*

'And when did he return?' His mouth felt dry.

'Oh – it must have been more than three years ago, in the summer of '93.'

Josse tried to take it in. He was in no doubt that Gerome de Villières and the English monk's lord were the same person. He was wondering what Thibault's reaction would be when faced with the news that he had discovered Gerome's identity when something struck him.

'Isabella,' he said, 'I am most grateful for this information. But how do you come to be such an expert on the de Villières family and their doings?'

She smiled. 'Gerome de Villières is distantly related to my Brice; Gerome's grandmother Hewisa was Brice's grandfather's sister. We know Editha de Villières quite well,' she added, 'she is Olivar's godmother.'

Although Isabella pressed him to wait for Brice's return and stay to eat with the family, Josse declined. He felt guilty; having extracted from Isabella everything she knew about the de Villières family, it was not good manners to bolt before he had, as it were, sung for his supper by staying to talk to Brice over a leisurely meal.

But Isabella seemed to understand. 'This matter is clearly important to you,' she said as she saw him out.

'Aye,' he agreed. 'There have been two killings,' he added, lowering his voice, 'and we have not seen the last of the violence yet, for something very important lies at its heart.'

'Something that it is worth killing for must be important indeed,' she whispered. Then, enfolding him in a sudden hug: 'Be careful, dear Josse!'

He returned the hug. 'I will,' he promised. 'There's no threat to me, Isabella,' he added.

She muttered something under her breath. 'Don't tempt provi-
dence,' she warned. 'I shall keep you in my thoughts.'

He thanked her, kissed her and took his leave.

He raced back to Hawkenlye Abbey. He had been sorely tempted
to ride straight for Robertsbridge, seek out the de Villières lands
and speak to Gerome in person; however, in the end he had
decided against it. For one thing, Gervase de Gifford could well
be at the Abbey about to interview Akhbir, and Josse wanted
to be present. For another thing, it would be better to think
carefully rather than heading off like an arrow to the bull; a
little more reflection might suggest that an approach to Gerome
de Villières should wait until he knew exactly what it was that
he wanted to ask the man.

He reached the Abbey in the middle of the afternoon. He
was ravenously hungry – it seemed like hours since he had
eaten Tilda's marigold cakes – but he went first to seek out the
Abbess. As he knocked and went into her room she said, before
he had a chance to speak, 'Gervase de Gifford is coming up
to the Abbey this afternoon. I thought you were he.'

He could tell from her expression – carefully neutral – that
she was not best pleased. 'Is Akhbir well enough to answer
questions?' he asked.

'Sister Caliste says no; he is still lying with his face to the
wall. Sister Euphemia has been down to the Vale and she says
shock, grief, dehydration and hunger have sent him half out of
his mind.'

'What shall we do, my lady? I am prepared to try to reason
with Gervase.'

'I do not see that your reasoning with him should influence
him more than a command from the Abbess of Hawkenlye,'
she said frostily. Then, instantly: 'I apologize, Sir Josse. That
was unforgivable and untrue. It's just that . . .' She paused,
collecting her thoughts. 'We here at the Abbey have a duty of
care for those who come to us sick in body and mind,' she said
more calmly. 'It goes against our purpose to sit by and watch
while a man suffering as deeply as Akhbir has questions hurled
at him by an angry sheriff.'

'There have been two terrible deaths, my lady,' Josse said
quietly. 'It is Gervase's duty to seek justice for the dead just
as it is yours to care for the sick.'

She sighed. 'I know. I *know*.' She looked up at Josse. 'I have sent Sister Caliste down to the Vale to fetch Akhbir,' she said. 'I will permit Gervase to ask his questions, but it will be in here, and you, Sister Caliste and I shall be here while he does so. It is the best I can do,' she muttered. Then she said, 'But Sir Josse, what of your mission? Did Brice supply the names of local men with kin in Outremer?'

'Aye,' he admitted. 'It was Isabella that I spoke to. She told me of a certain Gerome de Villières, who surely is our man.'

'The timing fits? Our knight turned runaway monk might have been of de Villières's company?'

'Aye, he might well.'

'De Villières,' she repeated, half to herself. 'The name seems vaguely familiar. Where is their manor?'

'Near Robertsbridge.'

'I will think about it. Robertsbridge is not so very far from where I grew up. I shall endeavour to recall where I have heard the name before.'

Sensing himself dismissed, Josse went out and quietly closed the door.

Her head was thumping as if a demon were hammering at it with a red-hot hammer. She tried to set an imaginary boundary around it and isolate it in a corner of her consciousness; it was something the infirmarer had taught her. Sometimes it worked, sometimes not. It helped if she had something else on which to concentrate. Visualizing herself walking away from her contained pain, she thought about the name de Villières.

And presently she remembered.

Her father had at one time wanted to unite his family with that of the de Villières; it made sense, for Ralf de Swansford's lands were quite close to those of Guilbert de Villières and a marital tie between the families would strengthen both. He suggested a meeting between his elder son Rainer and Guilbert's second daughter, Maud. The pair were introduced and Maud appeared keen but it was too late for Rainer, already dreaming of someone else; every other woman had become invisible. The de Villières party swept off clutching their dignity to them like a cloak on a windy day and relations between the two families were ever afterwards cool.

Helewise thought about that embarrassing time. Rainer was

perfectly polite to the pretty, over-eager Maud but Helewise knew that his good manners were automatic. He was already deeply in love with Egelina Rich and he had in fact married her not long afterwards. They had enjoyed a particularly happy life together until her death in childbed. Dear Rainer, she thought. Memories of their childhood together, and with her younger brother and sister making up the quartet, flooded into her mind and she smiled. It had been a fine upbringing, and she—

No. She made herself stop. It was not the moment to lose herself in an indulgent visit to the past, however happy it had been. She had a problem on her hands and her duty was to deal with it to the very best of her ability. So, having done what she set out to do and remembered why the name of de Villières was familiar, she put the matter from her mind.

She heard the tramp of footsteps outside her door. There was a knock and at her response the door opened and Gervase de Gifford came in. Akhbir walked behind him, Sister Caliste at his side, watching him anxiously. Behind them came Josse, who closed the door and then stood with his back against it. For an instant he met her eyes and she gave him a quick smile.

She looked up at Gervase, who was stating formally that while the man Akhbir's condition had been explained to him, nevertheless he must speak to him and so had agreed to do so in her presence and that of Sir Josse and Sister Caliste. Helewise turned to regard Akhbir. He stood with bowed head, his arms hanging limply by his sides. She said, 'Akhbir?' and for a moment he looked up at her. His skin was ashen and the flesh of his face seemed to have collapsed against the bones of the skull. 'Would you like to sit down?'

She was not sure whether he understood; he did not reply but went on staring at her. She turned to Sister Caliste. 'Sister, has he accepted any food or water?'

'A little water, my lady. He refuses food.'

Helewise's instinct was to send the poor wretch back to wherever he had been curled up and tell him to rest and recover his strength. But she knew she could not do that. 'Gervase, proceed,' she said. 'Ask your questions.'

Gervase turned to Akhbir. 'Five days ago a man was murdered on the fringe of the forest.' He spoke slowly, enunciating his words clearly. 'You and your late companion were hunting a man of similar appearance to the dead man; a man who had stolen something from your master. It is our belief that you mistook the dead man for the man whom you were hunting; that you tormented him to make him tell you the whereabouts of the stolen treasure, and when he could not, you killed him and stole his clothes and belongings.'

Akhbir said nothing. With a brief, exasperated exhalation, Gervase went on, 'There has been another death. A fire was deliberately started in the guest quarters at the priory in Tonbridge, its purpose to disguise the fact that one of those within was already dead. The victim and his two companions were Knights Hospitaller who, like you and Kathnir, had come to England from Outremer to search for someone; in their case, a monk. We believe that the monk and the thief who stole from your master are travelling together and we further believe that you and Kathnir were—'

'*Not fire!*' Akhbir's voice rang out so loudly and unexpectedly in the small room that they all jumped. 'Not fire,' he repeated more quietly. 'Do not know of fire.'

'Then you admit to knowing of the murder of the Saracen?' Gervase instantly demanded.

Akhbir took a long, slow look all around him, as if searching for a means of escape. Then, his shoulders slumping, he nodded.

'Why did you attack him?' Gervase spoke quietly.

'Kathnir believe him man we hunt. This – 'Akhbir lifted a fold of his robe and then touched his headdress – 'this was like.'

'You mean he was dressed in the same way as the man you were hunting?' Josse put in.

Akhbir nodded. 'Kathnir say to follow. Wait for quiet place, then jump. We fight him, overcome him, bind him, take him under trees. Kathnir—' He swallowed, his face screwed up. 'Kathnir must follow orders. Kathnir must find master's precious treasure and take back.'

'But you had caught the wrong man,' Gervase said. 'No matter what Kathnir did to him, the man you had attacked could not tell you what you wanted to know.'

Akhbir nodded. 'He die.'

Josse had moved forward and now he faced Akhbir. 'The man you killed was a Turk,' he said. 'We found his broken

bow. You were hunting for someone like him whose name was
Fadil, weren't you?'

Helewise, closely watching Akhbir's face, saw that he knew
the name. But instead of fear or apprehension at hearing his
quarry named, he just looked puzzled. 'Fadil?' he repeated.
'Not Fadil!'

And for just an instant he smiled, as if the mistake amused
him.

'But you do know who Fadil is?' Helewise said.

Akhbir turned his large dark eyes on her. 'Fadil was prisoner,' he said. 'Fadil was beloved of my master and my master
pay any price to have him back. There was meet in desert but
men do not act true. Many killed and my master wounded.
Fadil taken away. My master lost that which he valued above
all else.'

He hung his head.

'And your master sent Kathnir and you to follow the thief
and regain the treasure?' Gervase said.

'Treasure . . .' Akhbir put a hand to his head. Then: 'Yes.
Kathnir given order: succeed or die. Now Kathnir is dead.
Kathnir die but he not succeed.'

'This fire,' Gervase began.

But a low howl was starting to echo round the walls and
Akhbir slumped to the ground. Instantly Sister Caliste went to
him, supporting his head before it could crash onto the stone
floor. She looked up at the sheriff, eyes narrowed. 'Enough!'
she cried. Swiftly turning to Helewise, she added, 'My lady, I
am sorry to speak out of turn, but this man is in my care.'

'Take him back to his cot in the Vale,' Helewise said. 'Sir Josse,
would you summon a couple of sisters to help her, please?'

He went outside and they heard him call out. Presently two
nuns and a lay brother tapped on the open door and, the nuns
taking up positions either side of Akhbir and grasping his arms
while the lay brother fell in behind, they followed Sister Caliste
out of the room.

Gervase watched them go. 'I should arrest him,' he said
baldly. 'He has just admitted to murder.'

'He admitted to being there while murder was done,' Helewise
corrected. 'He could perhaps have prevented it, which I suppose
is also a crime, but I think he was used to doing what Kathnir
said.'

'I agree.' Josse spoke up. 'I saw them together at New Winnowlands and Akhbir barely said a word.'

'He would have us believe that he is prostrate with grief for his dead companion,' Gervase said, 'yet he did not hesitate to reveal that it was Kathnir who carried out the torture and the murder. What do you say to that?'

Helewise waited to see if Josse would speak. He met her eyes and gave an encouraging nod; she said, 'I can think of two reasons. One, Akhbir has been trained to speak the truth. When someone asks him a question he does not stop to think but simply provides the answer. Two, he is a practical man. Kathnir is dead and beyond justice; he is still alive.'

'And with a mission to carry out,' Josse added. 'With Kathnir dead, we must presume that finding the thief and recovering the treasure is now up to Akhbir.'

'That may be so,' Gervase said curtly, 'but it does not mean he is going to be free to carry it out.' He looked at Helewise. 'With your permission, my lady, I shall set a guard over him in the Vale and as soon as he is fit enough, put him in a prison cell in Tonbridge.'

Helewise understood his reasoning. 'You hope to prevent another murder, should Akhbir be set at liberty and manage to track down his quarry.'

'I do,' Gervase confirmed. 'The hunted man may very well be a thief who deserves to have Akhbir catch him but I do not intend to let that happen. Akhbir will have no further role in this matter; we for our part must undertake a search and hope that we succeed where Kathnir and Akhbir failed. Now,' he added grimly, 'if you will both excuse me, I'm going down to the Vale to organize a guard.'

He closed the door after him with a decisive slam. Helewise waited for the echoes to die away, then she said, 'Sir Josse, what on earth can have gone on in the desert that night?'

'That it had such far-reaching consequences?'

She sent up a small wordless prayer of gratitude for his instant understanding. 'Yes. I am not familiar with the ways of war but I imagine that it is common practice to exchange prisoners and normally such matters are quickly done and swiftly forgotten?'

'Aye, my lady. Some of the more spectacular arrangements may warrant a line or two in the chronicles – if a king, a prince, a noble or a particularly large sum of money is involved, for example.' He glanced at her, raising his eyebrows.

'Quite.' She knew exactly which recent and very well-known event he referred to. 'So why have so many people travelled all the way from Outremer to England this time?'

'Let's see. The Knights Hospitaller – two of them, originally three; the two Saracen warriors; and an unnamed, unknown group that comprised originally at least three men, one of whom is the dead Turk. Oh, and the runaway monk and his prisoner.' Josse counted on his fingers. 'Nine men. Something very important or very valuable – maybe both – must have been involved,' he added slowly. 'Thibault implied that the Saracens tried to cheat the Hospitallers by attempting to get away with both the prisoner and whatever they were offering in exchange for him. Gervase suggested that the Hospitallers might have done the same. I do feel,' he went on before she could comment, 'that if he is right, then it only goes to support what you just said: whatever was at stake, it was important enough that even the noble and honourable Knights Hospitaller were prepared to abandon their principles and risk their hard-won reputation for honesty and fair play.'

'*What* could the fat man have bartered for his young brother?' she mused. 'We have asked ourselves before, but we are no nearer to an answer.'

'And why was the younger man so very valuable to his brother?' Josse said. 'My lady, did you mark Akhbir's reaction when the name of Fadil was mentioned?'

'I did,' she replied. 'I thought he seemed amused. He found it funny that we should believe it was Fadil whom he and Kathnir were hunting.'

'Why would that be funny?' Josse wondered. 'Because it was so unlikely Fadil would be here in England?'

'Perhaps because he could not take Fadil seriously.' The flash of intuition seemed to come out of nowhere. 'He knows Fadil and he doesn't think much of him; he cannot imagine that Fadil could possibly have evaded him and Kathnir for so long and over so many hundreds of miles.'

'If he does not think much of this Fadil, then he would be either amused or insulted by the suggestion that he'd been such an efficient and elusive quarry,' Josse agreed. He was regarding her with admiration in his brown eyes. 'A good suggestion, my lady.'

She barely heard him. 'Josse, supposing it's Fadil himself? Akhbir just said that Kathnir's orders were to find his master's precious treasure and return it. Supposing it was not an object that he was speaking of but a person?'

'Fadil is the fat man's brother. But if he does not have sons of his own, then his younger brother might be his heir and thus important to him.'

'Precious,' she repeated. 'Would a man refer to his heir as being precious to him? It sounds more like a term one would use for someone one loved very, very deeply and – oh!' She realized what she had just said.

So, evidently, did Josse. 'It would explain a lot,' he said quietly. 'Love makes men blind; it makes them lose all reason and all sense of proportion. If the fat man was driven by love and desire, not only would he be prepared to pay the highest price to redeem Fadil from the Hospitallers; he would also take whatever measures necessary to find him when he escaped and bring him back. Even to the extent of sending two Saracen warriors who would not hesitate to kill.'

'Yet they attacked and killed the Turk and they would not have killed Fadil,' she pointed out. 'Their objective was to take him back unharmed to their master.'

'Aye, but they knew the Turk *wasn't* Fadil,' Josse replied. Then: 'Fadil must be the other Saracen; it's just as we surmised. He *must* be the man known to me as John Damianos.'

'Why did Kathnir torture the Turk?' She could hardly bear to think about it. 'What did he think the poor man knew?'

'The whereabouts of Fadil?' Josse suggested. 'Or, if Fadil and the treasure are not one and the same, perhaps Kathnir believed the Turk knew the location of both.'

'I think,' she said slowly, 'that the missing Hospitaller – the runaway English monk – is looking after both prisoner and treasure, just as he has been doing for more than two years ever since that night in the desert. Don't you?' She stared at Josse expectantly.

After a moment he sighed heavily and said, 'Aye. I do. We've got to find him, my lady; as Gervase said, we have to succeed where Kathnir and Akhbir failed.'

'Can we do it?' she whispered.

He shrugged. 'We can try.'

Eleven

When Josse finally got to his bed he was exhausted and fell asleep quickly. But some time later he was awakened; his soldier's reactions warned him there had been a sound that did not belong among the safe night noises. He lay on his back with his eyes open, staring out into the darkness of the low room. The door and the two small windows were closed, the fold of leather in place keeping out the moonlight and the starlight. The fire in the hearth had burned down to glowing embers.

He listened.

Then he heard it.

From the far corner where they had put Akhbir came the sound of softly muttered but urgent words; it seemed that Akhbir was pleading with his God.

Barely pausing to think about it, Josse was out of his bedroll and padding across the cold, hard floor. Akhbir sounded as if he was in despair. He was all alone in a foreign land, the man who had been his senior and his companion had just died, he still had a mission to fulfil and he probably had no idea how to go about it. All of which was good enough reason for despair.

But desperate men tend to talk, Josse reasoned. Especially in the dark hours before dawn when courage and optimism are at their lowest ebb and when so many of the dying slip away to death. He knelt down beside Akhbir, who lay curled up with his face to the wall, and put a hand on the man's shoulder. Akhbir jumped in alarm, twisting round to look up into Josse's face.

'Do not be afraid; I wish to help you.' Josse pitched his voice low. Akhbir had been put in this far corner well away from the sleeping lay brethren, but Josse was aware that one or more of the brothers would wake if he spoke aloud. Even worse, one of the two guards that Gervase had sent up from Tonbridge might hear.

'You cannot help,' Akhbir hissed back.

Josse considered how to proceed. It depended on Akhbir's mood; there was so much that he needed to know, but Akhbir would only be likely to talk if he truly believed there was no hope for him.

'You will not be ill-treated when they take you down to the prison cell,' he began, choosing his words carefully. 'You will be put on trial for murder but the sheriff may speak for you if he believes that it was Kathnir and not you who killed the Turk.'

'What happen to me if not?'

'If they think you were equally guilty? You'll hang.'

A sob escaped Akhbir. 'I want to go home,' he whispered mournfully.

Home. I wonder, Josse thought.

'Would you be able to find your way back to Outremer?'

'Yes.' There was no doubt in Akhbir's voice.

'But what of your mission? What of the treasure your master sent you to recover?'

Akhbir said something in his own tongue; it sounded faintly disparaging. Then: 'I not know about treasure. Kathnir know; Kathnir not tell secret to me.' Then, in case Josse was still in any doubt: 'Kathnir my master. I serve him all my life but he dead now.'

Josse saw tears in his dark eyes, welling up and catching the dim light from the hearth.

'Perhaps you truly do not know what the treasure is,' Josse said softly. 'But there are many things, Akhbir, that you do know; things that I should be very grateful to be told.'

The dark eyes slid to Josse's. There was a calculating expression in them. 'Very grateful?'

'Very grateful indeed,' Josse said. Firmly putting from his mind what Gervase was going to say, he took a deep breath and said, 'Answer my questions and I'll let you go.'

Akhbir's teeth flashed in a brief smile. 'Ask,' he said simply.

Josse was ready and the first question shot out. 'What is the name of the fat man who wanted Fadil returned to him?'

'Hisham.'

'He is wealthy and important?'

'He is both.'

'Is he a great landowner?'

'He own much land. He is – merchant, of Tripoli, but also man of very great wisdom. He is—' Akhbir appeared to struggle to find the word but then, giving up, said something in his own tongue that sounded like *simyager*.

'And Fadil is his brother and heir?' Josse thought he knew the answer already.

Akhbir sneered. 'Not kin. Not heir. But *beloved*.'

Josse did not think he had ever heard the beautiful word spoken with such disdain and disgust. 'I see,' he murmured. 'You told us that Hisham had lost that which he held most dear. Did you mean Fadil? Or did you mean whatever Hisham was offering to get him back?'

Akhbir narrowed his eyes and an expression of extreme cunning crossed his face. He watched Josse closely and Josse could almost hear his thoughts. Then the moment of resistance was gone. Akhbir gave a soft sigh and said, 'I not sure but I believe he mean both.'

So it was true that the fat man *was* trying to cheat the Hospitallers, Josse thought. What did he do? Prepare a secret force to overcome the knights in that lonely desert spot? They all died – all except one – so it was likely. And it would have to have been quite a force; the Knights Hospitaller fought like cornered lions.

But Akhbir had leaned closer and was whispering again. 'One monk get away. He take Fadil. My master say he also take treasure. My master call Kathnir, tell him, follow monk and Fadil. Bring back Fadil. Kill monk and take back treasure.'

'You cannot do the second part of your mission now. You just said you do not know what the treasure is.'

'No.' A deep sigh. 'No.'

Would Akhbir try to go after Fadil? Josse intended to keep his word and get Akhbir out of the lay brothers' quarters and onto the road that led to the coast; but by doing so would he be putting Fadil – John Damianos – in danger? I *liked* the man, he thought. I will not put him in danger of being taken back to Outremer and whatever terrible life he had as the fat man's sex slave.

Something did not feel quite right. He pictured John Damianos and tried to imagine him as the subject of an older man's lust. It was all but impossible.

He recalled something the Abbess had said. It was when they

began to believe that John Damianos was the name that Fadil had adopted; Josse told her he'd imagined Fadil to be a younger man and she replied that two years on the run would have aged him. Perhaps the experience had also hardened him from a rich old man's plaything to a man who walked tall and strong.

A man who, from what Josse recalled of John Damianos, would be more than capable of dealing with the broken, lonely, grieving and homesick Akhbir.

But what about the runaway Hospitaller? Would a released Akhbir feel honour- and duty-bound to pursue him? He and Fadil seemed to have parted company – there had been no monk with John Damianos when he arrived at New Winnowlands – and Thibault appeared to have been searching for the runaway in the vicinity of Tonbridge.

Where was the runaway monk?

Where was Fadil?

Did Akhbir have any idea of the whereabouts of either? Because if so and if Josse followed him, then Akhbir just might lead him to one or both of them.

In the absence of a better one, it was quite a good plan . . .

'Wait,' he commanded Akhbir. Then he tiptoed back to his own bed, swiftly put on his outer garments, picked up his weapons and drew on his boots. Creeping back to Akhbir, he whispered, 'Get up, put on your cloak and boots and collect your belongings together.' Akhbir hastily obeyed. 'Come with me – ' Josse took hold of his arm – 'this way.'

He put the Saracen directly behind him as he began to walk slowly and steadily along the room. One of the guards stirred and, looking up, said, 'Sir Josse?'

Josse spread his arms, concealing Akhbir behind him. 'Too much ale last night,' he whispered with a grin. 'I'm bursting.'

The guard gave a gap-toothed smile and lay down again, turning on his side away from Josse. Edging Akhbir round, Josse pushed him in front of him – the man walked soft-footed as a cat – and, prodding him to make him hurry, got him to the door. He opened it and Akhbir went out into the night, Josse on his heels.

He took the Saracen's arm and, urging him to a fast pace, took him along the path that led along the Vale. There was a little-used track at the far end of the shallow valley that led up to the road. Josse hurried up it, Akhbir panting beside him.

They stood side by side on the road. Dawn was not far off now and Josse said, 'That way leads down to Tonbridge, where the sheriff has his cell waiting for you. That way – ' he pointed – 'skirts the forest and then turns south towards the coast.'

Akhbir stood quite still, as if he could hardly believe that Josse had really kept his word and was setting him free. 'Go!' Josse urged. 'Hurry and get down to the sea, then take a boat for France and go home.'

Slowly Akhbir turned to stare at him. Then without a word he started to run down the track.

Josse watched him. He looked back once or twice, then he reached the turn in the road and vanished from sight.

Josse set off after him.

He discovered that it was possible to keep Akhbir in sight while remaining just beneath the cover of the forest fringe. Akhbir did not look back; he kept up a quick pace, his head down, sometimes turning to look to right or left as if checking for way markers. For two or three miles he kept to the main track. Then, when it veered off towards the south and the coast, Akhbir branched off to the right onto a smaller path around the edge of the forest. Now he – and Josse, in pursuit – walked with undergrowth and winter-bare trees on either side. After perhaps another mile and a half, Akhbir increased his pace. Then suddenly he wasn't there.

He's seen me, Josse thought instantly, and his instinct was to break into a run, but his common sense held him back. If he was wrong and Akhbir did not know he was there, then his pounding feet on the frost-hard track would advertise his presence as clearly as if he'd yelled *Here I am!*

He crept on, barely breathing, his eyes fixed to the bracken and the tangle of bramble to his right. And his diligence was rewarded, for presently he came to a place where an animal track – boar or deer – broke away from the path.

It led right into the heart of the forest.

Without hesitation he set off along it.

After a while he felt he knew where they might be heading. He could see Akhbir now, perhaps eighty paces ahead, keeping to the narrow track and walking purposefully, like a man eager to reach his destination.

Josse tried to summon memories of the last time he had been here, if indeed he was right and this was the place that he had in mind. It was difficult because apart from the fact that one forest track looked very much like another, especially when the leaves were off the trees and everything seemed fast asleep, when he had been brought here for the first time he had been blindfolded.

Joanna had hidden in an old house in this area. The house had belonged to her great-aunt and uncle, and when she was small she had spent much time in their household. She had been cared for and taught by their house servant, Mag Hobson; it was many years later that Joanna learned who Mag really was. The house was modest, with a few ramshackle outbuildings. It belonged to Joanna now; not that she went there often, preferring to live in her little hut deep in the forest.

Had Kathnir and Akhbir stumbled on the old place and, finding it deserted, made themselves at home? Josse prayed that he was wrong, for he could imagine all too clearly what Joanna's reaction would be if she paid one of her rare visits to the house and discovered a strange Saracen in her hall. She would attack and—

A smile spread over his face. Aye, Joanna might be a woman pitting herself against a warrior but she had a power about her now and ways of not only defending herself but also attacking her enemy that might come as quite a surprise to Akhbir.

But on a visit to the house she'd undoubtedly have Meggie with her . . .

Grim now, he pressed on.

The faint ribbon of track broadened into a well-defined path, then into a road wide enough for a horse and rider. Josse was certain now: the old house was about a quarter of a mile ahead. He had Akhbir in view as the Saracen climbed a slight rise and stepped out into the clearing, then hurried towards the paved courtyard, overgrown with tufts of grass and weeds.

Memories of being here with Joanna flooded Josse's mind despite his efforts to keep them at bay. It was to this house, her secret hiding place, that she had brought him when he had been wounded. Here she had told him her poignant tale; here she had wept and he had taken her in his arms. Here, on fur rugs in front of the fire, he had intended only to comfort her but comfort had turned into mutual passion and they had made love for the first time.

Joanna.

He closed his eyes and suffered the mingled joy and pain of his memories. Then, ordering himself to get on with his present imperative task, he opened his eyes again. But memory was still in command. He thought he saw her, clad in her heavy, enveloping woollen cloak. Just for an instant she seemed to shimmer there on the path beside the house.

Then the vision was gone.

Less out of his sense of duty than to rid himself of the anguish of remembering, he took a calming breath and began to creep carefully forward.

It looked as if Akhbir and Kathnir had been living in the undercroft, for whereas the heavy wooden door to the hall was fast shut and had a strand of wild rose growing across it, the arched door beside the steps was ajar and there were signs that feet had been treading through the doorway.

There was a group of holly trees where the track joined the open space in front of the house and Josse crouched behind it. He was thinking hard. Someone was living here, or had been very recently. Had it been the two Saracens? Or did Akhbir know that someone else was here – Fadil, perhaps, or the runaway monk; both, maybe – and was he even now about to burst in on them?

He stood up and stared after Akhbir.

Whoever was in the house, Akhbir was wary of them; he had drawn his long, curved knife. He held it firmly in his raised right hand.

He broke into a run.

And then suddenly he stopped, skittered to a halt and collapsed on the ground, an arrow in his chest.

Josse broke cover and raced to the fallen man. The arrow had been fired at short range and the shot had been devastatingly accurate. The missile had gone straight through Akhbir's body and its evil head was sticking a hand's breadth out of his back.

He was dead.

Josse knelt by his side, Akhbir's warm blood soaking into the cloth of his hose. He reached out a hand and gently closed the wide eyes. He muttered a prayer; although he had no idea what a Saracen would wish said over his dead body, Josse was familiar with the Christian ritual and he did his best.

I must get his body away and back to Hawkenlye, he thought. I cannot carry him. I shall have to hurry back and fetch help. But before I go I must find something to cover him. Akhbir's cloak was bunched up beneath his body and Josse began to roll the corpse from side to side to free it. He pulled out a section of the hem and was just attempting to move the body again when he heard a whistling sound above him.

He looked up to see a second arrow flying in a lobbed trajectory high over his head. Losing momentum, it fell to earth and embedded itself in the ground about a foot from where he knelt.

Hurriedly he shoved Akhbir off his cloak, then draped the cloth over the dead man's face and chest. Another arrow struck the ground, slightly closer to him. With a cry of alarm, he grabbed at it, wrested it free and leapt to his feet. His hands and arms covering his head in a futile gesture of self-defence, he ran for the path that led away under the trees.

The longer track that ran around the forest might have been the wiser road to take but Josse had received a bad scare and, in addition, he knew he had to face Gervase as quickly as he could with the news that the sheriff's prisoner was dead. Consequently he took the direct route that led straight through the old forest.

He muttered under his breath as he hurried along, a random string of words such as *please* and *sorry* and short little sentences such as *I would not intrude but for dire necessity.* He was not quite sure who he was addressing: the forest people; the trees; the numinous presence that dwelt in the heart of this strange place. Whoever it was, it heard him and he was not only left alone but, as if by magic, he found his way along the swiftest tracks and paths without one wrong turning.

All too soon he was back at the Abbey.

The community was emerging from the church after tierce. The Abbess saw him and walked up to him. Wordlessly he inclined his head in the direction of her room and, with a nod, she led the way there.

'Akhbir is dead,' he said without preamble. 'I let him go in the hope that he would lead me to either Fadil or the runaway monk.'

'I see,' she said. 'And did he?'

'He led me to someone,' Josse answered grimly. 'That someone shot Akhbir through the heart and warned me off with two more equally well-aimed shots.'

'It is exactly what happened when you and Gervase found the makeshift shrine to the dead Turk!' she exclaimed. 'Whoever shot at you then has already murdered Kathnir and now they have killed Akhbir too.'

'But—' he began.

'I shall send word immediately for Gervase,' she announced, striding over to the door. 'Sister Ursel!' she called loudly. '*Sister!*' She hurried out into the cloister and Josse, following, saw the porteress run towards her. There was a brief conversation, Sister Ursel nodded then hurried away in the direction of the stables.

'One of the young lay brothers is mucking out for Sister Martha,' the Abbess explained as she came back into the room. 'Sister Ursel is going to dispatch him down to Tonbridge immediately.' She looked sympathetically at Josse. 'Have you had breakfast?' He shook his head. 'Then come with me to the refectory, and while we wait for Gervase I shall order food and a warming drink for you.'

When he had finished Sister Basilia's excellent breakfast and expressed his thanks, he and the Abbess returned to her room. She seemed disinclined to question him further until the sheriff was with them, and as they settled down to wait he said, 'Someone has made a temporary camp out at the old house where Joanna's great-aunt and uncle lived.'

She knew straight away why he had told her that. 'Any sign of her?' she asked quietly.

'No. The door into the hall looked as if it hadn't been opened in months. Whoever is living there is using the undercroft.'

'I wonder why?' She was, he thought, doing her best to distract him from thoughts of Joanna by presenting a small puzzle. 'If you're going to borrow someone's house without permission, why not do it in style? He – or they – could have lit a fire in the hall and there must be furs and rugs and so on and—'

She must have noticed his expression. He had very precious and extremely intimate memories of fur rugs and a roaring fire in Joanna's hall.

'Well, it's odd to use the undercroft instead,' she hurried on. Her cheeks had flushed a little, as if she were aware of her error. 'Perhaps whoever it is knew they were doing wrong and were keen to keep the offence to a minimum . . .'

Silence fell. Although Josse was not keen to face Gervase and explain why he had released Akhbir and positively encouraged him to run away, still he found himself almost looking forward to the confrontation. Anything would be better, he thought miserably, than sitting here feeling the Abbess's sympathy coming at him in waves and being unable to do what he longed to do.

Which was to share with her the less personal of those precious memories. To open his heart and pour out all the pain that he was suffering.

But she was Abbess of Hawkenlye and they were trying to find out why two people – three now – had been murdered. He kept his peace.

When Gervase arrived, Josse gave him his reasons for having let Akhbir go succinctly and honestly. The sheriff was more surprised than angry. He said, 'I respect your judgement, Josse, and in fact you didn't do anything wrong since Akhbir wasn't exactly under arrest, merely under guard. But he didn't do what you expected, did he? He didn't lead you either to Fadil or to the English Hospitaller. Instead he seems to have run straight into the same bowman who killed Kathnir.'

'He didn't,' Josse said quietly.

'He didn't what?' Gervase demanded.

'It was not Kathnir's killer who fired the shot.'

'Josse, you're asking us to believe that there are *two* expert archers out there hunting down stray Saracens!' Gervase exclaimed, looking across at the Abbess with an exasperated smile. 'That is stretching credibility, is it not, my lady?'

'It would appear so,' she said guardedly.

'I have not told you it all yet,' Josse said.

'Then please do so!' cried the sheriff.

'Kathnir was killed with the same type of arrow that was fired at us, Gervase, as we stood at the spot where the Turk died, and we concluded that whoever killed Kathnir did so out of revenge for their fallen comrade. Also, that they did not want our presence at a spot that they revered like a shrine to the dead man.'

'Yes,' Gervase agreed.

'I believe that someone else killed Akhbir,' he said gravely, 'for he was shot with a crossbow bolt.'

'You are certain of that?' Gervase demanded.

'Aye. The bowman did not want me to linger over Akhbir's body and he fired two more shots to warn me off. I brought one of them away with me. It's in the gatehouse with my weapons.'

'You of all men ought to know the difference between a longbow arrow and a crossbow bolt,' Gervase admitted.

'Aye. I do,' Josse agreed.

'Cannot a man be efficient with both?' the Abbess asked. 'Is not the crossbow a better weapon for short-range fire?'

Josse turned to look at her. It was a surprising piece of knowledge for a nun, but then, as he often reminded himself, she had not always been a nun. 'That is so. As to whether a man can be as good a marksman with both weapons, I have not experienced such a thing. The two types of bow require different skills, use different muscles, and it is normal for a man to train in the use of one or the other. But it's not impossible.'

'Unlikely?' the sheriff persisted.

'Aye.'

'So those who wished to avenge the Turk's death by murdering the two Saracen warriors were not responsible for this morning's death,' the Abbess said. 'Who was, then?'

Josse, who had the advantage over his companions of having known for very much longer how Akhbir had died, had given a great deal of thought to the question. 'There are two obvious possibilities,' he said. 'Akhbir was involved in the mission to find Fadil and take him back to the fat man. He and Kathnir were also commanded to retrieve the stolen treasure with which the fat man intended to buy him back. We believe that Fadil and the English monk came to England together but that they have parted company. I suggest that either Fadil – John Damianos – is living out in the house in the forest alone, or else that he's got the Hospitaller with him. One of them must have fired the shots that killed Akhbir and sent me running.'

'You said that John Damianos was alone when he came to New Winnowlands,' the Abbess observed.

'Aye, I know. I thought of that too. But just because they

had separated then does not necessarily mean they have not joined forces again now.'

Gervase was shaking his head. 'What are they doing out there?' he said. 'Is it simply that, all too aware there are people hunting for them, they are lying low?'

'There are fewer people on their trail now,' the Abbess said. 'The two Saracens are dead. Thibault of Margat and Brother Otto are lying in their beds here at the Abbey recovering from the effects of the fire.'

'Aye, that is true, my lady,' Josse agreed, 'but we still face a third pursuing party which is perhaps the most dangerous of all.'

'How so?' asked Gervase.

Josse smiled grimly. 'Because, except for these facts – that they originally had a Turkish bowman with them, that there are at least two of them and both are expert archers, and they appear to be involved in the pursuit of Fadil and the English monk – we know absolutely nothing about them.'

Twelve

Before Josse left the Abbess she mentioned that Thibault was restless, asking repeatedly how soon he might be able to go on his way. 'But Sister Euphemia tells me he is still far from well,' she added. 'His burns are still raw and, apart from the dreadful pain, if he tries to move he risks infection.' Josse offered to call in and talk to Thibault and the Abbess accepted with gratitude. Accordingly, he made his way to the infirmary as soon as he had wished her good evening.

He parted the curtains and went inside the recess. Brother Otto was dozing but managed to open his eyes briefly and give him a weak smile. Thibault was propped up on pillows, clean dressings on his many wounds, his face tense with anxiety.

'I hear you wish to leave us, Thibault.' Josse perched carefully on his bed.

'I have a job to do,' Thibault replied. 'All the time I lie here, the man I seek flees further from me.' He had been looking straight at Josse but his eyes slipped away.

Josse thought he knew why that was.

'But he will not leave this area,' he said softly.

Thibault shot him a sharp look. 'What do you mean?'

'I mean that he is not likely to set off to other parts of the country when it is here that he has friends,' Josse replied.

Thibault licked his lips nervously. 'Friends?'

'Aye. The runaway monk went out to Outremer with Gerome de Villières. And Gerome de Villières has his manor near Robertsbridge, less than ten miles away.'

He could have sworn that Thibault relaxed with relief, although why this should be he had no idea. After some time Thibault said, 'You may be right.'

Aye, I might, Josse thought. 'And if I go to this Gerome,' he said, 'and ask about a certain young knight who left his service in Outremer to join the Knights Hospitaller, he will know exactly who I mean?'

Thibault hesitated. 'I knew him by a name different from that under which he enlisted in the service of Gerome de Villières.'

'Are you able to tell me either of those names?'

Thibault looked at him for several moments. Then he said simply, 'No.'

'Because you don't know them or because you won't reveal them?'

Thibault went on looking at him but he did not answer the question. But then he said, 'The man I seek is not at the manor of his former master and nobody in the vicinity has seen a solitary Hospitaller. Brother Otto and I went there shortly before we met up with Brother Jeremiah. The track from the de Villières estate joins the road from the coast to the north of Robertsbridge.'

'The de Villières family had received no word of him? He had not visited nor contacted them?'

'No, Sir Josse.' Thibault was watching him intently. 'That is the truth, and I give you my word on it.'

Was he telling the truth? It might well be that Thibault had his own reasons for not wanting Josse to visit Gerome de Villières, in which case telling him that the family had neither seen nor heard from their former knight was a good way of ensuring he didn't. On the other hand, a senior member of the Order of the Knights Hospitaller had just given his word.

On balance, Josse reckoned he believed him.

There was something about what Thibault had just related that called for Josse's attention. Thibault had relaxed into his pillows and closed his eyes and swiftly Josse went over their conversation to see if he could pick out what it was.

After some concentrated effort he thought he had it.

Nobody there has seen a solitary Hospitaller, Thibault said. And, *Brother Otto and I went there shortly before we met up with Brother Jeremiah.*

Thibault and Brother Otto were not the only ones hunting for the runaway monk and his companion. Kathnir and Akhbir had been after the monk's companion, Fadil, which meant they were also following the monk since he was travelling with Fadil. In addition, there was also the pair of bowmen who had avenged their Turkish companion's death by killing Kathnir. And now there was a mysterious crossbow-wielding archer as well . . .

Could one of these parties have been close enough to Thibault and Brother Otto to witness the visit to Gerome de Villières? They must have known that the two Hospitallers were looking for one of their own, and if their intelligence was good, they could also have known that the runaway went out to Outremer with de Villières and would be likely to seek sanctuary there. Supposing one or other of these pursuing groups saw Thibault and Brother Otto *before* Robertsbridge and the visit to Gerome de Villières, when it was just the two of them, and again *after* Robertsbridge, when all of a sudden they had a third monk with them? Surely the pursuers would reach the obvious conclusion: that Thibault and Brother Otto had found the runaway hiding at the home of his former master and that now they were taking him on up to Clerkenwell to face the judgement of his Order.

Oh, it made sense! Josse thought triumphantly. Then whoever it was – the Saracens or the two bowmen – had followed the Hospitallers first to Hawkenlye Abbey and then on to Tonbridge, where they had lodged in the guest wing. Still believing poor innocent Brother Jeremiah to be the man they sought, they had marked which bed was his, then slipped in at night and killed him, starting the fire to cover the murder.

The more he thought it over, the more he was convinced he was right. Had Thibault reached the same conclusion? The poor man had had long enough to think about it; had he too worked it out? There was only one way to find out.

'Thibault?' Josse said softly.

He thought the Hospitaller had dropped off to sleep but Thibault's eyes shot open and he said, 'What is it?' There was a wary look on his face.

'I believe I know why Brother Jeremiah was killed.'

Thibault watched him steadily. 'Go on.'

Josse outlined his theory. He did not mention the Saracens or the bowmen specifically, merely referring to them as parties on the trail of the runaway. Thibault did not interrupt, and when Josse finished he gave a heavy sigh and said, 'I believe you are right. This is how I too have reasoned.' He shifted slightly, wincing. 'Brother Jeremiah was young, eager and, as far as I could judge on so brief an acquaintance, had lived an innocent life. He chatted freely to Brother Otto and me as we walked up from Robertsbridge and we learned a great deal about him. He gave us the impression that he was a man with nothing to hide and I have not been able to think of any reason why anyone should have wished to kill him. Unless they thought he was somebody else.'

'Such as your runaway monk.'

'Exactly.'

Something else was stirring in Josse's mind; slowly he teased it out. He did not believe that Brother Jeremiah was murdered by the same hand that killed the Turk, for the method was quite different. The killer had tried to extract information out of the Turk; Brother Jeremiah's killing had been more of an execution. Either the killer knew that the man for whom they had mistaken Brother Jeremiah did not have the information they were after – which was very unlikely – or else they were not after the information.

They had a different reason for wanting the runaway monk dead.

Dear God, Josse thought, his head aching with the intense concentration, but it's a tangled business!

'Sir Josse?' Thibault's voice broke into his thoughts.

'Aye?'

'Brother Otto and I were not the only men pursuing our

runaway,' Thibault said. 'I know of one other party and I suspect the presence of a third.'

'Why are you telling me this?' Josse asked.

'Because I am forced to remain here,' Thibault said with poorly suppressed, frustrated anger. 'I fear for my quarry, Sir Josse. We wish to apprehend him and take him to our superiors for interrogation, for he has—' Thibault shut his mouth like a trap. 'If we catch him and overcome him there will be punishment but there is no danger that his life will be forfeit. I cannot say the same for others who pursue him.'

'What will happen if they get to him first?'

Thibault sighed. He seemed to be wrestling with himself over how much to reveal and Josse was sure that he would not be giving away anything at all were it not for the fact that his injuries kept him in his bed. He seemed to murmur a brief prayer then, his eyes on Josse, he said, 'I have decided to tell you something in the hope that you will agree to take my place and hunt down my missing monk.'

'I am more than willing to do so,' Josse said promptly.

'Thank you.' Then, picking up where he had earlier left off: 'After the disaster in the desert, our prisoner's brother was as desperate to recover his young sibling and his treasure as we were to find our runaway monk. The elder brother was wounded but he immediately selected two trusted warriors of his household and sent them on the trail of the monk.'

'And the prisoner,' Josse added.

Thibault pursed his lips but did not respond. 'These two men are almost certainly now in England,' he said, 'and, I sense, close on our runaway's heels. They must not find him, Sir Josse. They are desperate to get that which he— They know what happened in the desert that night and they will try to make Brother— They will force him to give up that with which he was entrusted.'

Irritated all over again by Thibault's stubborn refusal to reveal the whole truth, Josse said curtly, 'They will not find him or make him talk. They are dead.'

'They are – *dead*?'

'Aye. One – the leader – took an arrow in the chest. The other was shot through the heart with a crossbow bolt.'

'You are sure?'

'Aye. I saw them both die.'

'And there is no doubt that they were the two Saracens sent by – sent by the prisoner's elder brother?'

'Sent by Hisham?' Josse smiled grimly. 'See, Thibault: I know his name. And there is no doubt they are Hisham's warriors. With their deaths, one threat to your runaway has been removed.'

Thibault sank back into his pillows. His relief was evident and Josse saw the ghost of a smile on his face.

It was time to leave him to rest, Josse thought. In the morning he would return and see if Thibault had managed to persuade himself that if Josse was to find his runaway before anyone else did, then it made sense to reveal a few more facts. For now, Thibault should sleep.

He got up and stepped across to the curtains. As he parted them something occurred to him. 'Thibault?'

'Sir Josse?'

'You speak Arabic?'

'I do.'

'Can you tell me what *simyager* means?'

'Where did you hear this?' Thibault whispered.

'From one of the Saracens. He was describing his master Hisham and he said he was a merchant from Tripoli and then he said he was a *simyager.*'

Thibault said, 'It is not Arabic but Turkish.' Then with an indifference that was just too studied to be genuine, he added, 'It simply means merchant.'

'I see.' Josse twitched back the curtain and stepped out into the main ward. 'Sleep well, Thibault. I will visit you again tomorrow.'

He hurried down to the Vale. It was fully dark now and very cold. He sent up a prayer for Fadil and the runaway monk. Wherever they were, he hoped they had a fire. In the lay brothers' quarters he sat before the dying hearth with Brother Saul and Brother Urse for a short time, sharing the last of their mulled ale, then he excused himself and made his way over to his bedroll.

As he settled down, he wondered what the real meaning of the word *simyager* might be. He knew it did not translate as merchant. Before he uttered the word, Akhbir had just said in his halting English that Hisham was a merchant so why would he repeat it in Turkish? Whatever it meant, it referred to something that Hisham was, or perhaps did, that Thibault did not want him to know.

It was, he thought sleepily, just one more thing to worry about.

He went to see the Abbess early the next morning. There was something he needed to do – now, before anyone could try to stop him or demand to come with him – and his instinct was to slip off without telling anybody. But there might be danger, in which case it was probably better that someone knew where he was going.

As soon as they had greeted each other he said, 'My lady, last night Thibault asked me if I would take up his task of hunting for the missing Hospitaller and I said I would. Accordingly, since I believe that it may be he and Fadil who are hiding at the house in the woods, I am going back there this morning.'

'To the place where Akhbir was killed?'

'Aye. I need to—'

'You must not do any such thing, Sir Josse! Yesterday someone shot at you there, and although you maintain they were merely warning shots, still it is perilous. They do not want you there and they may shoot to kill this time.'

'I do not believe that I am in any real danger.' His voice was calm.

'How can you possibly say that?' she demanded.

He smiled. 'For one thing, whoever is hiding there knows their presence is no longer a secret. Akhbir knew where to find them, or him, and now he has led me there too. They do not want to be found, so they will have already fled. And for another thing—' He stopped. He had been about to say that if one of the men camping out in the undercroft was indeed Fadil – John Damianos – then he didn't think the man would harm him. I *liked* John Damianos, he reminded himself, and I am sure he liked me too. But it was slim reasoning with which to convince a beloved friend who was gravely worried for his safety.

'For another thing?' she prompted stonily.

'Gervase will want to turn the place over,' he said. Even if it was not what he had been going to say, it remained perfectly true. 'Akhbir may have deserved death for his part in the murder of the Turk, but Gervase will say that it is for the courts to award punishment. He will wish to find and arrest whoever fired that crossbow bolt, and he'll probably ask me to show him the way to the house in the woods as soon as he's rounded up some of his men. I want to get there before him, my lady,' he added.

It was apparent that she was not convinced. There was nothing left but the truth. 'I sheltered John Damianos at New Winnowlands and I feel compelled to protect him. If he and the runaway Hospitaller are still at the house, I would like the chance to speak to them before they are arrested.'

Now she understood. 'You do not believe that these fugitives have done anything wrong, do you?' she asked softly. 'We have been told that the runaway monk abandoned his dead and dying comrades out in the desert; that he abducted the prisoner and made off with the treasure that was to buy the young man back. At least one pursuing group wanted him dead, and Thibault wishes to take him to the Knights Hospitaller at Clerkenwell to be punished. Yet you, Sir Josse, wish to protect him?'

He tried to think of a soundly reasoned, rational reply. He couldn't. So he just said, 'Aye.'

Her face remained serious but he could see a smile beginning in her eyes. 'It's strange,' she mused, 'but ever since I heard tell of this John Damianos of yours, I have warmed to him. Probably it is because you have turned yourself into his champion. Very well, Sir Josse,' she added decisively, 'go. Take care – oh, do take care! – and if you have not returned by this afternoon I shall send out a search party.'

'You do not know where I'm going,' he pointed out.

She sat up regally. 'Then you had better tell me.'

He and Horace set out a short time later. He preferred, for reasons that he did not explore, to take the long road that skirted the forest rather than cut through it and he kicked the big horse into a canter. Gervase might set out for the house without him – it was possible that one of his men knew the place. Well, if he was there when Josse arrived, there was nothing he could do about it. He put it from his mind.

He reached the place where the path to the house led off the track and rode in beneath the trees. They were quite thin here and, by keeping to the wider paths, he was able to go to within perhaps two or three hundred paces of the house. He and Joanna had ridden right up to it before, but that had been a long time ago. Now, like some strange, vigorous growth encouraged by a magical spell, the undergrowth sprawled in places right over the faint line of the path. Dismounting, he tethered Horace to a birch tree and walked on.

The house on its rise came into sight. He was approaching at a different angle from yesterday and his view of the courtyard was obscured. This, no doubt, was why he could not see the body. But then he emerged out into the open.

The body had gone.

He stood absolutely still. A shiver of dread crept up his spine; what unearthly presence could make a body disappear . . . ? Then reason returned. Either the crossbow man disposed of the body straight after he drove Josse away, or else he, or others, returned later. Perhaps it had been the forest people. They might have different views on burials and funerals but he was sure it was not their custom to leave a dead body out in the open.

He made to walk on. It felt for a moment as if he was up against some powerful but invisible force trying to hold him back: *This place is not for you.*

'I have to look,' he said aloud. To his faint surprise his voice sounded quite level. He pushed against the invisible force. It yielded and he stumbled forward.

Before his courage could desert him, he went straight to the spot where Akhbir had fallen. There was a little blood, and he could make out crushed areas of grass, as if footprints had passed to and fro. He tried to detect a trail. It was faint but it was there. Akhbir's body had been dragged across the courtyard and into the woods. Breaking into a trot, Josse went in under the trees and presently came to a spot where the earth had been disturbed. The area of bare soil was roughly man-shaped. He had found Akhbir's burial place. Slowly and thoughtfully he walked back to the house.

The low door of the undercroft was closed and bolted. He pushed back the bolts. The door did not open; it must be locked. It made sense, he thought, that the undercroft could be bolted to keep livestock in and also locked to keep intruders out. But where was the key?

Whoever had been camping there had not broken down the door, for it showed no sign of damage. It was highly unlikely that they had been given the key – did Joanna even possess one? – so it must be concealed somewhere. Where, Josse mused, would I hide a key?

He looked around. He picked at one or two loose corners on the paving slabs close to the door but found nothing other than a handful of woodlice. He saw a crack in the wall, but his probing fingers found nothing inside. He frowned, turning in a slow circle, searching.

The rose that grew across the hall door at the top of the steps had its roots in the soft soil between their base and the side of the house. In the thick tangle of the rose's intertwining stems there was a blackbird's nest. The strong, dense cup of grass, roots, moss and twigs was lined with dried mud, and as Josse reached into it his fingers closed on the cold, hard shape of a key. He put it in the lock of the undercroft door. It turned easily, as if it had been recently used, and the door opened.

He pushed the door fully open to admit the light and then stepped cautiously inside. There was a short flight of half a dozen shallow steps. Slowly he descended. Despite the open door it was dim down there, for the undercroft had no windows. He waited while his eyes adjusted, then looked up at the vaulted ceiling. The room was well built and, despite the house having stood empty for so long, felt sound and dry.

He lowered his gaze and inspected the stone floor. There was a ring of hearthstones, encircling an area blackened with ash, soot and smoke. The makeshift fireplace had been swept clean; nearby was a neat stack of logs and kindling. Other than that, the room was bare.

Kneeling, he put his hand on the hearthstones. He detected warmth. There had been a fire there not long ago. But they had gone, that fugitive pair who had come so far; Akhbir's arrival, with Josse on his heels, had sent them running.

Slowly he straightened up, mounted the steps out of the undercroft, closed, bolted and locked the door and returned the key to its place in the blackbird's nest.

Sent them running . . . Were they on foot or did they have horses? Making his way to the stables, he pushed the door open and went in. He looked inside the short row of stalls and at first saw no sign of recent occupation. But then he discovered that, unlike the others, the two stalls furthest from the door had been recently mucked out. The floors were swept clean. He hurried out of the second, his searching eyes fixed to the ground.

Just inside the entrance he found what he was looking for: hoof prints. Two horses, one slightly bigger than the other, had recently passed out through the stable door.

He ran outside, closely examining the ground, and found more hoof prints leading out across the courtyard. But then he came to the line where stone gave way to grass and found no more. They have gone, then, he thought. The English Hospitaller fired those crossbow shots and then, once I had run off, yelled to Fadil that their hiding place had been discovered and they must leave without delay. Fadil, perhaps down in the under-croft preparing food over the hearth, stamped out the fire and threw his belongings in his pack. Perhaps he packed the monk's bag too, since his companion would have kept watch in the courtyard in case I came back. Then the pair of them raced round to the barn, saddled up the horses and fled.

Where to? Josse wondered. 'Where did you go, John?' he said aloud.

But there was no answer.

Thirteen

On arriving back at Hawkenlye, Josse went straight to the Abbess to announce his safe return. He strode along to her room to discover Gervase was there, and interrupting him in mid-sentence – he was declaiming Josse's action as fool-hardy and careless of his own safety – Josse said, 'Thank you for your concern, Gervase, but as you see, I have survived without a blemish.' Gervase raised an eyebrow at the gentle irony. 'I can report that whoever was out there has gone. They've left the undercroft clean and tidy, the stalls have been swept out and there is no sign save a little residual warmth in the hearthstones to say that anyone was there.'

'What of Akhbir?' Gervase asked.

'There's a new grave out in the woods. Whoever shot him has buried him.'

Gervase regarded him, his expression grave. 'This is not the end of the matter, Josse. Akhbir should have been arrested and made to answer for his crime. To shoot him dead is a criminal act in itself, and I must now find this mysterious crossbow man and question him.'

'It is not a crime if you kill a man who would otherwise kill you, is it, Gervase?' the Abbess asked.

'No, my lady,' he said courteously. 'The law recognizes a man's right to kill in self-defence.'

'Thank you. So, if the man hiding in the house in the woods saw Akhbir approach—'

'Wielding his sword,' Josse put in helpfully.

' – with his sword in his hand,' she went on, 'then, knowing what Kathnir and Akhbir did to the dead Turk, would he not be perfectly justified in shooting Akhbir?'

'Yes, very probably,' Gervase said, 'but he must give me an account of these events himself! I am not unreasonable and neither is the system of justice in which I am involved. I will not send a man to be hanged if he killed in self-defence. You have my word on it.'

'I did not think that you would,' the Abbess said gently. Then, addressing Josse: 'Sir Josse, you have undertaken the search for the missing Hospitaller on Thibault's behalf while he lies abed.'

'Aye, my lady.'

'I propose that we visit him now and ask if we are right in our supposition that Fadil is travelling with the English monk; moreover, if he has heard any rumour that Fadil has adopted the name John Damianos. You reason, Sir Josse, that it is Fadil who has been living at the house in the woods. Since you only missed him there by a hair's breadth, it would be reasonable to say that you have been doing your best to carry out your mission. In all fairness, I think we may now demand a little more frankness from Thibault.'

Josse grinned. 'We may demand it, my lady. Whether or not it will be forthcoming, I would not like to say.'

She had risen to her feet and was sweeping across the room towards the door. 'I shall at least try,' she said. 'Come along! Gervase, you had better accompany us.'

Gervase and Josse exchanged a glance. Then they meekly fell into step behind her.

* * *

Helewise did not intend to let either Josse or Gervase question Thibault. As Sister Euphemia ushered her into the small recess, she positioned herself very firmly by the bed so that neither of them could stand in front of her. Then, smiling down at Thibault – who, she could not help noticing, was regarding her with a certain amount of apprehension – she said, 'Thibault, you asked Sir Josse to search for your missing monk. This morning he has, on your behalf, made a dangerous journey. He believes he knows where your runaway has been hiding. He further believes that this man's companion earlier took refuge at Sir Josse's own manor of New Winnowlands.' She paused to let that sink in.

'Sir Josse has—' Thibault looked past her at Josse. 'You already knew of this man that I seek? Yet you did not mention this to me?'

'You did not tell us his name,' Josse said. 'All you revealed was that your man was dressed like you and your companions. The man who came to New Winnowlands was not your monk for he was a Saracen, dressed in the traditional style. But he was in the habit of going out secretly at night and' – as Helewise watched, a sort of brightness lit up his face – 'I would guess that his excursions might well have been to meet up with his long-time travelling companion. Your monk,' he added, in case it was not sufficiently clear.

'You believe that this man who stayed with you was Fadil?' Thibault looked astounded.

'Aye.'

But Helewise was watching Thibault's face and she could see that for some reason he found this suggestion laughable. 'Why should Fadil come to England?' he asked.

'Your monk brought him,' Josse said eagerly. 'When the exchange in the desert went so fatally wrong, your man believed that for some reason he could not take his prisoner back to Margat. As the only surviving Hospitaller of the group, he took – or had put on him – the duty of getting the prisoner Fadil and the ransom to safety. Which he is still trying to do.'

Thibault had put his head back and seemed to be staring at the ceiling. 'It is absurd,' he said flatly.

Helewise, stung on Josse's behalf, said coolly, 'Thibault, you ask for Sir Josse's aid and yet, far from giving him any assistance, you seem to go out of your way to increase the mists of mystery that surround this matter. What is your monk's name? What does he look like? Can you not at least answer these questions?'

Thibault looked at her and she was sure she read regret and, strangely, pity in his expression. 'I am sorry but I cannot, my lady,' he said. 'As another of the avowed, you will appreciate that it is not for us to make independent decisions when we have been given clear orders to follow.'

Oh, yes, she thought. I appreciate that all right. And how very convenient for Thibault to be able to produce such an unbreakably sound reason for not telling us what we so much want to know.

Josse was addressing Thibault. She made herself listen.

'Your monk,' he was saying, 'is a fighting man?'

'He is,' Thibault replied warily.

'He uses which weapons?'

'Lance and sword.'

'Can he shoot a bow?'

'Most men can shoot a bow.'

'Aye. I am asking if he is a good shot.'

Thibault shrugged. 'Average, perhaps. I cannot say.'

'And if a Knight Hospitaller such as he were to use a bow, of what type would it be?'

'Probably the longbow.'

'So you do not think it likely that your runaway is a deadly shot with the crossbow?'

'If he is, I never heard tell of it,' Thibault said decisively. 'And if he were as good as that, then those in charge of his training would have discovered the talent and put it to use.'

'Thank you,' Josse said.

Helewise shot him a quick look; he raised his eyebrows at her and she nodded.

He had just established that if the shots that had killed Akhbir and driven Josse off had been fired by the fugitive monk and his Saracen prisoner, then the bowman had to have been Fadil.

For the first time Gervase spoke. 'Thibault, I have taken note of all you have said and I am inclined to believe that your monk did not fire the shot that killed Akhbir. However, we – that is, my lady Abbess, Sir Josse and I – are convinced that he is involved in all four of the deaths that have recently occurred in this area. I will join forces with Sir Josse in our hunt for your runaway. If he is found, he will have to answer to the law of this land before he can be called to account by your Order.'

Helewise could see that Thibault objected to this statement. Perhaps Gervase realized it too for, before Thibault could say a word, he had turned smartly on his heel and could be heard marching away out of the infirmary.

Josse appeared to be concentrating very hard on Thibault. Helewise wondered why; the question was answered as Josse spoke. 'I am going hunting,' he announced. 'First I shall ride over to New Winnowlands, keeping my eyes open and asking anyone I meet if they have seen two strangers, one dressed in a Saracen's garb and the other in the robes of a Knight Hospitaller.' Thibault regarded him steadily. 'Then,' he went on, 'I shall go to Robertsbridge and speak to Gerome de Villières.'

If Josse's intention was to provoke a reaction, Helewise thought admiringly, he had succeeded surely beyond his wildest hopes. Thibault paled and shot out a bandaged hand, grasping at Josse's sleeve as if he would detain him by force if he had to. But his self-control was excellent and his turmoil was not evident in his tone of voice: 'I would not bother going there,' he said calmly. 'Brother Otto and I spoke to Gerome de Villières, as I told you. The man whom we seek is not there and there is no likelihood at all that he will visit in the future.' There was a small and, Helewise thought, telling pause. 'There was a dispute,' Thibault went on. Then, grudgingly: 'The runaway caused grave distress to the family's household out in Antioch. The lady Aurelie, a distant cousin of Gerome, had cause to report in the most reproachful terms to her English kinsman. Believe me,' he concluded earnestly, 'you would be wasting your time, Sir Josse, if you went there.'

Josse nodded. 'Thank you for that advice.' Helewise noticed – and she was quite sure Thibault did too – that Josse did not say whether or not he was going to take it.

'We will leave you to rest, Thibault,' she said. She glanced down at Brother Otto, who was looking at her out of dazed eyes. 'You too, Brother,' she added softly. She touched his shoulder very gently with her fingertips and the monk gave her a smile. 'How are you feeling?' she whispered, bending down over his bed.

Brother Otto tried to say something, but all that emerged was the whistling sound of air passing out through his lips.

'His throat was burned,' Thibault said. 'He cannot speak.'

Helewise crouched down beside Brother Otto. 'We will help you,' she said. 'Have faith, try to keep your spirits up and we will do all we can to make you better.'

Brother Otto nodded his thanks. Then he closed his eyes.

Helewise led the way out through the gap in the curtains, Josse behind her. On the way out of the infirmary she caught the eye of Sister Euphemia who, understanding that it was a summons, stopped what she was doing and came over to give her superior a bow of reverence. 'My lady?'

'Sir Josse and I have just been visiting Thibault and Brother Otto,' she said. 'How are they?'

'Thibault is determined to be out of his bed and off about his business as soon as he can,' the infirmarer replied, 'and his resolve certainly seems to be aiding his recovery. His burns are healing well and he has insisted that we reduce the amount of pain relief. Although I am quite sure he suffers a great deal, his mind is much less clouded.'

'I see. And Brother Otto?'

'That poor young man has lost the power of speech. We are treating him with soothing herbal drinks to heal his burned throat but only time will tell if we will be successful.'

'And the burns to his body?'

'He progresses, but it is very slow. So far we have managed to keep infection away, thanks be to the good Lord,' – and to your and Sister Caliste's scrupulous care, Helewise thought – 'so there is a good chance that he will make a reasonable recovery. It will take time, however.'

'Thank you, Sister.' Helewise patted the infirmarer's shoulder. 'We will leave you to your work.'

Outside, she and Josse stood in the cold morning air and she noticed that, like her, he too was taking deep breaths. Even in an infirmary as well run as Sister Euphemia's there was no avoiding foul smells.

'So, Sir Josse, you ride now to New Winnowlands?' she asked.

'Aye. John Damianos came there for refuge before, and now he has been driven away from the house in the woods, there is a chance he may come back.'

'You still believe that he is Fadil?'

'Aye, I do. Thibault has said that his monk does not use the crossbow, yet whoever killed Akhbir and fired those carefully aimed bolts at me was a first-rate exponent of the weapon. Which means that it must have been Fadil, an assumption that is reinforced by—' He stopped abruptly.

'Yes, Sir Josse? Reinforced by what?'

He looked bashful. 'Well, Fadil – John Damianos – must have recognized me. He might well have wanted me to back off, but he did not want to hurt me. I just think – I mean, it's likely that—'

'Of course he did not wish to hurt you,' she said warmly. 'You took him in; your Will made up a comfortable place where he could rest and Ella cooked good, nourishing meals for him. You acted in the true spirit of loving kindness, Sir Josse, and whatever Fadil may be or may have done, it would be a thankless, vicious man who turned on his benefactor.'

'Or a desperate one,' Josse said glumly.

She thought about it. Yes, he was right. There were circumstances under which one might have to do such a terrible deed: to save one's own life, perhaps. Or that of a loved one. 'Take care,' she said, reaching out to take his hand. 'Oh, do take care, dear Josse. Will you take one or two of the lay brothers with you? Brother Saul and Brother Augustus have often accompanied you into danger.'

'It is a kind thought, my lady, but I prefer to go alone. We would be more of a threat riding three abreast and I do not want Fadil to think we mean him harm.'

'I understand,' she said. 'God bless you, and return to us soon and safe,' she murmured.

'Amen.' He gave her a swift bow, then turned and strode off towards the stables. Her heart heavy and with a strange sense of foreboding, she returned to her room.

Josse made good time to New Winnowlands; Horace seemed to appreciate the crisp, sharp air and the frost-hardened ground under his big feet. The ride was exhilarating and as the familiar landscape came into view, Josse felt as if he had been given some powerful elixir that stepped up his brain function and encouraged him to action. He had seen few people on the way and those whom he had questioned had to a man – and a woman – shaken their heads and said no, they had seen neither a black-robed monk nor a swathed Saracen. Even the series of negative replies had not discouraged Josse. He told himself that he would have been most surprised if anyone *had* seen either of the men he was searching for. They were just too good at hiding.

Will greeted him with his usual total lack of surprise. He went with Josse into the hall, called out to Ella that master was home, hungry, cold and thirsty. As Ella bustled about stoking up the fire and preparing food and drink, Josse explained why he had come back and asked Will if there had been any sign of their former guest.

'No,' Will replied. Then, lowering his voice and with a quick glance to make sure Ella was not in earshot, he said, 'If it's all the same to you, sir, could you *not* ask the same question of Ella? She's well over that business now and it'd be a shame to bring it all up and set her to fretting and worrying again.'

'Aye, it would indeed,' Josse agreed, 'and I won't mention it, Will.' There was no point, he thought. If Ella had any idea that the man she knew as John Damianos might return, she would be plunged back into the agitated state she had exhibited before. He was content to take Will's word for it.

When Ella, having deposited a tray laden with bread, cheese, strips of dried pork, some berries and a jug of spiced wine, disappeared off in the direction of her kitchen, Josse indicated that Will should stay.

'Where would you go, Will,' he asked, 'if you needed a safe refuge in the winter?'

Will gave the question considerable thought. 'I'd go to a trusted friend.'

'Supposing you did not dare trust anyone? If, for instance, you carried with you something of great value that you had to keep safe?'

Will frowned. 'If there was not one single person I could ask for help, I reckon I'd find some out-of-the-way place and build a shelter. I'd cut stout poles,' he went on, warming to his theme, 'and fix bracken and branches of evergreen over them to keep out the rain and the wind. I'd find stones and make a hearth, then I'd scour the land for firewood. I'd risk a bit of poaching to feed myself and when night fell I'd barricade myself in and hope for the best.'

It was a long speech from the usually taciturn Will and, amused at the romantic, imaginative streak in his servant that had created such a colourful and optimistic image of life in the wilds, Josse hid a smile. 'You may be right, Will,' he said seriously. 'Perhaps our former guest has done just that.'

'You'll never find him if he has,' said Will sagely. 'There's a whole forest full of out-of-the-way places not five miles from here. If he's gone to ground in there, that'll be that.'

Josse sighed. Although it was an unwelcome conclusion, he had a suspicion that Will might well be right.

Will excused himself and went back outside. Josse finished his food and drained the jug of wine and as the nourishment and the fire's warmth relaxed him, he found his optimism beginning to creep back.

Fadil and the monk might well have done what Will suggested and hidden themselves away deep inside the forest. But they could not stay there for ever. If they were going to hide for the rest of their lives they could have done so out in Outremer. No: the monk had a clear purpose in coming to England, a purpose that was not going to be fulfilled by sleeping rough in the depths of the Great Wealden Forest. If Josse was right, the Hospitaller was aiming to get both his prisoner and the ransom safely to the headquarters of his Order at Clerkenwell. While he waited for them to emerge, there were other things that he could do and he intended to set about one of them immediately.

He stood up, brushed down his tunic and gathered up his cloak from where Ella had spread it to warm in front of the fire. Wrapping it round him with a dramatic flourish, he went outside, called for his horse and set off for Robertsbridge.

Part Four
The Lady

Fourteen

As he rode Josse thought how best to make his approach to Gerome de Villières. If Thibault had been telling the truth about a dispute between Gerome's erstwhile knight and the de Villières family out in Antioch – and, unless this was a ruse to keep Josse away from the Robertsbridge manor, there was no reason for him to lie – then there was no point in posing as a friend or relative of the missing monk. If they were not prepared to receive the man himself, they would not welcome one of his relatives. It was not much of an idea in any case, Josse decided, since the subterfuge would become evident as soon as they asked him what his supposed kinsman's name was or what he looked like, Josse having absolutely no idea of either.

I will say that I am from Hawkenlye Abbey, he thought in the end, the appointed representative of the Abbess. That was the truth. He would say that two Knights Hospitaller had been badly burned and were in the infirmary; that too was true. He would explain how he had offered to take on the Hospitallers' search for a missing monk but he would make out that he did not know Thibault had already visited the de Villières family. He would give the impression that Thibault could barely speak. He would let Gerome de Villières assume that enquiries were being made at every manor in the vicinity, implying that he did not know of Gerome's connection with the runaway.

Satisfied, he kicked Horace into a canter.

He obtained directions for the de Villières manor and found it quite easily. The house was generously sized and attractive, set in a fold of land to the west of Robertsbridge. Tree-clad slopes sheltered it from the prevailing south-westerly winds and orchards grew on south-facing hillsides. The huddles of peasant dwellings seemed in good condition and the bare earth in the fields looked fertile and rich.

The house and courtyard were enclosed by a stone wall in which there was an arched gateway. Riding in, Josse called out and almost immediately a lad came to take his horse and an older man to ask his name and his business. He listened to Josse's carefully prepared reply and invited him to come up into the house. Josse was ushered into an imposing hall with a wide central hearth and a raised dais on which there were a long table, two chairs and a couple of benches. A thin-faced woman of perhaps forty sat at the table, an embroidery hoop in her hand; a younger woman of about twenty sat beside her.

They watched as he approached the table and bowed. The older one said politely, 'My brother will be with us presently. Will you take some refreshment?'

'Aye, my lady, thank you.'

She nodded to the serving man who had brought Josse in and he bowed and went out through a doorway at the far end of the hall. Josse, beginning to feel slightly awkward beneath the two women's scrutiny, gave a diffident smile and said, 'Lovely bright day, isn't it?'

'It is,' the older woman agreed. She did not venture any further remark that might have picked up the conversation and helped it along. It was a relief when the sound of footsteps came from the passage and the manservant and his master came into the hall. While the servant poured mugs of wine, the master strode up to Josse and said, 'I am Gerome de Villières. This is my sister, the lady Maria, and this is my daughter Editha.' The younger woman gave Josse a shy smile. 'How can I help you?'

Gerome was a short, stout man who had probably once been strong but whose body was running to fat. Under his remaining grey-streaked brown hair his round, ruddy face wore a smile that creased up his light hazel eyes.

'I have come from Hawkenlye Abbey,' Josse began.

'Yes, so my manservant tells me,' Gerome replied. 'We hear great things of the Abbey, Sir Josse.'

'I am sure that they are all true,' Josse said. Then: 'There are two wounded Knights Hospitaller lying in the infirmary, Sir Gerome. They have come to England from Outremer searching for a runaway monk of their Order. Since neither is able to leave his sickbed, I have volunteered to search for the missing monk.'

'Two Hospitallers,' Gerome said, his eyes narrowed. 'They

have already been here.' His sister made as if to say something but with a gesture of his hand Gerome silenced her.

'They came to Hawkenlye,' Josse said, 'and then on to the priory at Tonbridge, where a fire in the guest wing killed a third monk who had joined them on the road after they left Robertsbridge.'

'How terrible!' Gerome seemed shocked. Then, his worried eyes meeting Josse's, he said, 'And was this fire an accident, Sir Josse?'

It was, Josse thought, a strange question. 'Why do you ask?'

Gerome eyed him candidly. 'Because there is much more to this tale of a missing Hospitaller than you know.' He turned to the dais and gave his sister and his daughter a bright smile. 'We will not further disturb your sewing, my dears – our male chatter may make you misdirect your needles!'

'You do not disturb us, Gerome,' said his sister, 'and indeed we should prefer to hear—'

But Gerome, it seemed, had made up his mind and was not going to allow anyone, even his sister, to be a party to a conversation that he deemed unsuitable for their ears. 'Sir Josse and I shall take a turn in the walled garden,' he said firmly, 'for it is sheltered there and we will not be interrupted.'

The final five words, Josse thought with a private smile, had the force of an order. He bowed to the women and followed Gerome across the hall and down the steps into the courtyard. They went through an arch in the wall and along a path, then through an opening in a second wall, on the far side of which was an area of low hedges and beds, the latter at present just bare earth. The sun shone on the far wall and there was a bench set in a recess. Gerome strode over to it, invited Josse to be seated and then settled himself beside him.

'I am sorry I had to bring you out here,' he said.

'I do not mind,' Josse replied. 'The sun makes it feel more like spring than winter.'

'You are charitable,' murmured Gerome. 'My sister is a good woman but she does not have enough to do. She loves to speculate and she insists that she knows best. Oh, it isn't that I do not love and respect her! It's just that—' He shrugged helplessly.

'Just that you like a quiet life?' Josse suggested.

Gerome beamed. 'Precisely. My beloved wife died, you see,'

he plunged straight into the revelation, leaving Josse still grinning inappropriately from the last exchange, 'and my two elder sisters are wed, although one is ailing . . . ' He frowned. 'Which is why my sister Maria runs my household, and very efficiently she does it. My needs and comforts are attended to in the most solicitous fashion and I can't complain. My dear Erys succumbed to the fever, you see.'

'I am sorry to hear it,' Josse said gravely.

'We were *very* happy.' There was a catch in Gerome's voice. 'Erys bore my daughter Editha, whom you just met, and then we had Columba, and then Erys had poor little Maella, only she lived but a few hours and then she died. Two days later, her mother was also dead. Columba was but four years old and not strong, Sir Josse, and she too succumbed to the fever. So I lost three of them in a week.' Gerome stared straight in front of him and Josse saw tears rolling down his face.

'You have my deepest sympathy,' Josse said. 'I cannot begin to imagine what it was like.'

Gerome wiped his eyes. 'The Lord gives, the Lord takes away,' he muttered.

It seemed to Josse scant comfort. But it was not for him to comment; if Gerome derived consolation from his faith, so much the better.

Gerome seemed to have recovered his cheerful spirits. With a smile he said, 'You are probably wondering why I tell you these things, Sir Josse. There is a reason, believe me.' He paused, as if weighing his words. Then: 'I have kin in Outremer. My great-grandfather won lands in Antioch in the course of the crusade of 1096 and they were left to his elder son, with this manor – ' he waved an arm – 'left to the second son, whose descendant I am. Godfrey – the son who inherited in Antioch – married and his wife gave birth to two daughters and one son, Raymond, who was sickly and who died young, having sired two daughters and no sons. His elder daughter, the lady Aurelie, is, however, a formidable woman and in many ways the equal of most men. She was advantageously wed to Count Hugo of Tripoli but the lack of boy children has continued even into her generation, for although she did bear her count a son after two daughters, the little boy – his name was Hugo – died of a flux of the bowels before he reached his first birthday.'

'Your family been cursed with bad fortune,' Josse said.

'Cursed?' Gerome queried the word. 'Perhaps. Yet these things are all too common, Sir Josse, especially in Outremer, where the climate really does not suit us. Anyway,' he said, with the air of a man picking up the thread of his tale, 'my cousin Aurelie's lands were threatened in the dangerous times that culminated in Hattin – you know of Saladin's great victory there?'

'I do.'

'Well, Aurelie and her count sent word to us here in England that she was hard-pressed and needed our assistance. I have no sons of my own but I have men who owe me allegiance and, like many another with kin in Outremer, I was willing to go and help. I'll freely admit that my motives were not entirely selfless. My cousin and her count are fabulously wealthy and I knew full well that her gratitude would be expressed in a manner that would do a great deal more than reimburse my expenses, as indeed has proved the case.' He glanced down at his golden brown, butter-soft leather boots polished to a high shine. 'There is little, Sir Josse, that my womenfolk and I lack these days.'

Josse smiled but did not comment.

'I arranged to take a party of twenty-five knights out to help my cousin defend what is hers,' Gerome continued. 'Aurelie's desperate appeal came in the summer of '85.' He drew a steadying breath but nevertheless his voice trembled. 'It was four years since I had lost my wife and my two youngest daughters but still I grieved. It was selfish, I know, for poor Editha was as affected as I was, but when Aurelie's plea came, I jumped at the chance to get right away from this place which, at that time, gave me nothing but memories of what I had lost and could never regain. The cure worked, Sir Josse.' He met Josse's eyes with disarming frankness. 'When I returned, my manor and my life here were washed clean of sorrow. Or perhaps it was I that was washed; I do not know. I still remember my beloved Erys – not a day passes that I do not think of her – but now I picture her alive and laughing instead of – well, never mind.'

He was, Josse thought, a man made for happiness. What a blessing that he had been allowed to find it again.

'My sister and my daughter are now the sole recipients of my love,' Gerome was saying, 'and they seem to manage quite well to share out between the two of them that which once encompassed more. But enough – this isn't what you came to hear.'

Picking up the cue, Josse said, 'There was in your company a young knight who, I understand, wanted to continue with the fight after you – er, after you had returned to your kin in Antioch.'

Gerome chuckled. 'After I decided that battle and war were not for me,' he corrected. 'I admit it freely, Sir Josse. I was not born for fighting. I was at Hattin, you know. King Guy was captured, as were the majority of our leaders, and worst of all the Saracens took the precious fragment of the True Cross, which was both our inspiration and our rallying point. We were demoralized at Hattin, Sir Josse, and as we were driven back towards the coast the fighting was at best half-hearted. Although I am ashamed that I could not discover a brave warrior spirit within myself, I was not alone in preferring to creep away to lick my wounds. I was in fact wounded,' he added with a touch of pride. Unfastening the ties at the neck of his chemise, he drew back the soft, fine linen to reveal a deep, purplish oval scar.

'Spear thrust?' asked Josse.

'Yes. It hurt like the very devil, but our medical men got hold of some stuff the Arabs used and managed to restrain the infection. They said I'd have died otherwise, so in a strange sort of way, I owe my survival to my enemy.' He gazed across the frosty fields, a faraway expression on his face. 'Funny how life goes.'

'Aye,' Josse agreed.

'Then, of course, the loss of Jerusalem made our King Richard set out to win it back,' Gerome continued, 'and we all know how *that* ended up. God bless him,' he added, although the pause was too long for it to have been anything but an afterthought.

'You returned to your cousin's house in Antioch to recover?' Josse asked.

'Hmm? Yes, yes, that's right. Aurelie and her girls made a great fuss of me and I confess I thrived on the attention. Oh, Sir Josse, you should have seen that house! Aurelie has lived all her life in Outremer, the fourth generation to make a home there, and, typically, her house shows the Eastern influence – well, it makes sense to adopt local ways. The place has a strong outer wall that shows a formidable face to the world, but once through the gates, you enter heaven on earth. She has inner courtyards where fountains play and where jasmine and roses scent the air. To keep you cool there are silk-draped divans set in the shade to catch the breeze. Her servants pad about on bare feet and they know precisely when you want an iced sherbet or a cool cloth on your forehead. And they all seem so happy, Sir Josse! I was a stranger but they cared for me with kindness and a smile on their dark faces.'

The great torrent of words stopped as Gerome paused for breath. Then he said sheepishly, 'I am sorry. I loved Antioch, you see, and once I begin speaking of my time there, the images and the memories come flooding back and I can talk all day if someone doesn't stop me. Usually it's Maria,' he added resignedly, 'but then she has heard it all so many times.'

Josse had been carried along. But now he said, 'I am fascinated by your descriptions, Sir Gerome. But I need to know more about your young knight.'

'Of course you do! Well, like you say, he wasn't at all happy about being dragged away from the fighting. You see, Sir Josse, I made a mistake. Hattin was so frightful that I thought my men would be *pleased* I was pulling them out! It never occurred to me that one of them would want to go on fighting. Anyway, he came to me and told me and I said he must go with my blessing. I said he knew where I'd be if he needed me and I wished him God's protection.'

'He intended to join one of the military orders?'

Gerome frowned. 'It's odd, because I'm sure I remember he said— Well, it doesn't matter and obviously I was wrong. He was going to go straight to Crac des Chevaliers – it's about a hundred miles from Antioch – and offer his services to the Knights Hospitaller. That would have been in the late summer of '87.'

'So he joined the Order before King Richard took up the fight,' Josse remarked.

'Yes. They taught him much and turned him into a first-rate fighter with many skills.'

'Could he use the crossbow?' Josse thought he knew the answer, having already asked Thibault.

'The crossbow? No, no; he was a mounted knight and he used

the lance and the sword. He might have been able to use the longbow, I suppose.'

'You saw him in action?'

'Yes. King Richard arrived and won the great victory at Acre, and his successes alongside the French fellow' – Josse was amused that Gerome did not even dignify King Philip with a name – 'put new heart in us all. I marched my men south from Antioch to Acre and we joined King Richard's great push from Acre to Jaffa. I heard word of my knight again on that long road, although they told me that he now wore the habit of a Knight Hospitaller and was known as Brother Ralf. We met up and prayed together on the eve of Arsuf. Oh, Sir Josse,' he exclaimed, 'what a time that was! We'd been marching through the Forest of Arsuf and we were all spooked by the rumour that the enemy was going to fire the trees and burn us all to death. Then we came out into the open and saw them there, great long rows of them, and I was frankly terrified. We set up our camp that night and they were so close that we could see the flames of their cooking fires under that vast, dark sky.' Slowly he shook his head. 'We all knew what would happen the next day. I was so glad to see Brother Ralf's familiar face; he was four years older and infinitely more mature than when I'd last seen him, and his quiet confidence and firm resolve did me more good than all the prayers and exhortations of the priests.

'Next day we rode into battle. It was a joyful victory, as of course you know.'

'Yet you were unwell,' Josse said.

'Yes, I was. I had dysentery and I thought I would die. I do not recall much, being barely conscious during the worst of it. They said I was too weak to go on with the army and I was sent back to Acre, then on to Antioch to rest and recuperate with my kinfolk. They treated me very well, Sir Josse, in return for having been generous with them. They undertook to make sure I reached Aurelie's home safely. To my surprise – I imagined he'd want to forge ahead with King Richard – one of my escorts was Brother Ralf.' Gerome smiled. 'He was not best pleased to exchange the nursemaid's role for the warrior's, but it was an order and he had no choice. He carried it out with a smiling face, caring for me as if I'd been his own father.' He sighed. 'And I who have no male children of my own loved him like a son. I always did and I always will.'

There was a contradiction here, Josse thought, for Thibault had given a very different picture. *Brother Jeremiah and I spoke to Gerome de Villières*, Thibault had said. *The man whom we seek is not there and there is no likelihood that he will visit in the future . . . the runaway caused grave offence to Gerome's kin in Antioch . . . the lady Aurelie had cause to report back in the most gravely reproachful terms to her English kinsman.*

He stared at Gerome. 'I have been told that you and Brother Ralf had fallen out because he had offended your kinswoman Aurelie,' he said flatly. 'How can you love him like a son if this is true?'

'One does not stop loving a son because of one rebellious act,' Gerome said quietly. There was a long pause. Then he said, 'I am not sure whether I should confide in you, Sir Josse, but I have been on this earth for a good many years and I flatter myself that I am a fair judge of men. I warm to you and I am inclined to tell you the truth. I hope, however, that by doing so I shall not endanger someone I care for.'

'I cannot give you my word to act solely in your interests,' Josse said quickly. 'I am entrusted by the Abbess of Hawkenlye to take up the task of Thibault of Margat, Knight Hospitaller, and that is my prime concern.'

'I understand,' Gerome said, giving Josse a calculating look. 'Well then, I shall say but this: Thibault of Margat has his own reasons for catching up with Brother Ralf and these reasons are not necessarily – to use your phrase – in Ralf's best interests.'

'I know that he has with him something of very great value,' Josse said. *I suspect* would have been more accurate, but by assuming a certainty he did not have he was hoping to flush out information.

But Gerome was too experienced to fall for the ruse. 'Do you, now?' he said with a grin. 'Well, that's as maybe; perhaps you do, perhaps you don't. This Hospitaller of yours has his orders, Sir Josse. Things are not always as they seem, and there is very much more at stake here than meets the eye.' Abruptly he stood up. 'Now we will return inside, for the sun is sinking and we shall soon be in shadow. We will draw a jug of the best wine and presently you will eat the evening meal with us and sleep in our best guest room. My sister and my daughter receive too few visitors in this chilly weather, when folk prefer their own firesides, and they will blossom in the company of a handsome and courteous knight such as yourself. What do you say?'

Facing the full force of Gerome de Villières's open-hearted, generous and hospitable nature, there was only one response. Josse said, 'Thank you. I'd be delighted to accept.'

As he walked back to the house beside Gerome – who was now explaining in his customary detailed way just where the inspiration for his garden had come from and how they had made it – Josse reflected on the man. He was affectionate, gossipy and, on the face of it, a sybarite who lacked backbone. But that was only half of it. Beneath that amiable exterior there was steel, for here was a man who did not hesitate to take his knights and his men on a hazardous journey of well over a thousand miles to go to the aid of his beleaguered kinswoman. He might not have liked the experience of fighting, but then that applied to a great many men and Gerome had not been raised as a soldier.

Aye, there's strength there all right, Josse decided.

Which for his present purpose was not the best conclusion. He was quite sure that Gerome de Villières had not revealed everything. But he was in no doubt that, having made up his mind not to divulge any more about what happened between himself, his kinswoman, the Knights Hospitaller and Brother Ralf out in Outremer, Gerome would not be persuaded to say another word.

Fifteen

As soon as Josse set out from the Abbey, Helewise shut herself decisively in her room. She had been preoccupied with all that had been happening and her regular duties had suffered. She worked swiftly through the many fat ledgers for several hours, breaking off only for the office. By the time she set off to the church for vespers – with the exception of compline, with its satisfying sense of completing the daily round, her favourite office of the day – she felt that she had just about caught up.

She returned to her room after the evening meal, intending to work until every task was finished. She thought it would not be long; however, she became engrossed in studying a proposed scheme to market wool from sheep on the Abbey's lands to the north of Romney Marsh and several hours passed.

One of the candles on her table flickered and went out. Looking up in surprise, she saw from the little that remained of the second just how long she had sat there. She leaned back in her chair, stretching luxuriously and feeling the taut muscles at the base of her neck crack in protest. She looked down at the manuscripts that she had been studying and at her own notes, written in her tidy and space-saving hand on a piece of scrap vellum. Confident that she now knew enough about the proposal, she tidied away manuscripts and writing materials and, lighting her little lantern from the dying candle, left her room, closing the door quietly behind her.

There was still a light in the infirmary but it was dim; it would be the shaded lamp of whichever sister dozed at her post on night duty. Elsewhere the Abbey was dark and silent. Helewise looked up at the night sky. There were wisps and tatters of cloud beginning to paint their soft veil over the stars. The wind had changed, bringing warmer air up from the south-west. In the south-east, Orion was still unobscured; Helewise stared up at him and then followed the line of his belt down to the horizon and found the brilliant Dog Star.

It was a long time since she had contemplated the glory of the heavens. Aware that her preoccupation with the recent dreadful events and, this afternoon, with catching up on her work had left her little time for her devotions, she decided to spend a quiet, precious interlude alone with the dear Lord and then slip up the night stairs to the dormitory.

She strode past the end of the infirmary and on to the church. The great west door was locked but the access to the side of it was open, as it always was. The gates were fastened and bolted; there was no need to put a lock on God's dwelling place. She pushed the small door open just a crack, slipped inside and quietly closed it.

The air was heavy with incense, and in the soft glow of the sanctuary light she could see smoke from the censer lying in strata. She looked down the length of the nave, then raised her eyes to the vast wooden beam of the rood screen that swept from north to south above the transept, marking off the chancel beyond with its new double rows of choir stalls, beautifully carved out of local oak. Slowly she walked up the nave, pausing beneath the rood screen to look up at Christ on the cross high above her, then on between the choir stalls until she knelt before the altar. Closing her eyes, she stilled her mind in the hope of hearing God's voice.

Some time later, she opened her eyes once more. Feeling peace all around her as if loving arms had placed a soft blanket on her shoulders, she rose to her feet. She heard a noise. She stood quite still, listening to see if it would come again, but there was nothing. Probably a mouse scouring the stone slabs for drops of wax. It was quite amazing what mice ate . . .

She walked on.

The soft, small noise came again.

She crossed to the end of one of the choir stalls and, holding up her small lantern, shone its light down on the shelf where the cresset lamps were kept ready for services after dark. She lit the five separate wicks – there was still plenty of oil in each depression – and, holding the lamp in one hand and her lantern in the other, slowly began to walk around the church.

She saw it when she was still several paces off. There was nothing particularly alarming about it at first sight, nothing to warn her; it was just that it was there where it should not be.

It was in a recess in the rounded wall behind the altar. There was a large wooden chest there with stout locks where the sacristan nun kept altar cloths, candlesticks and the precious beeswax candles. There was something on top of the chest. It looked like a bundle of clothes.

Helewise fought a sudden dart of fear. I am in the house of the Lord, she told herself. The gates were locked at sunset and there is nobody within to harm me.

Holding both lantern and cresset lamp high, she approached the chest.

She had been right in her guess, but from one end of the bundle protruded a sturdy boot. It was not very large and it showed signs of hard usage. The heel was worn down at one side, as if the wearer walked on the outsides of his feet, and the sole had been mended. Helewise moved her light to the other end of the bundle. Leaning down, she could make out the sound of deep, regular breathing. She sent up a swift and heartfelt prayer of gratitude, for in that first moment she had feared yet another dead body.

The sudden relief giving her courage – *anything* else was better than another murder! – she put down her lantern and, with her free hand, picked at the very edge of the cloak, or perhaps it was a blanket, that covered the sleeping man's head. But the action did not reveal very much, for he wore an enveloping headdress that swathed his head, came down low right over his brows almost to his closed eyelids and covered the lower part of his face, ending in a fold across the bridge of his nose. He had cushioned his cheek on his leather pack and one hand was tucked under the pack as if even in sleep he would not relinquish his hold.

She stared down at her unexpected guest. What she could see of the skin around his eyes was dark, although smooth and unlined. He was a young man, then. She looked down at the hand tucked under the satchel; it was palm up, and the satchel covered it as far as the wrist. The flesh of the inside of the wrist looked pale; she could see a blue lace of veins and there was the faint bump, bump, bump of a steady, regular pulse.

This poor man is exhausted, Helewise thought.

What shall I do?

He must have come into the Abbey in the stream of those seeking our help and then crept in here once the community had left after compline. He must, she thought with a frown, reckon on waking up and slipping out before matins . . .

She was inclined to leave him. He was warmly wrapped up, he looked quite comfortable – the wooden chest would undoubtedly offer a friendlier bed than the hard stone floor – and quite obviously was in dire need of sleep. She would go to her own bed, she decided, but she would not undress. She would make sure she was up at the first stroke of the call to matins so that she could get down here first, wake him up and perhaps offer him the care of either the infirmarer if he was unwell or the refectory nuns if, as undoubtedly he would be, he was hungry.

Pleased to have resolved the small matter, she bent down to pick up her lantern.

It was some tiny difference in the man's breathing that alerted her, but it was too late: a hand shot out from the heaped garments and grabbed her wrist. The man on the chest sat up, shrugged off his blanket and cloak and swept up his other hand, in which she saw a long, curved knife. Its wicked point was a hand's breadth from her throat.

Summoning every bit of her courage, praying that her voice would not give away her fear, she said, 'I mean you no harm. I do not know how you come to be here in the church but clearly you need to sleep and I was going to leave you here until morning.'

The knife was held steady as a rock but she thought – hoped – that the man had lowered it a little.

'This is God's house and all who love him are welcome,' she went on in the same calm, level tone. 'It may be that you do not wish anyone to know you are here, in which case you could claim sanctuary and be safe from violence or arrest.'

The shadowed eyes watched her warily but still the man did not speak.

'I am sorry that I startled you,' she went on. 'It must have given you quite a jolt, to wake up suddenly from profound sleep and find someone bending over you!' She forced a laugh. 'I would have been quite terrified, under the circumstances.'

At last the man spoke. In a low, hoarse, hesitant voice that she had to strain to hear, he whispered, 'I am not afraid of you.'

'Good, that's good,' she said. She held up the lamp so that he could see her face. 'I am in holy orders, as you can see, and we are vowed to love our fellow men. We do not do them harm.'

He nodded; a quick, curt movement, his eyes fixed on hers.

'Will you not accept a more comfortable bed?' she suggested. 'There will be a nun on duty in the infirmary. I could take you there – it's not only the sick who sleep within. When they are in need, the healthy accept its comforts too.'

'*No*,' the man said in a low growl. 'I do not – I did not want anyone to know I was here.'

'But now I know,' she pointed out.

'You not tell!' he hissed.

'No, very well,' she agreed. 'But why are you here? Are you in truth in hiding? Do you wish to claim sanctuary?'

He regarded her steadily. Now the knife was pointing at her heart, although she was almost sure he had no intention of harming her. 'In hiding, yes,' he said. His eyes glittered in the light of her lamp; she could see five tiny flames reflected. Then he drew away, pulling the headdress still lower so that his eyes were in its shadow.

She thought suddenly, we could be here all night in this stand-off. She had guessed who he was and she said decisively, 'You are Fadil, aren't you? You came here to England with a monk from the Order of the Knights Hospitaller, whose prisoner you once were, and not long ago you asked a man who lives near here if you could stay in his outbuilding. You told him your name was John Damianos. Isn't that so?'

His reaction greatly surprised her. In a strange echo of Thibault's response when Josse suggested it was Fadil who turned up at New Winnowlands, this man too seemed to be amused. He went further, however, and she thought she heard a faint and muffled laugh. 'Fadil?' he said. Then, curtly, 'Fadil not here.'

'But you have been travelling with the English monk, haven't you?' she persisted. It suddenly struck her that taking this man to the infirmary was not a good idea, since Thibault and Brother Otto might well recognize their monk's companion; she said, 'Two of the runaway's brethren are looking for him. They are called Thibault of Margat and Brother Otto. They were hurt in a fire and they are recovering here in the infirmary.'

'I know,' he whispered. She tried to catch the cadence of his voice but it was difficult when he spoke so softly and huskily. She thought he was young, his voice not long broken to manhood.

'Others were hunting you too, weren't they?' She longed to put out a hand to touch him but she did not dare; he might have lowered the knife but he still held it. 'There were two Saracen warriors called Kathnir and Akhbir and they killed a man they thought was you. They tormented him before they killed him and we assume that was because they thought he – or, rather, *you* – carried a precious object that they were desperate to find.'

His eyes widened in surprise. 'You – have discovered much,' he rasped.

'We think there is a third group who hunt you,' she went on, her confidence growing. 'Men of their number are skilled with the bow. It was—' She had been about to say that one of the unknown group had killed Kathnir, but she stopped. It was not wise to reveal too much too soon.

'You think correctly,' he muttered. Then, putting down the
knife, he said, 'There is abbess here?'

'Er—' Should she tell him who she was? Again, caution
prevailed: 'Yes, that's right. Abbess Helewise.'

'She is good woman?'

How, Helewise wondered, should she answer that? 'They
say so,' she said guardedly.

'And fair? Just?'

'She would not condemn anybody without hearing what they
had to say,' she said firmly. 'Even then her inclination would
be towards mercy rather than condemnation, for she does her
best to follow in the steps of her master, Our Lord.'

'This is what I have heard,' the man whispered.

'Why do you ask?'

He looked at her for what seemed a long time. She sensed
tension in the air like crackling frost. Then he growled, 'I have
come a very long way and I have been threatened over every
mile and at every turn by these three parties. One party alone
hunts for me. The others search for the Englishman.'

'The runaway monk,' she said, wanting to be quite clear.

'He is not—' The man stopped. 'Yes.'

'Is he close by?' she whispered. Something went through
her – some strange sense of heightened awareness – as she
spoke the words. When, very slowly, the man nodded his confirm-
ation, she had the peculiar sense that she had already known.

'He cannot come here,' the man said softly. 'It is not safe.'

'Because of the presence of Thibault, yes, I understand.'

'Not—' Again he stopped. Then: 'Yes, Sister, that is so.' She
thought there was a different quality in his voice: he sounded
almost . . . regretful.

Letting her instinct guide her – after all, thinking and
reasoning did not seem to be getting her very far – she said,
'Would you like to meet the Abbess?'

There was a pause and then slowly he nodded.

'Come, then,' she said. 'I will take you to her.'

Again he shrank back. 'It is late. She will be sleeping.'

'She has been working late tonight.' That at least was the
truth. 'I will take you to her private room, where there is a
small fire and candles for light. There you may reveal to her
why you are here.'

'I cannot—' He seemed to be debating with himself. Then,

once again, he nodded. Sliding the knife into a sheath on his belt, he swung his legs down, gathered up his satchel, swirled his wide cloak around him and, jumping off the wooden chest, stood beside her.

He was perhaps her own height; possibly just a little taller, but then she was a tall woman and stood eye to eye with many men. He was lightly built and, as they moved off, she noticed that he was catlike on his feet. Even in the heavy boots he made little noise.

He told me he is not Fadil, she thought, and from his re-action I am quite sure that he is not. But he *must* be John Damianos: the style of dress, the hesitant speech of a foreigner speaking an alien tongue, it all matches. I'm pretty certain he's been brought back from Outremer and abandoned, Josse had said. Well, if this young man was in truth not Fadil then perhaps Josse had been right in the first place. The runaway monk could easily have brought a Saracen body servant with him.

They had reached the great doors and she led the way out through the smaller side door. Very aware of him walking beside her, she strode on past the infirmary and into the cloister, then along to her little room.

'Now, sit here on this stool,' she said, pushing it forward, 'and I will add firewood to the brazier. It was banked down only recently and the embers will soon ignite the new fuel.' She worked swiftly and, when the flames caught, held out her hands to the warmth, watching him out of the corner of her eye.

He was staring around him, as well he might. 'Where is she?' he demanded, careful to keep his face away from the light of the fire. 'Where is the Abbess? You said she would be here!' There was a faint but definite note of suspicion – of fear? – in the low voice.

She walked around her table and lit the candle she had been using earlier. She had brought the cresset lamp over from the church and she put it down beside the candle. She glanced at the man. He was sitting on the stool, hunched into himself. His headdress was still drawn closely around his head and she could barely see anything of his face.

This will not do, she told herself. We are circling each other like two wary dogs.

She drew out her throne-like chair and sat down. Then she

said, 'I am Abbess Helewise. Tell me who you are and what you want of me.'

Sixteen

The young man seemed to take her revelation in his stride although since she could see so little of him it was hard to tell. When he spoke it was in the same gruff voice.

'Thank you,' he said.

'For what?'

'I ask to see you. You see me.'

She inclined her head. 'You are welcome.'

He had turned away and when he spoke again, he appeared to be addressing the wall rather than her.

'I tell you of Fadil,' he announced.

It seemed an odd place to start but at least he *was* starting. 'Very well.'

'Fadil fight with Muslim army and is taken prisoner. He is beloved of man named Hisham. Hisham claim Fadil is his young brother but this is not so. Relationship is – different.' He hesitated. '*Bad.*'

'I see.' Helewise thought she knew what he meant.

'Hisham approach Knights Hospitaller and make offer to exchange Fadil for something of very great value. Knights agree and meeting in desert at night is arranged. But knights and Hisham are alike. Both wish to keep prisoner *and* ransom. Very bad things happen – I cannot describe for I not there – and Hisham is wounded and many of his servants die but Hisham very clever, very devious, and he hide more men – fighting men – and more horses out in dark desert. These men help others to kill knights. They take Hisham away to where healers treat his wounds.'

'Both parties tried to cheat?' Helewise asked.

'*Very* much at stake,' the young man said. 'Even good men will do bad things in such circumstances.'

Helewise had noticed something. Careful so as not to alert him, she said, 'The monk who survived took the prisoner – Fadil – and fled, didn't he?'

'Yes. He take ransom as well.'

She nodded. 'So Hisham sent his men Kathnir and Akhbir to chase after them and the Hospitallers sent Thibault and his companions. Both pursuing parties wanted to recapture the prisoner and take possession of the ransom. Is that not so?'

The young man turned his swathed face her way and just for an instant the light of the candle flames illuminated his eyes.

Had Helewise not been paying such close attention and waiting tensely for just such a chance, she would have missed it. As it was she saw: just a glimpse in a split second. Her suspicion was confirmed.

Whoever this young man might be, he was not a Saracen. For one thing, as he told his tale the halting speech of someone speaking an alien language vanished. For another, Helewise was fairly certain that Saracens did not have jade-green eyes. He must not know that I have seen, she thought. For some reason it is very important to him that I believe in this false identity.

'Two parties pursue, yes,' he was saying. 'But only one cares about Fadil.'

'Hisham wanted his – er, his—'

'His boy,' supplied the young man. Helewise would have sworn that he was amused by her discomfiture.

'He wanted him desperately enough to have offered something of great value in exchange,' she said.

'He did, but it was never his intention that the thing he offered would be given away. Thirty fighting men of his household hidden out in the darkness beyond the circle of light would see to that.'

'So the monk and Fadil galloped off into the night,' she resumed. 'Then what?'

'Fadil did not wish to be returned to Hisham. He had become a fighter to get away from his particular form of servitude, and when he was captured and imprisoned he hoped that by the time he was released Hisham would have found another sexual slave and forgotten all about him. When Fadil was told that Hisham was going to buy him back, he was so desperate

that he thought about taking his own life. But he did not and
in the end he was very glad, for the monk took him far away
from the desert and Fadil will never see Hisham again.'

'Where is he? What happened to him?'

'When the Knights Hospitaller were attacked and slaugh-
tered by Hisham's men, Fadil slipped to the ground and went
over to where Hisham had been lying on his divan. Hisham
was intent on the fight, so Fadil helped himself to his purse.
It contained not only a large sum of gold but also very valuable rings which Hisham had removed before he drew his knife.
Hisham has fat hands,' he added, 'and the jewels that he wears
are set in wide bands of gold, so it is hard to grip a weapon.

'Fadil made a deal with the monk, who wished to take him
back to Margat. But Fadil knew that if this happened, it would
only be a matter of time before Hisham made another attempt
to buy him back. Fadil said he would give the monk a third of
what he had stolen from Hisham in exchange for his freedom.
The monk agreed.'

'Why?' Helewise cried. 'Surely his orders were to guard the
prisoner closely and return him to his cell?'

'That is true,' agreed the young man. 'But the monk understood what was waiting for Fadil in Hisham's house and in his
bed and he did not wish to condemn him to such horror. What
Hisham did to him is a *sin*,' he added primly. 'Besides, the
monk knew that what he had in his pack was inestimably more
valuable, both to his Order and to everyone else, than any
number of prisoners.'

What he had in his pack . . . She burned to ask but the moment
was not right. 'What happened to Fadil?'

'The monk took him as far as Constantinople, where they
crossed the Bosporus together. There Fadil felt safe at last and
they parted company. Fadil had distant family in Constantinople
and he was in no doubt that they would take him in. He was
a rich man now, remember, and wealth has a way of smoothing
the road.'

'It has,' Helewise murmured. So Fadil didn't come to England,
she was thinking. Josse and I were wrong. The monk's companion
was not Fadil but this man who sits so calmly and self-assuredly
before me. 'So,' she said, carefully, 'the monk decided that whatever Hisham had offered as ransom for Fadil was too dangerous
to take to Margat or any other fortress of the Order?'

'That is true. It is— That is to say, there were good reasons why he knew he must bring it to England.'

'To the English headquarters of the Knights Hospitaller at Clerkenwell?'

He shrugged. 'Perhaps. Yes.'

'And how did you come to be travelling with him?'

'I am his manservant.' The young man bowed elegantly from the waist.

Helewise said nothing.

The young man raised his head and looked at her. She studied what she could see of the face and took in the green eyes in the smooth skin. She observed the graceful way in which he held his head. She remembered that pale, translucent skin on the inside of his wrist.

'Stand up,' she said.

Hesitantly, eyes on her all the time, he did so.

She was sure.

'Before you knew who I am I told you that the Abbess of Hawkenlye was more inclined to mercy than to condemnation,' she said quietly. 'I also said that this Abbey offers sanctuary to those who flee. That beneficence is not in my gift, for it is the same in any religious house. Unless you have done or proceed to do something that I know to be a mortal sin, I shall not advertise your presence here to those who pursue you. Even if you were to confess that you have committed some crime, then it would be to our sheriff that I would give you up, and he is a just man.'

The man's eyes had widened in alarm when Helewise had spoken of those who pursued him but as she concluded her short speech, he looked calmer. He said, 'I have done wrong, but not without dire need.'

It is as I thought, Helewise said to herself. Then, rising, she walked slowly around her table until she was standing right in front of him. Again moving unhurriedly, her movements smooth and steady, she raised her hands and began to unfasten the headdress.

There was no reaction.

She unwound what seemed like yards of cloth from around the head and presently the smooth, honey-coloured hair came into view. Then she drew the folds away from the lower face and chin. Finally, she pulled the last length of the material from where it was tucked into the top of the robe.

She looked at what she had uncovered. And, with a wry smile, a green-eyed, dark blonde and rather beautiful young woman looked back at her.

Josse left the home of Gerome de Villières early the next morning. He had been right in predicting that Gerome would not refer again to the matter that had taken Josse so urgently to his house; however, he and his womenfolk entertained Josse to such an enjoyable evening that he could not complain. Indeed, as he settled for sleep on a luxurious feather mattress with sheets of finest linen and thick, warm woollen blankets, replete after an excellent meal and some even better French wine, he realized that it had been a relief to have a few hours' rest from his abiding preoccupations. Then, of course, he felt guilty because others – Abbess Helewise, for instance – would not have been given any such respite. They certainly wouldn't have enjoyed that delicious meal and the wonderfully soft, warm bed.

As he left, Gerome came out to the courtyard to see him off. 'I wish you good luck, Josse,' he said. 'I don't know what to hope for in the case of Brother Ralf. In a way he's damned if the Hospitallers catch up with him and damned if they don't.'

'Damned?'

Gerome waved a hand. 'Not literally, or at least I pray not! No; I merely meant that if they find him they'll punish him, but if he manages to evade capture then he'll be on the run for as long as there are people out there who know what he's done.'

'*Tell* me what he's done!' Josse said.

But Gerome shook his head. 'I cannot. I—' He made a face. 'I wish to live here in peace,' he said. 'I am sorry, Josse, and no doubt you think me weak, but this house has seen enough of tragedy and I will not willingly invite it back to my door.'

'But I could—'

'*Go*, Josse!' Gerome exclaimed with a short laugh. Then, as Josse gave him a valedictory salute and edged Horace off towards the gates, he called out, 'Come and see us again!'

'I shall!' Josse called back. 'Farewell!'

He was keen to get back to Hawkenlye to tell the Abbess what he had discovered and he set Horace off at a good pace. The morning was warmer than the previous few days and the white frost that had held the earth in its hard grip had melted, except on the verges of the track that did not receive sunshine. As Horace cantered along, Josse noticed the prints of his hooves going in the other direction. He was reflecting what huge feet Horace had when he noticed something: alongside Horace's hoof prints there was another set. They were considerably smaller and their spacing suggested a horse with a shorter stride.

As he rode to Robertsbridge, somebody had been following him.

It could be innocent. Many people used that road and it was likely that another rider had been travelling behind him, bound on some independent quest. He reached the place where the narrower and lesser-used track from New Winnowlands joined the road and rode along it. Again, he found Horace's prints; again, that smaller horse had been following him, perhaps all the way from his own home . . .

He was torn. He wanted to get back to the Abbey but his curiosity was piqued. He was also perturbed. There were violent men about, and he was alone. He told himself firmly not to be a coward. Then he dismounted and, leading Horace, he retraced their journey of the day before until, about two miles from New Winnowlands, he found what he was looking for.

There were Horace's prints. And there, coming in from a path to the right of the road, were those of his pursuer. Without hesitation he mounted and turned Horace onto the path.

It did not seem to be going anywhere. He was very close to the borders of his own land yet, ashamed, he admitted to himself that he had never been this way before. It began to rain. He drew his hood up over his hat, pulling it forward to shield his face.

Open ground gave way to woodland and presently he rode through a beech grove. Giant slabs of golden-yellow sandstone stood out from the leaf-covered ground and the breeze stirred the bare branches of the trees high above him. He could not see the horse's prints and he hoped that he had not missed the place where they joined the path. Then he came to a muddy stretch of track and there they were once again.

He looked ahead and could see no dwelling; not so much as a tumbledown hovel, hut or outbuilding. Should he give up the chase? It was tempting. He might ride all morning and find nothing and he had business elsewhere.

He pulled Horace up, turned him and set off back the way he had come.

It happened as he entered the beech grove.

There was no warning, or if there was it came all but instantaneously with the sudden dread as someone jumped down from the trees onto Horace's back, put an arm around Josse's neck and said, in a surprisingly normal voice, 'Do not go for your knife for mine is already at your throat.'

Josse made himself relax. He could sense Horace tensing as he felt this new weight on his back and he reached out to pat the strong neck.

'Be still!' his assailant said.

'I am calming my horse,' Josse replied.

'Very well. But remember my blade.'

Josse felt pressure on the flesh just over his windpipe. 'I will.'

'Why are you following me?' the man demanded.

'Why were *you* following *me*?' Josse countered.

The blade was removed from his throat. There was a brief pause, then: 'Who are you? Remove your hood and let me see your face.'

He did as he was ordered. The man behind him craned forward and Josse turned to look at him.

He was staring at a man perhaps in his late twenties. He wore a faded and mud-stained robe and at his side there was a leather satchel, its strap across his chest. His light brown hair had a reddish tinge and his eyes were grey-blue. He was lean-faced, clean-shaven and around his throat and jaw he wore a grimy bandage. Josse had never seen him before but he knew who he was. He had thought he recognized the voice and now the bandage made the man's identity certain.

Which was odd, for he had been convinced that John Damianos was a Saracen.

'John Damianos,' Josse said. On the man's tunic there was the outline of a cross; the emblem had been torn off, leaving its shape in an unfaded area of the black cloth. And, as the few facts he thought he knew collapsed in little pieces around him, he added incredulously, 'Also known as Brother Ralf.'

'Sir Josse.' John Damianos sheathed his knife and slipped down off Horace's back. 'I am sorry. I followed you yesterday to Robertsbridge and I was pretty certain it was you retracing our horses' prints this morning. But you had covered your face and, although I recognized your horse, a man can steal another's mount and pretend to be someone he is not. I cannot afford to be careless.'

'I believe I understand that now,' Josse replied.

John Damianos looked up at him, the beginnings of a smile on his face. 'Won't you dismount? It makes my throat hurt like the devil to stand staring up at you.'

'Aye, I will.'

He got down and stood facing John on the soft ground of the beech grove. The rain had intensified. John said, 'We should talk, Sir Josse. I badly need a friend and I am hoping that you are one.'

'I make no promises,' Josse warned. 'I serve the purposes of both Abbess Helewise of Hawkenlye and Gervase de Gifford, sheriff of Tonbridge, and I am a King's man.'

'I know both your credentials and your reputation, Sir Josse,' John said quietly. 'Why do you think I sought refuge with you when I was in dire need?'

'I – er, I'm glad that I could help,' Josse muttered.

'I have a shelter nearby,' John said. 'Let's get out of the rain.'

'Very well.'

John set off back along the track and Josse followed, leading Horace. Soon John turned off to the left down a path that descended into the narrow valley of a stream and presently the path gave out. John pushed his way through the undergrowth and, not without difficulty, Josse and his horse followed. John, he noticed, was constantly alert, looking all around him and occasionally putting up a hand to stop them so that he could listen. Eventually they came to a clearing where a bend of the stream had all but cut off an apron of land. Close by there was a hollowed-out space in the sloping side of the valley. In it a chestnut horse was tethered.

Josse stared at the animal. It was a gelding, smaller than the large and heavy Horace and quite beautifully formed. John, observing the direction of Josse's fixed and fascinated stare, said, 'His name is Cinnabar. He comes from a land a very long way away.'

'You have ridden him all the way from Outremer?'

'I have. Lead your horse into the shelter; there is water there and a place where you can tether him.'

Josse tied Horace's reins to a stout branch. 'The human accommodation is in here,' John said, and Josse followed him to a deeper hollow, its roof formed by an outcrop of sandstone. At the entrance there was a circle of hearthstones and, just inside, firewood and a small cooking pot. There were other objects within but Josse could not make out what they were.

John indicated a couple of cross-sections of tree trunk and said, 'Sit down. It's dry in here, at least.'

'How did you know I would be there on the track?' Josse asked.

'I didn't. I realized you were going to see Gerome yesterday and thought you would remain there. I keep a regular watch up in the beech grove when I use this shelter and you just happened to ride along.'

'I saw your horse's prints following mine,' Josse said.

'Yes, I know. I was careless.'

There were so many questions that Josse wanted to ask and he did not know where to start. Begin at the beginning, he thought.

'When you came to New Winnowlands,' he said, 'you were dressed differently and I took you for a Saracen.'

'Among the men on my trail are a trio of Knights Hospitaller,' John said dryly. 'I do not have many garments other than this tunic and my Saracen disguise. Given that I knew Thibault was close, I decided on the second.'

'That decision could have cost your life,' Josse said. 'Soon after you left us, a man dressed very similarly was tortured and killed close to Hawkenlye Abbey. I thought he was you.'

John had gone very still. 'How did you discover you were wrong?'

'I explained to the Hawkenlye infirmarer that I thought the dead man was John Damianos, who had come to lodge at New Winnowlands. She had treated a man of similar appearance, and when she looked at the body she said this was not the man she had treated because *he* had a burn on his throat. So we concluded that you were the man she had treated and the dead man was someone else.'

'His name was Touros,' John said, 'and he was a Turkish mercenary. He and his two companions followed me from Antioch. Although Touros did not deserve to die in such a terrible way, it may be some consolation to you to know that had he and his companions caught me, they would have killed me without a qualm.'

'Why did you flee from New Winnowlands?' Josse was not ready to comment on what John Damianos had just said.

'Your serving woman, Ella, is Pandora reborn,' John replied. 'Her curiosity about the man in the outbuilding got the better of her, and once she told you that I wasn't there and you concluded I was in the habit of going out at night – why else would I need to sleep all day? – then I could not stay.'

It was just as Josse had thought. He nodded.

'I saw the woman approach the outbuilding,' John said thoughtfully. 'I am sorry I scared her.'

'She thought you were some sort of night spirit,' Josse said.

John laughed. 'I have been many things, but not that. Yet,' he added.

'Where did you go? What did you have to do every night?'

John looked at him. 'I can't tell you. I hope I shall be able to, but for now it is too dangerous. What you don't know, Sir Josse, you can't tell.'

'I would not betray you,' he protested.

'You might,' John said. He must have seen Josse's reaction. 'I am sorry. I mean no offence.'

'Those who murdered the Turk are both dead,' Josse said.

'Yes, I know.'

'Did you kill them?'

John turned to stare at Josse and his grey-blue eyes were clear and honest. 'No.'

'One was killed with a longbow. I think the shot was fired by one of Touros's companions and that it was in revenge for his death.'

John nodded. 'That is very likely. The men who travelled with Touros are called William and Tancred. They are Franks from Outremer. They are in the employ of a ruthless and wealthy man who wants me dead. Touros was their best weapon. They will sorely miss his prowess.'

'They made a shrine to him,' Josse said. 'They did not have his body – he was buried at Hawkenlye – but they made a special place on the edge of the forest and stuck his broken bow in the ground.'

John shrugged. 'Well, perhaps there was some sentiment there after all and Touros was more to them than a useful servant.'

'They killed a man they believed was you,' Josse said softly.

'The Hospitaller? Yes, I suspected it, and I am sorry. They must have thought Thibault had found me at Gerome's house and was taking me to Clerkenwell.'

'They murdered the Hospitaller in his bed and then set fire to the place.' Josse was not sure whether or not this would be news to John Damianos; he seemed to be remarkably well informed.

'They have their orders and they will not rest until those orders are carried out. They are commanded to hunt me down and kill me. They believed that poor, innocent monk was me and they do not waste time asking questions.'

'Do you think they have discovered their mistake? Are you still in danger from them?'

'I wish it were not so, but the answer to both of your questions is yes.'

'How do you know?' Josse demanded.

John hesitated. Then he said, 'Again, I am sorry, Sir Josse, but you will just have take my word for it. I can't tell you.'

Josse had had enough. With the Abbess's and Gerome's help, so many of the pieces of the puzzle had been fitted together. But he knew they had not reached the core of it. Thibault knew much that he was not telling them; so did Gerome; and now here was John Damianos, who seemed to be at the heart of it all, calmly saying, *I can't tell you.*

'You have led me quite a dance,' he said coolly. 'I believed you to be a Saracen travelling in the company of the Knight Hospitaller sought by Thibault. I thought he was this runaway English monk who had been at the meeting in the desert, and that you – the Saracen – were Fadil, the prisoner who was being exchanged. Now I find that you are the English monk known as Brother Ralf.'

'You called me that earlier,' John observed. 'Did Gerome tell you the name?'

'Aye. That was one of the few things he *did* tell me. Where's Fadil? He's here, isn't he? You've brought your prisoner all the way to England and you—'

'I last saw my prisoner, as you call him, in Constantinople,' John interrupted. 'Fadil wasn't my choice of a travelling companion and I was very glad to see the last of him.'

'Why did you let him go? You should have taken him back to Margat or Crac des Chevaliers!'

'I should indeed. But something strange happened out there in the desert. I had a sort of vision of what he would be going back to if we returned him to his master. I couldn't be responsible for forcing him back into that life, Sir Josse, so I took him to where he wished to go and then said goodbye.'

Josse was shaking his head. 'This is all too deep for me. You were being hunted by three separate groups, one of which we may discount because both Kathnir and Akhbir are dead; another of which is out of action while Thibault of Margat and Brother Otto lie in the infirmary at Hawkenlye recovering from their burns. Only one of these groups therefore remains, and yet you—'

'And yet I continue to be evasive and secretive and I refuse to satisfy your curiosity by telling you everything?' John's voice was bitterly angry. 'Sir Josse, one group out of three may not sound much to you and, indeed, those who would have made me suffer torment before they killed me are in their graves. But do not dismiss these Frankish mercenaries. Their purpose in searching for me so doggedly and relentlessly is what I dread the most, for—' He stopped. He watched Josse intently for a moment and then, as if he read Josse's honesty and something in him yearned to confide, he gave in. 'They are the most dangerous of my enemies, Sir Josse, because it is not only I whom they seek. There is another quarry; and if by so doing I could guarantee her life, I would willingly die.'

Seventeen

Helewise persuaded her unexpected visitor to sleep in her own private room. She offered to fetch bedding but the young woman refused. 'I am used to sleeping on hard ground and my cloak and blanket are adequate, thank you.'

'You may lock yourself in,' Helewise suggested, and the young woman looked relieved. 'I shall return first thing in the morning. I am in no doubt that you need my help and I am prepared to give it to you, if *you* in turn are prepared to explain yourself to me.' The woman had made no reply. 'Think it over,' Helewise advised. 'Sleep well.'

Then she closed the door. As she walked away she heard the key turn in the lock.

She returned shortly before prime. She had collected food and drink from the refectory and now she tapped softly on the door. 'Hello? Are you awake?'

The door opened a crack and the young woman's face appeared. Seeing Helewise, she looked relieved. As she saw what Helewise was carrying, relief turned to wide-eyed appreciation.

'That is a welcome sight, my lady Abbess,' she said politely. She was wrapping the enveloping cloak around her as she spoke and Helewise caught a glimpse of the tunic and thick woollen hose she was wearing beneath. 'I am ravenous.'

She seemed to be waiting for permission, so Helewise said simply, 'Eat.'

Despite her very evident hunger, the young woman folded her hands, closed her eyes and muttered a short prayer before falling on the bread and dried meat. Well-brought up, Helewise observed, despite the fact that she has been masquerading as a man. No doubt she has her reasons . . .

'I must go,' she said. It was time for the office. 'I will be back soon.'

The young woman hastily chewed what seemed to be a huge mouthful, managed to swallow it down and then, getting to her feet, bowed and said, 'I shall be here.' Then, looking up and meeting Helewise's eyes, she added, 'I am ready, my lady.'

Hoping very much the woman meant she was prepared to tell her story, Helewise nodded and hurried away.

She returned immediately after prime. The young woman must have been listening out for her because the door opened as Helewise approached. She entered, sat in her chair and said, 'I am listening.'

The young woman settled on the stool, the wide skirts of her cloak pooling gracefully on the stone floor around her. She had braided her long hair and arranged it neatly. She must also have used some of the water provided to wash her hands and face, for she looked almost presentable. As soon as this is over and I have heard what she has to tell me, Helewise thought, compassion stirring, I shall offer her a bath.

'I was born in Antioch,' the young woman began, 'and until recently spent all my life in that sunny land. My childhood was idyllic, for my family did not lack means and my mother ensured that I spent time each day on my formal education and also on many other lessons. I learned to ride as well as any boy and I was instructed by masters in their craft in such skills as flying a falcon and playing chess. But it all changed when childhood came to an end. As I matured, I came to realize that I was a rich heiress and that my parents, having no son, were anxious to wed me advantageously.'

'Were you an only child?' Helewise asked.

'No. I have a younger sister' – Helewise detected by the tone of voice that there was no great affection between the sisters – 'but she was not as marriageable as I, for she was an awkward child and she has grown into an introspective woman who makes little of her looks and has a spiteful and self-seeking nature. My parents soon abandoned their attempts to encourage her, for they had me,' she went on bitterly, 'and already my mother had singled out the man whom she wanted me to marry.'

'You did not care for him?'

'No, my lady Abbess, I did not care for him at all. Let me describe him to you. I was first presented to him in the summer preceding my sixteenth birthday. He was a man a little past his prime. He was a native Armenian prince of Edessa; extremely rich, extremely powerful; and an alliance between his family and mine would have been highly advantageous to my father.'

'I did not realize there were such marriages between the Christians and the local nobility.'

'Indeed so, my lady. Moreover, this prince – his name is Leo Rubenid Anavarza – is Christian and many such as he take wives from the ranks of the Frankish settlers. For some, the main attraction is the money,' she added. 'There are many among the local nobility, as you call them, who try to survive and maintain their dignity and their position on a title alone. I speak as one who knows,' she added, 'for before my mother enticed Leo Rubenid into her web, many such men were paraded in front of me.'

'What did he look like, this Leo?' Helewise asked, drawn to the story.

She smiled. 'He was squat and swarthy. When we met, it was clear that I was considerably taller than him, and the next time he came he must have been wearing wedges in his shoes for suddenly he was only a hand's breadth shorter.' The smile developed into a laugh. 'Even that was barely noticeable, for he wore a ridiculous puffed-up hat that added inches but also gave the impression that he had an abnormally huge head.'

She laughed again, a happy, musical sound. Then her face fell. 'My lady, when I picture him now I see a figure of fun but, believe me, he is far from that. I *could* have persuaded myself that marriage to a man old enough to be my father with greasy hair, a sweaty, pockmarked face, several missing teeth and extremely bad breath was tolerable. There were advantages, after all; I would be a princess, I would be given the best of everything and my life would be one of pampered idleness. But I discovered something about Leo Rubenid that turned him in the blink of an eye from someone I just *might* have married into a man whom I would not have touched had he been the last man on earth and the survival of the human race up to the two of us.'

'Goodness!' Helewise exclaimed. 'Whatever was it?'

'I discovered that he was a monster,' the young woman said calmly. 'Let me tell you a little more about him. He was fifteen years older than me and he came from a family of many brothers. He had been wed before; he married young and his wife gave him four sons with a reputation for troublemaking. One took offence at some remark made by a prostitute in Ayas and he sliced off her lips. Another tried to raise a mercenary force to fight against his own father. These men and their brothers would have been my stepsons, even though I was but a year older than the eldest. My lady, you will have noted one factor in my mother's choice of a husband for me?'

'Yes,' Helewise answered. 'The preponderance of boy children in Leo's line, which your mother must have hoped would spread to your own family when you wed.'

'Yes, quite right. Leo was always son-hungry. His wife died giving birth to a fifth son conceived much too soon after the birth of the fourth. But Leo Rubenid is not a man to take a doctor's or a midwife's word that his wife has suffered internal

injuries which must heal before he beds and impregnates her
again. Had I agreed to marry him, he would have swept me
off to his fortress in Cilicia, which is a hundred miles north-
west of my family's home and a turbulent land in which a
cauldron of races and religions bubbles in constant enmity.
Dwellings must be like Leo's, for the only way to survive is
behind high, stout walls. There is no urban sophistication whatsoever. Once inside my husband's castle, there I should have
stayed, reclining on my silken cushions and listening to the
fountains splash into their copper bowls, all the time waiting
for the moment when I should be summoned to my husband's
side. To his bed.' She looked down.

'You said you discovered that he was a monster?' Helewise
prompted.

'Yes; yes, I did.' The young woman seemed reluctant to go
on. But then she raised her head and said, 'There was a boy
in my father's employ. He was very sweet, very young – well,
about my age, in fact, but he had not had my sophisticated
childhood – and he was a jongleur. You know what that is, my
lady?'

'An entertainer, I believe.'

'Yes. The jongleurs are professional entertainers who sing,
play instruments, dance, tumble and juggle. The boy of whom
I speak was a lute-player, a singer and a poet. He made up his
own songs and he was very popular, for often the songs poked
gentle fun at the great and the good. He—' She blushed suddenly
and once again looked down. 'He thought he was in love with
me, my lady. He wrote a love song for me, and when I made
it clear that although I was flattered I did not and could not
love him, he wrote another song that was a thinly veiled attack
on Leo Rubenid.' Her voice was shaking. 'Leo got to hear about
it – any number of his obsequious friends and acquaintances
would have made sure of it – and his men waylaid my little
lute-player as he ran an errand for my mother late one night.
His body was found the next day. They had cut off his hands,
my lady, and stuffed them in the opposite sleeves, as if to
emphasize that he would never play the lute again. Then, so
that he would never sing again either, they slit his throat.'

Helewise sat in stunned silence. Then she said, 'You are in
no doubt that Leo Rubenid was behind this atrocity?'

'None at all. Without actually admitting anything, he made

sure I knew that he ordered it and witnessed it. It was horrible!'
She dropped her face in her hands and her shoulders shook
with silent sobs. Then, recovering, she straightened up and said,
'Would *you* have accepted such a man as your husband?'

'Of course not.' An image of her dear Ivo swam before
Helewise's eyes. 'My husband was a very different man and I
loved him dearly.' Noticing a sudden spark of interest in the
young woman's face, she added firmly, 'But we are not here
to speak of him. Could you not persuade your parents that Leo
Rubenid was unsuitable? Surely if you had told them what you
knew they would have viewed him with new eyes?'

'My father, yes; for he has always been inclined to listen
to me and believe what I say. But my mother had made up
her mind and nobody, not even my father, can divert her from
her path once that has happened. She is not a bad woman, my
lady; it is simply that she sets herself a task and she *will
achieve* that task, even when she realizes it was not the wise
course she initially believed it to be. She is a very strong
woman. She would say, I am sure, that she has had to be for
she has borne a greater weight of responsibility for her family,
its lands and its possessions than many a man.'

'That is very often the case,' Helewise remarked. 'We are
spoken of in disparaging terms as the weaker sex, the fragile
vessel, and men proceed with their wars and their squabbles
without so much as discussing them with us, never mind actually inviting our opinion. Yet do we not also live in this world?
Should we not be a party to what is done upon it?'

'Of course we should,' the young woman said firmly. 'As
for being weak and fragile, what about giving birth? I'd like
to see a man do that without yelling for his mother.'

Helewise smiled. 'So, you pleaded not to marry Leo Rubenid
but your mother said you must?' She wanted to hear the rest
of the story.

'Yes. I do not know how it would have ended – I hope I
would have had the courage to *kill* myself rather than take that
man as my husband – but something happened and suddenly
everything changed.'

'What was it?'

'I fell in love. It was very swift and, as I said, afterwards
absolutely *nothing* was as it had been. Then I understood what
being married to someone really meant and, because I loved

my man totally and with all my heart, body and soul, I *knew* I would rather die than marry Leo Rubenid.'

'Who was the man?'

'He was a knight. He had come out to Outremer to fight for his lord's kin against the Saracen threat. His lord had abandoned the fight and he, wishing to continue, went off to ally himself with a military order.'

'The Knights Hospitaller,' Helewise said. 'My dear, I know something of this tale and, although I have not met him, I believe I know the identity of your man.'

'*Do* you?' breathed the young woman. Then she shook her head quickly and in a different tone said, 'Yes, he offered his services to the Hospitallers and they were grateful to accept him. But later he encountered his lord again and the lord was very sick, so he escorted him back to the home of his kin. That was my home, my lady, in Antioch. My mother is a cousin of this sick lord and she and her ladies nursed him back to health. While this was going on, I had met my knight and we had fallen in love.'

'He was a vowed monk!' Helewise was shocked. 'He had no business falling in love with anyone, especially the delicate young daughter of his lord's kinswoman!'

'He was not,' the young woman said levelly.

'Not what?'

'He fought *with* the Knights Hospitaller and he took a name in religion; he was known as Brother Ralf. But he was not *of* them. He did not take his vows.'

Helewise wondered whether this was the truth. Was it not all rather convenient, that she should fall in love with a man she believed to be a monk, only to discover that he wasn't?

The woman seemed to read her thoughts. 'I *am* telling the truth, my lady. I give you my word.'

But I do not know you, Helewise thought. Your word may be worthless. 'So you and this Brother Ralf ran away together?'

'Not then. For three years we were mostly apart and we tried to live our own lives. He was fighting with his warrior monks; I was desperately trying to create new reasons why I should not yet proceed with my marriage to Leo Rubenid. He – my knight – visited me quite frequently, for his lord was still living in my house and he was permitted to attend him. We used to wonder if the magic would fade away during the long periods when we had to be apart but it never did; in fact our love grew. Then we learned that King Richard was sailing for home and our kinsman announced he would go too. There was no more reason for my lover to come to my home and we did not know what to do.'

Helewise had a dozen questions buzzing in her head but she said nothing. The narrative was compelling and she did not want to interrupt.

'Then,' the young woman went on, 'the man known as Brother Ralf was selected for a secret mission. There was a young prisoner of the Hospitallers called Fadil who was to be ransomed back to his master. Only the payment for him was not gold or coin; it was something far more valuable and potentially very dangerous. The prisoner's family had no intention of parting with this precious thing and the Hospitallers were planning to keep both prisoner *and* payment. Of the monks, Brother Ralf alone survived. He fled across the desert with Fadil and he had the ransom in his satchel. He knew he had to keep it out of the hands of all of those who so badly wanted it; he must take it so far away that they would *never* find it. He came for me, my lady, for he had to leave Outremer and go back to England, never to return. He could not go without me and one night he was there in the little courtyard below my window, and he said I must put on travelling clothes and steal a pair of stout boots, then pack up just a small bag for we had to travel fast and far.'

'And that is what you did?' Helewise was incredulous. 'You abandoned your home and your family and you left?'

'I loved him; I love him now,' she said, her face softened by emotion. 'Yes. I packed, dressed in my riding clothes and my travelling cloak, took my horse, my knife and my weapon and, before anyone even knew he was there, I joined him and off we went.

'We rode by night and hid by day and in about a month we reached Constantinople, where as I told you we said farewell to Fadil. Lord, what a relief – I've never known anyone complain like Fadil! Brother Ralf and I had everything to lose if we were caught but so did Fadil, for he would have been returned to Hisham and Hisham would have found exquisitely awful ways of punishing him for running away. Yet, despite that, he constantly moaned that he was hungry, he was tired, it was uncomfortable to ride for such long hours at a stretch and why did we have to ride at night in the dark?' She smiled. 'The three of us shared a farewell meal in Constantinople, which Fadil paid for, and what a feast it was! After a month on short rations, it was wonderful to eat such delicacies and we wolfed them down. I paid for my greed, though. I was sick as a poisoned dog all night.'

Helewise liked the young woman's frankness. 'So then it was just you and Brother Ralf on the long road home?'

'Yes. A month to get from Antioch to Constantinople; two years to travel from there to our eventual destination. It has been a hard journey, my lady.'

That, thought Helewise, was an understatement if ever she had heard one. 'You must have been frightened sometimes,' she said. 'You knew you were being followed.'

'We did and I was,' the young woman agreed. 'Brother Ralf was incredible. He developed an instinct for danger – perhaps it is common among fighting men; I do not know – and for the most part he led us safely. By the time we reached Greece we had identified the three groups who were on our trail and Ralf thought our best bet was to take ship across to the kingdom of Naples and then make our way up through the Papal States to Lombardy and north across the mountains. We found a ship but we were caught in a storm and blown ashore on the island of Sicily. We had to stay there for almost three months because, of all the evil luck, one of the groups pursuing us had also ended up on Sicily and we had to hide till they left.'

'I am amazed that these separate parties who pursued you did not lose you on the road,' Helewise said.

'They frequently did,' the young woman replied. 'We didn't reach England via the same route. But it wouldn't have worried any of them if they did lose us because they knew where we were going. They were all aware of Brother Ralf's English origins and they knew where he was bound.'

'Then why did you not make for a different destination? You could surely have evaded your pursuers and settled in some foreign land, safe from capture?'

'We could have done, except that there was an imperative reason why Brother Ralf had to come here.'

'Because he—'

But with an apologetic smile the young woman interrupted. 'I cannot tell you, my lady. I am sorry.'

Helewise wondered why not. She thought for a few moments and then said, 'There were the two Saracens sent by Hisham after Fadil and the ransom, the trio of Knights Hospitaller hunting their runaway monk, and who else?' She thought she already knew the answer.

'Leo Rubenid is not a man to suffer an insult in meek silence. As soon as he discovered his betrothed had fled with her lover, he selected two of his most ruthless and efficient Frankish mercenaries – their names are William and Tancred – and a Turkish bowman called Touros to go with them. It was this trio who landed on Sicily and, for me anyway, they presented the worst threat.'

'Naturally so, for they would have taken you back to Leo and to a marriage you did not want.'

The young woman was watching her, one eyebrow slightly raised. 'It would not have been marriage that awaited me, my lady,' she said. 'Leo would only accept a virgin bride, and the moment he discovered I'd had a lover he would not have wanted me any more. He would, however, have been determined to punish me. He would have made sure nobody knew he'd captured me and then he would have offered me to his men and watched as one by one they raped me. Then he would have had what was left of me sent down to one of the brothels on the coast and ordered some whoremaster to chain me up in a very small cupboard for the exclusive use of those men who were too diseased and too repulsive for the other prostitutes.'

'You – how can you know this?' Helewise whispered.

'Because that is what he did to the girl he wished to marry before me when he found out that *she* had taken a lover.'

'And still, knowing this, your parents were keen for you to marry him?' she asked incredulously.

'They did not know it, my lady. Please do not think worse of them than you probably do already.'

'How did you find out?'

'It was I who was being forced to marry him; it was up to me to discover all that I could about him and so I found people who, for a price, would root out such things. As I told you just now, I kept hoping that I would come up with something that would change my mother's mind, and indeed I suppose I did, only it became irrelevant because I fled with – with Brother Ralf.'

A look of intense sadness crossed her face. Helewise believed she knew its cause and she got up and stood by over the young woman, putting out her hand. After a moment, it was grasped and tightly held.

'Your mother would understand if she knew the truth,' she said gently.

'I keep hoping so,' the woman said. 'I torment myself with the thought that my mother and my dear father believe me to be an impulsive ingrate who abandoned them without a backward glance.'

'If you love them and they you, then they will feel in their hearts that cannot be true.' Helewise squeezed the hand and the young woman squeezed back; her grip was surprisingly strong. 'They have known you all the years of your life. Their understanding of you will have told them what you are and I believe they will be well aware that whatever made you run away, you had no choice.'

There was a short silence. Then: 'Thank you, my lady. Your words console me.'

Helewise returned to her chair, moving slowly and giving the young woman time to recover herself. When once more she was seated, she considered what she was about to say. Then, meeting the young woman's eyes, she began, 'I do not suppose that you are aware of it, but there are two Hospitallers lying in the infirmary here. They are the surviving members of the group that followed your Brother Ralf all the way from the desert outside Margat. One thing puzzles me: if Brother Ralf was not an avowed monk in their Order, why should they have gone to such lengths to try to catch him and punish him? Did they not know that he had not taken his vows?'

The young woman's green eyes were steady and she did not look away. She said, 'Thibault of Margat knew all about Brother Ralf. He was well aware that in fleeing Outremer Ralf had committed no crime against the Knights Hospitaller.' She leaned forward, her expression intense. 'My lady, it is not Brother Ralf that the Knights Hospitaller want so desperately to get their hands on. It is what he carries with him.'

Eighteen

'So just who is it,' Josse demanded, 'these Frankish mercenaries whom you fear so much wish to find?'

John Damianos looked into his eyes. 'She is the daughter of Gerome's kinswoman Aurelie and her husband, Count Hugo of Tripoli. She was betrothed to a man who regarded her already as his wife and whose men, if they find us, will kill me and take her back to Outremer and to the very worst sort of captivity.' He paused, then added softly, 'Her name is Paradisa.'

Several pieces of the puzzle fell into place. Josse said, 'So, in addition to the other reason for your flight from Outremer – to take your prisoner to safety and deliver up the treasure to whoever you thought should receive it – you also had to ensure that this Paradisa escaped from her would-be husband.'

'Correct,' said John Damianos. 'I love her,' he added.

Josse grinned. 'So I imagine.' Then – for this was no time for levity – 'Where is she?'

'There is an abandoned house deep in the Great Forest,' John replied. 'We came across it when we were making for Hawkenlye Abbey, where I had to go because – where I was hoping to have my wound treated.' Josse was sure he had been on the point of saying something else but he did not press the matter. 'We found a key and let ourselves into the undercroft. We knew we were doing wrong and had no business living in someone else's house, even in the undercroft, but we were careful and we kept it very clean and tidy. We intend to—'

'When did you last see Paradisa there?' Josse interrupted.

'Three days ago,' John replied. 'I left her while I sought another hiding place – this place – and I told her I'd return as soon as I had found somewhere.' There was sudden anxiety in his eyes. 'Why do you ask?'

'I have been to the house in the woods,' Josse said. 'I followed Akhbir there early in the morning the day before yesterday.'

John Damianos shot to his feet and grasped Josse by the collar. 'You let Akhbir escape? How could you be so careless? Dear God, but I must get to her—' He lunged out of the shelter but Josse grabbed his arm and held him tight.

'*Wait*, John!' he cried. 'Listen. Akhbir knew where the house was. Either he followed your tracks or he had already discovered it. Anyway, he was striding up to it when he was shot and killed by a bolt from a crossbow.'

John had subsided. He looked at Josse, his eyes wary. 'He's dead? You are absolutely sure?'

'Aye, I swear it's true. I returned the next day and discovered someone had buried his body in the woods. I too found the key but the undercroft was empty. The hearthstones were still warm so whoever had been there cannot have long gone.'

John said nothing.

'John, you must tell me what has happened!' Josse cried, exasperated. 'Who shot the crossbow bolt? I am quite prepared to believe it was in self-defence, or rather in defence of Paradisa, but who is it that's such a deadly shot? He was confident enough in his skills to fire a couple of warning shots that landed far too close to me for comfort.' Still John did not speak. 'Tell me! Who is guarding Paradisa while you are away?'

John raised his face and looked straight at Josse. 'Nobody. It's just the two of us, as it has been all the way from Constantinople.'

'Then who fired the shots?'

'Paradisa.'

'But she – she's a woman!'

John smiled suddenly. 'Indeed she is,' he murmured.

'Women can't fire crossbows! It's unheard of!'

'*You* might not have heard of it, Sir Josse. Paradisa was born into a family that longed for sons and she was encouraged in activities traditionally reserved for boys. Her father bought her a falcon and she was taught how to fly it. She also wields a knife very effectively and a foot soldier who came out with the crusaders was employed to teach her how to use the crossbow.'

Josse was shaking his head in disbelief. 'She killed Akhbir,' he muttered. 'Killed him stone dead with a bolt through the heart!'

'Good for her.' John Damianos's tone was rough. 'He would have killed her, had she not fired the first shot.'

'Aye, I realize that,' Josse said hurriedly. 'I do not question the action, John. It is merely that I am staggered to learn whose hands performed it.'

'She is strong,' John said, his tense face relaxing into a smile. 'In many ways any man's equal. But we must find her, Josse!' He leapt off in the direction of the horses. 'She is probably back at the house,' he called back, 'but I have been away from her much too long. Come!'

As they rode, Josse turned over in his mind where this woman with the romantic name might have gone if – as he strongly suspected – they did not find her at the house in the woods. She will have fled, he thought, because she'll reason that if Akhbir managed to find her there, then others – specifically, the Frankish mercenaries so dreaded by John Damianos – might do so as well. She may have made her way to Hawkenlye Abbey, he thought hopefully, encouraging Horace to a fast canter as he pounded behind John Damianos. She'd have known of its existence because John obviously did: he went there to have his wound treated. What terrible conflict caused that frightful burn? Josse had no idea. Had there been an attack by one of the pursuing parties? He could not imagine how such a wound could be inflicted . . .

Paradisa would know she would be safe at the Abbey. Even if she had learned that the Knights Hospitaller were in the infirmary, surely she had nothing to fear from them? It was their runaway monk they were concerned with, not her. Anyway, she would be aware of the rules of sanctuary. If she hid in the Abbey church then the Abbess and the Hawkenlye community would uphold her right not to be taken away.

So she might have gone to the Abbey. But there was another possibility: on her way there, Paradisa might have encountered the forest people. They would have been aware of her – they always knew when Outworlders were in the forest – and might have offered to help her and take her in. Josse was trying not to be specific about just which forest dweller it might have been who had acted so kindly. He was all too aware that such an action was typical of Joanna.

They reached the forest fringes and rode in under the trees. John Damianos appeared to know a different route to the old house. It was the slightest of paths, heavily overgrown, and Josse, following him, had to lie right down against Horace's neck to avoid being clawed out of the saddle by low branches.

They reached the clearing and rode up the rise to the house. John swiftly dismounted and ran to the undercroft. He reached up for the key, turned it and, pushing the door open, looked inside. Almost instantly he closed and locked the door again, replacing the key. Then he ran round to the outbuilding and quickly reappeared.

'She's gone,' he said. Then, in a tight voice suggesting he was controlling his emotions only with great difficulty, 'Where is she?'

'She may have gone to Hawkenlye Abbey,' Josse said re-assuringly. 'She would not have felt safe here after Akhbir came to the house and she would have realized the Abbey was a place that you knew too and where you might reasonably expect her to go.'

'Yes, that makes sense,' John agreed. Mounting up, he said, 'Is there a way through the forest?'

Josse hesitated. There *was* a way and he was fairly confident of finding it; he knew the forest better than most Outworlders. But the forest people did not like people tramping through their territory, and for personal and very good reasons he did not wish to offend them.

But a young woman's life could be in danger.

'Aye, there is,' he said decisively. 'Follow me.'

It was difficult riding through the heart of the forest, although progress was easier than it would have been when the trees were in full leaf. The sense of trespass – of assault – was increased by riding a large horse through the secret, sacred groves. Josse's senses were heightened. Very aware that the forest people knew he and John Damianos were there, he maintained a careful watch ahead, around and, at first, behind him. Then John, obviously realizing the need for caution even if he did not understand the reason, said very quietly, 'I will guard our rear.'

They rode on.

They were deep in the forest now, riding a path where nobody went save the forest dwellers. Joanna's hut was away to the left.

Josse wondered if she was there. Did she know *he* was there, riding stealthily through her domain on a mission in which a young woman's life was at stake? He spoke to her silently. *Help us, Joanna. We do not come here for any frivolous reasons but to look for Paradisa. If you find her, look after her. Please, Joanna, help us all. Do not let any harm come to us.*

And he thought he heard her voice. She said, *Ahead, on your right!*

He jerked Horace's head to his left, and the arrow that would have pierced Josse's throat embedded itself harmlessly in a birch tree.

Josse slid off Horace's back and ran for the meagre shelter of the stand of birches, drawing his sword as he ran and yelling out to John, 'Enemy on the right! Arrow fire!'

John was already off his horse and crashing through the undergrowth to join him. 'Get behind me,' he panted, 'it's me they want, not you!'

But Josse had scented the fight and would not stand down. 'We'll face them together,' he replied.

John gave him a quick, flashing grin and then side by side they turned to face their enemy.

It would be a fight to the death: Josse knew it instinctively. There were only two men who would have attacked them there in the forest and he knew who they were before a glance at the arrow confirmed it.

'William and Tancred,' hissed John. He pointed to two dark, cloaked outlines, just visible through the trees. 'William is on the right – he is the taller and the better shot.' Two more arrows came whistling towards them. 'They are pinning us down,' John said softly. 'They are probably unsighted, merely making sure we stay where we are.'

'What weapons have you?' Josse asked.

John held up his sword. 'This, and my knife. You?'

'The same. No bow, unfortunately.'

They waited.

They could hear the sound of stealthy movement. The Frankish mercenaries were coming closer.

Josse moved very quietly until most of his body was sheltered by a birch tree; John did the same. 'Keep them in sight,' Josse said, 'and keep the tree trunk between you and them. If we can frustrate their attempts to kill us by arrow shot, eventually they will have to close in and then we shall have our chance.'

It was dreadful, he thought, to listen to arrows fly past. The narrow birch trunk was not as wide as his shoulders and he tried to stand sideways. An arrow grazed the top of his arm; almost instantly the blood began to flow. He made himself ignore the sudden burning pain. The Franks were closer now. Did they know *exactly* where he and John were? Had they lined up their sword points on the very two trees behind which they were hiding?

He leaned forward very, very cautiously and looked.

The shorter of the two Franks stood ten paces away. He was not looking at Josse's tree; he, like his companion, was closing on the one John stood behind. Both had drawn their swords.

They are going for him, Josse thought. They know precisely where he is and they will lunge at him, one on each side, and he will not stand a chance.

He let the two men come closer. Closer. He did not dare keep a constant watch in case they saw him, for then he would lose the advantage of surprise.

Six paces away now. Five. Four.

With a yell Josse leapt out from behind his tree, his sword in his right hand and his long dagger in his left. The two Franks spun to face him and as his weapons met their swords John rushed out and leapt in to the attack.

They were wrongly paired, Josse thought. He was the heavier and slightly taller man and should have taken on the bigger of the two Franks, but it was too late now. John must look after himself; very soon Josse realized that he had more than enough in his hands with the smaller Frank. He knew he was matched with a swordsman who was at least his equal.

Again and again Josse defended himself from the savage swipes. There just did not seem to be an opportunity to turn defence into attack. Josse felt his enemy's sword slice into his arm just below where the arrow had scorched it and hot agony shot through him. He was losing blood fast now and he could feel himself weakening . . . Then, lunging forward for the kill, the Frank trod on the end of a dead branch and flipped its opposite end up into his face; it did no more than halt him for a split second, but it was enough. Josse dropped his knife, took his sword in both hands and, raising it high in the air, brought it down on his opponent's head.

The skull sliced open under the huge assault and the Frank fell dead on the ground.

Swiftly Josse turned towards John. He was hard-pressed, but he was skilled and he was fighting like a bear. Steadily he pushed his adversary back.

The Frank risked a glance over to where his companion had been fighting. His eyes widened as he took in the dead body and the ghastly wound to the head.

Then, with a howl, he turned and ran.

'We must run after him! *Come on!*' shouted John. Josse had slumped against a tree; John tried to pull him up.

Josse looked up at him. He had a long cut above his left eye and blood was pouring down his face. He had also taken a wound across the front of his right shoulder and that too was streaming blood. Already his face was ashen.

Josse felt in no better shape. He was intensely grateful that their opponent had not appreciated how weakened both of them were, for he knew that neither he nor John was capable of fighting even one determined assailant.

And he also knew that he couldn't *run* anywhere.

He clutched at John's wrist as the young man attempted to get him to his feet. 'No,' he said. 'No, John. We are both hurt and we must seek help before we hunt for him.'

'He will go after Paradisa! We have to find him before he gets to her!' John shouted.

'Aye, I know that and we will go after him, you have my word, as soon as we stop bleeding.'

John's pallor had increased and suddenly he sat down beside Josse. He put up a hand to wipe his face and then looked in amazement at it; it was covered in blood. Then he glanced down at his tunic, saturated with glistening red. 'Oh, God,' he muttered.

'Can you mount your horse?' Josse asked.

'Yes.' John sounded determined.

'Very well. Come with me. I know someone close at hand who will help us.'

They went slowly over to the horses. Horace and the chestnut stood together, pacing nervously, ears laid flat against their heads. Josse was not sure which out of him and John was supporting the other. They managed to clamber onto their horses' backs and then, praying that she would not only be there but be prepared to treat them, slowly Josse led the way to Joanna's hut.

Sometimes he had trouble finding it. Sometimes he could not locate it at all. But today perhaps she felt his desperate need and helped him, for he rode straight to it.

He drew rein in the clearing and fell off Horace's back, and she was there to catch him. He sensed her helping him as he collapsed to the ground and then she went to John and held out her arms to him.

It was odd, but Josse thought he saw a look of recognition on her face as she looked up at John Damianos. Perhaps she knew he was on his way, too, he thought dreamily. He would not have been surprised if she had seen both of them in her scrying bowl . . . He closed his eyes.

But there was no rest yet. All too soon she was back, pulling and dragging at him, saying breathlessly that he and his friend must come inside before shock combined with the wet ground and the cold made them even more unwell than they already were. And, although movement was agony, he knew she was right.

She laid them on the floor of the hut beside the central hearth. Where was Meggie? Josse wondered. He looked around for his daughter and saw her peering down from the bedding platform above his head. She whispered joyfully, '*Josse!*' and he said, 'Hello, little Meggie.'

Joanna must have decided that John's wounds were the more serious for, having given both men some hot, herbal-smelling drink that she had hastily prepared, she turned her attention to him. Josse was quite content to lie there in the warmth of the fire with a blanket over him and a soft pillow under his head. The pain in his wounds was already lessening – bless Joanna for her magic remedies! – and he was feeling relaxed and muzzy. When Meggie took advantage of her mother's preoccupation with her patient and crept down the ladder to cuddle up to her beloved father, his happiness was complete.

Nineteen

Josse awoke to the dim dawn light. He was still lying beside the hearth. Joanna must have got up during the night to put on more firewood, for there was still plenty of warmth from the glowing embers. He stretched carefully, closing his wounded left arm into a fist and opening it again, then raising the arm a few inches. There was pain – quite a lot of it – but its sharp edge was absent. He would, he decided, begin using the arm as soon as the cut began to heal.

He glanced across at John Damianos. He was still asleep and the long cut above his eye had been closed with a row of small stitches. On his shoulder a thick dressing was held in place by a bandage wrapped around his chest. Yesterday's frightening pallor was gone.

Josse lay on his back looking up at the ceiling. The smell was unique: he would have known blindfold that he was in Joanna's hut. It was a blend of all the plants she used for her remedies and not at all unpleasant; rather the reverse. He could not see Joanna on the sleeping platform but one of Meggie's feet was sticking over the edge. He smiled. Perhaps she would come down to him when she woke. He was vaguely aware that she had stayed with him for much of the night, curled up against him like a kitten, but at some point Joanna must have—

The night. Something happened during the night. What was it? *Think!*

There had been a noise – a crashing noise, quite close – and he had tried to go and investigate, only his head had swum so badly he had thought he would be sick. Then Joanna had said calmly, 'It is nothing. We are safe here. I will go and see.' She had briefly gone outside then, returning, closed the door and said softly, 'Go to sleep, Josse. There is nothing to worry about.'

Still fighting the nausea, he had been all too willing to obey. Now, with the morning approaching, it was a different matter.

Very cautiously he raised his head and, when that seemed to be all right, levered himself into a sitting position. So far, so good. He pushed back the soft blanket and got up into a crouch. There was a stab of protest from his wounded arm and for a moment he felt dizzy, but both sensations passed. Then he stood up.

He found that as long as he put a hand on something solid to steady himself, he could move quite well. He opened the door and stepped outside into cool air, a rapidly brightening sky and a day that promised a mild breeze from the west and perhaps rain. He looked around, smiling involuntarily at the scene before him. Joanna must work incredibly hard, he reflected, for even now she had obviously been busy in her little patch. The beds were clear of weeds and dead vegetation, the paths between them swept and the grass verges neatly clipped. The fruit trees and bushes had been pruned so that waving branches did not catch the winter winds and damage the plants as they were torn off. Everywhere spoke of her careful husbandry and he—

The horses had gone.

Joanna had told him last night that she had removed their tack and put them in a hazel-hurdle corral. It had not sounded very secure but he had been too far gone in pain and drug-induced confusion to care. At some time during the night – he remembered the crashing – they must have pushed their way through the hurdles. But Joanna had gone to check! Why on earth had she not reported that the horses were missing? Because she knew you would get up and try to catch them, answered his logic, and she knew you were nowhere near up to it.

She could have gone, he thought disloyally.

He went back inside the hut.

Joanna was awake, leaning on one elbow and watching out for him. 'I did not go after them because I knew they were safe,' she said softly; both John and Meggie were still asleep.

'How can you be so sure?' he whispered back. 'There are all manner of strange beings in this forest, including the man who put those savage cuts on *him*.' He nodded in the direction of John Damianos.

'It was not he who was close by last night.' Joanna spoke with such certainty that he believed her. 'I know who it was, though, which is why I said we were safe. He was patrolling among the trees, guarding us. He was curious about the horses, for as you probably know my people do not have a great deal to do with them, although we greatly respect them because one of our Great Ones is revered in the form of a white horse.'

'Aye, that's as maybe, but are they safe?' he demanded.

She smiled. 'Perfectly safe. As I was saying, the being outside was curious about them and he probably called to them.'

'I did not hear any call!'

'No, dearest Josse, you wouldn't have done, for it would have gone directly to their minds. They too were undoubtedly curious about him, which was why your old Horace pushed his way out of my admittedly inadequate pen and went to have a look, and the other horse followed.'

'He's called Cinnabar. He's John's horse.' It was about the only thing Josse could think of *to* say.

'Well, Horace and Cinnabar probably had a fine time with our guardian, then I expect they ambled off to look for food. Your Horace knows the Abbey well, doesn't he?'

'Aye.'

'Then that'll be where he's gone, and Cinnabar with him. Don't worry, Josse – ' she swung her legs over the edge of the sleeping platform and jumped down – 'they'll be quite all right. When you leave, I'll help you carry the saddles and bridles to the edge of the forest.'

'They're heavy,' he said dully. It was better to think about the practicalities. The alternative was to contemplate going away from her again so soon and that hurt, especially when he hadn't even seen his daughter yet this morning.

'I will manage,' she said. She added, with an attempt at a smile, 'And you each have one good side with which to bear a load.'

Their eyes met. To his joy he saw an answering regret in hers. He knew that she too was wishing this day was going to be just for the three of them.

'Come back soon,' she whispered. 'We will be waiting for you; I promise.'

She did not make promises lightly. With a grin that seemed to spread all by itself, he nodded.

'Now,' she said, 'I am going outside to wash and then I shall prepare medicine, food and drink, and have a look at my patients' wounds.'

*   *   *

Josse and John both drank more of Joanna's pain-killing brew, although Josse – who had been given her remedies before – detected that this morning the element that had sent them so deeply asleep last night was absent. Joanna inspected the cut above John's eye and then she lifted the dressing on his shoulder, sniffing at it.

'Recently I have not had the chance to bathe as thoroughly as I would like,' John said, clearly embarrassed, 'for which I apologize, my lady.'

She looked up at him and smiled. 'My name is Joanna,' she said, 'and I am not sniffing at you but at your wound. There is a particular smell when infection is present and, if I detected it on you, I should have to do something about it. But it isn't there. This wound, and the one over your eye, are both clean.'

'Oh. Oh, I see.' John was looking at her with interest. 'I have seen Arab doctors with their patients,' he said. 'They too place this emphasis on keeping a wound clean and they even go so far as to wash their hands and instruments in a special solution before and after they examine a patient!'

Joanna was nodding. 'Yes, I have heard that their skills are far ahead of those of the West. Have you noticed anything else?'

'Well,' he said after a pause, 'I was told that they use maggots in an infected cut, although surely that can't be true?'

'It probably is,' she replied. 'You have observed maggots on dead meat?'

'Ye-es,' he admitted. Josse, watching, hid a smile. He remembered very well his own reaction when he had first encountered Joanna's extraordinary ideas.

'Well, a severe wound may contain flesh that is dying because of infection. The maggots clean out the wound by consuming the pus and the putrid flesh, leaving a clean space for new, healthy skin to grow.'

John looked quite sick. 'I see,' he said faintly. Then, rallying, 'I am even more relieved, then, that you smell no infection in my shoulder.'

Joanna laughed. 'I do not use maggots. I would take it as an affront to my medical skill if any patient of mine needed them. Now I am going to look at you, Josse.'

Josse felt the familiar touch of her fingers and winced as she gently probed the wound. It too had been stitched. 'No infection there either, my dear love,' she said in satisfaction.

She called me *my dear love*, he thought. John Damianos heard and now he is watching us with a rather peculiar look on his face. Why? Simple human curiosity? Maybe; only why should Josse have received the distinct impression that for some reason he disapproved?

It was puzzling.

I am not ashamed of my love for Joanna and Meggie, Josse thought, nor of theirs for me. Perhaps I shall have a quiet word with him . . .

But Meggie was awake and yelling that she was hungry. Joanna set about preparing food and, as Meggie came flying down the ladder and climbed delicately on to Josse's lap – Meggie understood about being very careful with wounded animals and people – he forgot about John Damianos and his frown in the pleasure of being with his child.

Soon after prime a very worried-looking Sister Martha came to Helewise to report that Sir Josse's Horace had turned up accompanied by another horse, neither wore saddle or bridle, there was no sign of Sir Josse and the smaller horse had blood on its mane. It was only after Sister Martha had delivered her message that she noticed there was someone else in the room. The young woman was standing to the right of the door and the nun had not seen her.

'Thank you, Sister,' Helewise said calmly. 'I am sure there is a simple explanation. You may go, and I will come across to the stables presently to decide if anything should be done.'

'But, my lady, he might be—'

'Thank you, Sister Martha,' Helewise said firmly. The nun bowed, backed out through the door and closed it.

'I did not wish to discuss possibilities in the presence of Sister Martha,' Helewise said very quietly, 'since it seems certain that this news is connected to your situation.' She watched the young woman steadily, a query in her eyes.

'I agree,' the young woman said. 'And I am very much afraid that it does not bode well.'

'Come with me.' Helewise got to her feet. 'The first thing is to see whether you recognize this other horse.'

They walked together along the cloister and to the stable block. Helewise eyed her companion, reflecting that yesterday's bath and change of clothing, together with a solid meal and a good night's sleep, had done much for her. During the day she had asked if she might go out and fetch her horse, which apparently she had hobbled and left nearby. Helewise had agreed, but only on the condition that she take a couple of lay brothers as escort. The horse – a beautiful bay mare – was now in the Hawkenlye stables.

She had revealed, as Helewise had again left her in her private room for the night, that her name was Paradisa. Helewise had never met anyone called Paradisa before but already she was coming round to thinking that it quite suited her . . .

Paradisa had tried to persuade Helewise yesterday to send out search parties to look for her Brother Ralf, and when Helewise had refused on the grounds that they had no idea where he was and she did not have enough people to scour the entire region, Paradisa had said she would take her horse and go and look by herself.

'You cannot,' Helewise had told her very firmly. 'If your Ralf is out there and in danger himself, how much worse would he feel if he knew you were riding recklessly alone? You have had the good sense to come to us. Please stay here, where we can keep you safe.'

The mention of Ralf's name had done the trick, as Helewise had hoped. Paradisa had grudgingly given in.

But this morning had come this unwelcome news about Josse's horse. As they approached the stables Paradisa broke into a run and Helewise lengthened her own stride and followed.

There was no need to ask if the horse belonged to Brother Ralf, for already the animal was nose to nose with Paradisa's bay and it was perfectly clear that they were old friends. Paradisa, with an arm around both necks, said softly, 'This is Cinnabar, my lady. He and my Seraphina are brother and sister, or at least so we think, because—' She had been about to say something concerning her lover; Helewise was sure of it, for the young woman's expression was tender, as if she contemplated some sweet memory. But suddenly her face crumpled and tears filled her eyes. She said urgently, 'Cinnabar has blood on his neck, my lady. Brother Ralf must be hurt.'

And if he was hurt in some fight when Josse was with him, Helewise thought, as seems likely since their horses arrived together, then without a doubt Josse would have fought alongside him.

Was Josse too hurt?

Was he – oh, surely not! – was he *dead*?

No, no, he can't be!

But Horace has abandoned his master. Would he do that were Josse still alive? Josse would not let his horse go if there was anything he could do to prevent it. Very afraid, she met Paradisa's eyes and read exactly the same dread in them.

I am her senior by many years, she told herself, and I have a position of the highest authority here. I must put aside my anxiety and act appropriately. She took a breath and said, 'Now is the time to send out search parties, for it may be possible to discover from these horses' tracks which direction they came from. I shall send a group of my people out on foot and tell them to be very careful not to obliterate any signs. I will ask—'

'I'm going,' Paradisa stated flatly. 'I will not stay here while others search for him – I just can't.'

'Neither can I,' Helewise agreed. 'I was going to say that I will summon Brother Saul and Brother Augustus, tell them to bring four other lay brothers and that you and I shall go with them.'

For the first time since Sister Martha had brought the news, Paradisa smiled.

They set out not long afterwards.

Brother Augustus, who was the best tracker, found the prints quite easily, for quite soon they veered away from the muddy and much-used road and went off at an angle through the short grass.

The tracks led towards the Great Forest.

Silently Helewise and Paradisa followed Gussie and Brother Saul. Helewise was aware of the four other lay brothers behind them. Each one carried a cudgel. She hoped that such a precaution was unnecessary, but she was well aware that Josse had been very wary of those who stalked the runaway monk. If any of them were lurking nearby, it was better to be safe than sorry.

They moved slowly up the long slope that led to the forest.

The small party set out from Joanna's hut mid-morning. She had administered another light dose of painkiller and the two men said they were more than capable of carrying their own saddles.

'Very well,' Joanna had said, 'but all the same Meggie and I will come with you to the forest fringes.'

Josse did not want that. The remaining Frankish mercenary was out there somewhere. Even if he had not come near the hut last night, it did not mean he would not attack today. Joanna seemed to have picked up his fear for her safety and she had summoned a friend to care for Meggie.

Josse was relieved. 'I cannot persuade you to remain here too?' he said.

She smiled. 'I know the forest even better than you do, Josse. I'll take you to the outside world along paths nobody else knows. It'll be all right.'

There was no changing her mind. He kissed Meggie, told her he would see her soon, nodded a greeting to Joanna's friend Lora and then they set off.

He regretted the weight of Horace's saddle and bridle before they had gone a mile, and from the set expression on John Damianos's face, guessed he felt the same. Joanna was leading the way. Josse recognized that it was a very roundabout route to the Abbey, which must lie over to the north-east. Still, if she kept them safe, then an extra few miles was well worth it, even carrying a saddle.

Presently they came to an area of woodland that he thought he knew and with huge relief he realized they were not much more than half a mile from the open ground where the forest gave way just above the Abbey. He called out softly, 'Joanna? May we rest?'

She turned round, looking quickly at him and then at John. 'Of course. I am sorry; I have been pushing the pace and I should have had more consideration for your hurts.' She handed a water bottle to Josse, who drank deeply and passed it to John. 'We are almost at the edge of the forest,' she said encouragingly, 'and already back on the better-known paths, so we should make haste.'

John gave a grimace as he hefted up his saddle again. Josse caught his eye. 'Not far. Good news, eh?'

John nodded. Then they fell into step behind Joanna and set off once more.

Helewise and Paradisa had caught up with the lay brothers on the edge of the trees. Augustus was bending down and examining the long grass, Saul beside him. The other brothers were staring ahead into the shadowy forest, cudgels in their hands.

Helewise heard voices.

One was Josse's; she recognized his deep tones and relief flooded through her. *Oh, thank you, thank you!* If he was talking, he wasn't dying.

Thank God!

The other voice was female and belonged to Joanna. Helewise narrowed her eyes and tried to make them out. There appeared to be someone else with them. It was a man, and he wore an enveloping, hooded dark robe. Was it John Damianos? Or was it the runaway monk? With his hood drawn up, she could not see his face and did not know if he was a Westerner or a Saracen.

The trio passed out from the narrow path between the trees and into a clearing. They were close enough now to have seen the search party, had any of them thought to look. Josse and the other man seemed to be carrying saddles and bridles . . . Of course, she thought; their horses had already had their tack removed when they ran off.

Paradisa was staring intently at the second man. Then, before Helewise could stop her, she had leapt over the low bank that marked the edge of the forest and was running along the track towards the clearing.

The man had seen her. Flinging down the saddle, he raced to meet her. They met in the middle of the clearing and were instantly wound in each other's arms. A beam of sunshine penetrated the low cloud and shone down into the glade as if its sole purpose was to illuminate them.

That, said Helewise to herself, just has to be Brother Ralf.

Smiling, affected by their evident joy, she walked on into the glade. Josse and Joanna were entering it from the opposite side. In that happy moment danger seemed irrelevant. Helewise had forgotten all about it and so, it seemed, had everyone else.

But danger was still there.

The Frankish mercenary known simply as William was watching. He had an arrow to the bow and the young man in the hooded robe was in his sights. He knew who he was. He knew he had robbed the great Leo Rubenid Anavarza of his bride. William had a mission; he had lost his colleague and his friend but he could not return to his master all those long miles away unless he had the woman with him. He stared at Leo Rubenid's bride. In order to take her he would have to kill the man.

Slowly he lowered the bow. Even had he killed the young man – and he did not doubt that he could – there was little point, for the big knight who had slain poor Tancred was just behind him. There were also two more women in the clearing, one of them a nun, and six monks armed with stout sticks.

The odds were too great.

Stealthily, he crept away.

Twenty

Helewise did not see Joanna go. One minute she was standing just behind Josse, then when she looked again she had gone. She has been caring for them, Helewise thought. They were wounded and she tended them and sheltered them during the night. She knew that she should be thankful for Joanna's skill but just then gratitude was not the foremost of her emotions.

She instructed two of the lay brothers to relieve Josse and Brother Ralf of the heavy tack and then she led the company down the long slope to the Abbey. Paradisa and her lover had their heads close together and were talking urgently in low voices. The young man had not yet been presented to Helewise but she knew it was not the moment to stand on ceremony, for both he and Josse had walked all the way from Joanna's hut, wherever that might be, and they were exhausted. She led them in through the Abbey gates, where Sister Martha and Sister Ursel, the porteress, came out to greet them. Sister Martha had tears in her eyes as she squeezed Josse's hand.

They went on to the infirmary.

Helewise realized that it would cause uproar if Josse's companion were put anywhere near Thibault and Brother Otto and so, with a look at Sister Euphemia, who nodded her understanding, Helewise led him and Josse to the recess at the far end of the long ward. Sister Euphemia saw her new patients inside then, drawing the curtains, turned to Helewise and Paradisa and said firmly, 'I will care for them now. My lady Abbess, they must be stripped of their soiled garments and bathed, then we will see to their hurts. When we have finished'– there was a slight emphasis on *when* – 'I will send word.'

The infirmarer evidently did not think such tasks were fit for any woman except a professional healer. Helewise hid her amusement. 'Very well, Sister,' she said. She glanced at Paradisa, who was fuming. 'Come, Paradisa.' Helewise turned it into a command. Turning, she walked away. After a moment she heard Paradisa's footsteps following behind her.

'It isn't *fair!*' the young woman burst out as she and Helewise stepped into the open air. 'He and I have cared for each other for two years and a thousand miles! There is little that I haven't done for him or he for me.'

'I do not doubt it,' Helewise said soothingly. 'But now you are at Hawkenlye Abbey and you must do as everyone else does and abide by its rules.'

'Which I don't suppose include women intimately tending their lovers in the infirmary?' There was a faint smile on Paradisa's face.

'No, they do not.' Helewise tried to keep a straight face. 'Come with me, young Paradisa. We shall go and say a prayer of thanks that these beloved men are safe, and then you shall come with me on my rounds and meet my nuns.' Paradisa hesitated. 'Do not worry,' Helewise added gently, 'Sister Euphemia knows she must send word the instant we are permitted to see them.'

With that, Paradisa had to be satisfied. She fell into step beside Helewise and together they went into the church.

Josse and John Damianos were put in adjoining beds. Nursing nuns stripped them, washed them and dressed them in clean linen shifts, careful not to disturb their wounds more than necessary. Josse noticed that John tried to keep a hand on the strap of his leather satchel and as soon as the nuns had finished, he picked it up and put it on the bed. The infirmarer came into the recess and gave both men a thorough examination.

After her first close look at her patients' wounds she met Josse's eyes and said, 'I believe I recognize the skilful hand that tended you.'

'Aye.'

Sister Euphemia gave a brisk nod. 'What luck that you were nearby when your urgent need arose.'

To which, Josse thought wearily, the only response was to say 'Aye' again.

But he noticed a frown on Sister Euphemia's face as she put her hand on John's forehead. She said bluntly, 'You, young man, have a slight fever. I shall give you a sedative. You, Sir Josse, could do with a good rest as well. I shall send word to the Abbess that I would prefer you not to have visitors before tomorrow morning.'

John looked aghast. 'But I must talk to Paradisa!'

The infirmarer looked at him compassionately. 'And she is just as eager to talk to you. But you will both have to wait.' With that she left the recess, drawing the curtains together very pointedly after her.

'She means it, I'm afraid,' Josse said quietly.

'And Abbess Helewise will do as she says?'

'In matters concerning the health of Sister Euphemia's charges, aye, she will.'

Silence fell. A nun came in with John's sedative and put it beside him. 'Drink it all,' she said as she turned to go. 'I shall be back for the empty mug.'

John looked at it. Then he threw it under his bed.

'You must take your medicine!' Josse whispered urgently. 'You have a fever!'

'It is but slight,' John said. 'I've had fevers before and recovered. I can't possibly *sleep*, Josse. If I am forbidden to speak to Paradisa, then I must talk to you.'

Josse looked into the light eyes, now clouded with fever and with anxiety. Knowing there was no alternative, he said, 'What about?'

'I've told you, or you've guessed, much of my story,' John began, 'and now I shall tell you the rest. Well, most of it,' he amended, 'for the last piece is for another to hear first. You know, Josse,' he went on before Josse could query that, 'how I went to Outremer with Gerome de Villières and left his service to fight with the Hospitallers, meeting up with Gerome later and escorting him to his kinswoman, where I met Paradisa. You know I was involved in that prisoner exchange and had to abandon my brethren to escape with Fadil and the incredible thing that was to have paid for him.'

'Aye,' Josse agreed. 'All of that is clear, as are the identities and the purposes of the three groups that pursued you back to England.'

'England,' John said softly. 'Yes. It had to be England.'

'Why?'

'I will explain, but not yet. For now, let me tell you how I escaped death in the desert when all my brethren died.' He smiled grimly. 'It was quite simply because of childhood greed.'

'*What?*'

'When I was a little boy I stole a batch of marigold, saffron and cinnamon cakes and ate every single one. Not only was I punished but I was sick for the rest of the day and ever since I have not been able to abide the smell of cinnamon, let alone eat or drink anything flavoured with it. Out in the desert they gave us poison, Josse; the fat man's smiling servants handed round pretty glasses of a cinnamon-flavoured drink and every monk but I drank it. Hisham intended to kill us all. He had only offered his treasure for Fadil to make absolutely sure we agreed to the exchange. He never intended us to take it away.'

'You did not consume the drink?'

'No, I poured it away in the sand beneath the rugs and when the servants offered more, I held up my empty glass and then poured that away too.'

'It has been suggested that the Knights Hospitaller also intended to deceive,' Josse said. 'Was that why you fled? Because you could not trust your own Order with either Fadil or this treasure offered for him?'

'Yes. But Josse, strictly speaking they are not *my* Order. I never took my vows.'

'Then why,' Josse hissed, leaning close, 'have those two Hospitallers lying there at the other end of the infirmary gone to such extraordinary lengths to catch you?' Light dawned in a flash and he said, 'They aren't after *you* at all, are they?'

And John Damianos patted his satchel and said, 'No.'

Josse leaned back against his pillows. 'You have to tell me what it is,' he said. Or else, he added silently, my intense curiosity might just kill me. 'Whatever it takes, whatever promises of secrecy you have to break, I *must know*.' Turning his head, he fixed John with a piercing glare.

'Yes, I appreciate that,' John said quickly, 'and you of all people have earned the right to be told.' He paused, as if deciding exactly where to begin, and then said, 'There were two special reasons why they selected me for the desert mission. One of them was that I was unavowed – not one of them – and therefore expendable. The other . . . Once again, it refers to my childhood. I was taught to read and write, Josse, and those skills are rare outside the ranks of the clerics. So there I was, the very person the Hospitallers needed for the mission that night. I was ordered to join the group as night fell and we rode out to the meeting place. Then as we all sat down, something extraordinary happened: my commanding officer turned to me, handed me a piece of parchment, a quill and a brass pot of ink and, nodding in the direction of the fat man on the divan, he said quietly, "When the fat man starts to speak, write down exactly what he says."

'I sat there straining my ears to catch every word. The fat man was reading from a manuscript and he made no attempt to speak slowly or clearly and I was scribbling faster than I had ever done in my life before. I was fervently hoping for the chance to write out a fair copy before handing it over, otherwise nobody would have made any sense of it at all.'

'It must have been nerve-wracking,' Josse said. Barely able to write, he readily understood the demands and the horrors of John's task.

'The main problem was that although I recognized most of the individual words, together they made no sense. Many of them were Latin words. I did not try to understand but merely scrawled them down just as the fat man spoke them. I kept thinking, if only I could have a respite! A few moments to go over what I had written so far and try to extract some meaning! If I'd had an inkling of what it was about, I would have stood a better chance of getting the rest right. But no such respite came. The fat man's voice went on and on. My hands were damp with sweat and the effort of concentration was making my head pound, but I went on scribbling.

'After an eternity, the fat man at last stopped speaking. It would probably be some time before I could study what I'd written and I was really worried that I wouldn't be able to decipher it. I decided to have a look there and then, when everybody was cheerful and friendly and my monks were innocently sipping those lethal drinks. So I smoothed out the parchment and studied it.

'All the time I'd been writing, I was so preoccupied with not missing anything that I hadn't considered the piece as a whole. Now I read it right through and for the first time I understood the full import. As I sat there the heat died out of me and my sweat cooled on my skin. I sat in the brilliant luxury of that tent, looking down in horror at my piece of parchment, and my blood felt like ice in my veins.'

'What had the fat man dictated?' Josse asked in a whisper. Something came back to him – a word, spoken what seemed a long time ago. 'John, what does *simyager* mean?'

John's eyes widened in surprise. 'It's a Turkish word. It's what Hisham is. However do you know it?'

'*What is he?*'

There was an instant of perfect silence.

Then: 'Hisham is an alchemist. The treasure with which he lured us into the desert that night was a deadly formula he's discovered.'

'What is this formula?' Josse whispered fiercely. '*What does it do?*'

John was watching him as if, even now, he was reluctant to confide the secret that he had borne for so long. Then with a sigh he said, 'It makes a black powder. If it is compressed and set alight, it explodes. If the balance of materials and the method of operation are accurate, it hurls a heavy object with incredible force.'

Dear God . . . The soldier in Josse conjured up instant images. Heavy objects hurled with great force into buildings. Into men. Blasting them apart. 'It's the devil's work,' he breathed.

'I don't believe in devils other than human ones,' John said calmly.

Josse still could not accept what he was hearing. 'But – are you sure?' he demanded. 'You only have this Hisham's word for it, and—'

John interrupted. 'Hisham arranged a demonstration that night,' he said. 'And to make sure I wrote it down correctly, I have tested it myself more than once. My latest attempt was not long before Paradisa and I arrived in England.' He pointed to the huge wound on the underside of his chin. 'I was careless, though, and I almost blew myself up too.'

'How do you make it?' Josse whispered. Horrified though he was, still he was fascinated.

'You mix brimstone, saltpetre and charcoal in a very specific ratio. It's difficult to get the right quality of saltpetre – it's that stuff that seeps out of cellar walls, which is how it got the name salt of the stones – and usually it has to be manufactured out of urine and excrement. I wrote all this down. Hisham was very thorough because he knew his formula was not going beyond those silken walls. It didn't matter if his servants heard because, as I told you, much of it was in Latin and they did not understand. As for the monks, Hisham knew we'd all be dead soon.'

'As indeed you would have been but for your childhood greed,' Josse said slowly. He was trying to take it all in. 'And you have this piece of parchment still? The formula is safe with you and nobody else has had access to it?'

'I have it and until this moment I have shared it with no one but Paradisa.'

'But the fat man – the alchemist Hisham still has it!'

John shrugged. 'He does not have the parchment from which he read it. I destroyed that. I threw it on the fire and watched it burn. He may have another copy but I doubt it; I judge by how desperately he tried to capture me that I now have the only one. His motive in sending Kathnir and Akhbir after me may have been simply to make sure the secret of the formula remained his alone, but I have come to think that it was more than that.' He paused. 'I said that Hisham had discovered this terrible thing, but I believe it was someone else's discovery. All Hisham had was the formula, and God alone knows how he got his hands on that.' His light eyes on Josse's, he said quietly, 'I do not think he can make this powder by himself. I believe that he needs my copy of the formula and I will not let him have it.'

There was a short silence. Then Josse said, 'Kathnir and Akhbir have failed. They will not catch you now.'

'That is true.'

'And Thibault, for all that he lies but the length of this room away, has no idea that you and what you carry are right here within his grasp.'

John shrugged. 'I have eluded Thibault this far. I am now very near to the point when I shall give the formula into the dependable hands I envisaged back in Outremer. Then it will be safe at last and I can rest.' He closed his eyes.

Questions threw themselves around Josse's head but most of them could wait. Very quietly he said 'John?' and when the young man grunted a response, he said, 'They must not be allowed to have this frightful weapon, must they? If it is as terrible as you make out, it must be kept from the Saracens *and* the Hospitallers.'

'It *is* terrible,' John said, his eyes still closed. 'Warfare out in Outremer is a constant, brutal, savage and cruel waste of human life. If this black powder were to be added to the weaponry of either side, I believe that the entire Holy Land would be blown to pieces.'

'In which case it must be kept from them,' Josse said, half to himself. Then: 'John, wherever these dependable hands that you spoke of are located, I will help you take your secret to them. I give you my word.'

It seemed to him that John Damianos smiled faintly. Then shortly afterwards a soft snore emerged from his slightly parted lips.

It was dark when Josse woke up and at first he did not know what had awakened him. He heard a quiet voice say in his ear, 'Do you want to see it in operation?'

Then he knew where he was, who was talking to him and what the words meant. With a nod he got out of bed and, throwing his cloak over his linen shift, picked up his boots. 'There's a small door just along here,' John whispered. 'I've already checked and it's possible to unlock it.'

They slipped out between the curtains. The nun on night duty was dozing in her chair and did not wake up. They crept past another curtained-off area and then Josse saw the little door. John was already working on it and very soon it stood open. John hurried out, Josse behind him, and they paused to put on their boots. John's satchel hung at his side beneath his cloak.

The sky was still partly cloud-covered but the moon was waxing towards the full and gave adequate light. John, Josse noticed, had a pitch torch in his hand. They walked quickly over to the high wall and John went unerringly to one of Sister Tiphaine's fruit trees where it was possible to shin up and climb over to the world outside. Josse wondered as he jumped rather painfully down the other side how they would get back in again. He asked John, who replied, 'There's a place I know. Trust me, Josse.'

They made their way south, where the open ground soon broke up into hillocks and shallow valleys. They came to a little dell, separated from the Abbey by a narrow ridge crowned by a trio of birch trees. John ran down into it and opened his satchel. He found a piece of flattish stone and, concentrating hard, took out three small, lidded earthenware containers. Using a little wooden spoon, he measured three separate piles of the contents: one was black; one was silvery-white; the third was bright yellow. He mixed the three together until their separate identities had disappeared and they formed a fine black powder. Then, moving away from the stone and turning his back, he struck a flint and lit the pitch torch. He said to Josse, 'Stand back.' Then he put the flame of the torch into the black powder.

There was a brilliant flash, a loud bang and a sudden acrid-smelling cloud of smoke.

'Dear God!' Josse breathed. 'You have harnessed the devil, John!'

John grinned. 'No I haven't. This is an entirely human discovery. Hisham is an alchemist and he deals with other men like him. Someone must have discovered this formula when investigating the possibilities of three separate substances.'

'It's similar to what they call Greek fire, is it not?'

'No, it's nothing like it,' John replied. 'Greek fire is a mix of tar, brimstone, resin, oil and quicklime. It burns fiercely and if you throw water on it you simply make it burn all the harder. They shoot it out of tubes fixed to the bows of ships, or else put it in pots which they hurl on the ballista. It's a fire that doesn't go out, Josse, and it has been known of for a long time. This black powder – ' he indicated the stone, whose surface was bare and now bore a large dark stain – 'is unique because it has a secret force in it.'

'A force?'

'Yes. Watch.'

John delved in his satchel again, this time coming up with a brass tube about the length of his hand and as wide as his two thumbs. Carefully he mixed more of the black powder, crouching over his task so that Josse could not see what he was doing.

He straightened up and turned to Josse. 'It isn't that I don't trust you, Josse,' he said apologetically. 'But this part I worked out for myself from references in Hisham's long description and, if you don't mind, I won't reveal what I've discovered, even to you.'

Touched by that *even to you*, as if he had become someone special in John Damianos's fugitive life, Josse said, 'Aye, I understand. And I don't mind.'

John nodded. Then he took a breath and squared his shoulders. With a nervous grin, he said, 'This is how I burned myself. I tried to do this with a wooden tube and it blew up.'

'You mustn't—'

But Josse never finished his protest.

John had somehow touched the torch flame to the black powder inside the brass tube, for there was another loud bang and a bright gout of fiery smoke flew out of the end with the speed and the brilliance of a shooting star.

Josse stood, amazed.

'And look what else it can do,' John said eagerly. Once more crouching down so that Josse could not see, after a moment he held up the tube again and this time as the powder inside exploded, something small and hard shot out of the end of the tube. Josse heard a thump as it embedded itself into one of the trees.

'What was that?'

'Just a stone. Want to see it again?' John was smiling broadly now and Josse found that he was too.

'Aye!'

'It's nowhere near accurate,' John said as he mixed his powder, 'and in these small amounts the propulsive force isn't very great, but just think of the potential.'

'I prefer not to,' Josse said gravely. Watching these experiments was all very well but already he understood why John had to protect this incredible secret. And why Hisham should have sent his warriors so far to get it back.

John had prepared his tube again and was on the point of putting the flame to it. Then a dark figure appeared from between the birch trees. He carried a sword and a knife and he was advancing down the slope into the dell. He said, 'You should not have made yourself so visible, Brother Ralf. Your loud sounds and flashing lights have drawn me to you like a moth to a candle.'

Josse was not wearing his sword. He was armed with nothing more lethal than his knife. He stood at John's left shoulder, just behind him.

'You have your knight with you, I see,' said the man. 'No matter. I recognize him and I shall kill him too, for he murdered my companion Tancred.'

'Your Tancred would have killed me!' Josse protested, adrenaline making his voice loud and fierce. 'It is not murder when a man kills in self-defence.'

'No, indeed, but Tancred is dead all the same.' The man was close now. It could only be a matter of moments before he was within sword's length.

'Go back, William,' John said. He sounded surprisingly calm. 'You are here only because Leo Rubenid pays you to do his foul deeds. Paradisa would suffer an unspeakable fate were she to be returned to him, as you very well know. Can you not find pity in your heart for her and let us be?'

William shrugged. 'I do as I am commanded,' he said coldly. 'If people suffer, it is not my concern.'

'How do you plan to get her all the way back to Outremer, even if you manage to kill me and Josse here and then remove her from an abbey full of nuns without anyone stopping you?' Still John sounded calm.

'I know where she is sleeping,' William said coldly. Josse felt a shiver of dread. 'I can be inside that room and render her senseless before she knows what is happening. Then down to the coast and a ship in which to sail home. Bound, gagged and locked in a cabin to which only I have the key, there will be no escape for her.'

'You have it all worked out,' John said, still in that reasonable voice. Only Josse, standing right beside him, could tell what an effort it was.

'Of course,' William replied. 'I am a professional, hired and well paid to carry out my task. I do not intend to forfeit the remainder of my reward.'

'You speak of a living, breathing woman.' Now there was emotion in John's tone. 'Have more respect!'

William laughed. 'Respect? Picture her in a few months' time when the scum of the ports of Outremer have been through her. She'll be naked, humiliated, filthy, poxed and foul. There won't be anything left to *respect* then.'

Josse sensed John go tense. 'In that case,' he said, calm once more, 'I shall just have to kill you.'

The bang and the flames followed so quickly on his words that Josse could not work out how he had done it. But William lay on the ground with a small hole above his left eye. It was rapidly filling up with blood.

John flung down the brass tube and swooped down on his victim. 'Is he dead?' Josse demanded.

'No. He is still breathing, but shallowly.' Without turning round John held out his hand. 'Your knife, please, Josse.'

He was proposing to slay an unconscious man. That could not be. 'No,' Josse said quietly. 'I am sorry, John. I cannot provide the weapon that murders a defenceless man.'

John had spun round, his face furious. 'But you just heard him say what he'll do if he escapes! Would you have my death and the knowledge of what will happen to Paradisa haunting you as William slays you?'

'We will bind him and take him to Gervase de Gifford for judgement and punishment!' Josse cried. 'That is the right thing to do, John. I will not be a part to this cold-blooded murder which—'

William thrust himself up off the ground. With incredible speed he clasped John firmly around the neck and, rapidly moving his knife from his left hand to his right, slashed it at John's wounded throat.

He is going to kill him before my eyes, Josse thought.

Then there was no more time for thought.

He drew his knife and with all his weight and power behind it drove it down into William's chest, coming in from immediately to the right of where John lay clasped against him.

He must have struck the heart.

William's knife fell away from John's throat and the encircling arm relaxed and dropped with a soft thud to the ground. John got slowly to his feet. He stood staring down at the dead man for a few moments. Then he turned to Josse and wordlessly put his arms around him.

John packed up his satchel while Josse covered William's face with the man's cloak. There were now two of them to bury; William and Tancred had been companions in life, so it would be a charitable gesture to bury them side by side. I'll make sure

I mention it to the Abbess, Josse thought. He felt cold, strangely distant from all that had just happened, and the wound in his upper arm was hurting so much that he wanted to moan.

Presently they climbed out of the dell and walked back to the Abbey.

Twenty-One

There was no need to make their way back inside the walls by whatever clandestine means John had worked out. Lights were burning and the gates were wide open.

Josse made out the figure of the Abbess, at the head of a group of monks, lay brothers and nuns. The men were armed with sticks or clubs and Sister Martha was wielding her trusty pitchfork.

The Abbess strode out through the gates, her expression stern and fixed.

Oh, dear, Josse thought.

With John Damianos beside him, he walked towards her.

Helewise had thought at first there must be a storm brewing. Awakened by a loud crash, she assumed it to be thunder, only it came again and it didn't really sound quite like thunder . . .

She lay drowsily in her bed, on the point of falling asleep again – it was, after all, only thunder – when suddenly she was filled with a stab of such horrified fear that it shot her up into a sitting position. It was as if something quite terrible was going to happen and she *knew* it without any doubt. The sense of foreboding was so undeniable that she got up, dressed swiftly and hurried outside.

Others had also heard the strange sounds and ventured out into the chill pre-dawn air. Sister Martha and Sister Ursel had unfastened the little spyhole in the gates and were peering out. From the rear gate down to the Vale came a party of monks and lay brothers led by Brother Saul and Brother Urse the carpenter, carrying an axe.

'I can see two men approaching over there in the distance – ' Sister Ursel pointed – 'but there were *lights* out there, my lady!' she gasped. 'Brilliant, flashing lights! The dear Lord alone knows what devilry is going on, but—'

'Sir Josse and the young man are missing from their beds,' said Sister Euphemia's clear voice. She strode up to Helewise's side. 'My lady, the nun on duty in the infirmary felt a draft and noticed that the small door at the far end of the ward was ajar. She checked on her patients and found the two beds empty.'

I knew, Helewise thought. I knew there was danger. But somehow something did not seem quite right . . .

'Open the gates, Sister Ursel,' she said calmly. 'We shall go out and help them.'

'It might be dangerous, my lady,' protested Sister Martha. 'Should you not let the rest of us go while you stay here where it's safe? They could be battling with vicious enemies!' She was clutching her pitchfork in her strong hands as if she just could not wait to plunge it into whoever had the effrontery to threaten Josse.

'Then all the more reason for us to make haste,' Helewise replied. 'Come along!'

Sister Ursel drew back the heavy bars and opened the gates. Helewise led her party outside.

She saw Josse coming towards her. Beside him was the slighter figure of another man who must be John Damianos. The infirmarer had reported that he was running a slight fever, which would not have been helped by this excursion out into the cold night . . .

John Damianos. Brother Ralf.

She frowned. Her eyes were on the young man beside Josse. His face was in the deep shadow cast by the hood of his cloak. She experienced an odd feeling, as if – as if— She gave up.

'Sir Josse,' she said as the two men stopped in front of their rescue party, 'are you all right?'

'Neither of us has received further injury, my lady,' he said. Then, meeting her eyes, he added quietly, 'It is over now.'

She nodded her understanding.

'Go back to the infirmary, both of you,' she said, addressing the two men, 'for you are wounded and one of you at least has a fever. We will—'

'My lady, I am sorry to contradict,' came a low voice, 'but I must speak privately with you.'

Josse, she noticed, gave the younger man a quick, sympathetic glance before turning to her. 'It is important, my lady,' he said. 'And – ' he eyed the gathered monks and nuns behind her – 'it's rather a delicate matter.'

'Very well,' she said, controlling her surprise. 'Go along to my room, Sir Josse, and take your companion with you. Paradisa is sleeping in there but I expect the commotion will have woken her up already. I will join you shortly.' She watched the two men set off. Josse, she noticed, seemed to be clutching the wound in his arm.

Then she turned back to her monks and her nuns. Filled suddenly with gratitude, for there they all were, ready and eager to fight for the community and to defend its Abbess to the very best of their ability, she smiled lovingly at them.

'Thank you, all of you,' she said simply. 'The Abbey is very lucky that such courageous and devoted men and women live within its walls. Now, go back to your beds. Soon it will be morning.'

They parted into two ranks and she walked between them. There were one or two mutterings of, 'God bless you, my lady.' Reining in her impulse to run after Josse – run after the strange, disturbing man who strode beside him – she walked sedately back into the Abbey.

She entered her room and firmly closed the door. The young man and Paradisa were locked tightly in each other's arms and Josse was looking on with an indulgent smile. The brazier had been poked into life and several candles were burning.

'So, what is this important matter that demands my attention before it is even light?' she demanded, seating herself in her chair. John Damianos, she noticed – or was he really called Ralf? – had buried his face in Paradisa's hair, but both Paradisa and Josse were staring at Helewise.

It was Paradisa who spoke.

'I told you, my lady, that Thibault of Margat has followed Brother Ralf all this way not because of who he is but what he carries.'

'You did, yes.'

'In that satchel is a secret formula. It was Hisham's great treasure. He has discovered the secret of how to make a deadly black powder that bursts into life when it is set on fire and which has a magical force to it, a special sort of energy that—'

'There is nothing *magical* about it,' Brother Ralf interrupted, his face still averted.

'Well, it looks magic to me,' Paradisa said. Holding the young man's face in her hands, she looked into his eyes and said softly, 'It's evil, too. Don't try to deny it. You could have been killed that time it blew up in your face and then I should have had to contemplate the awful prospect of life without you.'

It was a moment of deep intimacy. Helewise felt almost guilty for observing it.

'So, the Hospitallers wished to relieve you of this formula and utilize it for their own purposes,' she said briskly, 'and the two Saracens were sent by their master to recover it and take it back to it to him. And the last of your pursuers simply wanted to return Paradisa to her betrothed husband. Is that right?'

'Quite right, my lady,' Paradisa said politely.

'None of them is a threat any more,' Josse said. 'All except the two Hospitallers are dead.'

'Dead,' Helewise repeated. Then: 'I understand the importance of this . . . *thing*. Those flashes and bangs just now were, I presume, a demonstration of what it can do?'

'Aye.' It was Josse who spoke.

'But what I cannot understand,' she went on, 'is just why, Brother Ralf – John – you should have brought it here to England?'

Paradisa stepped a little apart from the young man. It was, Helewise thought vaguely, as if she knew that he must explain this alone . . .

His face still covered, he said, 'I had to take it to a place of safety.'

'Why not just destroy it?' she demanded.

She sensed that he was smiling as he replied. 'That is a good question, my lady. Because it is possible that if, against all my hope, Hisham manages to recreate the formula, he may give his secret to the Saracens. If that unthinkable event comes to pass, I would wish also to provide our side with this weapon.'

She nodded. It was a frightful thought. It was bad enough to think of one side having this awful thing, let alone both, but in a ghastly way it made a sort of sense. And, she thought, what do I or any woman truly know of warfare? A sudden image flashed through her mind of women . . . of one woman, a deity figure, loving, caring, nurturing . . . but then as swiftly it was gone.

She felt strangely disturbed and it was only with an effort that she remembered where and who she was and what had just happened.

'But why bring this thing here?' she asked again. 'Surely there were other safe havens on the long road from Outremer?'

'None that I could think of that was safer than Hawkenlye Abbey,' the young man said.

It was an extraordinary answer. 'You – you know about Hawkenlye?' she asked faintly.

He threw back his hood and at last she saw his face. He was smiling. 'I do,' he said softly. 'I also know its Abbess. There is no woman on earth that I trust more.'

She was up and out of her chair, brushing both Paradisa and Josse out of her way, although she registered a fleeting impression that both were smiling and neither seemed to mind. Then the young man was in her arms and she was clutching him to her as if she would never let him go. She felt his strong arms go around her to return the hard embrace. She reached up to kiss his wounded throat and, as he bent his head, put her lips to his cheek. Pulling away slightly, she stared at him. He was tanned by the sun and there were lines of maturity on his handsome face; its bones and its shape were those of a grown man now.

But she would have known him anywhere.

'Dominic,' she whispered, 'oh, my Dominic!'

Then, turning to Josse, she said, 'Dear, dear Josse; this is my son.'

Postscript
21 December 1196

It was not the traditional season for a wedding, but the young bride and bridegroom had waited quite long enough and it was high time that their union was formalized.

Dominic had asked his mother, and she had asked the priest, and Father Gilbert had said that little would give him greater pleasure than to perform, at Hawkenlye Abbey, the ceremony that would unite the Abbess's younger son in matrimony with his radiant bride.

The wedding would take place on the shortest day of the year. To honour their beloved Abbess and show off the Abbey to the very best of their abilities, the nuns, the monks and the lay brothers threw themselves into the preparations. The news spread swiftly that Abbess Helewise's son was home again after countless decades bravely fighting the Infidel in Outremer – it was only eleven years, but wild exaggeration spiced up a tale – and many people made up their minds to go to the Abbey and show their respect for its Abbess by cheering the young couple and wishing them well.

It was just as well that the Abbey could accommodate a crowd.

Helewise had ordered Dominic to face Thibault of Margat with the truth. Together mother and son went to see the Hospitaller, who, although slowly recovering, was still very unwell, and Dominic explained that he was going to entrust the formula to the safest place on earth. Thibault might have guessed where that was. He made a desultory attempt to question Dominic but soon gave up.

Looking at him with deep compassion, Helewise realized that the fight had leaked out of him. The single-minded, fierce and powerful man had gone, perhaps burned away in the fire that almost killed him and forced upon him this agonizing convalescence. He had been dosed and dosed again with Sister Tiphaine's potions, wielded with a determined hand by Sister Euphemia. Their strength might be diminishing but the quantity that Thibault had consumed must now be considerable. And, as both the herbalist and the infirmarer often pointed out, you just did not know what else a powerful remedy did besides relieve pain.

Helewise studied Thibault as he looked up at the young man whose footsteps he had dogged so far and for so long. With a faint smile he said, 'This thing . . . It is too powerful. I have seen what the lust for it will make men do and I've had enough of it all.' He sighed. 'I will not see Outremer again, for I shall never now voyage so far. When Brother Otto and I are able to travel, we shall go to Clerkenwell. I shall request a private meeting with the Grand Master and I shall report that the formula is gone.'

Dominic studied him for several moments, and it seemed to Helewise that he was thinking hard. Then he said very softly, 'It could be retrieved, you know, were there to be incontestable need.'

The Hospitaller gave a small gasp. Then he nodded. He understood.

Josse went out to the forest to keep his tryst with Joanna. When he revealed the true identity of the young man whom she had known as John Damianos, he had the clear impression that it was not in fact news at all.

'You knew, didn't you?'

She smiled. 'Yes.'

'How?'

'Remember when Abbess Helewise was so sick and we thought she might die?'

'Aye. You called her back to life.'

'I – well yes, sort of. But in the place where she was, she could see things that were going to happen, although I don't think she realized it then or recalls it now. And one of the things she – we – saw was Dominic's return. So when you brought him here to my hut, I recognized him.'

He shook his head in wonder. I ought to be used to her and

her weird powers by now, he thought, but I'm not. I'm not sure if any normal, human man ever could be. The thought that swiftly followed – if a human couldn't hope to understand Joanna, then what did that make her? – slipped in and out of his consciousness so swiftly that he barely noticed it. It was dark, Meggie was fast asleep and Joanna was lying in his arms.

He had other things on his mind.

The dead had to be accounted for.

Gervase de Gifford was satisfied that in several cases the murderer was dead: Kathnir killed the Turk Touros and died at the hands of William and Tancred, who were also responsible for the death of Brother Jeremiah and the fire in Tonbridge Priory's guest wing. Tancred died fighting Josse and John Damianos, and William was slain by Josse to save John's life.

'Except that he's not really called John Damianos, is he?' Gervase said with an ironic lift of his eyebrows. He and Josse were riding out to the old manor house in the forest, Dominic and Paradisa behind them.

'No,' Josse agreed.

Gervase looked at him through narrowed eyes. 'I must get used to calling him Dominic Warin, I suppose,' he said. Then, bitingly: 'And I only have his and your word, Josse, as to how these two Franks were slain.' Pretending surprise, he added, 'Both killed by you, as it happens, fighting for your life, you say, alongside this son of your extremely good friend Abbess Helewise.'

Josse waited until he had his anger under control. Then he said, not for the first time, 'Tancred would have killed me had I not struck the fatal blow before he did. And William virtually had his knife in Dominic's throat and was about to kill him.' He added stiffly, 'I will swear to it if you wish.'

There was quite a long pause. Then Gervase said, 'Your word is enough.'

The mood between them was definitely chilly. Gervase had been intensely curious about that strange, round indentation in William's forehead and Josse's explanation – that William fell on his face and the stone must have embedded itself, only to fall out and roll away into the grass – sounded feeble, even to Josse's ears. He was tempted to say more but it was not his secret to tell.

They rode on in silence until at last – and it was not nearly soon enough for Josse – the old manor came into view.

Paradisa told her story and again Josse noticed the scepticism in Gervase's eyes. It was as if the sheriff was thinking, ah, but it is too easy! These people all swear that the killings were justified, done in self-defence or in defence of the innocent, but since they all bear witness for each other, how am I to decide if they speak the truth?

Paradisa led them to the place in the trees where she had buried the body of Akhbir. Gervase stared down in silence and then observed that it was a long way for a woman to carry the body of a grown man.

Paradisa said tonelessly, 'I did not carry him. I tied a rope around him and fastened the other end to my horse's saddle. I dragged him to his grave, and I bitterly regret both the treatment and the fact that I was not able to dig the grave deep enough. I have had dreams of his body being dug up and eaten by wild creatures.' A sob escaped her, hastily suppressed, and she put her hands up to hide her face. Dominic put his arm around her. Gervase went on staring down at the man-shaped mound of earth. Then abruptly he turned away.

He and Josse rode back towards Hawkenlye without a word being spoken. When they reached the place where Gervase's road down to Tonbridge branched off, he drew rein. He looked Josse in the eye and, nodding in the direction of the young couple, said, 'You can tell them I'm satisfied.'

'I will,' Josse said. 'Thank you.'

'But, Josse, next time—' Gervase bit off whatever he had been about to say. Then: 'Just remember who's sheriff around here.'

He touched his cap, put spurs to his horse and cantered away.

Perhaps Sabin de Gifford had sufficient tact and understanding to reason the sheriff out of his bad mood at what he clearly saw as a challenge to his authority, if not worse. Either that or he came to his senses by himself. Sabin sent word that she and Gervase would come to the Abbey on Dominic and Paradisa's wedding day to add their congratulations and good wishes.

Josse learned of this with relief. Gervase was just too good a friend to lose.

*   *   *

The day of the wedding began misty and dank and there was a soft, chilly rain in the air. The nuns and the monks, eyeing the weather and trying to smile, endlessly repeated the old saying *rain at dawn, sun by mid-morn*, and at least some of them believed it. The sceptics were proved wrong. As the church emptied after sext, the congregation looked up to see that the clouds had cleared. By the time Dominic and Paradisa stood side by side at the church door, the sun was shining brightly down from a pale winter sky.

Dominic was the first to make his vow, saying in a strong voice that carried right to the back of the crowd, 'I do take you, Paradisa, as my wife,' and straight away she echoed the words. Rings were handed to Father Gilbert to be blessed, and then he returned them to the young couple and they placed them on each other's hands. The priest led them into the church and up to the altar, where they knelt while he prayed. Then he blessed them and the entire congregation broke into joyous song.

After the ceremony came the celebration.

Josse moved among the crowds spilling out into the cloister, the stable yard and every other available space. He had a pewter mug of excellent French wine in his hand. He was grabbed and greeted by many people: the Abbess's elder son, Leofgar, was there with his wife Rohaise, four-year-old Timus and his two-year-old sister, Little Helewise, the children dressed in their best and bubbling with excitement. Leofgar looked pale and Rohaise confided to Josse that her husband and his brother had been up most of the previous night catching up on the years of Dominic's absence, 'and talking is such thirsty work, is it not, Josse?' she added with a lovely smile.

He moved on, stopping – or being stopped – with increasing frequency. Among the guests were former patients who had been treated in the infirmary, including some who had been plague sufferers; ordinary people who had cause to be deeply thankful to Hawkenlye Abbey and who had come to express their gratitude on this special day. They all wanted to wring Josse's hand and he was moved at being among so many people who seemed to regard him as a friend. It was quite something, when you considered that—

He saw Joanna.

She was standing just inside the Abbey gates, Meggie holding her hand and looking eagerly about with wide eyes. On Joanna's other side stood a slim, erect figure cloaked in grey. As Josse approached, all three turned to look at him – Meggie shouted with delight, 'Josse! *Josse!*' – and he saw that the Domina had come to bestow her good wishes on the newly married couple.

He greeted the Great One with a deep, respectful bow. As he straightened up and met her strange, other-worldly eyes, he hoped he was not the only person there who knew just what an honour this was. Joanna murmured that she would escort the Domina over to where the Abbess sat beside her son and his bride, on a bench in the sunny cloister. 'Of course,' Josse said.

The two women moved away, Meggie between them turning to give her father a beaming smile. Just for a moment Joanna turned, too. She looked straight into Josse's eyes and mouthed the one word, *Later*.

With a secret smile, he continued on his round. Joanna had just made the day perfect.

Late in the afternoon, Josse found himself sitting beside Dominic in the refectory. Not entirely sure how he came to be there, Josse turned with what he hoped was a sensible and sober face and said, 'Well, Dominic, what a wonderful day!'

Dominic gave him a happy smile. 'Yes,' he said quietly. He glanced at Paradisa, sitting on his other side. The neckline of her deep green velvet gown had slipped a little and the tops of her breasts were exposed, the skin pale cream, the flesh firm and rounded. '*Yes*,' he repeated.

There was a sudden fierce erotic charge in the air.

'Have some more wine,' said Dominic, reaching out for the jug and topping up Josse's mug.

'Thank you.'

There was a pause while both men sipped the excellent wine. Then Josse said, 'Why did you not bring Paradisa to New Winnowlands when you came in the guise of John Damianos? It must have been dreadful to be separated when you knew she was in such peril.'

'It was,' Dominic said quietly. 'But I felt that her peril was even greater if she was with me. I hoped to keep the hiding place in the undercroft a secret from the entire world. I believed one or more of my pursuers would pick up my trail in the end and I wanted to make sure it led somewhere else.'

'You succeeded,' Josse said. 'And it was to see her and check on her safety that you slipped away each night?'

Dominic met his eyes. 'Yes, Josse. Although that was not *all* I did.'

Aye, Josse thought with a smile. The Abbess was quite right to insist that this marriage take place without delay . . .

There was something he wanted to say. It concerned a very important matter and he had not been able to find a suitable moment. Now, quite drunk, the suitability no longer seemed important. 'What do you think of New Winnowlands?' he demanded.

Dominic looked surprised. 'Your estate? It's fine. A good place, with rich pasture. Your people seem all right, too.' He leaned closer. 'You might do better moving your sheep to the higher ground during the winter. That way you'll rest the summer grazing on the marshland. It's fertile soil but sheep can damage it in the wet months. Also I reckon some of your land might be suitable for wheat. It might be an idea to keep some of the pasture back for making hay for winter fodder.'

Josse sat back in amazement. 'You know all that, just from the short time you were there?'

Dominic smiled. 'I just kept my eyes open. Most of it's pretty obvious, Josse.'

'It might be obvious to you but it certainly isn't to me,' Josse said ruefully. 'I'm a soldier. I know nothing about farming the land.'

'You don't really need to all the time you have Will,' Dominic remarked.

Josse fell silent. What he had just heard made the matter he wanted to put before Dominic all the more imperative. Without further thought he said, 'New Winnowlands is too big for me and I don't give it the devotion it deserves. If you and Paradisa need a home, I would like you to come and live there. There's plenty of room but if you'd prefer to have the main house to yourselves, I'll build a smaller place on the other side of the courtyard.' He grinned. 'I might even move into your outbuilding.'

Dominic's expression turned swiftly from shocked surprise to laughter. 'Oh, I see. You were joking.'

Josse grabbed his arm, spilling quite a lot of Dominic's wine. 'No, I'm not. Will you come?'

Dominic fixed Josse with a very direct stare. 'Do you mean it?' 'Aye.'

Dominic frowned. 'It's true that we are in sore need of a home. My brother Leofgar and his wife have offered to put us up until we find a place to settle but to be honest, Josse, it's not the start to married life that I'd envisaged, what with us being so used to it being just the two of us. Don't think I'm ungrateful – it's very generous of him and Rohaise to have made the offer. But . . .' He trailed to a stop.

Josse understood his misgivings. 'Come to New Winnowlands, then. Make it your home.'

Dominic lowered his head and Josse guessed he was thinking hard. Letting his eyes roam around the room, Josse spotted the Abbess, sitting beside the Domina – good Lord, was she still there? – talking animatedly. The Abbess. Helewise. It was as if his heart had suddenly altered, becoming softer, kinder. She's the sort of woman, he thought, who—

He did not finish the thought. Dominic was leaning over towards him and he spoke directly into Josse's ear. 'I was just about to ask you,' he whispered, 'why you were making this incredibly generous offer. But I don't think there's any need, do you?'

Guiltily Josse wrenched his gaze away from the Abbess. Too late; he was quite sure Dominic knew exactly where he had been looking. Then he thought, why should I feel guilty? Why should I try to hide my feelings, even if I could, from this perceptive, intelligent son of hers?

He turned to Dominic. 'I love your mother and have done so for years,' he said quietly. 'It is true that I would do anything within my power to help her or to make her happy. But I would not have offered you New Winnowlands if I couldn't abide the thought of having you living so close. Fortunately I can.'

Dominic watched him intently for a moment. Then a smile spread across his face. Lowering his voice and leaning closer to Josse, he said, 'May I tell Paradisa? You're not going to change your mind when you're sober?'

Josse grinned. It was true he was drunk, but not that drunk. 'I won't change my mind. Tell her as soon as you like, and with my blessing.'

*   *   *

Helewise had gone outside into the last of the late afternoon light to take some fresh air. She went along the cloister and sank down onto a bench. Presently she saw with pleasure that Josse was weaving his not entirely steady way towards her. She smiled up at him, patting the bench beside her. He returned her smile and sank down.

For some time they did not speak. Then she said, 'I wish he had come here openly when first he visited Hawkenlye. I – we could have helped him.'

'He could not risk making himself known to you,' Josse said immediately.

'Why?' she demanded.

She thought she heard Josse sigh. Then he said, 'Because he would have put you in the position of defending him from his many enemies, whether or not you wanted to.'

'Of course I would want to!'

Now the sigh was very audible. 'Helewise, how could he know that? You're the Abbess of Hawkenlye, a respected authority figure with considerable power. One of the men pursuing Dominic was a Knight Hospitaller. Even your own son might just recognize a possible conflict of loyalties.'

'I would never have given him up, no matter who demanded that I should!' she cried hotly.

'No, of course you wouldn't,' Josse agreed. 'But as well as that, there was the danger. Those others – the Franks and the Saracens – were utterly ruthless. Had Dominic come openly to the Abbey, innocent people might have got between the hunters and their quarry.' He paused and then said softly, 'People such as you.'

'But—' She struggled with her indignation. She still felt hurt that Dominic had not brought his problems, perilous and terrible though they were, straight to her. It was like plainly stating he could manage quite well without her.

Josse said gently, 'My lady, he is still and will always be your son. But he is a grown man, a fighting man who has been in grave danger and who, by his own wits, courage and common sense, has lived to tell the tale.' Then, softly: 'Let him go.'

She choked on a sob. She reached for Josse's hand and he took hers in his big, warm palm. It was immeasurably comforting.

After quite some time she said, 'A part of me knew it was him long before he revealed himself.' Josse did not speak but waited for her to go on. She struggled to put her thoughts into words. 'I felt – *odd*, as if something momentous was happening, and I did not understand why.' Smiling, she shook her head. 'And, of course, there was his name.'

'His name? What, John Damianos?'

'No, no. His name in religion. He took the name Brother Ralf.'

Her smile deepened. She could all but hear Josse trying to work it out and failing. 'What of it?' he asked.

She squeezed his hand, leaning against his reassuring bulk. 'Ralf was my father's name. Dominic was always very fond of his grandfather.'

Much later, the newly married couple were led by a lively, ribald escort to their marriage bed in the guest quarters. The nuns had made up the bed with fine linen and warm blankets, and decked it with lucky charms and bunches of dried herbs. The priest had sprinkled it with holy water to sanction the union.

Finally the last of the happy, tipsy guests were shooed away and the gates firmly closed. The celebration was over and it was time for the lanterns and the candles to be blown out and for the night to descend.

Josse had been waiting for this moment.

When everyone had settled and all was quiet, he slipped out and hurried away to the forest. Joanna was waiting for him, sitting cross-legged on the floor beside the hearth. Meggie was deeply asleep up on the platform, warmly wrapped, her thumb in her mouth.

Josse leaned down and kissed Joanna on the mouth, then settled beside her. He put his arm around her and she leaned into his shoulder.

'You smell of wine,' she murmured.

'I'm not surprised. I have drunk rather a lot of it.'

'It was a great celebration, wasn't it?'

'Aye.' He put a hand to her jaw, raising her face so that he could look at her. 'I am very glad that you and the Domina put in an appearance. It was a profound honour for her to give the young couple her blessing.'

'Yes, it was. She did it, I think, because of the respect she has for Abbess Helewise.'

'Dominic and Paradisa had been living in the forest, in your house. Yet the forest people made no protest?'

'No. We recognized they are good people. They were in danger and no threat to us. Why should they not use the forest as a refuge?'

'Mmm.' He kissed her sweet-smelling hair as she nestled against him. It was beyond him even when sober to attempt to fathom out the strange ways of her people. He certainly wasn't up to it tonight.

He realized how tired he was. 'Sweeting, shall we go to bed? I fear I am too weary for more than a hug, but it would give me great pleasure to have you sleep in my arms.'

He felt her tense. 'Yes, Josse, of course.' She pulled a little away from him, turning her head so as to look him in the eyes. 'But first I—' She broke off.

'What?' He felt alarm swiftly rising in him. '*What?*'

She looked down. 'I may have to go away.'

'But you often go away!' He tried to make light of it. 'You're frequently not here when I come looking but you always turn up again.' He forced a laugh.

She did not join in.

'This time it is different,' she said neutrally. 'I have to – they have told me I must go to a place which is of vital importance to us. To my people, I mean. Something is happening there. It's under threat and we must protect it.'

'Why you?' he demanded. It was the first thing that flew into his head.

She smiled. 'Oh, Josse. Dear, lovely Josse. Because I'm powerful now. I can do something about this threat. I won't be alone,' she hurried on. 'They'll choose the very best of us for the mission. I won't be very important – others will do what is necessary. I'll just be there to make up the necessary numbers.'

He looked straight into her dark eyes.

He did not believe her.

She was either being modest or, more likely, telling him this to comfort him. Trying to minimize the danger.

'Where is this place?' he said gruffly. 'Is it far?'

'Northern France.'

'That is a big area. Can you not narrow it down?'

She grimaced. 'No, Josse. I'm sorry. I can't.'

Anger burst out. Keeping his voice down so as not to wake his daughter, he hissed, 'Always so mysterious! Always *I've got to do this* or *I have to go away so I won't see you!* But

I'm welcome enough when you are here and you do want me, aren't I? I'm very useful as a stud in your bed to keep you warm and give you pleasure!'

He heard his furious words and instantly wished he could draw them back.

But she took his face in her cool hands and, bending her head, kissed him. Then, breaking away, she said, 'It's the way it has to be. It's never my wish to hurt you or to use you.' A tiny pause. 'Actually I love you.'

Once he would have been filled with joy to hear her say so. Once it would have been enough to keep him happy, keep him returning to her, patient, faithful and true.

Once . . .

He stood up.

'You're not leaving?' She sounded aghast.

He gave her an ironic smile. 'No. I'm going to bed.'

He went outside to relieve himself, then dipped his hands in the pail of water by the door and splashed his face and neck. Back inside, he found that she had climbed up onto the platform. She had moved over to the far side to make room for him. Meggie was curled at her feet.

He had imagined they would not speak to each other again that night. But after a while she said, 'Josse? Are you still awake?'

'Aye.' As if he would be able to sleep!

He sensed that she was nerving herself to say something important. When it came, it was not what he had imagined.

'I won't be taking Meggie with me,' she whispered, her mouth right against his ear. 'She doesn't know but I'll have to leave her here. Lora will look after her, and Tiphaine says she'll visit when she can. There will be others too, of course, who will share her care.'

Oh, dear God, he thought. He tried to speak, failed. Tried again. 'When are you going?'

'I don't know. Perhaps next year, even the year after. It depends on – on many things. They haven't told me much yet. There are preparations that must be made. Ceremonies,' she added vaguely.

'So why are you telling me this now?'

'Because I can't rest till I know you'll help!' she said in a fierce whisper.

'*Help?* What help can you possibly want of me?'

'Josse, I want Meggie to be with you,' she said in a rush. 'She'll miss me and she won't understand why I'm not here. If she has you instead she won't mind.'

He opened his mouth to speak but found he had absolutely nothing to say.

'Josse?' Joanna said urgently. 'Will you do it? Will you give me your word that you'll do what I ask?'

He put his arms round her and drew her to him. The kiss was long and, in time, grew passionate.

When they were both satiated, he said, 'Aye.'

He slept for some time and then was suddenly wide awake. It was still dark and he could tell from their breathing that Joanna and Meggie were sound asleep.

His mind was full of Joanna.

Where was she going? What would she be ordered to do? It must be dangerous if she was not allowed to take her child.

Joanna was going away. Not yet, but in the future. When she had gone he would slip into his daughter's life. Oh, he was there already; he knew that the child loved him and, as for him, he adored her. But this would be different. Joanna would be far away and those in whose care she had left Meggie would be told that Josse was going to take up the role of parent. They all knew he was Meggie's father; it was his right to care for his own child.

Meggie.

Joanna would be gone but she would leave their daughter with him. Perhaps he would take her away to live at New Winnowlands? He could find a pony for her, a nice, safe, well-mannered pony, and teach her to ride. Will would help – Will knew where to find good horses. And maybe Josse would get Ella to fix up a special chamber with a proper bed and pretty hangings. He could buy her clothes, shoes . . . Or perhaps she would be able to live temporarily at the Abbey? The details did not matter. He would work something out. The important thing was that the two of them would be together.

In a corner of his mind a voice that just might have been his appeared to be cheering.

Historical Note

It is said that gunpowder was first discovered in China, where, as early as 1161, an explosive of some sort was used in 'noise makers' that might have been firecrackers. In the West, the formula was undoubtedly discovered by alchemists in their endless and ultimately fruitless attempts to turn base metals into gold. The theory was that if only the accretions could be sloughed off, what remained would be pure gold. Newly discovered substances would be tested and combined with other substances, and it was probably by accident that someone stumbled on the result of mixing the right proportions of charcoal, saltpetre and brimstone. Because the alchemists of the Arab world were in general far in advance in their learning than their western counterparts, it seems reasonable to propose that the secret of the 'black powder' in the west originated with them.

The Church rigidly disapproved of science in general, and of the science of warfare in particular; in the twelfth century, an anathema was laid on those attempting to make or use 'fiery substances', and this probably referred to Greek Fire (a mixture of naphtha, bitumen, pitch, sulphur, oil and quicklime). The Knights Templar, however – who were universally suspected of dabbling in alchemy – apparently took no notice of the Church's disapproval, and it is reasonable to suggest that their brothers in arms, the Knights Hospitaller, may also have been able to put aside their scruples when faced with the prospect of such a momentous discovery as the 'black powder'.

It was not until around 1250 that gunpowder became known in England. Roger Bacon, born in 1212 or 1214 and curious about the nature of the world around him from the day he became aware, became known for his enquiring mind and his interest in the diverse and the bizarre. He seems to have discovered gunpowder in around 1247, where he makes a cryptic reference to it in a manuscript. In a later work he proposes the correct mixture as being seven parts saltpetre, five parts charcoal and five parts sulphur.

Gunpowder as the force to propel missiles was first recorded in the middle of the fourteenth century. It is said that the English at the Battle of Crecy in 1346 used some sort of explosive powder to propel bolts (with very little accuracy) from tubes. Men were very wary of it; the powder was so unstable that apparently it exploded if you stamped on it.

Alys Clare